5 plus 2

Seven Plays with a Light Touch

Ron Blicq

Seven Plays with a Light Touch

5 plus 2
Seven Plays with a Light Touch

This is the second book of a two-volume set containing twelve plays written by the same author. It features seven plays with appeal primarily for adult actors, although the first three plays also include roles for teens.

Five of the plays have already been produced, some in the UK and some in Canada, which has provided me with the opportunity to include Production Notes with each script. The notes describe some of the factors affecting the early performances.

The earlier book in the series is titled *Five Plays for Young Actors* and contains plays for actors aged 7 to 15. It was published in 2014.

There is a further adult two-act play by the same author, which is being produced worldwide. Titled *Closure*, it has been published by Samuel French Inc. and can be ordered directly from them. Alternatively, it can be ordered from any local bookstore or online through Amazon.

All of the plays in the two books are available for production by either professional or amateur theatre groups. Because they are copyright, however, approval has to be obtained first from the publisher. Turn to page 319 for details or go to our web site at **www.r-group.ca**.

Seven Plays with a Light Touch

First published in Canada in 2015 by
R-Group Publications, 569 Oxford St, Winnipeg MB R3M 3J2
(a Division of The Roning Group Inc)

Copyright © 2015 Ron S. Blicq
First Edition

All rights reserved; no part of this publication may be
reproduced or transmitted by any means, electronic,
mechanical, photocopying, or otherwise, without
prior permission of the publisher.

ISBN Hard Cover: 978-1-4602-7044-8
ISBN Paperback: 978-1-4602-7045-5
ISBN eBook: 978-1-4602-7046-2
ISBN Paperback UK: 978-0-9686989-3-8

North American Version Printed by
FriesenPress, Inc
Victoria, BC, Canada, V8V 3K2

British Version Printed by
Melody Press
L'Islet, Guernsey, UK

Distributed to the trade by The Ingram Book Company

Cover photographs
Upper front cover: *Closure* – John Gaisford
Lower front cover: *The Sicilian Wine Test* – The author
Back cover : *Choosing Home* – Peter Frankland

Seven Plays with a Light Touch

Acknowledgments

This book and its seven plays would not have been possible without the help of many people who encouraged me to write them or who performed in them. On this page I want to thank all of you who have so generously given much of yourselves to ensure our audiences have had a happy experience.

I would like to list everyone here but, as there are so many of you, will you please forgive me if I just say a very big **Thank You**? ('You' are the over 150 actors, directors, stage managers, sound and light technicians, stage crews, and countless front-of-house staff I have had the pleasure to work with.)

I also want to recognize how much I appreciated the trust that the Guernsey Amateur Dramatic and Operatic Club *(GADOC)* in the British Channel Islands invested in me, as a new and relatively unknown playwright, when they chose to produce my as yet unperformed plays, such as *Closure, Choosing Home, The Sicilian Wine Test,* and *You Will Write, Won't You?* GADOC also premiered plays from the first book with equal success, such as *The Railway Children* and *Five Children and a Psammead*.

In Winnipeg I shall never forget the tremendous effort by the actors who worked so hard to make five of the plays in this book so enjoyable for audiences attending the Winnipeg Fringe Theatre Festival.

Thank you so much, all my friends.

Books by the Same Author

Theatre
Closure
Five Plays for Young Actors
Seven Plays with a Light Touch

Novels/Biography
Choosing Home
The Spirit of Giving
Au Revoir, Sarnia Chérie
(Good-bye, Dear Guernsey)
You Will Write, Won't You?

Education
On The Move
Technically-Write!
Administratively-Write!
Communicating at Work
Guidelines for Report Writing

Seven Plays with a Light Touch

Contents

About the Plays	1
Part 1 – Plays for Adults and Teens	5
Choosing Home	7
You Will Write, Won't You?	59
Sudoku Fever	101
Part 2 – Plays for Adults	135
A Touch of Gray	137
The Sicilian Wine Test	197
Just a Two-cent Stamp	229
Chords, Accords and Discords	239
Obtaining Performance Rights	319
About the Author	320

Seven Plays with a Light Touch

"Make them laugh, make them cry,
but make them wait."
W. Somerset Maugham
1874-1965

When a radio interviewer asked what factor he considered most made his stories so popular, Maugham replied: "You always have to keep your audience in mind," and quoted the above ten words.

(Heard on the BBC, c 1956)

About the Plays

The seven plays presented here fall into two categories:

Classic Dramas, which address a problem that needs to be corrected or a situation that needs to be improved, and work toward a resolution. Four of the plays fall into this category:

>*Choosing Home*
>
>*You Will Write, Won't You?*
>
>*Sudoku Fever*
>
>*A Touch of Gray*

Anecdotes, which describe an event or events that have happened, often in the form of a light comedy. These are:

>*The Sicilian Wine Test*
>
>*Just a Two-cent Stamp*

In longer plays the anecdotes may become a dramatized documentary, often referred to as a **Docudrama**, as in the seventh play:

>*Chords, Accords and Discords*

All the plays in this volume are intended mainly for adult audiences. The first three plays also will appeal to teen-agers, who will understand and empathize with the situations faced by the teens in them.

I have labeled the front part of the book 'Plays for Adults and Teens.' The first play, *Choosing Home*, has been—and continues to be—my most-produced one-act play. Its popularity stems from a real-life situation affecting an 8-year-old girl who became an evacuee during World War 2 and was unable to communicate with her parents for five long years. She was lodged with a middle-aged couple in rural England, grew to love them, and was readily accepted by the children in the village.

After the war ended in 1945 she was sent home, now a teen-ager, only to discover that she and her parents hardly knew each other and certainly didn't understand one-another. So after four months she asked if she could return to England and continue living with her war-time 'parents,' because she felt they were more like real parents to her. The play follows the difficult deliberations that ensued, culminating in a decision that could be happy for only one set of 'parents.'

The second play, *You Will Write, Won't You?*, also involves a difficult decision affecting a teen-ager, but this time occurring in the Prairies of Western Canada. It has been performed four times: twice in the UK and twice in Canada.

Sixteen-year-old Melissa lives on a remote farm in Saskatchewan and is expected to marry a local boy, the son of a successful farmer and landowner. But her teacher in the country school she attends has identified that she has the capability to be a creative writer, and encourages her to apply for a scholarship to attend a prestigious Youth Writers' Institute for the summer, 500 km away. She wins the scholarship, but her mother, her boyfriend, and her boyfriend's parents all try to dissuade her from attending, each insisting she should work on the farm for the summer and gain more agricultural experience. Only her grandmother and her teacher support her.

The serious theme evident in the previous two plays is followed by a comedy, *Sudoku Fever*, in which a 17-year-old girl announces to her family that she wants to go to university and become a mechanical engineer, which means she will have to leave home and move to the city. As in the previous play, her wish is resisted: this time by her single-parent mother, her aunt, and her grandmother. Her grandfather, however, plots a way to help her achieve her plan.

The second half of the book I have labelled 'Plays for Adults.' The first play in this section, *A Touch of Gray,* like the three earlier plays, also requires a decision. Well-educated Frankie, who is single, has been assigned to undertake a two-year research project in a remote area of Peru, likely to be followed by a second two-year project in Central Africa. She is carrying out online research in readiness for her departure when she discovers she is pregnant. Because it will be impossible to take the baby with her, she decides to assign the child permanently to her brother and his wife, who are childless and want to adopt it. But her ex-boyfriend demurs: he is the father of the child and demands that the child come to him and his new partner. A conflict ensues between the two parties.

About the Plays

The next play, *The Sicilian Wine Test*, is a comedy in which we meet Barry, who is seeking the 'right' woman to marry. Yet he is cautious, for he fears that each seemingly bright young woman he dates may develop into an opinionated, cantankerous person in later life. He has discovered a Sicilian wine which, when imbibed in sufficient quantity, loosens the tongue and shows a less-controlled side to the person's character. He invites happy, cheerful Shelley to dinner, serves the wine, sees her display traits he dislikes, and so decides to terminate their relationship. Then he meets delightful Lorraine, who passes the wine test (twice!) and Barry is ready to propose. But there is a side to Lorraine the wine has not yet revealed....

Then comes another comedy, *Just a Two-cent Stamp,* which clearly fits the 'anecdote' label because it plays for only 10 minutes. It belongs to a relatively new genre known as Pint-sized Plays, which originated in the UK and now is gaining worldwide attention. The plays are performed in informal settings such as the corner of a pub, and so are limited to no more than three characters.

The primary character is George who, when Canada first abolished the one-cent coin, discovers a loophole which he believes will enable him to buy one- and two-cent stamps at no cost. His attempts confuse a young postal clerk, but in a neat twist she finds a way to 'turn the tables' on him.

The final play, *Chords, Accords and Discords*, is a full-length musical. In a sense it is a docudrama, since it contains a series of linked anecdotes. The story tells of the sometimes turbulent relationship, for close to two decades, between playwright William Schwenk Gilbert and composer Arthur Sullivan, who between them created the d'Oyly Carte operettas such as *H.M.S. Pinafore, The Pirates of Penzance* and *The Mikado*. Yet it's more than just a historical narrative, because many of the favorite songs from the operettas are integrated into the storyline.

All the scripts are followed by biographical notes describing the characters' backgrounds and their relationship with other characters. For five of the plays there also is a section called Production Notes, which describe events that occurred or factors that had to be accommodated during the first (and sometimes subsequent) productions. Because *Just a Two-cent Stamp* and

Chords, Accords and Discords have not yet been performed, they do not have detailed Production Notes.

If you wonder why the book's title has been preceded by the subheading *5 plus 2,* it signifies there is a dividing line between the first five plays, which have been produced successfully, and the last two plays, which are 'standing in the wings' awaiting their first venture onto the stage.

My choice in having two separate editions of each book has evolved from the differences that exist in terminology and spelling between American and British English. The spelling differences are well-known, such as *color/colour, center/centre,* and *enroll/enrol,* but other differences are less obvious. For example:

- In the US and Canada, the word *program* is always spelled 'program,' but in the UK this spelling is used only when referring to *software programs.* In all other cases, the spelling in the UK is *programme,* as in *theatre programme* and *conference programme.*
- We speak on a *cell phone* in the US and Canada, but they speak on a *mobile phone* in the UK.
- In the US, the word *presently* normally means 'right away,' whereas in the UK it more often means 'shortly' or 'in good time.'
- For *Mr.* and *Ms.* the period following the abbreviation is always present in the US, but is omitted in the UK (where it is referred to as a 'full stop.' The same applies to similar abbreviations.
- Dates in the US are consistently shown as month-day-year (July 28, 2015) with punctuation, whereas in the UK they are shown as day-month-year (28 July 2015) without punctuation.
- In the US and Canada we spell the rubber exterior of a car wheel as tire, but in the UK it is spelled *tyre.*

These, and other subtle differences, have been incorporated into the narrative of this Canada/US edition.

Ron Blicq
April 2015

Part 1

Plays for Adults and Teens

Seven Plays with a Light Touch

Play No. 1

Choosing Home

Synopsis

Shortly before her eighth birthday, in June 1940, Rosalind was evacuated from the British island of Guernsey (which became enemy-occupied territory during World War 2) and was sent to the rural village of Somerford Keynes in Gloucestershire, in southwest England. For the next five years she lived with and grew to love the middle-aged couple who harbored her. Now it's November 1945, Rosalind is 13, and four months ago she was returned to her family in their fashionable home above Fermaine Bay in Guernsey. She feels lonely and unhappy, as did quite a few evacuees who were billeted with, and lived as an integral part of, a private family in England. But, out of deference to her parents, she has said nothing and has lived silently with her unhappiness.

As a 'thank you' gesture, her parents have invited the Gloucestershire couple to visit. Shortly after their arrival, Rosalind announces she wants to return to Somerford Keynes and live with them permanently, rather than continue living in Guernsey with her birth parents.

Rosalind's mother is incensed and suspects the Gloucestershire couple have coerced Rosalind, so she asks an elderly distant cousin, who once was a respected Legal Advocate (lawyer) to investigate. In the ensuing, sometimes heated, discussions he elicits the truth. He then presents his findings to both parties but refuses to make a decision, or even offer an opinion, because he says the choice must be made by the person who is directly affected.

Rationale

The idea to write the play emerged in the late 1990's, when I heard that some evacuees, now that their parents were no longer present, had felt it was acceptable to divulge the unhappiness they had experienced on their return to Guernsey, which they had quietly concealed for close to 50 years. Their return home was expected to be joyful, yet for some it proved to be a very lonely experience.

In their book *Islands in Danger*, Alan Wood and Mary Seaton Wood described how

'...there were heartaches as well as happiness. For often they were different children with a new outlook, even a new language (picked up in different areas such as Lancashire and Glasgow). *Their mothers and fathers realized that the five years had turned their own children into strangers, and made a gulf that might never be bridged.'*

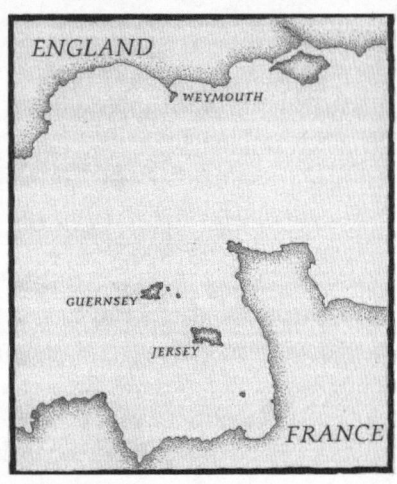

The distance between Guernsey and Weymouth is approximately 60 miles (92 km). To France it's 17 miles (25 km).

I felt this little-known element of Guernsey history needed to be heard, and so created *Choosing Home* to record the story.

History

The play was written originally for the Guernsey Amateur Dramatic and Operatic Club's (GADOC's) 2005 One-Act-Play Festival, to celebrate the 60th anniversary of the repatriation of Guernsey's children at the end of the war. Since then the script has been updated in several ways:

- For broadcast as a five-part radio play, by BBC Guernsey in February 2006.
- For presentation at the Fringe Theatre Festival, in Winnipeg, Canada, in July 2011.
- For presentation as an entry in GADOC's 2015 One-Act-Play Festival, to celebrate the 75th anniversary of the evacuation and the 70th anniversary of the return of the children.

In 2007, the playscript was also converted into a novel bearing the same name, in which the story was extended to describe what happened to Rosalind in the years following her choice of parents.

Choosing Home

Characters

The original play had seven roles. Subsequent versions have had eight, with Rosalind appearing twice: as she was in 1945, when she was 13; and as she was in 2010, at age 78, to describe the situation and events for audiences less familiar with the evacuation.

	GADOC, 2005	*Winnipeg, 2011*
The Le Page Family		
Rosalind, 13	*Caitlin Sullivan*	*Iris Dyck*
Wesley, her brother, 16	*Charlie Morvan*	*Scott Austin*
Celia, her mother, 44	*Susan Costley*	*Ali Everett*
Gerald, her father, 48	*Steven Molnar*	*Bill Pats*
Rosalind, 78	--	*Dorothy Talman*
The Chipman Family		
Bernard *(Chips)*, 51	*Tony Riddle*	*Bill Moore*
Beryl, 52	*Pauline Telford*	*Janet Taylor*
The Advocate		
Vincent Hargreaves, 73	*John Gaisford*	*Ron Robinson*
The Play was directed by:	*Jane Blower*	*The author*

Steven Molnar, Pauline Telford, and John Gaisford will appear again, in their original roles, in the 2015 production. It will be directed by Bob Thompson.

Character descriptions start on page 49.

The Set

The living room of the Le Page home in a fashionable area of Guernsey, populated by financially comfortable residents. It is November 1945. There is mid-1930s furniture. The entrance stage left leads to other rooms and the front hall; the entrance stage right leads to the back of the house and the garden. There is a sofa stage left and two armchairs stage right; the sofa has thickly padded arms that can be sat on. There are two chairs and a small dining-height table center stage, with a vase and ornament on the table. For the opening and closing scenes, a spot illuminates downstage extreme right, for the introductory opening and closing remarks by Rosalind today. A second spot illuminates extreme downstage left, for the brief opening scenes by the Le Page parents and by Beryl and Bernard Chipman, and the closing scenes with Wesley, Celia, and Gerald. More notes about the production start on page 56.

Seven Plays with a Light Touch

Approximate Length: 65 minutes

Video Prop

A DVD of children singing *Wish Me Luck as you Wave Me Goodbye* and *We'll Meet Again* (each 70 seconds long) is available.** One of the songs can be screened to open the play. The DVD depicts children waiting in their classroom, in June 1940, for the moment when they would be transported to the harbor and board a ship for evacuation to mainland England. They are dressed in 1940 clothing and have old suitcases, sandwich packs, and gas marks with them.

Some Script Guidelines

Throughout the script, two symbols are used occasionally at the end of a piece of dialogue to indicate how the sentence ends:

... An ellipsis at the end of a statement means the speaker just trails off and leaves his or her thought hanging in the air (possibly accompanied by a shrug).

— A dash at the end of a statement means the speaker is interrupted by the next speaker, so that the first speaker's statement is incomplete. Sometimes there is an italicized continuation of the statement *(within brackets)* immediately following the dash, to help the actor sense where the sentence was going.

v.o. Means that the words are spoken by someone off-stage.

Three of the place names used in the play are listed below. They are real, yet may prove difficult to pronounce correctly. The correct pronunciations are:

        Pleinmont   *Ply-mont*
        Portelet   *Port-a-lay* *
        Jerbourg   *Jer-berg*

* The pronunciation is correct for the time of the play (1945). Today the name has (sadly) been Anglicized to 'port-a-lett'.

** For source information, contact rgrouppubs@gmail.com

Children Awaiting Evacuation

The photograph is a clip from a DVD, made by John Gaisford in 2004, for the first performance of *Choosing Home* at the GADOC One-Act-Play Festival in 2005. The children were students in levels 4, 5 and 6 at Notre Dame du Rosaire Primary School in Guernsey. They were dressed in clothing suitable for 1940 and carried small suitcases and the inevitable gas mask. Their voices singing 'We'll Meet Again' provide an emotionally moving moment when the DVD is screened immediately after the lights go down and the audience hushes in readiness for the play.

Seven Plays with a Light Touch

Script: *Choosing Home*
© 2003, 2014, Ron Blicq

(A 70-second video is projected onto a large screen upstage, showing children at La Rosaire primary school, all dressed ready for evacuation in 1940, singing 'We'll Meet Again'.)

(A spotlight comes up on **ROSALIND Sr.** *downstage right. She addresses the audience. It's 2010.)*

ROSALIND Sr.: As a parent, how would you feel if you were told that you should send your children away— immediately—so they will be safe, out of reach of an approaching enemy? Would you let them go, without knowing where they will be going, or for how long, and that you will be unable to visit or write to them, or even text or phone them? Or would you choose to keep them with you, at home, even though they could be facing unimaginable dangers?

Because that's what my parents had to do. In 1940. For me and my brother Wesley.

(Bring up spot at downstage left, on **GERALD** *and* **CELIA**; *it's 18 June 1940, evening.).*

*(***ROSALIND Sr.** *turns and watches them.)*

GERALD: I'm not happy about it, Celia. Rosalind's too young to be going on her own.

CELIA: Think of it as if we were sending her to boarding school.

GERALD: She's only seven.

CELIA: Oh, Gerald. She's nearly eight.

GERALD: I'd be happier if she could go with Wesley.

CELIA: No, that won't be possible. He'll be with his own school.

GERALD: Then *you* must go with her.

CELIA: She'll be with her school, Gerald! With girls her own age. Anyway, I shall stay with you.

GERALD: But—

CELIA: It'll only be for a month or two.

GERALD: Not if it's anything like the last war. Four years!

CELIA: Yes, but it's different this time.

GERALD: I wish I could think like that. *(pause)* How soon will all this happen?

Choosing Home

CELIA: Tomorrow.

GERALD: Tomorrow!

CELIA: The children have to go right away. The Germans aren't going to wait patiently until we're ready for them.

(Fade stage-left spot to black.)

(ROSALIND Sr. turns to the audience.)

ROSALIND Sr.: We lived on the island of Guernsey: one of the Channel Islands off the coast of France. British territory, really, but too far away for England to defend.

Already, Nazi troops had swept through Western Europe and were poised along the Normandy coast, ready to invade the islands.

(Slight pause.)

The very next morning Wesley and I were driven to our respective schools, each with a suitcase of clothes—small, because we would have to carry it ourselves everywhere we went—a ration book, and of course a gas mask.

By dusk that evening, forty-three-hundred of Guernsey's children had marched down to the docks and had been crammed into the holds of smelly old cargo boats. Already they were heading north toward England, feeling the effect of the heaving sea beneath them.

My brother was sent to Derbyshire with his school, in the north of England. I was sent farther west, on my own, to a little village in rural Gloucestershire, where I first met dear Beryl and Chips.

(Bring up spot downstage left on BERYL *and* BERNARD. *They face the audience, but address their remarks to a child supposedly standing at their door, right in front of them.)*

(ROSALIND Sr. turns and watches them.)

BERNARD: 'Ello, my ducks.

BERYL: Are you...?

(BERYL searches in her apron pocket, pulls out a slip of paper.)

BERNARD: Rosie, isn't it?

BERYL: No, Bernie: it's Rosalind. Rosalind Le Page. *(to imaginary young Rosalind)* Is that how you say it, my dear?

(ROSALIND Sr. nods 'yes'.)

BERNARD: Then come on in, love.

BERYL: Take 'er case for 'er, Bernie.

BERNARD: *(reaching for the case)* We were about to 'ave our tea. You're just in time.

(Fade stage left spot to black. ROSALIND Sr. *turns to the audience.)*

ROSALIND Sr.: That's how it all started: my five wartime years with Beryl and Chips. They didn't *try* to make me feel at home. They just treated me like I was one of their own. It was so warm, so comfortable.

Did I miss my parents? Of course I did. At first. But, after a while, only in a remote way. The children in the village drew me into their circle and in no time I began to feel just like one of them; I even talked like them: 'Are you goin' to Ciren, love? See you at the shops?' My mother would have been appalled.

Eventually, of course, the war was over and I was told I would be going home.

Home? I had become so accustomed to living with Beryl and Chips, I felt I was about to be evacuated all over again.

(As ROSALIND Sr. *speaks, lights come up on the living room of the Le Page home in Guernsey, in November 1945.)*

*(*ROSALIND Jr. *is sitting near stage left at a small side table, doing homework. On the table, she has spread out schoolbooks. A satchel stands on the floor, leaning against a table leg. A vase of flowers and a table ornament are under the table.)*

By then I was thirteen and when we met I...I hardly knew my parents, could barely remember them. And they...they didn't seem to understand how I felt. So lonely...lost...out of touch.

Then, after four months my mother unwittingly came to my rescue. She invited Beryl and Chips to visit—like a 'thank you' for having me all those years.

Oh, it was *wonderful* to see them again. You can imagine how I hurried through my homework when I came home from school, just so I could be with them!

(Lights fade to black on Rosalind Sr.; she exits.)

(From here until the final scene, ROSALIND *means 13-year-old Rosalind.)*

ROSALIND: With names like Geometry and Trigonometry—and Pythagoras and his theorem!—how *can* they expect me to understand...

(She erases something she has written. Enter WESLEY stage left, dressed in Elizabeth College grey slacks and white jersey bearing a college emblem engraved on the left front.)

Oh, Wes: This is impossible! Can you help?

(WESLEY leans over the table.)

WESLEY: You know what mother's going to say, don't you?

ROSALIND: Only too well. *(imitates Celia's voice)* "Now, Rosalind. This is no place to be doing your homework. You have a perfectly good desk up in your bedroom."

WESLEY: Then why do you?

ROSALIND: It's friendlier down here. Not nearly so cold...so isolated.

(Pause, as WESLEY peers at Rosalind's notes.)

You have no idea, have you? What it's like to feel so...alone.

WESLEY: But you're not alone, Ros. *(points to page)* You've taken the complement of the angle. Should be fifty-three degrees, not thirty-seven.

ROSALIND: I don't mind ordinary arithmetic, but this stuff!

(ROSALIND sniffs at WESLEY's jersey.)

You've been smoking!

WESLEY: Ugh!

(He backs away, crosses toward door, stage left.)

I'd better change, before mother—

(CELIA enters stage left, followed by great-uncle VINCENT.)

CELIA: Before mother...what?

WESLEY: A-a-h...Before your visitor arrives. *(indicates VINCENT)*

CELIA: How did you know I had a visitor?

WESLEY: Uh... Cook told me: 'Seven for dinner.'

CELIA: Oh. *(to VINCENT)* Vincent: this is my son, Wesley. *(to WESLEY)* Let me introduce you to what for simplicity I will call your great-uncle: Vincent Hargreaves.

(They shake hands.)

WESLEY: How do you do, sir?

VINCENT: How do you do, Wesley?

CELIA: And this is my daughter, Rosalind. *(to* ROSALIND*)* Your great-uncle Vincent. He's my mother's cousin, which makes us second cousins.

ROSALIND: How do you do, sir?

VINCENT: Ah, yes, Rosalind. I don't think we have met before, but I have heard about you. *(to* CELIA*)* A 'Rosalind' for your 'Celia'? From 'As You Like It'?

CELIA: Not intentionally. Although, temperamentally, one could say there is a likeness.

VINCENT: *(to* WESLEY*)* But we have met before, ten years ago. In 1935. The Silver Jubilee of King George the Fifth.

WESLEY: I'd've been six then.

VINCENT: I took you with me on one of the decorated boats, in the harbor.

*(*VINCENT *and* WESLEY *mime conversation.)*

CELIA: *(to* ROSALIND*)* I've told you before, Rosalind, your homework is to be done in your room, on your desk. Not in here.

ROSALIND: Yes, mother.

*(*ROSALIND *gathers up her books and satchel.* CELIA *lifts flowers and ornament from the floor, sets them on the table.)*

CELIA: *(to* WESLEY*)* And you go upstairs and change.

WESLEY: Yes, mother.

*(*WESLEY *and* ROSALIND *turn to exit stage left.)*

CELIA: *(*to WESLEY*, a caution)* I'll talk to *you* later.

*(*ROSALIND *and* WESLEY *exit.)*

*(*CELIA *invites* VINCENT *to sit. She paces.)*

Did you notice anything unusual about Rosalind?

VINCENT: Can't say I did. But I have hardly had time to—

CELIA: She has been behaving so…differently. From the day she came home.

VINCENT: In what way?

CELIA: Withdrawn; uncommunicative; almost sullenly defiant.

VINCENT: You can hardly expect her to be the same girl she was five years ago. How old was she when she was evacuated?

Choosing Home

CELIA: Seven; just about to turn eight.

VINCENT: Then she's thirteen now?

(CELIA nods.)

Just entering puberty. Can be a difficult time, I'm told.

CELIA: No. I blame it on the people she was billeted with. They lost their only daughter in 1941, in an air raid near Brighton. Rosalind seems to have become a convenient replacement.

VINCENT: Aren't you assuming...?

CELIA: No, I don't think so. *(brief pause)* In the nearly five months she has been home, not a peep out of her about wanting to go back there. Then the Chipmans arrive—

VINCENT: Chipmans?

CELIA: The people she was billeted with.

VINCENT: They're *here*?

CELIA: Of course. I thought I'd told you. We sent them tickets. A way to say 'thank you' for having her all that time.

VINCENT: I see...

CELIA: They'd hardly been here five minutes, when Rosalind announces she wants to go back with them. Stay with them. Go on living there!

VINCENT: Without any— *(premeditation)*

CELIA: How do you think that makes me feel? I'm her mother!

VINCENT: So what did you say to her?

CELIA: Not to be ridiculous!

VINCENT: Were the other people...?

CELIA: The Chipmans.

VINCENT: Were they there, too?

CELIA: Oh, yes. Young Rosalind knew exactly what she was doing.

VINCENT: And you said: "Don't be ridiculous." Just like that?

CELIA: Well, not in so many words. I think I said something about it being impracticable. That this was her home now.

VINCENT: And what did Gerald say?

CELIA: Oh, he was his usual non-committal self. Thinks it's just temporary; it'll blow over.

VINCENT: On what grounds?

CELIA: Says we must give her more time.

VINCENT: For what?

CELIA: To make friends here, at school.
VINCENT: In four months, she hasn't...?
CELIA: She says they laugh at her. At the accent she's acquired. Didn't you hear her?
VINCENT: Can't say I noticed.
CELIA: I keep telling her to articulate correctly. Like we do. Like her brother does.
VINCENT: Oh, Celia! You know what I'm hearing? Your mother's voice. Twenty years ago. Saying that about you.
CELIA: Oh, Vincent! Hmm...perhaps that's why I'm so concerned for her. I don't like seeing her like this, as if she's hurt, in pain. I wish she would open up more, talk about it.
(Pause.)
VINCENT: So...you've invited me here...?
CELIA: I want you to talk to her. Find out what prompted such a sudden outburst.
VINCENT: Can't you do that? Or Gerald?
CELIA: She'd go silent.
VINCENT: You don't think Gerald's got a point? It will just blow over?
CELIA: No. It's much deeper than that. You'll need to talk to them too: the Chipmans.
VINCENT: But, Celia, this isn't a legal issue.
CELIA: You think not? If Mr. and Mrs. Chipman are coercing my daughter to live with them, in my book that's illegal.
VINCENT: But I'm retired.
CELIA: You were an Advocate, once.
VINCENT: Not any more.
CELIA: I want you to use your extraordinary questioning powers to elicit the truth. I used to watch you in court. You didn't always know I was there. You were brilliant: so gentle, so probing. You'd disarm the person you were questioning, and then you'd swoop!
VINCENT: You're not suggesting I hold a court-like inquisition?
CELIA: No, no. Just elicit some facts.
VINCENT: I'm not comfortable with this, Celia.
CELIA: I do need you to.
VINCENT: Once you start something— *(like this...)*

Choosing Home

CELIA: You don't have to make it obvious. All you have to do is—
(Sound of laughter and voices approaching from stage left. CELIA *urges* VINCENT *toward the door at stage right.)*
Come on. Let's find Gerald. Put him in the picture.
*(*CELIA *and* VINCENT *exit stage right.)*
*(*ROSALIND, BERYL *and* BERNARD *enter stage left.* ROSALIND *tends to speak with a country accent, as they do.)*
BERNARD: What the lads did, Rosie… *(laughs)* They moved Ma Chalmers' bike.
ROSALIND: They hid it?
BERNARD: No, no! Just moved it down one door, nearer the road.
BERYL: If I'd known what you were up to, Bernie…
BERNARD: You'd've 'id in the bushes with us, an' watched too!
(to ROSALIND*)* You know how Ol' Geraint boasts: no matter 'ow many pints 'e's 'ad in the pub, 'e can always find his door in the dark, even in the blackout.
ROSALIND: He lives in the row of alms houses?
BERYL: Aye. You know how dark it gets down there.
BERNARD: Every night….
*(*BERNARD *emulates Geraint feeling his way along the path.)*
'E feels 'is way forward, a step at a time… like 'e's a blind man…
BERYL: Which it really was like, in the blackout.
*(*BERNARD *takes two or three steps forward, pauses as though he's grasped something with his right hand.)*
BERNARD: Ah! Ma Chalmers' bike.
BERYL: She lives at number three.
ROSALIND: Aye. You had me take eggs to her.
BERYL: You remember that?
ROSALIND: Oh, yes. She'd lead me to the dresser in the kitchen, tell me to put me 'and in a jar. Always there were 'umbugs in it.
BERNARD: *(takes two more steps)* So the next door's mine…
ROSALIND: Ol' Geraint lives at number four.
BERNARD: You got it. 'E knew where 'e was, because every night Ma Chalmers'd lean 'er bike against the wall beside 'er door…

BERYL: Ready for the morning, when she'd cycle off to pick up the morning newspapers; deliver them.

BERNARD: But this night—

BERYL: No moon, mind—

BERNARD: Bloody dark! Young Moodie gets there first, moves the bike one door down, toward the road.

ROSALIND: To number two?

BERNARD: Aye. *(laughs)* We 'id in the bushes, could 'ear 'im coming down the road.

(BERNARD resumes his role, sings a bar or two from 'It's a long way to Tipperary,' starts feeling his way along.)

Ah! My door.

ROSALIND: Only it was Ma Chalmers' door?

BERYL: *(drawn out)* Right...

(BERNARD fumbles for an imaginary latch, pushes an imaginary door open, then closes the door with his rump.)

Up the stairs, then.

ROSALIND: He doesn't turn on a light?

BERNARD: No. 'E never does.

ROSALIND: Didn't Ma Chalmers *hear* him?

BERYL: She's a bit deaf, remember.

BERNARD: But 'er little Scottie did.

ROSALIND: That yappy little dog?

BERNARD: Comes bouncing off 'er bed, meets Ol' Geraint 'alf way up the stairs. You should've 'eard 'er!

ROSALIND: Did she attack him?

BERNARD: 'E didn't wait to find out.

BERYL: But by then young Moodie'd nipped in and moved the bike back in front of 'er door.

BERNARD: So when Ol' Geraint comes stumbling out the door, the first thing 'e bumps into is the bike!

ROSALIND: And he thinks he made a mistake?

BERNARD: 'E still does!

BERYL: You should tell 'im, Bernie.

(They laugh at the memory.)

ROSALIND: Oh, I wish I could've been there.

Choosing Home

BERYL: You'd've been in bed, fast asleep.

ROSALIND: But you'd've told me, Chips? Wouldn't you? Next morning.

BERNARD: A-a-h...perhaps.

ROSALIND: Oh, you! Of course you would.

(*ROSALIND puts an arm around each of them.*)

Oh, I *do* miss you!

BERYL: I know, but you're home now.

ROSALIND: It's not the same!

BERYL: Just give it time, love.

(*Brief pause.*)

ROSALIND: Oh, I'm not being a good 'ost *(host)*. Please...

(*ROSALIND points to the sofa; they sit.*)

Chips: did you finish the doll-house furniture I was making for Wendy. Give it to her?

BERNARD: No. She said she'd wait on you.

ROSALIND: To finish it?

BERNARD: Says it'll give you a reason to come back.

ROSALIND: As if I need a reason!

BERYL: For a visit.

ROSALIND: Not just a visit!

BERYL: No, Rosie. This has to be your home now.

(*ROSALIND shrugs a shivering 'no.' Slight pause.*)

BERNARD: Young Wendy: she does miss you.

ROSALIND: She was my best friend. Ever! Still is. We write, often.

BERNARD: Never known two girls giggle so much. *(imitates a girlish voice)* Whisper, whisper, whisper...he, he, he...whisper, whisper... he, he, he...

ROSALIND: Oh, Chips!

BERNARD: 'N me trying to get a bit o' shut-eye!

(*A shared giggle. Brief pause.*)

ROSALIND: D'you know, I lived with you for five years, one month and 21 days.

BERYL: You counted?

ROSALIND: Afterwards, here. I worked it out. Do you realise just how much of my life that is?

BERNARD: A pretty good chunk— *(I should think)*

ROSALIND: Thirty-eight point six percent.

BERYL: You never cease to— *(surprise me)*

ROSALIND: But it's different if I count just from when I was first *aware* of my surroundings, the first thing I can remember. We were at Portelet, fishing, and Wes was jealous and pushed me into the harbor. Fiona had to jump in and pull me out. In her Sunday clothes, too! That was on my third birthday, so the *memory* part of my life is three years less than my real age. Which means I was living with you for sixty point seven percent of my life. So is it any wonder that I want to...

(Enter CELIA, GERALD and VINCENT, stage right. CELIA carries a writing pad and pencil.)

CELIA: Is it any wonder you want to...what?

(Pause.)

BERYL: *(coming to the rescue)* Stop doing so much arithmetic in her head, I should think!

ROSALIND: It muddles my brain.

GERALD: Well, actually, it's Wesley who's a wizard with numbers.

VINCENT: He'll be joining you in your firm? As a chartered accountant?

GERALD: I'd like to think so. It'll depend on— *(what he wants to do)*

CELIA: Actually, Wesley's thinking of going into the army. With his experience with the OTC at the College, he'd be bound to get a commission.

VINCENT: I doubt whether the Services will be recruiting, now the war's over.

CELIA: Oh, they're always looking for promising young men like—

GERALD: When Wesley's ready. Then he can make up his own mind.

(Awkward pause.)

CELIA: *(to VINCENT)* Let me introduce you to our guests. I'd like you to meet Mr. and Mrs. Chipman. *(to BERNARD and BERYL)* This is Advocate—

VINCENT: No. No. Just Vincent, Vincent Hargreaves. How do you do?

BERNARD: *(shakes hands)* How do you do, sir?

BERYL: Rosie told us you were here.

Choosing Home

CELIA: Mr. Hargreaves is *Rosalind*'s second cousin, once removed, on my mother's side of the family.

VINCENT: Yeoman service you provided, for our two young people.

BERYL: Oh, just one. Rosie, here.

ROSALIND: Wes stayed with the College, up at Buxton.

VINCENT: Ah! I see.

CELIA: *(emphasizing their names)* Rosalind: where *is* Wesley? See if you can find him, will you?

(Exit ROSALIND.*)*

BERNARD: *(to* VINCENT*)* It was a real pleasure to 'ave Rosie ...er... Rosalind, stay with us.

BERYL: She's such a pleasure to be with. Always.

ROSALIND: *(v.o., shouts)* Wesley! Are you up there?

CELIA: Will she never learn not to—

ROSALIND: *(shouts)* Mother wants you down here.

BERNARD: Got a fine voice, that girl! Sings a treat, too. You should've seen 'er in the Christmas pageant.

BERYL: She had a special carol to sing. Did it just fine.

CELIA: Yes, I'm sure.

(Enter ROSALIND *and* WESLEY.*)*

(to ROSALIND*)* Were you too tired to walk up the stairs? Knock on Wesley's door?

ROSALIND: *(to* WESLEY*)* You heard me, didn't you?

WESLEY: Oh, definitely!

*(*WESLEY *and* ROSALIND *exchange a grin.)*

CELIA: Yes, well... Now, if you'd all be seated, if you wouldn't mind. Mr. and Mrs. Chipman: you stay where you were. Gerald and I will sit here. And, Rosalind, can you bring over a chair, sit beside Wesley? Uncle Vincent, I thought you would be more comfortable in the middle.

*(*CELIA *lifts the flowers and ornament from the small table from which* ROSALIND *has just removed the chair, places them on a bookshelf, carries the table to center stage, and places the pad and pencil on it.)*

*(*ROSALIND *carries her chair to the table [for Vincent's use], then pats the arm of the sofa on which Bernard and Beryl sit.)*

ROSALIND: I'll sit here.

CELIA: The arm of a sofa is *not* for sitting on.

> *(Pause.* ROSALIND *remains standing by the sofa.)*
> Oh, alright. So long as you don't make a practice of it.
> *(Pause.* VINCENT *looks questioningly at* CELIA.*)*

VINCENT: Am I to…just begin?

CELIA: You want me to introduce… *(the reason for the meeting?)*

VINCENT: I think that would be appropriate.

CELIA: I'd prefer you do it.

VINCENT: Oh. Alright, then.

> *(As he speaks,* VINCENT *clears the table top, placing the notepad and pencil on the bookcase. He turns to* BERYL *and* BERNARD.*)*
> Mr. and Mrs. Le Page—Gerald and Celia—have asked me to discuss, very informally, the wish expressed by young Rosalind that she be allowed to live in England with you, rather than continue to live here, in Guernsey.
> *(Brief pause as he turns to everyone, leaning toward each person in turn.)*
> So, rather than talk to each of you individually, I thought it would be better for everyone to be together, hear what is said, know everyone's opinion, so there will be nothing hidden.
> Before we start, I should make it clear that my role is *not* to make a decision, or even offer an opinion. No. My role is to elicit information, in a spirit of mutual understanding. And, I trust, cooperation.
> *(Reactions:*
> > CELIA *listens intently, nods at appropriate moments.*
> > GERALD *stands behind Celia's chair, feels uncomfortable.*
> > BERYL *and* BERNARD *look at each other, also uncomfortable.*
> > WESLEY *feels it's hardly his problem.*
> > ROSALIND *is annoyed with her mother for causing the situation, and embarrassed for the Chipmans.)*
> *(*VINCENT *senses their discomfort.)*
> So…who would like to start?

Choosing Home

(Silence. He turns to ROSALIND, *addresses her gently.)*

VINCENT: *(continuing)* This was your idea, wasn't it?

ROSALIND: *(misunderstands, gestures to the gathering)* This?

VINCENT: No, no. I meant that, two nights ago, you expressed a wish to go back with Mr. and Mrs. Chipman; to live with them.

ROSALIND: Y-e-s.

VINCENT: Can you give me an idea why?

ROSALIND: I like living there. I have friends there.

VINCENT: You don't have friends here?

ROSALIND: No. Not really.

VINCENT: Surely, at school...?

ROSALIND: No. They all know each other. They've been together a long time. I'm new. Not like them at all.

VINCENT: You are aware of this, Gerald?

GERALD: It's so difficult. I've hardly had time to get to know my daughter. And now, if she goes, will I ever?

ROSALIND: Oh, dad!...Father...

VINCENT: Celia?

CELIA: How do you expect me to feel? I'm her mother!

VINCENT: Wesley?

(WESLEY shrugs, looks away. Pause. BERNARD *makes a move to stand up.* BERYL *restrains him, a hand on his arm.)*

BERNARD: Would you mind if Beryl and me, we wait in another room?

BERYL: Of course, we'd be happy to have Rosie come back to us. But it's not for us to say.

BERNARD: We don't want to cause a problem.

CELIA: That's not the way I read it! As soon as you arrived, Rosalind announced she wants to—

GERALD: No, Celia. Wrong moment. Let Vincent do it.

(CELIA sits back, a little shaken.)

VINCENT: Well, please forgive me. I seem to have made a mistake, expecting an open, reasonably harmonious discussion to evolve. Frankly, I would like to drop the whole thing. But I can't very well now, can I? Can you see us all trooping in for a convivial dinner? Smiles on our faces?

VINCENT: *(continuing)* So, this is what I'd like to do. I will meet with each of you separately, and then we'll come together after and I'll sum up; tell you what I learn.

I won't be pointing fingers, laying blame. Nothing like that. I just want to clear the air, so we can go in to dinner with—how shall I put it?—warmer hearts.

(Brief pause.)

Alright, then, here's my plan. I'll talk to Mr. and Mrs. Le Page first. And then to Mr. and Mrs. Chipman. After that, to Wesley. And finally to Rosalind.

(Short pause.)

Celia! This will probably take longer than I expected. Can you delay dinner to, say, half past seven?

CELIA: I'll ask cook.

VINCENT: No. You stay here. Wesley can tell her.

(VINCENT raises an eyebrow to WESLEY, who nods. VINCENT turns to ROSALIND.)

Will you accompany Mr. and Mrs. Chipman? Wait in the front room. See if you can rustle up a cup of tea for them.

(BERNARD, BERYL, ROSALIND and WESLEY exit. VINCENT calls after them.)

And, please, see if you can find something else to talk about. Something less controversial.

(VINCENT takes his chair, places it in front of CELIA and GERALD with its back closest to them. He straddles it, facing them. It's something he does frequently.)

VINCENT: Is this what you expected?

CELIA: No. Yes. I'm not sure what I expected.

VINCENT: Couldn't you have just talked to them privately? Quietly?

CELIA: No. No, it's too contentious.

VINCENT: Contentious?

(CELIA turns away, won't be drawn.)

Gerald, you've been pretty silent. What's your view?

GERALD: Well, I'd rather not have precipitated—

CELIA: You'd have just sat there and let them—

VINCENT: Celia! Can you let Gerald...?

(Brief pause.)

Choosing Home

GERALD: I hardly know my daughter. Before the war I was so busy, trying to get the business off the ground. And then the evacuation: so abrupt; not time to think the alternatives through. *(to* CELIA*)* For all the hardships Rosalind would have faced here, sometimes I think we made the wrong decision, sending her away so young.

VINCENT: Do you feel the same way about Wesley?

GERALD: No. Strangely, no. He was older, already at the College, with boys his own age. If we'd chosen to send him to a boarding school in England—*(to* CELIA*)* we seriously thought about registering him, when he was still a baby—*(to* VINCENT*)* He would have thrived!

VINCENT: Rosalind's different?

CELIA: More introspective.

GERALD: I find it so hard to reach her. She's been back with us for four months and... *(shrugs)*

CELIA: You can't blame yourself for that. Being appointed to the reparations commission, takes so much of your time.

GERALD: I know...I know.

(Pause.)

VINCENT: *(to* CELIA*)* I want to go back. Why do you feel it's too contentious to talk personally to the Chipmans?

CELIA: Because it's so...obvious. They're trying to spirit Rosalind away.

VINCENT: Obvious? Can you be more specific?

CELIA: They're playing up to her. You saw them when we came in.

VINCENT: A-a-h. When did Rosalind first advance the idea she would like to go back there? Live with them?

CELIA: Tuesday.

VINCENT: Before, or after, the Chipmans arrived?

CELIA: After. That very evening.

VINCENT: You're absolutely certain?

CELIA: Oh, yes. The Chipmans arrived on the early morning mailboat. Gerald drove down to meet them.

VINCENT: Alone?

GERALD: No. Rosalind came with me.

VINCENT: Did the Chipmans say anything, right then, that might lead you to believe they were trying to persuade her?

GERALD: No. They were entirely circumspect. Shed a tear or two, Mrs. Chipman and Rosalind. Even he did. They were tired, hardly slept on the mailboat. You know what it's like.

VINCENT: *(to* CELIA*)* Did they say anything to Rosalind, during the day, that might lead you to think…?

CELIA: Difficult to say, really. Rosalind went to school, just for the morning. They had a sleep. Then after lunch I went to a meeting and Rosalind took them for a walk along the cliffs. To Jerbourg, I think.

VINCENT: So, when were you presented with the idea?

CELIA: During dinner, that night. We were having the sweet.

VINCENT: And who said it?

GERALD: Rosalind.

VINCENT: You're sure about that?

CELIA: Yes. She said: "Mother, Father: I'd like to go back to Somerford Keynes. Live with Mu—*(she is about to* say *'Mum Two')*…Beryl and Chips."

VINCENT: Just like that?

GERALD: Yes.

CELIA: The words are imprinted on my memory. Always they will be there.

VINCENT: Was Rosalind—think carefully about this—did she seem to be advancing an idea for consideration? Or making a statement?

CELIA: Oh, a statement. Definitely.

GERALD: I'd have to agree with that.

VINCENT: How did Mr. and Mrs. Chipman react?

GERALD: Looked a bit embarrassed, really.

CELIA: I felt they looked… *(shrugs)*

GERALD: I think they would have liked to have been somewhere else, right at that moment.

VINCENT: *(to* CELIA*)* You felt they looked…?

CELIA: A little smug.

VINCENT: You could *see* that?

CELIA: An impression I had. A strong impression.

VINCENT: *(to* GERALD*)* How did you reply?

GERALD: I didn't. I was caught off guard.

CELIA: I told her to be reasonable. That it was out of the question.

VINCENT: What was her reaction?

CELIA: Burst into tears. Ran from the room. Her way to get attention. I know her.

(VINCENT rises, paces. He's working up toward a courtroom-like interrogation.)

VINCENT: *(primarily to* CELIA*)* It's your contention, then, that Mr. and Mrs. Chipman have been urging Rosalind to return to England and live with them?

CELIA: Oh, absolutely.

VINCENT: Absolutely?

CELIA: Definitely.

VINCENT: What makes you so certain?

GERALD: It would appear that—

VINCENT: It would *appear*? That's hardly a certainty.

GERALD: The sequence in which things happened.

VINCENT: Up to that night, had Rosalind ever said anything, to either of you, to indicate she would like to go back and live there? Permanently?

CELIA: No.

GERALD: No.

VINCENT: On that basis you're convinced Mr. and Mrs. Chipman coerced her?

CELIA: Oh, definitely.

VINCENT: You feel you have sufficient proof that it was their idea? That they persuaded her?

CELIA: Isn't it *obvious*?

VINCENT: Did you—either of you—at any time *hear* Mr. or Mrs. Chipman suggest it to Rosalind?

GERALD: No. Not in so many words. In fact, Mrs. Chipman said to her: "That would be nice, Rosalind, but your home is here now."

VINCENT: *When* did she say that?

GERALD: At the dinner table. It was that, I think, that prompted Rosalind's tears.

CELIA: But it was the *way* she said it, like she was covering up, trying to show it wasn't their idea.

VINCENT: Aren't you making an assumption?

CELIA: You didn't hear her!

VINCENT: I repeat my question: are you not placing your own interpretation on Mrs. Chipman's words?

CELIA: Oh, I don't think so.

VINCENT: If I were to say that Mrs. Chipman's statement does not constitute evidence of her intentions, would I be correct?

GERALD: Yes. It could not be construed as evidence.

CELIA: But the *timing*, Gerald.

GERALD: I agree, the timing does seem more than a coincidence.

VINCENT: Ah! Let's consider that. *(paces)* For the four months she has been home, Rosalind says nothing to you about wanting to return there. Correct?

GERALD: Correct.

VINCENT: Then the Chipmans arrive and within twelve hours Rosalind announces she wants to live with them. Correct?

GERALD: Correct.

CELIA: Right.

VINCENT: Do you have *evidence* that they coerced her?

GERALD: N-o-o.

CELIA: It's obvious, Gerald!

(VINCENT presses hard on CELIA during the following sequence.)

VINCENT: But is it *evidence*?

CELIA: You don't need evidence!

VINCENT: Please answer my question: Do...you...have...evidence?

GERALD: Vincent! Do you really have to—?

VINCENT: Yes, I do. Let me finish. *(to* CELIA,*)* **Do...you... have...evidence?** Or are you only making an assumption?

GERALD: Really, Vincent, is there any need for you to act like this?

VINCENT: Yes, there is. *(now speaks personally)* Celia intimated to me earlier that, if necessary, she would be willing to take the Chipmans to court. I needed to show you how a counsel for their defense would treat her. Sorry my dear.

GERALD: So, you're saying we don't have a case?

VINCENT: The Chipmans may or may not have tried to persuade Rosalind. But you don't know. Even if they did, you have no proof.

Choosing Home

CELIA: Do you think they did?

VINCENT: My dear: my role is purely to elicit facts, not to offer opinions. If they did, I sympathize with you. If they didn't...

GERALD: You sympathize with them?

VINCENT: Yes, for we have placed them in an exceedingly embarrassing position. *(pause)* Now, apart from the filial factors, what would Rosalind lose if she were to go back there?

CELIA: Our lifestyle. Guernsey itself. Her friends here.

VINCENT: You said earlier, she doesn't seem to have friends.

CELIA: Y-e-s...

GERALD: *(to CELIA)* She still doesn't have any friends?

CELIA: She just needs more time.

GERALD: Can't you find a way to help her?

CELIA: I don't know. I've tried, but she won't talk about it.

(Pause.)

VINCENT: So, what else would she lose, if she goes away?

GERALD: Education. Definitely. At the Ladies College she'll have a solid grounding for when she's ready to go on to...whatever she chooses.

CELIA: A rural school in Gloucestershire? She'd come out with that awful accent! Have you heard her speaking to them?

VINCENT: Hmmm. Just because some Guernsey people think they have a pure BBC accent... *(shakes his head)* No, another time. I really must shepherd you out, or we won't have dinner until ten o'clock. And none of us will appreciate that. Especially your cook

(VINCENT ushers CELIA and GERALD out stage right. Then he exits himself stage left and returns with BERYL and BERNARD. ROSALIND follows close behind them, hesitates in the doorway.)

ROSALIND: Me, too?

VINCENT: No. Later.

(ROSALIND exits.)

Do sit. Please.

(BERNARD and BERYL sit on the sofa. VINCENT sits in front of them.)

I am so very sorry for the unfortunate...tone... that erupted earlier, which put you in a very uncomfortable position.

VINCENT: *(continuing)* It all came about because, as you know, two nights ago Rosalind suddenly announced she would like to return to Gloucestershire and live with you. *(slight pause)* That is correct?

BERNARD: Yes.

VINCENT: Unfortunately, and this has been rather overlooked, without realizing it Rosalind put you both in a very awkward position. You wouldn't want to hurt her feelings by countering with a definite 'No. Oh, no.' But on the other hand, you couldn't let yourselves sound too enthusiastic because your response might be misconstrued.

BERYL: I couldn't have said it better.

VINCENT: Quite understandably, Mr. and Mrs. Le Page were somewhat taken aback—as I expect you were—by Rosalind's unexpected announcement.
(Slight pause. he waits for a response.)

BERNARD: Y-e-s.

VINCENT: Because they felt it was difficult for them to deal with personally, they asked me, as an independent observer, to try to determine how serious her request is. So will it be all right if I ask you one or two questions, so I can get a full picture?

BERYL: Certainly. We'll answer as best we can.
(BERNARD nods in agreement.)

VINCENT: How did Rosalind come to be lodged with you? I thought she was evacuated with one of the schools.

BERYL: Oh, she was. To Cirencester. But it was a private school, just a little one, and almost right away the two teachers decided to close it.

BERNARD: They just shut the doors. 'Anded the dozen or so children over to the County Council.

VINCENT: Who brought what must have seemed like a little waif to your door?

BERYL: Never thought of it like that, really.

BERNARD: Nearly broke me 'eart, it did. Seeing 'er standing there. So tiny, a little suitcase in one hand, gas mask in t'other.

BERYL: We couldn't say no.

BERNARD: There was no question—

BERYL: We didn't want to.

Choosing Home

VINCENT: *(slight pause)* Do you have children of your own?

BERYL: Three. Well, two now.

(BERNARD rests a hand on BERYL's wrist.)

BERNARD: Two boys.

VINCENT: Did they mind, having a little…sister…being dropped on them like that?

BERYL: Oh, no. They were away. In the army.

VINCENT: Ah. Of course. So, with Rosalind, it was like you were starting all over again?

BERNARD: It…er…sort of, took some getting used to.

BERYL: She was a comfort, really.

VINCENT: Was she lonely, do you think?

BERYL: A little, for a while.

BERNARD: Didn't take long making friends.

BERYL: Children in the village—

BERNARD: Sort of adopted 'er

BERYL: A Cotswold village is, well, like an island really. But you'd know about that.

VINCENT: Everyone knows everyone else?

BERYL: And Rosie's real easy to get to know.

VINCENT: I'm interested you call her 'Rosie.' Here, she's Rosalind. Always.

BERYL: *(laughs)* That was Chips!

BERNARD: Rosie 'ad been with us about a week. An' we used to walk through the village of an evening…

BERYL: The summer in 1940 was lovely, so sunny. You could 'ardly believe there was a war on.

BERNARD: Took 'er friend Wendy with us. Same age. Lives just across the road.

BERYL: You've not been to Somerford Keynes, have you?

VINCENT: Not had the pleasure.

BERYL: Everyone grows roses—red, pink, yellow—and they hang over the stone walls beside the footpath.

BERNARD: Bobbing in the evening breeze. Like they were nodding at us.

BERYL: And little Wendy says to Rosalind: "Look, they're saying 'ello to you." Then Chips puts an arm over Rosalind's shoulder,

BERYL: *(continuing)* and says: "They're saying: 'Ello, Rosie. Welcome to our village.' Then 'e turns to 'er and says: "Is it all right if we call you Rosie, 'cause you're just like a little English rose?"

BERNARD: An' she looks up at me in that perky little way of 'ers and says—ever so quiet—"I'd like that."

VINCENT: Very nice. Very nice. Was Rosalind—Rosie—was she very homesick?

BERYL: Difficult to tell, really. She was so…so withdrawn at first, as if she was holding herself together.

BERNARD: Like she'd built a tight little shell around 'er.

BERYL: Then, gradually, once she'd started school in the village, she seemed to pull out of it. And it helped when Bernie took her into the woodshop with him.

BERNARD: Working with 'er 'ands, getting the feel of the wood.

BERYL: She made—carved—a little rabbit.

(BERYL stretches her forefinger and thumb 5 inches apart.)

Took it everywhere with 'er. To bed even, like it were a doll.

BERNARD: Even talked to it, like a special friend.

BERYL: Someone she could confide in. Privately.

(Pause.)

VINCENT: Did she talk much about her family.

BERYL: At first. Fiona, mostly. I thought Fiona was her mother!

VINCENT: Her mother?

BERYL: Fiona was their nanny.

VINCENT: Ah! *(to BERNARD)* She calls you "Chips."

BERYL: Everyone calls 'im 'Chips'.

BERNARD: 'Cause I work with wood, make lots of shavings, wood chips.

VINCENT: And when your name's Chipman…yes, of course! Did you suggest to Rosie that she should call you Chips?

BERNARD: No. No, she just did it 'erself.

VINCENT: And you didn't object? Feel it was disrespectful?

BERNARD: Lord, no!

VINCENT: *(to BERYL)* And did she call you "Mrs. Chips?"

BERYL: Oh, no. At first it was "Mrs. Chipman," but we felt that seemed too…impersonal.

Choosing Home

BERNARD: Actually, 'twere Rosie. We were turning wood in the shop. She asked if "Auntie Beryl" would be alright.

BERYL: Too formal.

BERNARD: And then just "Beryl."

BERYL: Too familiar.

BERNARD: Then she says: "Can I call 'er 'Mum Two'?" I didn't know what to say.

VINCENT: *(to BERYL)* You didn't mind?

BERYL: No. It helped her feel more at home, like her friends called their mums.

BERNARD: Then, after a time, the "Two"...sort of disappeared.

BERYL: But she never called me "Mummy." Never.

VINCENT: Out of deference to her mother, I should think.

BERYL: Perhaps.

(Slight pause.)

VINCENT: How did it feel, having to start all over again with a fairly young child, just at the moment when you were probably thinking you'd be having time for yourselves?

BERNARD: With Rosie, it was a real pleasure, she was so easy to 'ave around.

BERYL: You could sense she needed us.

BERNARD: And it, sort of...'elped us...just when—

BERYL: We had to get over it. We had to keep going...

BERNARD: The war, you know...

BERYL: For her—Rosie. Be as normal as we could.

BERNARD: I liked 'er coming into the woodshop with me. That she *wanted* to. Took my mind off... *(shrugs)*

BERYL: Jenny. Our daughter.

(VINCENT nods, refrains from commenting. Slight pause.)

VINCENT: Was it hard, five years later, to say 'good bye' to Rosalind... Rosie?

BERYL: We tried not to let it show. We'd come to think of 'er, like, she was one of our own.

BERNARD: Though we knew all along, the day would come...

VINCENT: Yes. Quite a wrench, I expect.

(BERYL and BERNARD nod.)

VINCENT: *(continuing)* I must congratulate you for creating an environment in which you made young Rosie feel so much at home. It shows. *(slight pause)* If, after all this, Rosie really pushes to come back—really pushes—and her parents were to agree, what would your answer be?

BERNARD: Yes. Aye, yes.

BERYL: We would love to have 'er back. Of course we would. But her home is *here* now.

(VINCENT gives an appreciative nod, rises.)

VINCENT: I very much appreciate your help; your understanding.

(BERYL and BERNARD stand.)

Would you mind re-joining Rosalind…Rosie!…just for a few more minutes.

(He ushers them out, stage left.)

And ask her to call her brother, will you? Send him in.

(VINCENT walks slowly across stage, deep in thought. Enter WESLEY. VINCENT indicates he should sit but remains standing himself.)

Ah, Wesley. With you, I'll come straight to the point. What's your impression of what happened earlier?

WESLEY: Storm in a teacup.

VINCENT: What made you say that?

WESLEY: It's what mother says, when people in the Women's Institute are fussing over something that's really of no great consequence.

VINCENT: *(laughs)* Did you make that up?

WESLEY: *(laughs)* No. I'm repeating her words. She's said it often enough.

VINCENT: Interesting…!

WESLEY: Do *you* think it's much ado about nothing?

VINCENT: Quoting Shakespeare now?

(WESLEY grins.)

I really don't know. It's what I'm trying to find out.

WESLEY: Do you think you will?

VINCENT: We'll see.

(VINCENT straddles the chair and faces WESLEY.)

How well do you know Mr. and Mrs. Chipman?

WESLEY: A little. Some.

VINCENT: I gather from your mother that you visited them while you were at school in Derbyshire.

WESLEY: About once a year. They'd invite me. During the hols.

VINCENT: Did you like it? Down there?

WESLEY: It was alright.

VINCENT: You weren't thrilled?

WESLEY: *(shrugs)* Gave me a chance to see Ros.

VINCENT: Did you feel she was happy?

WESLEY: Oh, yes. Yes.

VINCENT: Have friends?

WESLEY: Lots. They were always around.

VINCENT: She has friends like that here, too?

WESLEY: Couldn't say, really.

VINCENT: Hmmm... *(brief pause)* Did Mr. and Mrs. Chipman spoil her?

WESLEY: I suppose, a bit. Specially Mr. Chipman. But Mrs. was strict: no nonsense.

VINCENT: How did Rosalind like that?

WESLEY: Didn't seem to mind. She knew what she could and couldn't do. Her limits.

VINCENT: If you were Rosalind, would you want to go and live there?

WESLEY: Lord no!

VINCENT: Why not?

WESLEY: Boring.

VINCENT: Just...boring?

WESLEY: To be fair, Mr. and Mrs. were nice...are nice. But...

VINCENT: But...?

WESLEY: It's just a little village. Cotswold stone houses: cottages. Small and cramped. Toilet down at the bottom of the garden. Freezing!

(VINCENT laughs.)

No proper bathroom, just a wash-hand basin in a corner. They drag a big iron bath in from the scullery, plonk it in front of the fire, take turns.

VINCENT: Very romantic! But not your style?

(WESLEY *gestures to the house around him.*)
WESLEY: Hardly!
VINCENT: Do you think Rosalind *really* wants to live with them! Or is it just a passing fancy?
WESLEY: Hard to say. Perhaps she does.
VINCENT: Have you seen anything that might suggest to you that Mr. and Mrs. Chipman—?
WESLEY: Have been working on Ros? Trying to persuade her? N-o-o. Can't say I have. But, then, I haven't been around them much. Hardly at all.
VINCENT: *(stands)* Thanks, Wesley. I appreciate that you have been so open; so direct. That has helped. Is there anything you would like to add?
WESLEY: No. I don't think so.
(WESLEY *stands, turns toward the exit, then turns back.*)
Well, yes: Do *you* think Ros should be allowed to go?
VINCENT: Of all of us here, I'm the one person who cannot say what I think. Remember?...Ask Rosalind to come in, will you?
(WESLEY *exits.* VINCENT *paces, thoughtful. Enter* ROSALIND.)
Hello, Rosalind.
(VINCENT *indicates for her to sit.*)
You know. I'm not sure whether I should be calling you Rosalind, Ros, or Rosie! Do you have a preference?
ROSALIND: Oh, Rosie. Definitely. But not here. And only Wes calls me Ros. Mother doesn't like it, but...Wes is Wes!
VINCENT: And you call him Wes?
ROSALIND: *(nods, laughs)* But not in front of mother. If I remember!
VINCENT: Do you always call your mother 'mother'? Your father 'father'?
ROSALIND: Oh, yes. They prefer it.
VINCENT: They insist?
ROSALIND: No. It just hasn't...*(shrugs)* They've never said...
VINCENT: Wouldn't you like something less formal, especially for your mother?
ROSALIND: No, I don't think so. 'Mother' suits her.

Choosing Home

VINCENT: So be it. Now, Rosie: what makes you want to go back and live with Mr. and Mrs. Chipman?

ROSALIND: I like living with them.

VINCENT: Does that imply you don't like living with your parents?

ROSALIND: No.

VINCENT: No?

ROSALIND: It's nice here. But it's nicer there.

VINCENT: Nicer? In what way?

ROSALIND: It just is. They let me be part of their life. And I let them be part of mine.

VINCENT: Are you implying that doesn't happen here?

ROSALIND: Not in the same way.

VINCENT: Not the same?

ROSALIND: With Chips and Mum Two—Mrs. Chipman—we do things *together*.

VINCENT: Such as?

ROSALIND: Like, with Chips, in the woodshop. He and I, we help each other. He makes me feel like we're friends.

VINCENT: *(eases the interrogation)* What draws you into wanting to work with wood?

ROSALIND: Oh, the feel of the wood: it's lovely! You take a block of oak, mahogany...

(She shows the size with her fingers, about 6 inches long, 3 inches wide.)

You put it on the lathe, start turning it...

(She paddles her feet, as though pushing on lathe pedals.)

ROSALIND: *(continuing)* Gradually it starts taking shape. Then you take it off and start sanding it, and you can *feel* the shape in your hands, the smoothness, the texture, and you can see the grain as it becomes part of the shape. And part of you...

(She senses she has gone on too long.)

Sorry!

VINCENT: No, don't be. I needed to hear that, to understand. So, what do you do with Mrs. Chipman?

ROSALIND: Oh, we bake, and we shop together; do embroidery. I know it sounds like work, but she makes it fun. And she coaches me for the pageant, reciting and singing.

VINCENT: Now you're home, what do you do, special, with your parents?

ROSALIND: We...we walk the cliff paths; sometimes take a picnic to Pleinmont, or Lancresse.

VINCENT: I mean at home, around the house.

ROSALIND: Not much, really. Father spends a lot of time at the office, and Mother is either helping him or doing things with the Women's Institute. *(sighs)* It was different when Fiona was with us.

VINCENT: And who was Fiona?

ROSALIND: She was our nanny, until the evacuation. She did *everything* with Wes and me. Breakfast, lunch, walks in the lanes, bedtime stories—I was only little then. Oh, Fiona could tell the best bedtime stories!

VINCENT: Where is she now?

ROSALIND: Went back to Ireland, I think.

VINCENT: Alright. Now I'd like to go onto other things. My questions may be a little more difficult. Ready?

(ROSALIND nods.)

VINCENT: What makes you think Mr. and Mrs. Chipman would want you back?

ROSALIND: They said so.

VINCENT: When was that?

ROSALIND: When I asked them.

VINCENT: Yes, but when?

ROSALIND: The day they got here.

VINCENT: Had you been planning to ask them? Before they came?

ROSALIND: No, not really.

VINCENT: Then why the sudden...?

(Pause. ROSALIND sighs.)

ROSALIND: I didn't know how much I missed them. And then, there they were, and I knew.

VINCENT: Just like that! But you sounded them out first, surely, before saying anything to your parents?

ROSALIND: The same afternoon. We were walking on the cliffs, at Jerbourg.

VINCENT: You realize, don't you, that you created a dilemma for them? Put them in a difficult position? They couldn't very well

Choosing Home

say: "Yes, please, we want you back," out of deference to your parents. As parents themselves they'd be aware of that. But at the same time, they wouldn't want to give you a direct "No," for fear they might hurt your feelings. I'm sure they love you too much for that.

ROSALIND: *(very quiet)* I know.

VINCENT: Are you perfectly sure—absolutely sure—they would want you back?

ROSALIND: Yes...*Yes!*

VINCENT: *How* do you know?

ROSALIND: I just do. You can't live with people for five years, people who treat you like you're their own daughter, without feeling it, like it's a pain. I know them better—much better—than I know my own parents. And I have been trying so hard! So hard.

(Brief pause. VINCENT *waits, lets* ROSALIND *overcome a tearful moment.)*

VINCENT: The Chipmans seem to be very special.

ROSALIND: Oh, *they are*.

VINCENT: Have you given any thought to how your parents must be feeling?

ROSALIND: I knew you'd ask me that.

VINCENT: Well, have you?

*(*VINCENT *rises, paces.)*
How *much* have you?

ROSALIND: A lot.

VINCENT: Can you be more specific?

ROSALIND: They wouldn't like it, I know. Won't be happy about it.

VINCENT: Why didn't you talk to them, before shouting it out in front of everyone?

ROSALIND: I didn't shout. I said it quietly. Calmly.

VINCENT: Do you think it took them by surprise?

ROSALIND: Who?

VINCENT: Your mother and father.

ROSALIND: *(after a beat)* Yes.

VINCENT: Was that fair?

ROSALIND: Probably not.

VINCENT: Did it color their reaction, do you think?

ROSALIND: Probably.

VINCENT: Would it not have been better—more personal—to sit down with them beforehand? To talk it through?

ROSALIND: In 1940, they didn't ask *me* if I wanted to leave! They just sent me.

VINCENT: There was a war on. It was in your best interest. You were only seven.

ROSALIND: You have feelings when you're seven!

VINCENT: True. But now you're thirteen, and you should be able to see things differently.

ROSALIND: You make it sound so simple. So easy.

VINCENT: Well, wouldn't it have been better to talk first?

ROSALIND: You wouldn't understand.

VINCENT: I'm trying to.

(ROSALIND rises, paces.)

ROSALIND: They don't *listen!* It's hard enough finding the right moment. Father brings work home. Mother's off doing things. And Wes is out there in his own little college world, in the first eleven, planning events. *(sighs)* Nobody has time to *listen.*

(VINCENT has been standing, partly facing away. Now he turns toward her, almost with a flourish.)

VINCENT: A-a-a-h! That's...what...I...needed...to...hear!

(ROSALIND's tension is relieved.)

ROSALIND: You're just like Darrell Fancourt!

(She turns away from him, then swings back as though flinging a cloak behind her, speaks with a deep, guttural tone.)

A-a-a-h! *(sings, pacing toward him)*
>My object all sublime
>I shall achieve in time.

VINCENT: The Mikado! And would you be Yum-Yum?

(ROSALIND nods.)
>Ah, pray make no mistake.
>You are not shy...

ROSALIND : *(sings)* We're very wide awake,
>The moon and I!

(They laugh.)
VINCENT: Where did you learn…?
ROSALIND: At school, for the pageant.
VINCENT: And you were Yum-Yum!
ROSALIND: Yes. And then Mum took me to the New Theatre in Oxford. We went by bus, on a Saturday, just before V.E. Day. Darrell Fancourt was the Mikado. Mum loves the theater. Once or twice a year we'd go. Another time we saw *The Importance of Being Ernest*. So funny!
VINCENT: Just you and Mrs. Chipman?
ROSALIND: Chips? He only likes the Pantomime. Every year, between Christmas and New Year, he'd take us.
VINCENT: You *do* seem to have had an interesting life.
ROSALIND: Oh, yes. Yes!
VINCENT: Wait here.

*(*VINCENT *exits briefly, calls voice over [it's a shout].)*
Hello, everyone. Can you hear me? I'd like you all to come back in now!

*(*ROSALIND *giggles.* VINCENT *re-enters, perhaps gives her a mischievous grin. Then he turns, still smiling, as he greets the returnees. He invites them to sit. They take the same positions as before.* ROSALIND *offers* VINCENT *her chair, but he declines, indicates he will stand. She places the chair next to* WESLEY, *sits on it.)*

Let me say right away how much I have appreciated your individual openness and willingness to provide information. That has been an immense help.

(Brief pause.)

Now, I'm going to sum up my findings—present you with the facts. As such they need not be questioned. Or challenged. Consequently, I am asking you to bear with me and refrain from asking questions, or even passing comments, until I have completely finished.

(Brief pause, during which VINCENT *looks at each of his audience in turn, ensuring his request has been registered. No one answers.)*

Toward the end I may offer a comment or two, but I will *not* be making a decision or making a recommendation.

VINCENT: *(continuing)* Now: do I have your agreement—your acceptance—of the proposed modus operandi?

(VINCENT looks at each in turn and awaits a response. They either incline the head and murmur acceptance, or say "Aye" [BERNARD] or "Yes, sir" [WESLEY]. CELIA is last: she hesitates then inclines her head.)

Right, then. Here we go...

My first Finding: In the four-and-a-half months that Rosalind has been back in Guernsey, at no time did she inform her parents—or her brother—that she was unhappy and wanted to return to the mainland and live with Mr. and Mrs. Chipman.

My second Finding: On the afternoon of the 17th of November—the day that Mr. and Mrs. Chipman arrived—Rosalind informed them that she would like to return and live with them. However, there is no evidence that Mr. and Mrs. Chipman in any way coerced or encouraged her.

My third Finding: The element of surprise created by Rosalind's unexpected announcement caused reactions that virtually eliminated further reasonable discussion. Hence, the reason for my being here tonight.

My fourth Finding: Under the given circumstances, Rosalind's desire to return to live at Somerford Keynes is perfectly understandable.

(CELIA gasps.)

CELIA: How can you— *(possibly know that?)*

(VINCENT raises his hand; GERALD places a cautionary hand on CELIA's arm.)

VINCENT: I said "understandable" intentionally. It's not a decision. Neither is it a recommendation.

(Slight pause, he paces.)

Now, I want to enlarge on that last finding. Because it presents Rosalind with a dilemma.

(He stands behind Rosalind's chair, places his hands on its back, and speaks over her, toward the two sets of 'parents.')

Like quite a few Guernsey children her age, who were evacuated in 1940 and lived alone with a new family, without their own family siblings around them, Rosalind had to adjust to a completely new way of living.

Choosing Home

VINCENT: *(continuing)* May I remind you: Rosalind was only seven.

(Slight pause.)

Now, five years later, she has had to start all over again and adjust to another new way of living.

I said "another new way of living" intentionally. Because Rosalind's memory of her early years here—in this house—with Gerald and Celia and Wesley—is, to say the least, minuscule. Hence, Rosalind feels lonely and yearns to return to the lifestyle she knows best.

(VINCENT leans over and addresses ROSALIND.)

Am I not right?

(ROSALIND turns to face him and nods. He steps around her and directs his next remarks to the four adults.)

Now we—as adults—we have to ask ourselves which is better? For Rosalind to take her time and try to adjust to this new lifestyle? Or return to the lifestyle she is more accustomed to?

We also need to consider which lifestyle will create the least long-term trauma for her.

(VINCENT pauses, paces.)

Either lifestyle will launch Rosalind into her adult life perfectly satisfactorily, but each in a very different way. But can we... can we honestly say that *we* can confidently make that decision for her?

(VINCENT looks at each of the adults, in turn.)

No, because Rosalind is the *only* person who has lived both lifestyles. Shouldn't she—not you, not me—shouldn't she make that decision?

(There is a long pause. Then VINCENT turns to ROSALIND, speaks gently.)

I think, my dear, your two sets of parents will now accept your choice. The life you choose to live.

(Pause. Celia gives a slight 'no' shake of her head.)

ROSALIND: You really are like the Mikado, aren't you?

VINCENT: And you make a bewitching Yum-Yum.

(ROSALIND gives a nervous giggle. The others look vacantly at VINCENT and ROSALIND, aware they are not privy to the private exchange.)

VINCENT: *(continuing)* Go ahead.

(ROSALIND stands up, but slowly. VINCENT takes her chair.)

ROSALIND: Oh, this is going to be so…so difficult.

(She looks in turn at the two sets of parents, one on each side of her, then addresses BERNARD.)

Chips, will you sit beside my Father?

(She turns to CELIA.)

And Mother, will you sit beside…Mum Two?

(They look uncertain. Neither of them moves. ROSALIND waits a moment and then crosses to CELIA, leans over, kisses her. CELIA responds with a peck on ROSALIND's cheek. ROSALIND takes her hand and leads her across to BERYL. BERNARD stands; CELIA sits in his place.)

(ROSALIND takes BERNARD's hand, leans over and kisses BERYL, who responds by reaching up and holding the side of ROSALIND's head, and giving a warm, gentle kiss in return. ROSALIND then leads BERNARD to the seat that Celia vacated. He sits beside GERALD. ROSALIND leans over and kisses GERALD and then BERNARD. Each smiles but does not respond with a kiss. She walks to stage center, speaks almost to herself.)

ROSALIND: That's better. It's not two camps any more.

(Slight pause, then she turns to VINCENT.)

Do I have to?

VINCENT: *(impressed by her action, speaks gently, supportively)* You're doing fine. A step at a time.

ROSALIND: *(slowly)* Whichever I choose, I know it's going to hurt someone. If I stay here, Mum and Chips will be sad. If I go back with them, Mother and Father—and Wesley—will be sad too. Upset. Even if I promise to visit. Lots.

(ROSALIND pauses, sighs, turns to VINCENT.)

What you are saying, I think, is that I have to choose…what I feel will be best... *(quietly)* for me.

(VINCENT nods supportively. Pause.)

Then, that's what I will have to do.

(ROSALIND pauses, then turns and crosses slowly to BERNARD and GERALD. She takes BERNARD's hand and he stands. She pulls him gently toward the wives.

Choosing Home

BERYL *stands and steps toward them.* ROSALIND *takes her hand.)*

*(*CELIA *is distraught. She glances at* VINCENT *and shakes her head as if saying: "What have you done?"* VINCENT *raises his hands as though saying: "I did as you asked.")*

*(*CELIA *holds her hands out to* GERALD *and* WESLEY, *who approach and take them [*WESLEY *has an unusual moment of sympathy for his mother].)*

(Lights have come up on ROSALIND Sr. *downstage right. She is watching the scene. Lights fade on the living room and she turns to the audience.)*

ROSALIND Sr.: What prompted me to make that choice, when up to that moment I really did not know what I should do?

It was as simple as that kiss: the routine, perfunctory kiss from my mother, followed by the warm, giving kiss from Beryl.

(Pause.)

I left with Beryl and Chips the very next morning, on the mailboat to Weymouth. I didn't know what to expect when the time came to say good-bye. How painful it was going to be.

(In the following sequence, WESLEY, CELIA *and* GERALD *enter individually, in turn, downstage left and speak directly toward the audience. Each time,* ROSALIND Sr. *turns to watch them, and then turns back to speak to the audience.)*

Wesley was his practical, cheerful self.

(A spotlight comes up on WESLEY, *far stage left, putting on bicycle clips to protect his trousers.)*

WESLEY: It's the right move for you, Ros. It wouldn't work for me, I know. But then I'm not you.

(With a wave, he turns and exits. The spotlight remains on.)

ROSALIND Sr.: With my mother, I couldn't tell. She was her usual, efficient self, wouldn't let her feelings show.

*(*CELIA *enters the spot-lit area far stage left with a ration book and package of sandwiches, one in each hand, which she holds forward.)*

CELIA: Here: I made some sandwiches for the three of you, for when you're on the boat. And you'll need your ration book.

(CELIA turns away, but glances back briefly, painfully, as she exits.)

ROSALIND Sr.: Yet it took my normally reticent father to nearly break my composure. Nicely, though.

(GERALD enters the spot-lit area stage left. He leans forward slightly, a catch developing in his throat as he speaks.)

GERALD: Let me know any time you want to come home: I'll send you rail and boat tickets. No. that's not right, is it? It's really, when you want to come for a visit. Because, from now on, 'Home' for you will be with Chips and Mum Two. You'll be fine with them.

(Quick fade of spotlight over GERALD.)

ROSALIND Sr.: *(a catch in her throat, but also a smile)* And I was.

(Lights fade to blackout. Bring up music: children singing 'We'll meet again.')

CURTAIN

Choosing Home

Character Descriptions

The Le Page Family

Today, the relationship between the parents and the two children in the Le Page family may seem unreal, too 'distant'. Yet in the 1930's and 1940's it was natural for professional people, in what we now call the 'upper middle-class', to be affectionate in a rather withdrawn way. Recognizing this will help future directors and actors of the play understand that this does not represent an 'unfeeling' dimension in the characters of Gerald and Celia. It affects Rosalind because she experienced more obvious affection living with Bernard and Beryl during the war years, from shortly before her 8th birthday until she was close to 13. (Wesley did not experience this, because he remained billeted with his school and lived with the same boys for the duration.)

Rosalind (age 13, in 1945)

Rosalind can be an outspoken, determined person, yet she has been schooled by her family and the events that have occurred to be self-contained and to withhold her opinions. Essentially, she is a bright, cheerful, very family-oriented person, who wants (and needs) affection and to be loved.

Until she was seven she lived with her natural family in Guernsey. Her parents are professional people who are comfortably off financially and treat their children in a rather off-hand way, somewhat similar to well-off parents in England who send their children to a boarding school as early as possible and endure their presence during school holidays.

Two months before her eighth birthday, Rosalind was evacuated to Cirencester, where she was placed with Beryl and Bernard Chipman in a local village called Somerford Keynes. The Chipmans' adult children were away from home, so in effect she became an only child.

Rosalind was obedient, polite, but withdrawn at first, yet she sensed their warmth toward her and wanted to reciprocate. Gradually, as she realized that they accepted her as one of their own, she relaxed and let her normal, happy, sometimes exuberant self show. She was enrolled in the village school, where she quickly made fast friends with girls her own age. Suddenly she was experiencing a warm environment in which the girls popped in and out of each other's homes and were encouraged by their parents to do so.

In June 1945 Rosalind was returned to her family in Guernsey, where her reception with her family was happy but muted (privately, Rosalind felt it was like being adopted). She found her parents and brother were pre-occupied with their own activities and pursuits, and consequently she felt alone and out-of-place. Worse, her parents enrolled her in the Ladies College, where she knew no one and found the girls all knew each other, most having been together for at least five years. The Gloucestershire accent she had adopted also made her seem even more out of place, and she was embarrassed when the girls laughed at the way she spoke.

Rosalind missed Bernard and Beryl very much, yearned to return, and wrote to them often. She wanted to talk to someone, both about how alone she felt and her desire to return to Somerford Keynes, but hesitated. She didn't want to seem disloyal to her family, and she found it difficult to interrupt their busy schedules.

When we meet Rosalind she is feeling frustrated, a misfit, and constrained. She longs to be her normal happy self, but doubts that it will happen if she continues living with her family in Guernsey.

Rosalind (age 78, in 2010)

Rosalind carried her youthful directness and definiteness into her adult life, and now has carried the same traits into her retirement,

Iris Dyck and Dorothy Talman as the two Rosalinds in the 2011 production

although in a much milder form. Both have proved valuable in her work as a stage manager, mainly for provincial theatres.

The decision she made at age 13 carried her down a path that worked well for her (there was never any doubt in her mind that she made the right decision), resulting in a satisfaction with the life she has led and a comfortableness within herself as she enters her closing years.

Wesley

Wesley is approaching his 17th birthday and is accustomed to being independent, part of yet apart from his family. For the past five years he lived full time with the Elizabeth College boys near Buxton in Derbyshire, while the College was evacuated. It was a boarding school style of life, and he related well to it. He is self-sufficient and is being groomed to be a prefect at the College.

Wesley relates comfortably with his parents, mostly because they encourage his self-sufficiency. He is polite but outspoken with them, yet rarely asks their opinion; he goes to his peers at College for that, or sometimes his teachers. His relationship with Rosalind is comfortable yet a little 'distant.' He senses that she feels unhappy and 'out of place' in Guernsey, but doesn't understand why she should; neither does he know how to help her.

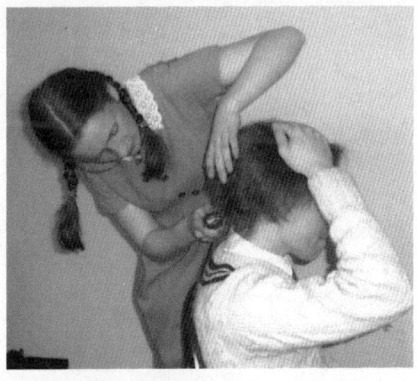

Rosalind (Caitlin Sullivan) trims Wesley's (Charlie Morvan's) hair moments before the first performance of Choosing Home, at the One-Act Play Festival in Guernsey, May 2005.

His manner is direct, definite and confident. He is comfortable with himself and his role in life.

Celia

Celia is a professional woman, having been trained to be an administrative assistant. She grew up in Guernsey, attended Ladies College, went to a business college in England, and on returning to Guernsey responded to an advertisement for an administrator in Gerald Le Page's firm of chartered accountants. She proved to be an excellent manager and eventually married the boss.

After marriage, she continued working until Wesley was born, then hired a nanny (they already had a cook/housekeeper) to look after him and subsequently his sister Rosalind, so Celia could work part-time. She joined the Women's Institute, where she was so efficient and so well respected that in her third year she was elected president. She headed the committee for the Silver Anniversary of King George V and the Coronation Celebrations Committee for King George VI.

If Celia and Gerald had lived in England, they would have sent their children to boarding schools. Having a cook/housekeeper and a nanny was a satisfactory alternative in Guernsey, because their presence freed Celia to continue working and take part in community activities, both of which she really loved doing.

Celia is well-groomed, an excellent organizer, yet only fair at delegating. She becomes frustrated and impatient with people who undertake a task but don't meet deadlines or fail to meet her expectations. She becomes angry with people who don't accept her approach or do things that run counter to the way she expects them to be done. She is not good at compromising and tries to avoid working with people who have different ideas; indeed she resents people who don't meet her standards.

She loves her children, but in a remote sort of way, which was not unusual among professional or moneyed people of that era (the first 30 or 40 years of the 20th century). She expects them to be there when she wants them, but often is not there when they might need her. If she senses they have a problem, she tends to defer dealing with it until later, or until Gerald gets home (and then forgets about it, and the children have learned to 'back off' and not push).

Gerald

Gerald inherited an accounting business from his father, who arranged for Gerald to be articled with a large chartered accountancy firm in the UK and then brought him back to become a partner and, eventually, owner of the firm. The firm is now the most successful chartered accountancy on the island and Gerald is financially very secure.

He is essentially a shy man who loves the privacy and detail of accounting and auditing. He is good at administrative work, although not a good business administrator himself. He is uncomfortable dealing with people problems (staff problems, not client relationships). Consequently he defers many such problems, including hiring, to Celia's good judgment and cool administrative prowess (the reason she continues to work part-time). Similarly, he leaves the running of the house to Celia. Until 1940 he was quite comfortable just seeing his children at mealtimes and, in the evening, when they were brought in by their nanny, bathed and dressed in their pajamas, and ready for a bedtime cup of Ovaltine and a goodnight kiss with each parent. Sometimes Gerald read a story to them (reading from a book rather than making up his own stories).

Since the children's return in 1945, Gerald's relationship with them has been even more distant. He provides solid financial support, likes having them around, but doesn't know how to be close to them. Of the two, he sees Wesley as less of a problem: Wesley is fully occupied with his school and does not seem to seek parental involvement, or even affection. With Rosalind, however, he is at a loss: he senses she is seeking affection and warmth, but he does not know how to provide it. (Privately, he wishes she was more grown-up, like Wesley.) When he gives her a good-night kiss it tends to be a duty, a custom, rather than a demonstration of affection or warmth.

The Chipmans

They married young, in 1915, during World War I. They have three children: Tom, born in 1916, now 30; Jenny, born in 1920, who was 20 when she died in an air raid in 1941; and Ben, born in 1922, now 23. All three children were away from home, in the military, when Rosalind joined the family in late June, 1940.

They live in a Cotswold-stone row house, one of three. It's small, with two cramped bedrooms upstairs and three rooms downstairs. The toilet is at the foot of the garden in a small 'outhouse' attached to the woodshop where Bernard does his carpentry work. There is a wash-hand basin off the scullery, and a large metal tub that is brought into the kitchen and filled in front of the fire. Very romantic, but a darned nuisance when it has to be emptied!

They show affection much more easily than Celia and Gerald Le Page. It is this ease with affection that draws Rosalind to them.

Beryl

Beryl is strict and firm, yet motherly. She is able to provide comfort and assurance, and a sense of being wanted, without being overly oppressive. She is a calm, capable homebuilder proud of her home without making it 'untouchable.' She holds a strong belief in the family and doing things as a family. Their children mildly resented/resisted her tendency to be in control, and to some extent left home early 'to be their own people.' (Yet Rosalind wallows in it, welcoming the warmth and closeness she had experienced previously only with the nanny in her Guernsey home.)

Beryl manages money well (there isn't much of it, but what there is, is spent well), and looks after the family's finances. Bernard welcomes this, for he tends to be artistic and can't be bothered with material things.

She was devastated by her daughter's death, but let it show less because Bernard was even more hurt. Having Rosalind there eased the pain to some extent and allowed Beryl to transfer even more affection to the young girl. She loves music and encouraged all her reluctant children to sing. Only Rosalind really jumped at the opportunity.

Bernard (Chips)

Bernard is a 'country lad,' quiet, easy-going, who loves working with wood and creating lovely pieces of furniture. He comes from a long line of craftsmen, mostly cabinet-makers, in and around Cirencester. He doesn't flare up easily, yet when he is crossed, or someone pushes him too far, he can be like a bulldog with a bone. He tends to be a very fair man who can see both sides of a question. He may have an alternative view, but holds it in rather than promulgates it.

Jenny's death upset him immensely. Having Rosalind there was a plus and a minus: she helped deflect his grief, yet because he had to 'keep a stiff upper lip' on her behalf, he didn't have an opportunity to come to terms with his grief for a long time.

He loves little Rosalind, and not just because she has helped assuage the pain of his daughter's death. He senses her love of working with wood, which allows a closeness to develop between them. This closeness grows into a very strong attachment, so that by the time Rosalind leaves in 1945, he is really hurt, feeling he is losing a second daughter. Yet he tries not to let it show, so as not to upset her and make her departure worse.

The Advocate (Lawyer)

Vincent Hargreaves

Vincent is Celia's great-uncle and he holds an honors degree in law. He came to Guernsey in 1899, joined a small legal firm, and became an excellent and highly respected Advocate. Until his retirement in 1938, he dealt primarily with business disputes, only rarely with family disputes.

He is a very upright man, acts with confidence, is a careful listener, and excels at drawing information from reluctant people. He senses when a person is prevaricating and can be impatient with people who try to side-step a question or conceal facts.

He is a widower: his wife died in 1930 and they had no children. Since then he has employed a live-in housekeeper to run his home. He is not comfortable with the task Celia has assigned him, but feels he has to do it because she is a distant relative.

A celebratory moment following the first production, at the 2005 GADOC One-Act Play Festival. At the front: Caitlin Sullivan (who played Rosalind), and Jane Blower (the Director). At the back: the author and John Gaisford (who played the Advocate, Vincent Hargreaves) The four awards were for best director, best actor under 18 (Caitlin), best male actor (John), and best original script.

Production Notes

Choosing Home, together with *Closure,* has become one of my most-produced plays. As I write (January 2015), Bob Thompson is already rehearsing the cast who will perform the play in the GADOC One-Act Play Festival in Guernsey in

Sitting, from the left: Mike De La Mare (Chips), Pauline Telford (Beryl), Micky Nicolle (Rosalind at 78), Abigail Dempster (Rosalind at 13), Sam Totty (Wesley), Claire Cathcart (Celia), Steve Molnar (Gerald). Standing: John Gaisford (Advocate Vincent), Bob Thompson (Director). Photo: John Gaisford

Every time the play has been produced, care has had to be taken to prevent the role of Celia from appearing too severe, too disconnected from her children, and so prejudice the audience into *expecting* Advocate Vincent Hargreaves to recommend that Rosalind should return to Somerford Keynes and live with Beryl and Bernard Chipman.

The difficulty evolves from the way parents in middle-class families tended to act toward their children in the first 50 to 60 years of the 20th century. They were much more formal in their relationship with their children, who simply assumed the formality was normal. Wealthier parents often employed a nanny, who frequently became a much warmer presence for the children. This is implied twice in the play, when Vincent is interviewing Rosalind:

Choosing Home

Vincent: Do you always call your mother 'mother'? Your father 'father'?
Rosalind: Oh, yes. They prefer it.
Vincent: They insist?
Rosalind: No. It just hasn't... *(shrugs)* They've never said...
Vincent: Wouldn't you like something less formal, especially for your mother?
Rosalind: No. I don't think so. 'Mother' suits her.

Rosalind: It was different when Fiona was with us.
Vincent: And who was Fiona?
Rosalind: She was our nanny, until the evacuation. She did *everything* with Wes and me. Breakfast, lunch, walks in the park, bedtime stories...

In such families the nanny would bath and dress the children ready for bed, who would then be paraded down to say good-night to their parents, when a peremptory kiss would be exchanged. (It's Celia's normal kiss to Rosalind, in the closing 'family' scene, compared to Beryl's warm kiss, with a hand raised to Rosalind's cheek, that really triggers Rosalind's decision.)

Gerald's and Celia's demeanor needs to be presented as closely as possible to the way they would have been in 1945, yet not appear too cold and distant. To help alleviate that impression, for the most recent productions I have inserted a brief remark by Advocate Vincent, in an early discussion he has with Celia, Rosalind's mother:

Celia: I keep telling Rosalind to articulate correctly. Like we do. Like her brother does.
Vincent: Oh, Celia! You know what I'm hearing? Your mother's voice. Twenty years ago. Saying that about you.

Wesley has retained his normal speaking manner because he and his school friends were billeted together during the evacuation, living in a large house in Derbyshire. Rosalind, however, was separated from the children she knew at school in Guernsey and was billeted with a rural family. She attended the village school, where she quickly made new friends and acquired a 'local' accent, which she used for five years, from just before she was 8 until she was about to turn 13.

Creating a 78-year-old Rosalind to introduce the play occurred first in the 2011 Winnipeg production, where the audience was not familiar with the evacuation (as a Guernsey audience was, in the first production). This also allowed Rosalind Senior to appear again at the end of the play, to provide a better closing moment than the rather abrupt one that existed in the first production. The story now has a closing scene that is natural for the way Wesley and Celia would say goodbye, yet also provides a moment for Gerald to show a previously hidden warmth in his character.

Play No. 2

You Will Write, Won't You?

Synopsis

Sixteen-year-old Melissa—who lives on a farm in a remote area of the Canadian Prairies—is excited to learn she has won a scholarship to a summer-long intensive Youth Writers' Institute. But her excitement is dampened by her family, and particularly by her boyfriend, who *expect* her to work on the farm in the summer, go on to agricultural college, and then return to help manage the farm. In a series of interviews with her teacher, her family, and her boyfriend Pete's family, she is simultaneously persuaded to go and dissuaded from doing so. Although Pete is particularly adamant he wants her to remain on the farm for the summer, he also is intuitive and instrumental in helping her make a decision.

Rationale

The idea for the play evolved while I was taking a course on how to write short stories for children. About 70% of my way through the course I was assigned to write a 1500-word story based on an illustration of a boy and a girl, both about 16, standing in a bus station with a bus waiting behind them. Their expressions showed they were coping with a problem: the girl was leaving and the boy clearly was not happy about it.

    The ideas fell into place neatly and I started writing. But soon I ran into a problem: the story just grew and grew until I could see there was no way I could convey the ideas I had in mind in less than 6000 words. Try as I might, I was unable to cut the story down to just 1500 words.

    By then I had developed clear histories of the two characters and the situation in which they were involved, and recognized that it would be better to create a stage play, rather than a short story, around the decision they were facing. The boy and girl would be my principal characters, around whom I would introduce others who had opinions on the situation and were trying to intervene.

History

The play on the following pages has been produced several times and a few changes have been made from the original script. Subsequently, I developed the story into a book bearing the same name and featuring exactly the same characters. There are, however, some differences.

The play is written for general audiences (both teen and adult). The book, however, is written for a teen audience, generally female. The book also continues the story from the moment the decision is made (where the play ends) and in two chapters describes what happened afterward and the impact it had on relationships.

The loneliness of living on the Canadian Prairies is accentuated in this photograph of Melissa taking her laptop into the fields to write. (The illustration is from the book cover, designed by Carol Kemp.)

Characters

The play is set in Hillsview, Saskatchewan, population 850, the focal point of a widespread farming community in the grain belt of Western Canada. The characters are:

Principal Characters
  Melissa Grandpré, 16
  Pete Sawatzky, 17, her boyfriend

Supporting Characters
  Sandra Dawes, 17, Melissa's friend
  Cynthia Grandpré, 45, Melissa's mother
  Louise Grandpré, 71, Melissa's grandmother
  Edgar Sawatzky, 55, Pete's father
  Doris Sawatzky, 53, Pete's mother
  Heather Collins, 32, Melissa's teacher
  Bus Driver, F, 40s *(can be played by the actor playing Doris)*

Although the setting is western Canada, the inaugural production of *You Will Write, Won't You?* occurred in Guernsey, Great Britain, on Thursday May 27, 2004, as part of the 56th One-

You Will Write, Won't You?

Act Play Festival held under the auspices of the Guernsey Amateur Dramatic & Operatic Club (GADOC). The first Canadian Production was performed by R-G Productions at the 2008 Winnipeg Fringe Theatre Festival. The cast in each case comprised:

Role	Guernsey 2004	Winnipeg 2008
Melissa	Charlee Hales	Megan Wilson
Pete	Nick Langmead	Kevin Carruthers
Sandra	Mary Selvidge	Julie Seroy
Cynthia	Caron Parker	Debbie Pomeransky
Louise	Chris Menhenitt	Evelyn Darrach
Edgar	Brian Corbet	Ron Robinson
Doris	Gillian Jackson	Betty Winterhalt
Heather	Clare Milner	Nicole Hargrove
Bus Driver	Mack Tachon	Betty Winterhalt
Director	John Gaisford	The author

Detailed character descriptions are on pages 92 to 97.

The following year, R-G Productions took the Winnipeg cast to Guernsey, to play both *You Will Write, Won't You?* and *Sudoku Fever* at the 2009 GADOC One-Act-Play Festival. (For that event the role of Heather Collins was played by Holly Steele.)

The Set

Stage left is the waiting room of a Greyhound bus depot in the small town of Hillsview. There is a single entrance stage left, which opens onto the road where the bus pauses briefly twice daily. A single large poster of a Canadian scene such as Banff hangs on the right wall and a notice board with pinned announcements hangs near the door. A large working clock is visible high on the back wall, set so the hands have moved to 3:15 when the bus is heard to arrive.

A bench that can seat two is set about 1.2 meters (3.5 feet) farther downstage, facing the audience. A strong light floods in from stage left, to replicate the sun shining on a gravel road and reflecting into the room through the open door.

Stage right is a blacked-out area in which the secondary characters appear briefly, spot-lit, as they enact previous conversations with Melissa and enlarge on what she and Pete are discussing; they speak directly downstage, toward the audience. When this occurs, Melissa and Pete freeze. However, when they need to respond to someone at stage right, they also speak downstage, as if the person is in front of them.

There are minor props for the secondary characters, such as an ironing board, a table, and an armchair, to convey the situation they are speaking from. Notes describing factors affecting previous productions start on page 98.

The bus depot, set up for rehearsal in a private home, prior to the Winnipeg 2008 Fringe Theatre Festival. On stage, it stood at upstage left, with a single entrance at downstage left.

Approximate Length: 50 minutes

Some Script Guidelines

Throughout the script, two symbols are used occasionally at the end of a piece of dialogue to indicate how the sentence ends:

- ... An ellipsis at the end of a statement means the speaker just trails off and leaves his or her thought hanging in the air (possibly accompanied by a shrug).

- — A dash at the end of a statement means the speaker is interrupted by the next speaker, so that the first speaker's statement is incomplete. Sometimes there is an italicized continuation of the statement *(within brackets)* immediately following the dash, to help the actor sense where the sentence was going.

v.o. means 'voice over' - the words are spoken by a speaker who is offstage.

'Waskesiu' is pronounced *wass-ker-soo*.

Script: *You Will Write, Won't You?*

© 2003, 2008, Ron Blicq

CURTAIN UP

(The waiting room is empty. Stage right is in darkness. Sound of a car pulling up, engine switching off, two doors opening, then slamming shut.)

MELISSA: *(v.o.)* Check, will you? See if anyone's there.

SANDY: *(v.o.)* Anyone?

MELISSA: *(v.o.)* Anyone I know.

(SANDY peers into the room. She is dressed in old, faded dark blue jeans and a T-shirt. She looks around, half enters, then turns back to face Melissa offstage.)

SANDY: *(calls)* It's alright, Mel. There's no one here.

(SANDY exits, then returns carrying a heavy medium-size soft-sided travel bag. MELISSA follows, carrying a sports bag and a shoulder purse. She is wearing clean, new, light-blue jeans, a soft-patterned blouse.)

SANDY: Whew! What've you got in there?

MELISSA: It's for two months!

SANDY: I know, but...

MELISSA: *(glances up at the clock)* Nice timing. The bus will be here in five minutes.

(MELISSA goes to the door, looks to the right, turns back into the room.)

With any luck, no one else will be getting on.

SANDY: Or off?

MELISSA: Doesn't matter. There'll be no time for questions.

SANDY: Just raised eyebrows?

(Melissa laughs, paces restlessly.)

Pete doesn't know?

MELISSA: No. He doesn't. I didn't know how to tell him.

SANDY: He's not going to like it. You just going off like this, not saying anything.

MELISSA: I know! I tried. I picked up the phone three times. Even dialed once, heard it ring, his mother answer, but I just...hung up. Couldn't find the words.

(MELISSA walks to the door, steps partly out, looks up the road. She turns back in, but is too restless to sit.)

SANDY: Why all the secrecy? I don't understand— *(why no one should know)*

MELISSA: *(sharp)* Because everyone will try to stop me from going.

SANDY: Try to talk you out of it?

MELISSA: Everyone!

SANDY: Even Pete?

MELISSA: Especially Pete.

SANDY: He can be that persuasive?

MELISSA: Yeah. *(brief pause)* I know he'll be disappointed. We'd made such plans for the summer. Work together all day on his father's farm. Long hours. Then once a month take off for a long weekend.

SANDY: Work hard. Play hard?

MELISSA: Mmm...yeah. The Folk Festival in Regina in July. Then drive up to Lake Waskesiu in August. Swim. Lie in the sun. Maybe a round of golf.

SANDY: Just you and Pete?

MELISSA: Uh-huh. His aunt's letting us have her cabin for the weekend.

SANDY: When we first came here, I was so jealous...

MELISSA: Of me?

SANDY: Of you and Pete. Your relationship. Your closeness.

MELISSA: I guess. As far back as I can remember, our families have just hung out together. They always have, since I was so high .*(MELISSA holds the palm of a hand out horizontally about two feet above the floor).*

Pete and I, we sort of grew up together. Like he's my brother.

SANDY: Your brother?

MELISSA: Uh-huh.

SANDY: Hardly! When I saw you two at the end-of-term dance...

MELISSA: Well, that was different.

(SANDY laughs. MELISSA goes to the door, peers out, stands in the doorway.)

SANDY: *(calls)* Have you...?

You Will Write, Won't You?

MELISSA: Slept with him, Sandy? Like you and Kevin?

SANDY: Well, that's different, too. We plan on—

MELISSA: I know: getting married, having a family. The traditional thing a Prairie girl does after she leaves school. Fifty years ago.

SANDY: So? What's wrong with that?

MELISSA: Alright for you, maybe...

SANDY: Well...have you?

MELISSA: *(slight pause)* No. Not yet. Pete wants to, I know. But...I'm scared. Not of being with Pete; nothing like that. It's just...it would be like a commitment. Like we'd agreed to...you know...

SANDY: Make it permanent?

MELISSA: Y-e-s. Yes!

SANDY: You two always seem so close; so well-matched. Everyone sort- of expects—

MELISSA: I know! My Mom sure does! So do Pete's parents. They've never said anything, but I can sense it. *(a giggle)* Can you see me surrounded by three snotty-nosed kids clamoring for attention? Washing diapers, mending torn jeans, making three meals a day? In the summer lugging sandwiches and lemonade out to the field crew when they're harvesting?

SANDY: Yeah, I can.

MELISSA: Oh, no!

SANDY: That's the image you project, Mel. *(slight pause)* Is that why you've decided to go away for the summer?

MELISSA: To the Writer's Institute?

SANDY: Are you trying to escape what will happen, when you and Pete head off on your own?

MELISSA: I already thought about that, when I agreed we'd go up to Waskesui. *(slight pause)* No, Sandy: this is the only way for me to find out if I'm good enough to be a writer. I have to go on this course.

SANDY: You really want to turn your writing into a career?

MELISSA: Oh, I don't know!

SANDY: Not stay here? Work on the farm?

MELISSA: ***I don't know!*** I won't get another opportunity like this. *(looks at the clock)* Where *is* that bus?

(SANDY crosses to the notice board, scans, reads a message, points to it.)

SANDY: It's late, Mel! Won't be here till three-fifteen.

MELISSA: Oh, no! *(paces)* Shit!...Shit!

SANDY: Who knows you're here?

MELISSA: Just my Mom. She's...*(shrugs).* Well, she *said* it's okay for me to go. But, actually, she's not happy about it. You can imagine! My gran knows too. She's the only one who thinks I'm doing the right thing!

SANDY: And your teacher.

MELISSA: Ms. Collins? Well, yes. If it wasn't for her...

SANDY: You wouldn't be going.

(There is the sound of an approaching motor bike; it almost screeches to a stop. They both look toward the door.)

That's not the bus!

MELISSA: *(apprehensive; knows who it is)* Oh, no!

(PETE rushes in, distraught. He has come straight from the farm, wears worn, soiled jeans, a dusty, sweaty check shirt, glasses with strong prescription lenses [optional], and a helmet with visor.)

PETE: Oh, you're still here! I was afraid I'd miss you.

(PETE pushes up the visor, looks accusingly at SANDY, then back to MELISSA.)

Mel! What are you doing?

MELISSA: Waiting for the bus.

(MELISSA touches one of her bags with the toe of a shoe.)

Isn't it obvious?

PETE: But *why?*

(MELISSA shrugs, turns slightly away. [She is scared he will dissuade her from leaving.] PETE removes his helmet during the exchange, hangs it on the back of the bench.)

Where are you going?

MELISSA: Banff.

PETE: You don't know anyone in Banff.

MELISSA: I will. Soon.

PETE: It's true then. You *are* going to the Youth Writers' Institute?

You Will Write, Won't You?

(MELISSA *nods.*)

PETE: *(continuing)* But we talked about it, Mel. Over and over. And you decided not to apply.

MELISSA: I know, but I...I changed my mind.

PETE: You changed your mind!?

MELISSA: I had to.

PETE: Without telling me?

MELISSA: I did tell you.

PETE: Oh, no, you didn't!

MELISSA: In my letter.

PETE: *What* letter?

MELISSA: My mother didn't give it to you?

PETE: I haven't seen your mother!

MELISSA: Then how did you know I was here? *(turns to* SANDY*)* It was you, Sandy! You two-timing, two faced—

SANDY: No, no! Not me!

MELISSA: Call yourself a friend! Saying 'Sure, I'll be happy to' when I asked you to drive me!

SANDY: No, Mel. I told no one—

MELISSA: And all the time you were going behind my back—

PETE: It wasn't Sandy, Mel. It...it was your mother.

MELISSA: My mother? But you said you hadn't seen her!

PETE: She phoned me. On my mobile, while I was out in the fields. Said if I moved fast, I'd be in time to catch you.

MELISSA: The bitch! The miserable, double-crossing bitch! She's using you, Pete! She wants you to stop me from going.

*(*SANDY *marches to the door.)*

SANDY: I'm outta here!

MELISSA: Oh, Sandy, I'm so sorry...

SANDY: I don't need any of this! You two sort it out!

MELISSA: I was so rude. But no-one else knew. I didn't think—

SANDY: Typical! Always jumping to conclusions—

MELISSA: Oh, no! I'm so sorry, Sandy. So very sorry.

SANDY: *(mellowing)* Alright. Alright.

*(*SANDY *glances at the clock.)*

I do have to go. Pick up Kevin.

(She pauses at the door, looks back.)

SANDY: *(continuing)* Have fun, you two!

(SANDY exits. During the following conversation we hear a car door open and close, and then the car start up and drive away.)

(PETE puts an arm around MELISSA and leads her to the bench. They sit, with MELISSA stage left of PETE. He is calmer and tries to calm her.)

PETE: Mel: I don't understand. What's going on?

MELISSA: It's so difficult to explain. I don't want to hurt you, Pete. I just didn't know how to tell you. *(pause)* I've got to try. Got to find out. I'll never know, otherwise.

PETE: We talked about it, Mel. Endlessly. And you decided you wouldn't...

MELISSA: I know. *(whispers)* I know.

PETE: Then why...? *(touches her travel bag with his toe)* Why all this?

MELISSA: It's so difficult— *(to explain)*

PETE: And you didn't tell me!

MELISSA: I couldn't, Pete.

PETE: Couldn't? Or wouldn't?

MELISSA: You don't know what it's like. With my mother. *(pause)* It's alright for you. When you say you want to do something, your family...they stand behind you. Like they're saying "Go on. Try it."

PETE: They'd do the same for you.

MELISSA: No, Pete. No, they can't. *(pause)* It goes back to that day Ms. Collins held me back after school.

(A spotlight picks out Ms. COLLINS stage right, standing beside her desk, holding three pages of forms in her hand. She speaks as though Melissa is standing directly downstage of her. Simultaneously, the lights dim slightly stage left. PETE and MELISSA freeze.)

Ms. COLLINS: Melissa: I really think this summer you should apply to go to the Youth Writers' Institute. Two whole months of concentrated writing instruction. They have such well-known writers teaching it: *(looks at the forms)* Monica Fields. James Calhoun. *(she holds the forms out, in front of her)*

You Will Write, Won't You?

Ms. COLLINS: *(continuing)* You could apply for a scholarship. You'd have a very good chance of winning.

(MELISSA stands and speaks directly ahead.)

MELISSA: But I've agreed to work for Mr. Sawatzky this summer. On his farm.

Ms. COLLINS: You've got to believe me, Melissa. You have the potential. There are many pieces you've written you could send in with your application.

(She searches on the desk, holds up two pages.)

Like this one, when you described that strange, imaginary boy in your class. *(reads)* "He marches toward the school steps with a slight roll to his body, as if he had just stepped off a merchant ship following a two-week journey over rolling seas. He shoulders his way along the locker-lined corridors, other students stepping to one side."

(She pauses, looks at imaginary Melissa.)

Remember?

(MELISSA nods. Ms. COLLINS continues to read. MELISSA follows the words and quietly starts to mouth them aloud, in synchronism. After a few words, Ms. COLLINS goes silent while MELISSA finishes.)

"He walks into the classroom assertively, confidently, pushes up the third aisle, and eases himself backward into his seat. He drops his books onto his desk..."

MELISSA: "... He drops his books onto his desk, briefly scans the already seated students, lays his hands palm-down onto the top surface of his desk, and looks up at the teacher. 'Right!' he announces. 'Let's get this show on the road'."

(They both laugh.)

Ms. COLLINS: You paint such evocative images! I can *see* that boy. And there's rhythm in your writing. Like music. At the Institute they'll help you develop that. Much more than I can. *(she holds the application forms forward)*

(MELISSA shakes her head.)

No? Well, at least promise me you'll think about it. The forms will be in the top draw of my desk.

(The spotlight extinguishes stage right. MELISSA returns to the bench as the lights return to full strength stage left.)

PETE: But Ms. Collins is only a teacher. She'd be off writing herself if she was any good.

MELISSA: No, Pete. She is good. I've learnt a lot from her.

PETE: Yeah, but writing for the school magazine—even for the local rag—it's not the same as...as... *(he searches for the word)*

MELISSA: Writing in the real world?

PETE: Anyway, I thought you were going to concentrate on the sciences next year, like my dad asked you.

MELISSA: Oh, I still plan to.

PETE: But if you start writing...will you even stay here?

MELISSA: I'm coming back. It's only for two months.

PETE: My dad really needs you on the farm.

MELISSA: I know that. I understand.

PETE: Not just for this summer. After you've been to agricultural college.

MELISSA: *If* I go to agricultural college.

PETE: If?

MELISSA: If I don't go to Banff now, how will I ever know if I'm doing the right thing?

PETE: As a writer?

MELISSA: Or in agriculture.

PETE: Dad thinks it's all arranged— *(that you'll study agriculture)*

MELISSA: I can't let your Dad pay for my education.

PETE: But he *wants* to.

(A spotlight picks out EDGAR *wearing a heavy check shirt and coveralls with straps over the shoulders. He is sitting at a table, stage right, a coffee mug in his hand. He speaks as though Melissa is sitting on the other side of the table, directly downstage in front of him. The lights dim slightly stage left.* PETE *and* MELISSA *freeze.)*

EDGAR: I need you, Melissa. The farm needs you. You're smart. After high school you go to agricultural college. Come back, be my...technical adviser.

MELISSA: *(facing directly ahead, still seated)* But shouldn't Pete do that? I mean, he's family.

EDGAR: I need Pete on the farm. Right now. Working with the machinery. He's good with his hands.

You Will Write, Won't You?

EDGAR: *(continuing)* He knows how to fix farm equipment. When a combine breaks down, he always seems to be able to rig up a temporary fix until the service rep drives out here. When we're harvesting, we can't afford to wait two, three days. With our short summers, every moment counts. And *you* know what it's like on a farm. You've worked here: three summers now.

That's why I want to sponsor you, Mel. Pay for your tuition. Lodging too.

MELISSA: *(murmurs)* No...no...no...

EDGAR: I'm not just being philanthropic, Mel. No way. I see it as an investment. I don't want to hire some citified, theoretical graduate straight out of college, who has no idea what it's like working out here in the summer heat. And the dust. Or how to face a drought. Or a host of grasshoppers munching away at the crop. Or cope with rust on the grain. He'll just give me textbook answers with lots of theory.

(Spotlight extinguishes stage right; lights return to full strength stage left.)

MELISSA: It's not right, Pete. Your father should be paying for *you* to go to college!

PETE: No, that was my choice. I *have* to start working on the farm. Right now. Get ready so I can manage it for Dad.

MELISSA: You could still do that, after college.

PETE: There's no time! *(brief pause)* He's got arthritis, Mel. Already it's affecting his work. I see him wince when he has to move a bale or grab a heavy tool. Sometimes he drops things, for no reason. I've seen it more than Mom has.

MELISSA: So you're going to step in, pick up the load? As though you want to?

PETE: I *do* want to. And Mom wants me to. And she agrees with Dad, about you going to agricultural college.

MELISSA: I know. She told me.

(A spotlight picks out DORIS *stage right, standing in front of a table. She is cutting up a cucumber and placing pieces into jars. She speaks as though Melissa is sitting on the other side of the table, downstage, directly in front of her. The lights dim slightly stage left.* PETE *and* MELISSA *freeze.)*

DORIS: Edgar has such affection for you, Melissa. You're like a daughter to him—the daughter he's always wanted.

You see, with Pete, it was a difficult birth. We just couldn't have any more.

He's not just being kind—benevolent, like—when he says, you know, he wants to pay for you to go to college.

He still misses your father, after all these years. They were such good friends. Your Dad gave Edgar so much good advice. About the crops, what to sow, how to get a good mix. Having a balanced farm, he called it. Now Edgar feels, through you, he can sort of give respect to your father.

(Spotlight extinguishes stage right; lights return to full strength stage left.)

MELISSA: I can understand your parents' wishes, Pete. But why are *you* so set against my going?

PETE: To the Writer's Institute?

(MELISSA nods)

It's just...it's just I can't see *why*. Why you need to.

MELISSA: *(puts a hand on his arm; gently)* No, Pete. It's more than that.

PETE: *(after a moment)* Well, we'd sort of planned...we were both going to work on the farm this summer. And take a break together, in Regina; Waskesiu. Then in the winter, my parents want to take you with us to Mazatlan. So we can learn scuba diving. Like we talked about.

MELISSA: And we still can.

PETE: When you haven't kept up your side of the bargain?

MELISSA: Bargain? What bargain? I get paid when I work for your father, just like the other workers. I just won't be paid this summer.

PETE: Then how are you going to pay for this...this Institute?

MELISSA: It's...it's all arranged.

PETE: Not by your mother?

MELISSA: Oh, no. She doesn't really want me to go.

(A spotlight picks out CYNTHIA *at stage right, at an ironing board, facing downstage. She irons clothes as she speaks, pausing slightly in her discourse as she turns or replaces clothes, and in her ironing as she makes a point.)*

You Will Write, Won't You?

(CYNTHIA speaks as though Melissa is standing in front of her, leaning against a doorpost. The lights dim slightly stage left. PETE and MELISSA freeze.)

CYNTHIA: You're chasing a dream, Melissa. You're being self-indulgent. Indulging in a whim. *(slight pause)* What are you going to use as spending money next year? You won't earn anything if you go to that Writing Camp. Summer's when you earn. And Edgar pays you well. You know that.

(MELISSA has stepped forward, speaks directly downstage. Now she is an irritating, belligerent teenager.)

MELISSA: Oh, don't go on and on about it!

CYNTHIA: I don't want you to make the same mistake I made. Waste all that time going to college and then not using it.

MELISSA: Mother! Going to a writer's camp for two months is nothing like going to teacher's college for three years!

CYNTHIA: Worse. There are no guarantees. All the time, I knew there'd be a job waiting for me. Guaranteed! They were clamoring for teachers.

MELISSA: But this isn't about you. It's about me. And, anyway, you didn't go on to be a teacher.

CYNTHIA: No. I didn't. *(a self-satisfied smile)* I met your father. And then you came along. *(pause)* Hmmm. I'd have been a good teacher. I was good with young people…

(Spotlight extinguishes stage right; lights return to full strength stage left as MELISSA returns to sit beside PETE.)

PETE: You're not taking out a loan, are you? Like from the credit union?

MELISSA: No, nothing like that.

PETE: My father would lend you the money.

MELISSA: Then I'd have to…I'd feel obligated to— *(work for him)*

PETE: He'd want to, Mel.

MELISSA: No, Pete. Don't you see? I'd *have* to follow through. Go on and take agriculture.

PETE: He wouldn't expect…he's not like that.

MELISSA: But I am. *(brief pause)* No, I have to do it on my own.

PETE: Then it must be your grandmother.

MELISSA: Nan? N-o-o. She'd like to, I know. But she's only got her pension.

(A spotlight picks out LOUISE *sitting in an armchair stage right, doing embroidery. Melissa is supposedly sitting opposite her, directly downstage. The lights dim slightly stage left.* PETE *and* MELISSA *freeze.)*

LOUISE: My dear, you've got to follow your heart; your intuition. Decide what's best *for you*. *(slight pause)* I mean, how do you see yourself in, say, five years? Ten years?

MELISSA: I wish I knew!

LOUISE: I'd like to tell you what I really think, but I can't. I don't want to cross your mother. We have to go on living together, whether you're here or not.

MELISSA: Why is she so set against my going?

LOUISE: It's hard for your mother to pull back, Melissa. To let go.

MELISSA: Of me?

LOUISE: Mother's can be like that, my dear.

MELISSA: So she'll hate me if I go?

LOUISE: She can't help wanting to see you settled.

MELISSA: Yeah, on a farm close by! So I can be a comfort to her, in her old age.

LOUISE: Don't be too hard on her, Melissa. You're all she's got.

MELISSA: I know. *(shakes her head, frustrated)*

LOUISE: If you were a boy, your decision would be straightforward: work on the farm, or learn a new trade, elsewhere. For a girl, it's different. You can stay and become a farm wife, as I did. Bring up the children, prepare meals for the hired help; become involved in the community. Be an anchor for the family. Perfectly respectable; very satisfying.

*(*MELISSA *steps forward, to stage front, goes down on one knee, as though appealing to her grandmother sitting in the chair in front of her.)*

MELISSA: That's what you think I should do?

LOUISE: Or you can let your heart dictate: move away and find other work. *(muses)* But only a few ever come back, except for a visit at Christmas. Or for a wedding. Or a funeral. *(pause)* So, my dear, how am I to advise you? *Of course* I'd prefer to have you stay here, but... *(*LOUISE *leans forward, reaches out)*

You Will Write, Won't You?

(MELISSA reaches forward, as though grasping the hand.)
LOUISE: *(continuing)* Let me put it this way. If your grandfather was alive, I know exactly what he would say: *(adopts a deep voice)* "Go for it, lass. Bite the bullet."
(MELISSA laughs. She rises, returns to PETE.)
(The spotlight extinguishes stage right; lights return to full strength stage left.)
MELISSA: Is it all that different? Me wanting to write? You wanting to fly?
PETE: No. Except I didn't. I couldn't.
MELISSA: But you would have...?
PETE: Most likely. Probably...it was a great dream. While it lasted.
MELISSA: *(persisting)* But you still would've gone to the Flying Academy?
PETE: Well, yeah, I suppose. But, Mel: it's no good crying over spilt milk. Like your Nan says.
(MELISSA laughs.)
MELISSA: Was your dad disappointed you couldn't be a pilot?
PETE: Mixed feelings, I guess. He gave me so much encouragement, even though he really wanted me to stay.
(A spotlight picks out EDGAR and DORIS sitting side-by-side at a table stage right, facing directly downstage. Each holds a cup of coffee. They speak as though Melissa and Pete are sitting on the other side of the table, directly in front of them. The lights do not dim stage left, and PETE and MELISSA do not freeze. They look straight forward, as if sitting at the table.)
EDGAR: From the time Pete was ten...even earlier...he wanted to fly. Be a pilot. He was obsessed with the idea. Fly with the Snow Birds. That was his ambition.
PETE: *(to MELISSA)* I think Dad was more 'for' it than I was!
EDGAR: Built all those model airplanes. Flying models. Not plastic. Made of balsa wood and glue, with a real engine inside. And radio control. No control lines. Sharp!
(EDGAR stretches his arms out sideways.)
Remember that Spitfire, Pete? It was *big!*
PETE: Four foot, eight inch wingspan.
EDGAR: Sleek! And fast!

MELISSA: *(to* PETE*)* I remember the Spitfire. It disobeyed your orders and flew across the fields! Wouldn't turn around and come back.

PETE: We chased after it, on our bikes.

MELISSA: It landed in Mr. Granger's wheat field.

PETE: He wasn't happy when we walked in after it.

MELISSA: Worried we'd ruin his crop.

(They laugh.)

DORIS: You wrote a wonderful story about it, Mel.

*(*DORIS *holds up a local newspaper, with a headline and a photo of Pete and the plane in the text; reads.)*

"A Spitfire that Flies Like a Bird!"

EDGAR: *(points to photo in paper)* You took that photo, too, Melissa. A real good one. How old were you then, Pete?

PETE: Thirteen…fourteen. Grade 8, I think.

EDGAR: You were so enthusiastic.

DORIS: You both were!

EDGAR: If only your eyes hadn't let you down.

(Fade light stage right.)

MELISSA: Oh, your eyes! *(holds her hands to either side of her head)* I'd forgotten about your eyes.

PETE: It's no big deal!

*(*MELISSA *is disoriented, disconcerted. She knows something about Pete's eyes that he doesn't, but with the sudden excitement of going to the Institute had forgotten about it.)*

MELISSA: Oh!…it's just…oh…I was sorry when you found out about your eyes. I knew you were disappointed.

*(*MELISSA *places a hand on* PETE*'s arm.)*

But, for me, it meant you wouldn't be going away.

*(*PETE *rests a hand over hers.)*

PETE: That's it, Mel. You see? That's why I don't want you to go to this writer's camp.

MELISSA: But it's only for two months. You'd've been gone for…years.

PETE: I'm afraid of what comes after. You could get a taste for this writing stuff. Go study writing instead of agriculture.

You Will Write, Won't You?

PETE: *(continuing)* And to do that you'd have to move away. And work away. And that'd be it. For us.

MELISSA: Oh, Pete. You really don't want me to go, do you?

(PETE shakes his head.)

You think I should just forget about going to Banff?

PETE: I don't know, Mel! I want what's best for you. Really, I do. But I also want what's best for me. And they don't...fit.

(MELISSA stands up, looks at the clock, walks to the door, looks out. She turns back, stands behind him, places her hands on his shoulders, and brushes her cheek against his hair. He looks up at her and we feel the connection between them. He stands and they embrace [but no kiss]. We sense that Melissa may have changed her mind and not go to the Writers' Institute.)

Oh, Mel...

MELISSA: But what am I to say to Ms. Collins?

PETE: Your teacher?

MELISSA: She wants me to go.

PETE: It's not for her to decide— *(whether you should go)*

MELISSA: She *expects* me to.

PETE: She'd understand.

MELISSA: She'd be so disappointed, after all she's done.

PETE: Mel: This isn't *about* Ms. Collins!

(Slight pause.)

MELISSA: *(slowly)* Y-e-s. Yes, it is.

(MELISSA delves into her purse, pulls out an envelope, opens up the letter inside it, hands it to PETE. He reads. He is surprised, but not congratulatory.)

PETE: You...won...a...scholarship?

(MELISSA nods)

You won a scholarship!

MELISSA: A *residential* scholarship. Travel, accommodation, all paid. The lot.

PETE: So that's how—

MELISSA: And Ms. Collins said— *(she was sure I'd win)*

PETE: Mel! How come you didn't tell me?

77

MELISSA: I didn't know.

PETE: There've never been secrets between us. Always, we share ideas, plans.

MELISSA: Pete! I didn't know!

PETE: *(sarcastic)* I didn't know! Of course you knew. All the time you knew. You've been planning this and you were going to sneak away— *(without telling me)*

MELISSA: It wasn't like that. I *really* didn't know.

PETE: Maybe you didn't know you had won the scholarship—not at first—but all the time you knew you'd put in for it; knew there was a chance.

MELISSA: Pete! *(stresses the words)* It wasn't like that!

PETE: I can't believe you'd do this. Not say a word!

MELISSA: I keep telling you—

PETE: I bet you weren't even going to write to me.

MELISSA: Of course I will.

PETE: If you can find the time!

MELISSA: Pete, please. Don't be like that.

PETE: There's no point in my staying here. You don't need me. You didn't even want me to be here, to say goodbye!

(PETE rushes to the door, turns back, strides across to the bench. MELISSA reaches out to him. He ignores her, retrieves his helmet, and exits. MELISSA runs to the door, exits, calls.)

MELISSA: *(v.o.)* Pete! I do want you to stay. Please! *(pause; shouts)* I know you don't like it, but—

(The motorbike engine starts, is put into gear, drives off. The sound fades into the distance. MELISSA returns to the waiting room, sobs.)

I do care, Pete. I do care.

(She stands upstage of the bench, the letter still in her hand, looks at it, shakes her head.)

Oh, Pete. You say: 'There've never been any secrets between us.' But you don't really know, do you?

(She paces, looks out of the door, comes in, paces.)

For eight months I've carried a secret. And I nearly forgot. After I'd promised your father.

You Will Write, Won't You?

(Lights come up stage right. EDGAR *stands behind the table, looking downstage toward Melissa, who is assumed to be standing on the downstage side of the table.)*

EDGAR: Sit down, Mel. Will you?

*(*MELISSA *looks toward the audience, steps around the bench, sits on it. She tilts her head up slightly as she listens. Similarly,* EDGAR *looks slightly downward, as* MELISSA *is now seated. He has difficulty finding the right words.)*

> *(ALTERNATIVE:* MELISSA *responds to* EDGAR*'s request, walks across to stage right, sits at the table. Lights black out stage left.)*

Look. I…I want to…to share something with you. Yes, share. Share it with you. *(leans forward)* But, first, I need a promise from you.

MELISSA: I…I don't understand.

EDGAR: Bear with me, will you, Melissa. Just for a minute.

MELISSA: Oh…uh…sure.

EDGAR: I want to tell you something about Pete. Because you and Pete…well, you're like special friends.

MELISSA: Y-e-s.

EDGAR: I mean, you've been Pete's girl…for a long time now. *(pause)* There's something you need to know. About Pete…

(Pause. EDGAR *waits for* MELISSA *to respond, but she only looks enquiringly up at him.)*

But it has to stay with you, Mel. You can't tell him. Or anyone. *Anyone.* Not even your mother. Or your gran.

MELISSA: I don't understand, Edgar. Pete isn't…I mean, he hasn't got something like… *(shrugs)*

EDGAR: Cancer? No. Nothing like that. *(slight pause)* Mel: Pete must hear this only from me. Or from his mother, should I not be spared.

*(*EDGAR *raises his hand slightly, as though saying 'Wait a minute'. He walks to stage right of the table, pulls out a chair, sits.* MELISSA *turns slightly to her right as she follows his movements. He reaches forward as though taking her hand. She leans her hand forward, as though grasping his hand.)*

(ALTERNATIVE: They engage hands.)

EDGAR: *(continuing)* It's about his eyes, Melissa. How—.

MELISSA: Oh. I...I do know about Pete's eyes.

EDGAR: *(taken aback)* You do?

MELISSA: How sorry I was, when Pete told me he couldn't be a pilot.

EDGAR: Ah. No. No, Mel. It's more than that. *(big breath)* Over the years, Pete's eyesight will go on getting worse. Slowly.

MELISSA: Worse! How...how much worse?

EDGAR: A lot.

MELISSA: I mean...how long before...?

EDGAR: Fifteen years, maybe. More if he's lucky.

MELISSA: You're not saying...Pete'll go blind? You're not, are you?

EDGAR: I wish I knew. Probably not completely blind. But—unless there's some sort of medical breakthrough—he won't be able to see all that much.

MELISSA: *(to herself)* Oh, Pete. I didn't know. You didn't say...*(to EDGAR)* He doesn't know?

(EDGAR shakes his head 'no'.)

EDGAR: It's a disease called glaucoma. Open-angle glaucoma. The onset will be slow. But it's...it's incurable.

MELISSA: *(drawn out)* O-h-h... You haven't told him?

EDGAR: No, Mel. No.

MELISSA: But why?

EDGAR: The ophthalmologist suggested we wait until—

MELISSA: Shouldn't he know? Be the first to know?

EDGAR: Doris and I—

MELISSA: They're Pete's eyes!

EDGAR: We decided it's...it's better—

MELISSA: It's *his* life!

EDGAR: It's better for him not to know. Not yet. *(slight pause)* We want him to enjoy what he's doing, while he still can. Enjoy being with you. *Seeing* you. We don't—

MELISSA: Then why're you telling me?

EDGAR: We don't want him to feel like he's living under a cloud—

MELISSA: But it's okay for me to? Live under a cloud?

You Will Write, Won't You?

EDGAR: Keep wondering how long he's got; how bad it's going to be.

MELISSA: Don't you think *I* will? Keep wondering?

(EDGAR holds up his hand to stop her.)

EDGAR: Mel: you're like family to us. And you and Pete, you're such friends...so close...you do so much together.

MELISSA: *(gently)* I know.

EDGAR: Me and Doris.... We feel it's only fair you should know.

(Pause.)

MELISSA: I don't know if I should be saying "Thank you" or "Why have you told me?" *(pause)* "Thank you," I guess.

(EDGAR inclines his head in acknowledgement.)

EDGAR: But, Mel, there is some 'Why'.

(MELISSA lifts her head: it's a question.)

You can help. Encourage Pete to get out of the house more. It's important for him to be outside, looking at things from a distance. Like when you're out on your bikes, or you're riding together on his motorbike. It's better for him to see things from far off, not peering up close. Like when he's working on his stamp collection.

And, particularly—you'll think this is strange—on a hot day try to prevent Pete from taking such long, deep drinks of water; or lemonade. You've seen him do it.

MELISSA: Yeah. Yeah, like when we were haying. Two weeks ago. I told him it's bad to drink so much so fast. You get bloated.

EDGAR: The ophthalmologist said big drinks sort-of speed up onset of the disease. She doesn't know why.

MELISSA: But, Edgar...how am I to...to not say anything? To him? How can I go on being the same with Pete? So he doesn't suspect... guess...I know something he doesn't?

EDGAR: You'll be able to handle it. You're very much like your father.

MELISSA: Oh, I don't think— *(that's true)*

EDGAR: You've got to believe me, Mel. I knew your father well.

(Pause.)

I guess you'll just have to push what we've been talking about, right to the back of that pretty little head of yours.

MELISSA: Oh, Edgar...if only it could be that easy.
(Fade light to blackout stage right.)
   (ALTERNATIVE: MELISSA *rises and crosses to stage left.)*
   *(*MELISSA, *thoughtful, goes to door, peers out.)*
   Pete? Pete? Come back. Please!
   *(*MELISSA *returns to the bench, sits, is disconsolate. She picks up the Banff letter, looks at it, inserts it into its envelope, and lays the envelope on the bench beside her.)*
MELISSA: *(continuing)* In all the excitement I'd forgotten about your eyes... Oh, if only Edgar hadn't told me. How can I say I'm going to Banff, now, when I know you're...*(a moan of distress)* O-o-h!
   (At stage right, a very bright spotlight fades in, from above, directed onto a single upright chair, empty, facing stage left. MELISSA *turns to face it.)*
   Dad...Oh, Dad...What am I to do now?
   (Pause, then submissive, as if agreeing.)
   Yes...I know. I have to decide for myself. But it's going to be so difficult. So hard. *(pause)* I love him, Dad. I think I love him.
   (Pause. The stage right spotlight begins to fade, slowly.)
   I miss you, Dad. Oh, I do miss you.
   (The light extinguishes stage right. Pause, then MELISSA *lifts her head and listens. She has heard something we have not yet heard: the sound of the motorbike approaching. The engine sound grows louder, then ceases as the bike pulls to a stop and the engine is switched off.* MELISSA *looks toward the door, then turns away and looks down.)*
   *(*PETE *runs in. He is still wearing his helmet, but with the visor pushed up. He pauses, then steps around the bench, drops to one knee in front of her, and takes her hands in his.)*
PETE: Mel...Oh, Mel. I shouldn't...I shouldn't— *(have gone off like that)*
MELISSA: I thought you might've been pleased for me.
PETE: Oh, more than pleased. Proud!
MELISSA: I wanted to tell you. I did try....

You Will Write, Won't You?

MELISSA: *(continuing)* Last night, when we went to close up the barn. Remember? But the words just…just wouldn't come. That's why I wrote to you. When I write, somehow the words…they say what I really want them to say. In my letter I told you how I feel about you. And why I have to go away. And I said it well. You'll see, when you read it. *(slight pause)* Though you won't need to now.

*(*MELISSA *is undoing his helmet as they speak. She pulls it off his head and hangs it on the back of the bench [it's clear this is something she has done before].* PETE *sits beside her.)*

PETE: You'll still let me see it?

MELISSA: You'll have to ask my mother. She has it.

PETE: On my way home.

MELISSA: There's something else you need to know.

*(*MELISSA *picks up the Banff envelope and thrusts it into his hand.)*

Look at the address.

PETE: *(reads)* "The Banff Centre for Youth Education in the Arts"—

MELISSA: No, no. Who it's addressed to.

PETE: *(reads)* "Ms. Heather Collins, Post Office box"— *(117 Hillsview)*

(Sound of doorbell. MELISSA *steps downstage, the envelope in her hand [hidden], and faces the audience. She reaches forward as though grasping a door handle, pulls it toward her.)*

(A spotlight comes up on Ms. COLLINS *downstage right, facing the audience.)*

MELISSA: Ms. Collins!

*(*Ms. COLLINS *holds out an identical envelope to the one Melissa is holding.)*

Ms. COLLINS: Hello, Melissa. This came for you.

MELISSA: For me?

*(*MELISSA *reaches forward with the hand holding her envelope, and 'takes' it from* Ms. COLLINS, *who lowers her hand as though the envelope has been taken, and conceals it.)*

Ms. COLLINS: Read it. I know what it says.

(Pause, MELISSA opens and reads the letter.)
MELISSA: *I've...won...a...scholarship?*
Ms. COLLINS: To go to Banff.
MELISSA: But *how*? I didn't...
Ms. COLLINS: I sent in the application. As your teacher. On your behalf.
MELISSA: But I said I didn't want to apply. You knew that!
Ms. COLLINS: You'll have to forgive me, Melissa. Knowing your talent, I just *had* to.
MELISSA: But you should've asked me first.
Ms. COLLINS: I did. Remember? And what would you have said, if I'd asked you again?
MELISSA: The same. No.
Ms. COLLINS: You don't have to accept the scholarship, Melissa. But you won't be eligible next year. You'll be too old.
MELISSA: I can't believe...
Ms. COLLINS: That you won?
MELISSA: Yeah. Yeah! That this is happening!
 (Ms. COLLINS inclines her head toward the door.)
Ms. COLLINS: How will...?
MELISSA: My mother take it?
 (Ms. COLLINS nods. MELISSA shakes her head.)
 I...I...
Ms. COLLINS: Would you rather I told her?
MELISSA: Could you? Would you?
Ms. COLLINS: It'll have to be tonight. You have to leave on Thursday.
 (Lights fade quickly stage right.)
PETE: You had only three days?
MELISSA: Two, actually.
PETE: Do my parents know?
MELISSA: No. Not yet. I asked my Mom to phone them *after* she gave you my letter.
PETE: Ms. Collins talked your mother into letting you go?
MELISSA: *(slight smile)* Well, it wasn't quite like that.
 (Lights come up stage right.)

You Will Write, Won't You?

(CYNTHIA and Ms. COLLINS *face each other, one on either side of the table.* CYNTHIA *is dressed in a casual business suit. She turns her head, addresses* MELISSA, *speaks directly downstage.)*

CYNTHIA: Melissa: Why didn't you tell me you had applied for this...this 'Institute'?

MELISSA: I didn't—

*(*Ms. COLLINS *turns downstage, raises her hand to stop* MELISSA, *then turns back to* CYNTHIA.*)*

Ms. COLLINS: Melissa didn't apply. I did it for her. She didn't know.

CYNTHIA: Wasn't that presumptuous of you?

Ms. COLLINS: Your daughter has extraordinary talent, Ms. Grandpré. I just couldn't let the opportunity slip by.

CYNTHIA: Even though she told you she didn't want to go?

Ms. COLLINS: That's not quite true. Melissa said she didn't want to *apply*. She did not say she didn't want to go.

CYNTHIA: Hmmph! You know she has a job for the summer?

Ms. COLLINS: Yes, I do.

CYNTHIA: Which means she will have to break her promise to Mr. Sawatzky.

Ms. COLLINS: I'm sorry about that.

CYNTHIA: Her job with Mr. Sawatzky will help her when she goes on to study agriculture.

Ms. COLLINS: Taking part in the Teen Writers' Institute will help Melissa, too, when she has to write term papers. At college. She'll express herself well; reap higher marks.

CYNTHIA: Hmmph.

(Pause. CYNTHIA *looks at* MELISSA *[downstage], then at* Ms. COLLINS.*)*

I appreciate what you have done for Melissa, even though it was without my approval, and especially that you have such confidence in her.

MELISSA: *(to* PETE*)* When my mother starts like that...nicely, like...it always means she's going to say "no." She winds you up and then... drops the bomb!

*(*CYNTHIA *turns and faces downstage.)*

CYNTHIA: Melissa! I think I'll have to call in sick tomorrow. You and I...we'll drive up to Saskatoon. Buy some clothes. For your trip *(she half-grins).*

MELISSA: Huh? You mean I can go? To Banff!

CYNTHIA: Ms. Collins seems to think you should.

(Lights fade to fast blackout stage right.)

PETE: Your teacher, she sure does believe in you. Doesn't she?

MELISSA: Yeah. I guess.

PETE: *(taps the envelope)* So do they.

MELISSA: I don't know how I'm going to tell her.

PETE: Tell who? What?

MELISSA: Ms. Collins. That I'm not going.

PETE: You're not going?

(PETE holds the letter out to her, then gestures to the room and to themselves, speaks with amazement.)

After all this, you're not going?

MELISSA: No, Pete. I have to be with you this summer.

PETE: You *have* to?

MELISSA: Ugh...I...I need to. I *want* to.

PETE: Mel: Just now you were saying you want to go to Banff!

MELISSA: I know, but... *(shrugs)*

PETE: I don't understand you, Mel. Why have you changed your mind? Ten minutes ago, you were *eager* to go. Now, you seem to be against it!

(PETE throws his hands in the air, in exasperation.)

What...has...happened?

(Pause. MELISSA *rests the palms of her hands on his chest.)*

MELISSA: I'm scared, Pete. I'm so scared.

PETE: That you'll be on your own?

MELISSA: No, not that. I don't want anything to come between us. To upset...to upset the way we are. With each other.

PETE: It'll only be for two months, Mel. Eight weeks.

MELISSA: Too long...too long....

PETE: Once you're there, doing your writing—

You Will Write, Won't You?

MELISSA: No, Pete. No. I'm...I'm thinking about your father. I mean, he *expects* me to be here.

PETE: No, I don't think— *(he expects; he'd just like...)*

MELISSA: Yes, he does. So I can learn more about the farm. For when—

PETE: All that can wait. Till next year.

MELISSA: No! No. He told me he wants to start training me. Right away. This year.

(PETE grasps her shoulders with both hands.)

PETE: Mel! Just listen to me! I'll explain to Dad—and Mom—why you *have* to go. Why it's so important that you—

MELISSA: But it isn't important. Not any more.

PETE: Just for *this* summer.

(MELISSA turns away.)

MELISSA: Oh, you don't understand.

PETE: Understand what?

MELISSA: Oh. I don't know. It's...it's just that I—

PETE: Wait!

(PETE pulls his cellphone out from his pocket, punches buttons.)

MELISSA: No, Pete. No!

(MELISSA tries to wrestle the phone away from him. They tussle. PETE pulls away, stands at the door with his back to the room, blocking MELISSA from reaching the phone.)

PETE: Dad. I'm at the bus depot, with Melissa. *(pause, listens)* She wants to ask you something.

MELISSA: Please, Pete. Don't push it. Please!

PETE: Go on: take it!

(PETE thrusts the phone into MELISSA's hand. He backs to the door, his hands behind him, but does not exit. MELISSA looks pleadingly at him, but he turns away. She holds the phone to her ear.)

MELISSA: Edgar?

(Lights come up on EDGAR stage right, sitting on a stool as though he is sitting at the wheel of a tractor. He faces

stage left. There is the sound of a tractor engine idling. He holds a cellphone to his ear.)

EDGAR: Yes, Mel.

(EDGAR leans forward, switches off an imaginary tractor engine. Silence.)

MELISSA: I'm waiting for the bus, to go to Banff.

EDGAR: Yes, Mel, I know. Your mother told me.

MELISSA: She phoned you too? *(slight pause)* I don't want to go, Edgar. I can't go. Can I?

EDGAR: Are you asking me? Or are you telling me?

MELISSA: I'm asking

(Pause. EDGAR waits.)

EDGAR: Go on.

MELISSA: I...I promised I'd...

(MELISSA glances at PETE, to check if he can hear.)

I...uh...I said I'd work in the fields for you, and now I can't. If I go to Banff.

EDGAR: Ah, I see. Don't let that worry you. There's always next summer.

MELISSA: Yes, but...I mean...

EDGAR: Are you really asking me something else?

MELISSA: Yes. *(glances at PETE)* Yes.

EDGAR: And you can't say anything because Pete's there? He can hear?

MELISSA: Yes.

EDGAR: Right. *(slight pause)* So you want to know what I think you should do?

MELISSA: Yeah. I guess.

EDGAR: What would your father have said, Mel, if you had asked him?

MELISSA: Oh. *(light laugh)* "Don't beat about the bush."

EDGAR: Right.

MELISSA: So...really what I'm saying is... *(glances toward PETE)* If I'm not here for a while... *(she waits).*

EDGAR: *(after a brief pause)* Can I be your eyes? Is that it? To help Pete.

MELISSA: Yes. Yes!

You Will Write, Won't You?

EDGAR: Of course I will.

MELISSA: So, you're saying it's all right for me to go, then?

EDGAR: Is that a question?

MELISSA: No. *(light laugh)* Not now. Oh, thank you, Edgar.

EDGAR: You're welcome, Mel. 'Bye— and good luck on that course.

MELISSA: 'Bye, Edgar.

(Light fades quickly stage right. MELISSA *switches off the mobile, hands it to* PETE.*)*

PETE: So Dad said okay?

*(*MELISSA *nods.)*

I knew he would.

MELISSA: But, Pete, I really want to be with you this summer.

*(*PETE *takes her hands.)*

PETE: I know you do, Mel. Just like I do.

(They hug. There is the sound of the bus approaching and pulling up. [The clock is now exactly on or close to 3:15] PETE *and* MELISSA *pull apart, but he still holds her hands.)*

You have to go, Mel. Or you'll live with it for the rest of your life, never really knowing. I don't want that to come between us. Ever.

MELISSA: No. No.

PETE: I'll wait for you. You know I will.

*(*MELISSA *mumbles a 'yes'.)*

And I haven't got someone hiding behind the hay in the barn, waiting to step into your shoes.

MELISSA: *(pushing on* PETE*'s chest)* I'd brain you if you did!

(They laugh and hug. The BUS DRIVER *strides in.)*

BUS DRIVER: Is that your bike?

(They pull apart.)

PETE: Yes.

BUS DRIVER: You've left it where the bus is supposed to stop.

PETE: Okay. Okay! I'll move it.

BUS DRIVER: No point now! Who's travelling?

PETE: She is.

BUS DRIVER: To where?

(*MELISSA goes to speak, but* PETE *has taken over.*)

PETE: Banff.

BUS DRIVER: How many bags?

PETE: Two. *(to* MELISSA*)* Right?

MELISSA: Yes.

(*The* BUS DRIVER *tears the ends from two of several luggage tags in her hand, gives them to* MELISSA.)

BUS DRIVER: Get aboard. I'm already late.

(*The* BUS DRIVER *exits, carrying Melissa's two bags.* PETE *and* MELISSA *exchange meaningful glances about her abruptness, almost a giggle.* MELISSA *moves toward* PETE.)

MELISSA: Oh, Pete…

(PETE *is silently urging her toward the door. They embrace. Suddenly* MELISSA *pushes* PETE *away from her, holds him at arms' length.*)

Look at me, Pete. *(slight pause)* **Look at me!** Take a photograph with your eyes, so you can see me any time you want to. Go on! Do it!

(*Brief pause. He looks at her.*)

PETE: Click. Photo taken, Mel.

MELISSA: No, Pete! Do it again. **Concentrate!**

(*MELISSA stands on tip-toe, to be closer to his height, looks him straight in the eye.*)

Look…at…me!

PETE: Okay. Okay.

(*Longish pause.*)

Click. It's not digital. But just as good.

MELISSA: *(laughs)* Better!

(*The bus horn sounds; they move apart.*)

PETE: Go on.

(*He urges her toward the door.*)

I'd rather not come out…d'you mind?

MELISSA: *(understands, gently)* No.

You Will Write, Won't You?

(PETE stands by the bench. At the door, MELISSA turns back, a tearful smile, a small wave, turns away.)
PETE: *(calls)* Mel!
(She turns back)
You will write, won't you? *(means: "You will write to me?")*
MELISSA: *(slight smile, through her tears, almost a twinkle)* Oh, Pete, of course. That's why I'm going. To write!
(MELISSA reaches into her jean pocket, lifts out a mobile phone, holds it up, taps it.)
MELISSA: I'll text you. All the time.
(They laugh lightly. MELISSA exits. PETE turns despondently toward the bench, sits, head in hands. As we hear the bus pull away, he lifts his head, looks toward the empty doorway. Then he removes his glasses, blinks toward the audience, rubs the glasses on his sleeve, puts them back on, peers forward, blinks again.)
(Fade slowly to blackout and bring up closing music [possibly 'I'll see you again'].)

END

Character Descriptions

Main Characters

Melissa

Melissa would be a strong character if she could come to terms with the two major contradictions in her life. Academically she is very bright, in the sciences particularly, and has won school prizes for her efforts. But she has an added capability—a gift—in that she has the ability to write well and creatively. This skill is thought to be of little importance by her family and friends ("It's nice, but not of much use in a farming family"), but her teacher recognizes her ability to inject music and rhythm into the words she writes.

Melissa is an only child. Her father, with whom she was very close, died in a grain elevator accident five years ago. Her mother works for the local Credit Union in Hillsview, while her grandmother (her father's mother) is a retired widow and lives with them. Money is not in abundance. Melissa has just completed Grade 11 and for the summer is expected to earn money for the winter by working on Edgar's farm (her boyfriend Pete's father), and then to concentrate on science-oriented subjects in her final year of high school.

Melissa's contradictions:

1. Her desire to follow her personal inclination and become a writer, rather than fall into the expected pattern for a country girl growing up in a farming community.
2. The urging of Pete, his parents, and her mother, that she go to agricultural college (for which, Pete's father will pay) and then become the agricultural and horticultural adviser for his farm. This, she realizes, will most likely lead to marriage with Pete and a houseful of children.

Her relationships:

- She has an ongoing conflict with her mother (it's mostly a typical mother/teen-age daughter type of conflict), who she feels is too controlling and opinionated.
- She has a close relationship with her grandmother and often turns to her for advice (see the description for Louise).

You Will Write, Won't You?

- She has a natural, easy-going relationship with Pete's parents, who treat her almost like a daughter (although she addresses them by their first names, and does it naturally). In some ways Edgar has become a substitute father for her, since her own father died when she was 11.
- She has an unusual best-friend yet close-boyfriend relationship with Pete, and generally they have no secrets from each other. Does she love Pete? She is fond of him—knows he's her greatest friend—yet she doesn't know if her feelings are love. She realizes that Pete loves her.

Decisions in Melissa's life always seem to have been made for her. Now she has to make her own and finds it difficult.

Pete

He is determined, definite in his statements and decisions, very sure of himself, knows exactly what he wants (and expects to get it or achieve it), yet without being overbearing. Once his mind is set, he doesn't adjust readily to change. He is moderately intelligent, a C (sometimes B) student, and recognizes it, has come to terms with it.

In rehearsal for the Winnipeg Fringe 2008 production of You Will Write, Won't You?

Pete (Kevin Carruthers) *is appealing to Melissa (Megan Wilson) as he tries to get her to change her mind and not go to the Teen Writers' Institute.*

Pete is the younger of two boys: the other is away at a computer school and is not interested in carrying on the farm that their father has built up so successfully. Pete has completed Grade 11 and has convinced his father that he should start working on the farm permanently rather than attend the final year of high school. He has had a major disappointment in his life—wanting to be a fighter pilot—but deterioration in his eyesight has prevented it. Yet he has adjusted successfully to it and now is strongly focused in a new direction.

Pete has grown up with Melissa, through the closeness of their families and their ages, and the relative remoteness of their family locations (reasonably close to each other yet not close to other farms). He has always imagined her in his life and in recent months has started looking forward—even expecting—to marry her. He knows his parents would approve.

In earlier years Pete felt Melissa was like a slightly younger sister, yet they never experienced sibling rivalry. Throughout their association they have become extraordinary friends. They have always confided with each other and have never had secrets from one another.

But now Pete realizes he loves her, cares for her very much. Yet it's not a self-centered love. He would like them to be lovers but, although he respects and thinks he understands her desire to 'wait for a more appropriate moment,' he is frustrated by it.

Supporting Characters

Sandy

Sandy is an energetic, outgoing young woman who has graduated from high school (she is one year ahead of Melissa and Pete) and next year she will move to the city to take a one-year course in catering and hotel/motel management. She will return to work in her father's motel (the only such facility in Hillsview).

Her father took over the motel four years ago and at first Sandy hated living in such a small community after living in the city (where he was assistant manager of a moderate-size hotel). For three years she envied Melissa's close relationship with Pete, until six months ago she met Kevin, who works on a neighboring farm, and in time expects to marry him.

She and Melissa are good friends, though not confidantes. As Sandy is a very definite, opinionated young woman, she has difficulty coming to terms with Melissa's indecisiveness.

Edgar

Edgar grew up on the Prairies, on the farm where he now lives. He was the third of four children, with two girls older and one younger.

You Will Write, Won't You?

When his parents retired and moved to a smallholding on Vancouver Island, Edgar took over the farm, buying it progressively.

That was 30 years ago, and since then he has continued to maintain the very successful operation he inherited. He married Doris, a daughter from a neighboring farm, 28 years ago, and they have two sons: Jonathan, now 26, and Pete, now 17.

When Pete showed an interest in aviation, Edgar supported him although he really hoped Pete would eventually take over the farm. Consequently it was a shock, yet a mixed blessing, when he discovered that Pete had an eye condition that would prevent him from becoming a pilot. Since then he has been more than just pleased to see that Pete really does want to take over the farm (although his delight has been offset by his concern for Pete's deteriorating eyesight). He hopes Melissa will play an important role in Pete's life, being with him and assisting him as his eye condition deteriorates.

One word best describes Edgar: 'Dedicated.' He is dedicated to running a quality farm, he is dedicated to and adores his wife, and he is dedicated to ensuring his sons' well-being and that they are launched successfully into life. He also has great fatherly affection for Melissa, who has become for him the daughter he and Doris will never have of their own. He genuinely wants the best for her and would go a long way to help her achieve it.

He seems to be easy-going and accepts others for the way they are. Yet he also has very firm ideas on how things should be done: he expects his farm workers to understand and meet his expectations, and has little patience with those who don't or who seem to think that inferior work is acceptable. He is not a person who loses his temper and shows his anger easily.

Doris

Doris is definitely 'married' to a farming life. She was brought up on a nearby farm, married the son of a farmer, enjoys the wide open spaces and distance between farms on the prairies, and would detest the confines of city living.

Doris has accepted the news of Pete's disability and expected worsening of Pete's eye condition more readily than Edgar, perhaps because she recognizes it will keep him at home on the farm, in contrast to their older son who has moved away permanently. She really regrets she was unable to bear a daughter and in one sense Melissa has filled that role for her and Edgar. She would like to think Pete and Melissa would become more than just close friends, but is realistic enough to recognize that others may intrude into their lives. She tries to instil into Melissa the comfortable role she could achieve staying on the farm, yet she does not do it overtly.

Cynthia

Cynthia was training to be a teacher in northern England when she met Paul Grandpré, a Canadian Grains Inspector on an exchange posting, married him three weeks later, and emigrated to Canada expecting to live in a city. But almost immediately Paul inherited a farm, gave up his Inspector's job, and they moved to rural Saskatchewan.

Consequently she became a reluctant farm wife. When Paul died five years ago, she considered returning to England with her 11-year-old daughter, but her now-diminished finances, a family in England who were cool to the idea, and the presence of Paul's widowed mother with no one else to turn to, quashed the idea. She leased much of the farm acreage to Edgar, and took a job with the local Credit Union. She carries a resentment within her about the way her life has panned out.

She desperately wants to keep Melissa on the farm and would welcome her marrying Pete and remaining in the community. As a result she carries a deep-down fear that going to the Youth Writers' Institute will open Melissa's eyes to a completely different career and Cynthia will lose her. She genuinely wants the best for her daughter, but on her own terms. She has difficulty managing Melissa's teen-age temperament.

Louise

Paul's mother Louise, like Cynthia, was a town-girl, but in her case she was born and grew up in a Canadian city. Like Cynthia, she met and married a farmer and became a prairie farm wife. She adapted to the change without resentment, and surprised herself on finding she *liked* farm life and did not miss the city or feel lonely.

She is a widow and has no living siblings or younger family, which means she is dependent on Cynthia for a home. She does not really understand Cynthia, resents her moodiness, but lives with it because this is her only choice (other than being lodged in an elderly people's home in a city, where she would know no one and receive no visitors.) She and Melissa have an easy-going relationship, engendered mostly because Louise knows what it is like to live, and like living, in both an urban and a rural setting. Melissa often turns to Louise for advice when faced with problems in her relationship with others.

Louise has an unusual sense of humor which Cynthia doesn't understand and so deprecates, but Melissa thinks is 'cool.'

Heather (Ms. Collins)

Heather is a brilliant teacher who has chosen to teach in a rural setting for three years to broaden her experience before returning to university to complete a Ph.D. (And also to earn enough to support herself when she is studying.) Although essentially a practical person, she also has strengths as a writer and is determined to write for general publication (not in the academic milieu, which she finds too restrictive). She is well-liked by her students, although other teachers tend to think her methods are a little strange.

She seeks out students' strengths and gives them exercises that build on their strengths rather than make them all 'fit' the accepted academic mold. She is innovative, a good speaker, firm (she won't accept difficult behavior but tries to deflect it rather than reprimand it).

She sees Melissa's strengths as a writer and is determined to open the door for Melissa to build on them. She also sees Melissa's indecisiveness and unsureness about herself, and so has to find a way to work around it.

Bus Driver

She is efficient but tends to be grumpy when behind schedule.

Production Notes

I have made changes to the script in tune with each production. Because the first production would be taking place on the Island of Guernsey, where no part of the island is more than 25 minutes' drive away, I realized it would be difficult for the audience to think in terms of miles between the immense farms that exist on the Canadian Prairies. So I added short references to distance in the dialogue to create the feel of that distance.

In another sense, however, there was a similarity: the need for a Prairie girl to go a great distance and live away from home to attend university would be understood by the Islanders, because their youth have to go to mainland England or into Europe to do the same. Indeed, following the performances in 2004 and 2009, audience members came up to me to talk about the similarity.

A remark by Adjudicator William Burns, following the first performance at the One-Act-Play Festival in 2004, prompted me to write an additional sequence which appears here and has been present in all subsequent editions of the script.

He said: "I really wanted to know more about Pete's eyes and why they should inhibit him from becoming a pilot. After all, many pilots wear glasses."

The first script simply said that Pete's vision was not good enough for him to become an air force pilot. That led me to research open-angle glaucoma and then write the sequence during which Edgar informs Melissa of the condition and warns her that Pete has not yet been told his eyesight will continue to deteriorate. This addition also supported Melissa's indecision about leaving Pete for two months, and provided a link to the moment at the end of the play when she asks Pete to look at her and 'take a mental photograph.'

We experimented during the most recent production, diverging slightly from the script during the sequence when Edgar informs Melissa about Pete's glaucoma. The script says that Edgar and Melissa both face directly downstage as they talk to each other from their respective sides. This we changed so that at the point where Edgar says "Sit down, Mel. Will you?" (top of page 79), Melissa rises from the bench at stage left and walks across to sit at the table across from Edgar. She remains there until the point where she says: "Oh, Edgar...if only it could be that easy." (at the top of page 82).

You Will Write, Won't You?

Although both approaches work well, for three reasons I now prefer to have Melissa join Edgar at the table. It helps show the warmth—the closeness—that exists between them, which in turn leads to Edgar's readiness to understand the quandary Melissa faces toward the end of the play, when she talks to him by mobile phone. Secondly, it's a long time—close to four minutes—to have them sitting apart and facing downstage to talk to each other. And finally it introduces a change into the sequence of memory flashbacks, with the family members and the teacher at stage right, and Melissa and Pete at stage left.

Having an open stage can cause the audience to be distracted by off-scene sounds and movement when stage right is being prepared for the next flashback sequence. Because the set has to be positioned and torn down very quickly, within 10 or 15 minutes for a one-act-play festival or fringe theatre presentation, the set has to be very simple and normally without dividing walls. Consequently, unless the stage is very wide, light tends to spill from the bus-depot scene at stage left onto the unlit 'flashback area' at stage right.

A rug on the floor at stage right is essential to dampen the sound of feet on the floor. Each prop, such as the ironing board used by Cynthia, needs to be prepared with everything in place, so that it can be simply carried in and positioned easily and quietly. Similarly, the table and chairs can be set permanently upstage and then used both as a kitchen table and the teacher's desk.

The play ends with Pete and Edgar helping Melissa make her decision, and then Melissa exits to board the unseen bus, leaving Pete on his own in the bus depot. Whether Melissa becomes a successful writer or returns to the farm and eventually becomes an 'adviser' to Edgar, is left for each audience member to decide.

When I converted the play into a book for teen-age readers, however, I knew they would *expect* to learn what happens. So in two chapters following the original closing scene, readers learn that Melissa's experience was successful and she learns she has the potential to become a creative writer. But, at the same time, her course advisers recommend, for financial reasons, it would be best to take the agricultural courses and become Edgar's 'farm adviser' and then write in her spare time.

Readers also learn that when Melissa returns from the Institute, she discovers that Pete's parents have informed him of his eye condition and the prognosis, and he has come to terms with it (although Melissa has not).

For romantic reasons, they also sense that Pete's and Melissa's relationship is developing well and it would not be unreasonable to assume they will marry. (I'm sure some people would have liked to see those additional moments appended to the playscript, but I felt it would change the focus and take away from the 'tightness' of the story as it now stands.)

The book has been published using the pseudonym Veronica Steele as the author.

The Winnipeg cast who presented You Will Write, Won't You? *and* Sudoku Fever *at the 2009 One-Act-Play Festival in Guernsey sit for a group photograph just before they leave La Villette Hotel to fly home. Seated, left to right, Julie Seroy, Morgan Winterhalt, Debbie Pomeransky, Ron Robinson, Evelyn Darrach, Kevin Carruthers. Standing, left to right: Holly Steele, Megan Wilson, the author, Lana Winterhalt, Betty Winterhalt. The photograph was taken by our twelfth member, Carol McKibbin, who was props manager. (Their trophies are on the table.)* Author photo

Play No. 3

Sudoku Fever

Synopsis

Three generations of the same family live together in a narrow, multi-story home in a small town 200 km (125 miles) northwest of the nearest major city.

The youngest is 17-year-old Regan, who is about to graduate from high school and wants to enroll in Mechanical Engineering. Her mother, grandmother and aunt all deplore her choice and try to convince her to enter a more conventional occupation that will keep her in town.

Regan's mother arranges for the Professional Engineering Association to send out an engineer to counsel Regan. She expects the engineer will be male and that he will dissuade her daughter from entering a field mostly populated by men. But an enthusiastic young *female* engineer appears on the doorstep!

The only male living in the house is Regan's step-grandfather who, although privately applauding Regan's choice, tends to be overwhelmed by the three adult females and remains non-committal. The arrival of the engineer prompts him to reveal a hidden factor from his past and offer an opposing opinion.

Rationale

This is the third play in which a central character is a teen facing a 'decision situation,' but this time it's a comedy.

There were few females among the Engineering Technology students I taught at Red River College, and even fewer males among the Early Childhood Education students I also faced. These two factors drew me into creating a play that addresses the issue. I chose to make it a comedy, because doing so would make the serious message it contains more acceptable.

The title *Sudoku Fever* at first may seem strange, yet it becomes a side issue that introduces much of the humor and tells more about the characters.

Seven Plays with a Light Touch

History

The first stage performance of *Sudoku Fever* was at the Forrest Nickerson Theatre, Winnipeg, Canada, April 25-27, 2009. The cast then flew to Guernsey, UK, to perform the play at the GADOC One-Act-Play Festival, May 19-21, and then returned to Canada for the Summer Theatre Festival in Gimli, Manitoba, August 16-18.

The cast won two awards at the GADOC Festival: the Joyce and Cecil Cook Trophy for the best play by a new director and the Burns Trophy for the best original unpublished play. The trophies are held for one year, inscribed with the winners' names, and then returned to be awarded at the next One-Act-Play Festival.

Characters

The play has a cast of six: 5 females and 1 male. The actors were the same for all three performances and are listed beside their character names:

Sheila Dubrowski, 72	*Evelyn Darrach*
George Dubrowski, 78, her husband	*Ron Robinson*
Marta Warkentin, 48, Sheila's daughter	*Debbie Pomeransky*
Katie O'Hanlon, 51, Marta's sister-in-law	*Betty Winterhalt*
Regan Warkentin, 17, Marta's daughter	*Julie Seroy*
Chris Fellowes, 27, a visitor *(female)*	*Holly Steele*

The play was directed by the author.

Sheila has been married previously, and so has her husband George, who is a paraplegic in a wheelchair. Both Marta and Katie are divorced and have not remarried. More information about the characters and their relationships starts on page 126.

Production Notes are on page 132.

Sudoku Fever

The Set

The action occurs in the living room of the house occupied by the family. There are three doors:

Upstage center: a door leading to the interior of the house.
Stage right: a door leading to the back of the house.
Stage left: a door leading to the front of the house.

Stage left has a small table with a laptop computer on it, where George sits in his wheelchair (the doors at stage right and upstage need to be wide enough for passage of the wheelchair). The rest of the room has a sofa, two armchairs, and a side table.

Props

The primary stage prop is a mock-up of an intentionally crazy contraption, which is supposedly to be attached to the back door to provide an automatic door opener for Rufus, the family dog, who will actuate it with his nose.

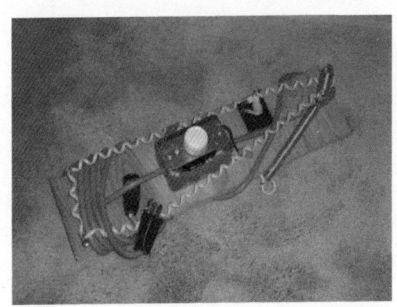

Approximate Length: 35 minutes

Some Script Guidelines

Throughout the script, two symbols are used occasionally at the end of a piece of dialogue to indicate how the sentence ends:

- ... An ellipsis at the end of a statement means the speaker just trails off and leaves his or her thought hanging in the air (possibly accompanied by a shrug).
- — A dash at the end of a statement means the speaker is interrupted by the next speaker, so that the first speaker's statement is incomplete. Sometimes there is an italicized continuation of the statement *(within brackets)* immediately following the dash, to help the actor sense where the sentence was going.

v.o. Means that the words are spoken by someone off-stage.

Seven Plays with a Light Touch

Script: *Sudoku Fever*
© 2009, Ron Blicq

(At curtain up GEORGE is in his wheelchair mid-stage left, a laptop computer on a small wheeled table in front of him. He is doing a Sudoku puzzle and entering numbers one at a time, each after a short thinking spell.)

GEORGE: Ah...if I put a seven in the third column...

(MARTA enters from upstage center, a cellphone to her ear. She is listening and speaks as she enters. Almost immediately she uses her other hand to start tidying the room.)

(GEORGE moves the wireless mouse, taps the '7' key, moves the mouse again, looks up when he hears Marta's voice, then looks down again.)

MARTA: You mean he's coming right now?...Already on his way?...Be here in fifteen minutes...Oh...Right...Well, thank you for making the arrangements, and so quickly. That was so helpful...Goodbye.

(MARTA smiles. She continues to plump cushions, tidy things on the side tables, and re-arrange George's books, as the conversation evolves.)

There! He's on his way.

(GEORGE taps a '4' then looks up.)

GEORGE: Who is 'he,' may I ask? And where is he on his way to?

MARTA: Oh, Dad, you chose not to listen, didn't you? Pretending you were concentrating on your Sudoku puzzle.

GEORGE: I was *supposed* to be listening?

MARTA: Why is it, when I'm having a *private* conversation you're all ears, never miss a syllable? Even if I'm in the next room. But when I'm having a general conversation— *(one that's not important...)*

GEORGE: You didn't answer my question.

MARTA: You asked two questions.

(GEORGE looks up with a grin; he is teasing.)

Alright! Alright! 'He' is Chris Fellowes, and he's an engineer with Central Power—

GEORGE: Send him back! Regan's working on the automatic door opener. She's got it all sorted.

Sudoku Fever

MARTA: That's not why he's coming.

GEORGE: So...?

(SHEILA *enters upstage center, carrying a purse, three books, and a library postcard. She speaks as she enters.*)

SHEILA: I'm going to the library, George. Any books you want me to take back?

GEORGE: Of course!

(MARTA *throws up her hands at the interruption, which happens often in this house. As* SHEILA *nears,* GEORGE *tosses a hardback book to her.*)

Utter crap! Never got past page 14. And *you* chose it!

SHEILA: It looked like— *(something you'd want to read)*

GEORGE: Written by a woman, of course.

MARTA: Dad! You shouldn't— *(talk like that)*

SHEILA: *(examining cover)* No, it isn't. *(reads)* "Winston Churchill: My Early Life." You couldn't get past page 14?

GEORGE: Of course I did, woman! Damn good choice. Great man. See if they've got "My African Journey."

SHEILA: Also by...? *(she points to the book cover)*

GEORGE: Who else!

SHEILA: You don't want that new book?

(SHEILA *reads from a library reminder postcard*) "Sudoku for Experts?"

GEORGE: Sheila! I am an expert.

SHEILA: Yes, George, we know. You're better— *(than expert)*

GEORGE: *(points to laptop)* Anyway, I can get it online.

SHEILA: *(to* MARTA*)* Have you any books to go back?

MARTA: No thanks, Mom.

(SHEILA *crosses toward the door stage right, is about to leave when* GEORGE *calls to her.*)

GEORGE: Marta's invited an engineer to have tea with us.

SHEILA: An engineer?

GEORGE: A *male* engineer. You didn't know?

SHEILA: *(to Marta)* We never have tea.

GEORGE: On our doorstep any minute now.

(MARTA *raises an angry cautionary hand toward* GEORGE.*)*

MARTA: *(to Sheila)* He's coming to talk to Regan.
SHEILA: To Regan?
MARTA: You know: what it's like to be an engineer.
SHEILA: I thought you didn't want her to be an engineer.
MARTA: I don't. No way.
SHEILA: Then why?

> *(REGAN enters from stage right, speaking as she enters. She crosses quickly to GEORGE. She is carrying a mechanical/ electrical contraption with a spring between two of the parts.)*
>
> *(SHEILA and MARTA, now upstage right, mime conversation while Regan and George talk.)*

REGAN: I think I've got it, Pops. Check it, will you, before I put it up?
GEORGE: Let's have a look.
> *(He turns the contraption over, examines it.)*

Where's the nose button?
REGAN: On the wall already, outside the back door.
GEORGE: Right. Show me how it works.
REGAN: You know how it works.
GEORGE: Just making sure.
> *(GEORGE grins mischievously at REGAN, who grins back. They have played this game before.)*

Because I'm sure going to have to explain it to your grandmother. *(gestures toward SHEILA)*
REGAN: *(easily, comfortably)* Okay. When Rufus puts his nose on the button—
GEORGE: Or his paw.
REGAN: On his nose?
GEORGE: On the button!
> *(They laugh companionably.)*

REGAN: It triggers an electromagnet—here—which releases the clamp holding this spring. Then the door springs open.
GEORGE: And Rufus wanders in, his tail wagging like a piston.
REGAN: And then the door closes after him.
GEORGE: For how long?
REGAN: Does it stay open?

(GEORGE nods.)

REGAN: *(continuing)* I've set it for six seconds.

GEORGE: Hmmm...bit short I think. Can't risk Rufus getting his tail caught in the door as it closes.

REGAN: Gran would go bananas! I'll make it eight seconds.

(GEORGE nods. REGAN pulls a screwdriver from her tool belt and adjusts the delay mechanism. They continue to mime examining the contraption. GEORGE touches a couple of computer keys.)

SHEILA: You think this engineer's going to change her mind?

MARTA: If he does what I want him to do. Tell her how engineers feel about women sneaking into their field.

SHEILA: Like a man going into nursing.

(GEORGE looks questioningly at SHEILA.)

MARTA: Yeah. The same.

REGAN: *(to GEORGE)* Time for a beta test?

GEORGE: Go hook it up.

(REGAN crosses toward the exit stage right. MARTA intercepts her. During the following sequence, SHEILA crosses to GEORGE and mimes talking to him and looking at his computer screen.)

MARTA: Regan: I need you to clean up.

REGAN: I will. I will. *(holds up the contraption)* I just have to screw this onto the wall.

MARTA: No. Now.

REGAN: And hook it up to the door.

MARTA: No. Right now.

REGAN: I've already got a broom out there.

MARTA: No, *You*. We've got a visitor coming.

REGAN: So?

MARTA: I want you to look good.

REGAN: I'll be working by the back door. They'll come in the front.

MARTA: I want you to meet him.

REGAN: Mother, I don't need to meet your house-hunting clients. You know that.

MARTA: He's coming to see *you*.

REGAN: What are you up to?
MARTA: Someone you should talk to.
REGAN: *(sarcasm)* Someone my age?
MARTA: Coming from the city.
REGAN: You're trying to hook me up again with— *(a guy, aren't you?)*
MARTA: No, no, no—
REGAN: Like that weird kid you invited over. From up on the estate!
MARTA: You were younger then.
REGAN: I'll choose my own friends, thank you.
(Slight pause.)
MARTA: He's from the A.P.E.
REGAN: The what?
MARTA: The Association for Professional Engineers.
REGAN: Ah! I get it!
MARTA: He wants to talk to you.
REGAN: Yeah: you want him to talk me out of going into engineering.
MARTA: Oh, no. He's only coming to tell you what it's like to be an engineer.
REGAN: After you've primed him!
MARTA: I've never met him. Never even talked to him.
REGAN: Why are you so set against my going into engineering?
MARTA: I'm not against it. I just want you— *(to hear both sides)*
REGAN: Oh, yes you are. Ever since I first said I wanted to—
MARTA: I just want what's best for you.
REGAN: Best? For me? Or for you?
MARTA: For you, of course.
REGAN: Not really. You keep saying things, doing things—like bringing in this engineer—to talk me out of it.
MARTA: Regan: just go and clean up, will you?
REGAN: If he's a good engineer, his hands'll be just as dirty as mine.
GEORGE: Take a look at what Regan's holding, Marta. What she's doing. Does that look as though— *(she needs advice?)*
SHEILA: Don't interfere, George.

REGAN: *(to Marta)* I'm not the one who needs an engineer. If anyone does, you do, Mum.

(GEORGE snorts derisively.)

SHEILA: Regan!

REGAN: Or Aunt Katie.

(GEORGE laughs.)

GEORGE: A male engineer, About 45 to 50. Unattached.

REGAN: Way to go, Pops!

SHEILA: You mind your tongue, young lady.

(REGAN shakes her head, exits stage right.)

MARTA: And you, Dad!

SHEILA: That girl...! *(slight pause)* Umm, if we're to have a visitor...*(to GEORGE)* Time to play Sudoku, I think.

(GEORGE nods, pushes the laptop table to one side.)

Want to play an easy game, or a difficult one?

GEORGE: Easy, I guess.

MARTA: He never really decides until he gets there. Sees all the books.

(SHEILA goes to take the wheelchair handle, but GEORGE waves her off. He wheels himself toward the upstage exit. SHEILA follows.)

GEORGE: No, I won't be long. Looking forward to meeting your engineer, hearing a *male* voice.

SHEILA: I know, George. You're suffering because you're surrounded by women.

GEORGE: Suffering? Suffocating!

(SHEILA and GEORGE exit.)

(Humming, MARTA whisks around tidying the room.)

(Sound of car arriving and stopping. Dog barks, stage right.)

MARTA: Oh! He's here.

(MARTA hurries with her tidying; puts a hand through her hair, goes to the door stage right; calls.)

He's here, Regan... *(pause, shouts)* Regan!

REGAN: *(v.o.)* I'm not deaf!

MARTA: Have you washed up?

REGAN: *(v.o.)* I don't need to.

(REGAN enters, stands in the doorway.)

REGAN: *(continuing)* It's only Aunt Katie.
MARTA: Katie? What's she doing here?
REGAN: She lives here!
MARTA: I know, but...
 (KATIE enters stage right, pushes past REGAN, who exits. KATIE is dressed in a nurse's uniform, and is obviously tired. She is carrying the mail, distributes it as she talks.)
 What're you doing here?
KATIE: Like Regan said, I happen to live here.
MARTA: Yeah, but...it's only two.
KATIE: Had to go in at 4 a.m. Emergency appendectomy. The Korvan boy.
MARTA: That cute, blonde 13-year-old?
 (KATIE nods.)
 He'll be all right?
KATIE: It was close. Only just in time.
MARTA: So it's bed for you.
KATIE: Sudoku first.
MARTA: George is in there.
KATIE: Oh, damn! Really, it's time we had a second Sudoku room.
MARTA: I know. I know. You've said it before.
KATIE: He'll be in there for ever.
MARTA: Unlikely. He's doing an easy puzzle.
KATIE: So I just have to sit here with my legs crossed.
MARTA: Sorry about that. *(she isn't)*
KATIE: If that drunkard husband of mine hadn't buggered off to Australia, like he did...
MARTA: Mine too. Taking all our money.
KATIE: I'd be out of here, like a shot.
MARTA: You're not alone there.
KATIE: Have my own place.
MARTA: With your own, private, Sudoku room.
 (They laugh.)
 (GEORGE enters upstage center, propelling his own wheelchair. He crosses to stage left, wheels around. SHEILA follows, then crosses to MARTA and KATIE.)

Sudoku Fever

MARTA: *(continuing)* That's something like a record, Dad. *(to KATIE)* I told you he'd be fast.

GEORGE: Don't want to miss meeting your engineer.

MARTA: Regan's engineer.

KATIE: What engineer?

SHEILA: Marta's invited—

GEORGE: When was the last time we had a man in this house!

KATIE: Don't you fit that description?

(GEORGE points to his wheelchair.)

GEORGE: Like this?

SHEILA: Now, George, don't start feeling— *(sorry for yourself)*

GEORGE: Here I am, surrounded by women— *(four of you!)*

KATIE: You should be so lucky!

GEORGE: Day after day…

KATIE: Most men would give their eye teeth— *(to have four women…)*

GEORGE: Like having a harem…manned by nuns!

KATIE: George: Nuns don't 'man' anything!

GEORGE: Exactly!

MARTA: You think we're like nuns?

GEORGE: Well, you can't deny you live a somewhat celibate existence.

KATIE: How would you know what we— *(do away from the house?)*

GEORGE: *(to* MARTA*)* With the exception of your daughter, perhaps.

MARTA: Regan? She'd better not be climbing into bed with some local farm boy!

KATIE: You've got to be realistic, Marta. She's nearly eighteen. It's not like when you were a teen-ager.

MARTA: Weren't you going to bed?

KATIE: No way. Not when a mystery man's about to appear on our doorstep.

MARTA: *(to* SHEILA*)* And you were taking books down to the library.

SHEILA: Later, Marta. Too much going on here.

GEORGE: Popular guy, this engineer.

KATIE: What's this all about? This 'engineer' thing.

MARTA: I want Regan to hear what engineers really think about women entering their profession. How protective they are.

GEORGE: *(to KATIE)* Your sister-in-law's asked the Engineers' Association—

KATIE: *(to MARTA)* He's coming from the city? All that way?

GEORGE: Marta asked them to send her an engineer who will persuade Regan not to—

SHEILA: No, George. It's really to encourage her to take up something like accounting. Or business administration.

KATIE: Or nursing. Even better!

GEORGE: Like our Katie!

KATIE: *(to MARTA)* He's coming over 100 miles to tell her that!

MARTA: Katie: weren't you desperate to play Sudoku?

KATIE: In a minute. In a minute. You don't even know this man?

MARTA: Only his name.

GEORGE: A giant step forward!

MARTA: Fellowes. Chris Fellowes.

GEORGE: And he works for Central Power.

KATIE: Big deal! But why someone from the city? I mean our town engineer would— *(do just the same)*

MARTA: Old Frank Williams? No way. Regan would be suspicious.

KATIE: Think you talked to him first?

GEORGE: Oh, Marta'd never do anything like that!

*(*REGAN *enters stage right.)*

REGAN: It's ready, Pops! You want to be the first to push the button?

GEORGE: Shouldn't Rufus?

REGAN: I'm still training him.

KATIE: George doesn't need training?

GEORGE: You're incorrigible, Katie.

*(*REGAN *takes the handles of the wheelchair and pushes* GEORGE *toward stage right. He does not insist he will push himself.)*

REGAN: C'mon, Pops.

SHEILA: Are you going down the ramp?

Sudoku Fever

GEORGE: How else do you get out there?

SHEILA: *(to* REGAN*)* Make sure he puts the brake on before— *(you go down)*

GEORGE: I know how to drive, woman!

SHEILA: Yeah. That's how you got into that wheelchair.

(GEORGE *gives a dismissive wave. He and* REGAN *exit.)*

MARTA: *(to* KATIE*)* There's no one in the Sudoku room now.

KATIE: Yeah, I know.

MARTA: Don't want to miss a beat, do you?

KATIE: Alright! *(exits upstage)*

MARTA: *(to* SHEILA*)* And, really, there's no reason why you shouldn't go to the library.

SHEILA: Give it a rest, Marta. I'll go when I'm ready.

(There is a screeching and bumping from offstage right. It's Regan's door-opening mechanism.)

What the devil's that!

MARTA: The automatic door opener for Rufus. So you won't have to get up every time he wants in.

SHEILA: I have to listen to that! I'd rather let him in myself.

(The screeching and bumping from offstage right is repeated as the door closes. There is a two-second pause after the noise stops, and then a bang as the door closes. SHEILA *throws up her hands in disgust.)*

(Sound of a motorbike pulling up stage left. The dog barks stage right.)

SHEILA: Is that him? Your engineer?

MARTA: On a motorbike?

SHEILA: Nothing would surprise me today.

MARTA: All the way from the city?

SHEILA: Or someone wanting to see your new listing?

(Doorbell sounds stage left. The dog barks again.)

REGAN: *(v.o. muffled, stage right)* Quiet, Rufus! Quiet!

MARTA: *(to* SHEILA) Let him in, will you.

SHEILA: Rufus?

MARTA: No, the engineer. I'll tell Regan he's here. *(exits stage right)*

SHEILA: Why bother? *(exits stage left)*

(The dog stops barking. Pause for 7 seconds. SHEILA *re-enters, followed by* CHRIS.*)*
SHEILA: *(continuing)* You've come to see Marta?
CHRIS: I think so. *(fishes in her shirt pocket)*
SHEILA: You're looking to buy a house?
CHRIS: I beg your pardon?
SHEILA: Marta will be right with you.
CHRIS: *(shakes head)* I...um...actually, I'm supposed to see your daughter.
SHEILA: She is my daughter.
CHRIS: But not about a house.
SHEILA: She *is* a real-estate agent.
   *(*CHRIS *shakes her head; unfolds the paper from her pocket, reads.)*
CHRIS: You are Ms. Warkentin?
SHEILA: No. That's my daughter.
CHRIS: Then I am in the right place. And you are...?
SHEILA: Oh, sorry. *(extends hand)* Sheila. Sheila Dubrowski.
CHRIS: *(shakes hand)* Chris Fellowes.
SHEILA: Oh, I've heard that name before...
CHRIS: It's Christina, really.
   (Enter MARTA *briskly, stage right. When she sees Chris she stops, surprised.)*
SHEILA: Ah! Here she is.
MARTA: *(slight pause)* You're here for the Westover Place?
   *(*CHRIS *shakes her head, 'no.')*
   It's in the new estate. On the west side of the valley.
CHRIS: I...uh...you phoned. You want advice, about going into engineering?
MARTA: N-o-o, that's my daughter.
CHRIS: Oh, it's *your* daughter I'm— *(supposed to see?)*
MARTA: You don't mean...? You're an engineer?
CHRIS: The Association asked me to— *(come up here and...)*
MARTA: They said they were sending a *Mister* Fellowes.
SHEILA: My dear, this is he. Her!
CHRIS: *(extends her hand)* I'm sorry. I should have introduced myself: Chris Fellowes.

Sudoku Fever

MARTA: Oh, God! You see I was expecting…

(MARTA shakes her head, trying to recover. CHRIS shows a ring on her little finger.)

CHRIS: I am an engineer. This is an engineer's ring.

MARTA: You mean, you came all the way from the city, on a motorbike?

CHRIS: The bike is correct. But not the city. From Newbury. Twenty minutes.

MARTA: From Newbury?

CHRIS: I'm on assignment there.

(GEORGE is wheeling himself in.)

GEORGE: It worked!

SHEILA: We heard.

GEORGE: And who do we have here?

(CHRIS walks to GEORGE, hand extended.)

CHRIS: Chris Fellowes. From Central Power.

(They shake hands.)

GEORGE: George Dubrowski. Glad to meet you, Chris. *(to SHEILA and MARTA)* This is rich!

(GEORGE erupts into a hearty laugh.)

SHEILA: If you've only come from Newbury, I guess you won't need the Sudoku room.

CHRIS: I beg your pardon?

GEORGE: It would have been more polite to ask.

MARTA: *(desperate; to CHRIS)* Let me take you out to meet my daughter.

CHRIS: She's in the…Sudoku room?

MARTA: Regan? No, that's Katie.

GEORGE: Explain!

MARTA: Katie's my sister-in-law.

GEORGE: *(to CHRIS)* Regan wants to be like *you*.

CHRIS: Like me?

GEORGE: Be an engineer.

MARTA: Dad: Let me— *(handle this)*

CHRIS: I was led to believe— *(I would counsel…)*

GEORGE: You can't believe anything you hear in this house!

CHRIS: I thought I was to talk to a student.

GEORGE: That'll be Regan. She'll be so glad to see *you*!
MARTA: Dad! *(to* CHRIS*)* Come with me.
*(*MARTA *and* CHRIS *exit stage right.)*
SHEILA: You shouldn't interfere, George.
GEORGE: You think *that's* interfering. You should see me when— *(there's really something to interfere about)*
SHEILA: It's for Marta to decide.
GEORGE: Shouldn't it be Regan?
SHEILA: *They* should. It really isn't our business.
*(*MARTA *re-enters.)*
MARTA: This isn't what I planned. Not at all.
GEORGE: So you planned it?
MARTA: Just go back to your computer, Dad.
*(*MARTA *draws* SHEILA *aside, confides.)*
I don't care how influential this woman engineer is, she's not going to change my mind.
*(*REGAN *and* CHRIS *laugh, offstage right.)*
Such a waste of effort. Completely wrong.
SHEILA: My dear, are you sure about this?
*(*MARTA *looks questioningly at* SHEILA.*)*
Your reason for wanting to dissuade Regan?
MARTA: Isn't it obvious?
SHEILA: You *really* want her to come into your real estate business?
MARTA: Of course.
SHEILA: So long as it's for the right reason. *(slight pause)* Are you pushing because, in time, you want her to take over the business? Or is it just a way to keep her here? Close by? Huh?
*(*MARTA *turns away, confronted with a truth she doesn't want to face.)*
MARTA: Mother, I don't need you— *(to tell me how to run my life)*
*(*REGAN *and* CHRIS *enter stage right.)*
REGAN: *(as they enter)* No, no! The Sudoku room is our bathroom. Our washroom.
CHRIS: Then why do you call it a Sudoku room?
REGAN: It's the only place in the house where we're allowed to do Sudoku puzzles. It was Pops' idea.

Sudoku Fever

GEORGE: Only because your Gran complained.

SHEILA: The whole house was a mess. Sudoku books everywhere. Couldn't move without stepping on them, sitting on them.

REGAN: We all do them.

MARTA: A house full of Sudoku fanatics.

SHEILA: George built it.

MARTA: A shelf at a time.

CHRIS: *(to GEORGE, pointing to his wheelchair)* You built it?

SHEILA: Before his accident.

GEORGE: I'll answer my own questions, thank you.

SHEILA: Except when you're in the Sudoku room.

MARTA: Now it's like a regular library in there.

REGAN: And everything we do in there is in code.

SHEILA: It's less embarrassing that way.

REGAN: If you're going in just for a pee, then you say you'll be doing an easy puzzle.

CHRIS: And if you need to stay longer, it's a difficult puzzle?

MARTA: Exactly. Except that *everyone* seems to have to do a difficult puzzle. You can never get in there!

GEORGE: All right, Chris: If, when I come out, Sheila asks me—

SHEILA: Did you put the puzzle book back on the shelf?

GEORGE: What's she really saying?

CHRIS: Did you tidy up before—

SHEILA: George? Tidy?

GEORGE: No. It's "Did you close the toilet lid?"

SHEILA: He always forgets.

GEORGE: Actually, I have a theory: it's women who forget. They never look back to see. Men do, because they're already facing that way.

SHEILA: Not you, George.

GEORGE: Another blow below the belt!

REGAN: *(to* CHRIS*)* So what do I mean when I say I've been cleaning up the numbers in the horizontal rows?

*(*CHRIS *shakes her head.)*

MARTA: "Brushing her teeth."

(Everybody pitches into the fast-paced fun.)

SHEILA: Erasing wrong numbers?

REGAN: "Taking a shower."
GEORGE: *(to* CHRIS*)* Redesigning the puzzle? *(slight pause)* Applies only to women.
CHRIS: "Putting on makeup?"
GEORGE: Oh, well done. See: that's an engineer for you.
MARTA: Darkening the entries in the top row?
REGAN: "Applying eyeliner."
CHRIS: So, who thought of all this?
MARTA: It all sort of...just grew. Like, we all contributed.
CHRIS: Which was yours?
MARTA: Tidying up the bottom line.
SHEILA: "Clipping your toenails."
REGAN: Mine was: "Putting two eights in the same row." *(pause)* "Being constipated."
CHRIS: I don't get it.
REGAN: Think how an eight is shaped: those two big, round O's...
CHRIS: Ugh!...Dare I ask: has anybody found a code for F-A-R-T?
REGAN: *(laughs)* No, not yet.
GEORGE: *(to* CHRIS*)* Can you?
CHRIS: Yeah, I guess... "Turn on the exhaust fan" ...No. How about: "False...Answer...Right...Top"... F-A-R-T?
(Laughter; congratulations.)
GEORGE: You've passed the initiation test, Chris. Consider yourself a member of the Sudoku club.
CHRIS: Well thank you, sir. I assume you're the chair?
GEORGE: Of course. Aren't I sitting in it? *(slight pause, then to everyone, firmly)* But enough!
(Surprised looks from everyone.)
The real issue isn't about the Sudoku room. It's about Chris. Why she's here.
SHEILA: George, I don't think this is the right moment— *(to talk about that)*
GEORGE: Yes. Yes, it is. *(to* MARTA *and* SHEILA*)* You've both had your say—and Katie has too. You three all feel it's inappropriate for Regan to go in for a degree in engineering. Right?
(Reluctant nods from SHEILA and MARTA.)

Sudoku Fever

GEORGE: *(continuing)* But so far I've held back; haven't offered my opinion.

MARTA: You always have an opinion!

GEORGE: Not about this. Not yet. So bear with me...Regan!

REGAN: Y-e-s, Pops.

GEORGE: I want you to do something for me. Go into the Sudoku room. Search for a special book. *(semi-confidentially)* Do you know where those old, old Mayerling books are?

REGAN: Yeah. Top shelf. On the left, as you go in.

GEORGE: Right. Go and pull a handful forward. Gently, because they tend to fall apart. Behind them, standing flat against the wall, you'll find Issue No. 7...October 1998. Don't open it. Just bring it to me.

REGAN: O-k-a-y...

(REGAN heads toward the upstage door, speaks to herself.)

Top left, Mayerling Seven...

(REGAN exits.)

SHEILA: George: Sudoku books are *never* taken out of the Sudoku room.

GEORGE: This one is!

MARTA: So it's okay for *you* to break the rule? Even though you made it?

GEORGE: Sheila's rule, really.

SHEILA: *(to CHRIS)* You can imagine what it'd be like, all those silly books cluttering up the house, lying around because no one can be bothered to put them back.

REGAN: *(re-entering)* I can't, Pops. Someone's in there.

MARTA: Katie. Might as well wait till tomorrow.

GEORGE: *(to REGAN)* Go pound on the door.

MARTA: Won't work, Dad. She'll just settle in; sit tight.

GEORGE: *(to REGAN)* Tell her it's an emergency. That I'm in dire straits; just gotta do a difficult puzzle. *(to MARTA)* She knows what happens if I don't get there in time.

MARTA: We all know!

SHEILA: George, you can't— *(play a trick like that)*

GEORGE: *(to REGAN)* Just do it!

*(*REGAN *looks at* MARTA, *who throws her hands in the air.* REGAN *exits.)*
SHEILA: She'll never forgive you.
GEORGE: She will.
(Sound of pounding on door.)
KATIE: *(v.o.)* Who the hell's that?
REGAN: *(v.o.)* It's me, Regan. Pops has just got to come in. It's an emergency!
KATIE: *(v.o.)* I haven't finished my puzzle yet!
(Pause. Sound of door opening.)
Well, where is he?
REGAN: *(v.o.)* In the front room.
*(*KATIE *enters upstage center, pauses in the doorway, strides over to* GEORGE.*)*
KATIE: What kind of trick are you pulling now?
GEORGE: No trick. You'll see.
KATIE: You spend hours in that room, not letting anyone in. Yet when I'm in there you always find a reason to— *(interrupt what I'm doing)*
GEORGE: Just for once, woman, will you hold your tongue!
SHEILA: George!
GEORGE: Or snip it out and ship it back to Ireland.
SHEILA: *(to* CHRIS*)* I apologize for my husband's attitude— *(but he's a little uptight today)*
GEORGE: She's an engineer! She'll understand.
KATIE: *She's* the engineer? Ha!
*(*KATIE *emits a raucous laugh, turns to* CHRIS.*)*
Sorry. I'm Kate. Regan's aunt.
CHRIS: Hi...Chris.
(They shake hands.)
(Enter REGAN *with large, old Sudoku book in hand; she holds it out to* GEORGE.*)*
GEORGE: No. You hold it.
REGAN: How'd you get it up there?
GEORGE: Before this happened *(taps his wheelchair).* Turn to page seventy-eight.
*(*REGAN *sits on a footstool, riffles through the pages.)*

Sudoku Fever

REGAN: There's something else in here. Glued down.

GEORGE: Open it up.

(KATIE and MARTA edge forward, try to peer over REGAN's shoulder.)

GEORGE: No, you two. Let Regan do it.

REGAN: It's a certificate.

GEORGE: Right. So, tell me...tell them...what does it say?

REGAN: Read it out loud?

GEORGE: How else?

REGAN: *(reads)* "The Province of Nova Scotia..."

(REGAN is impressed, glances at others.)

GEORGE: Go on!

REGAN: *(reads)* "This is to certify that...George, James, Wilberforce Dubrowski—"

KATIE: *(laughs)* "Wilberforce!"

SHEILA: You never said you had a third name!

GEORGE: Men with big handles are too large for small ships.

MARTA: *(to CHRIS)* He served in the navy. Thirty-one years.

CHRIS: Got it!

SHEILA: *(to GEORGE)* Did your first wife know you were called Wilberforce?

GEORGE: It was on our marriage certificate.

KATIE: Bet she laughed, too, when she saw it.

GEORGE: She certainly did not!

KATIE: No sense of humor?

MARTA: She was probably scared to!

GEORGE: *(with dignity)* When a good woman's name is "Wilhelmina," she doesn't laugh when her husband-to-be carries the name "Wilberforce."

REGAN: Good for you, Pops.

KATIE: *(giggles)* Wilhelmina...!

(SHEILA and MARTA glance scathingly at KATIE.)

GEORGE: *(to SHEILA)* Would you still have married me if you'd known my name was "Wilberforce?"

SHEILA: What difference would— *(that have made?)*

GEORGE: Or would you have laughed?

SHEILA: *(goes to him)* No. You're still my man.

KATIE: You're quite a force, George, wheeling around in your high-speed Wilberchair!

(Laughter.)

GEORGE: Enough! *(to REGAN, waves at certificate)* Continue.

REGAN: *(reads)* "George...etcetera, etcetera...has completed the training and successfully passed the requisite examinations, with the result that, from the Eighteenth of April, 1959, he is certified by the Province of Nova Scotia as a Fully Registered Nurse."

(The following three remarks partly overlap.)

MARTA: Nurse? You? A nurse?   )
KATIE: How could you possibly be…?)
SHEILA: You never said anything...   )

GEORGE: Hold it up, Regan. Let them see for themselves.

(Pause while the adult women peer at the certificate.)

SHEILA: Why didn't you say?

KATIE: I always thought...

GEORGE: Thought what?

KATIE: You served on a destroyer.

MARTA: And a submarine.

GEORGE: Correct. Both. At different times.

KATIE: *You* were the ship's nurse?

GEORGE: Correct again.

SHEILA: But you always said...

GEORGE: Said what?

MARTA: You did the electronics bit...depth finders. Didn't you?

GEORGE: Did I ever actually *say* that?

KATIE: You loaded torpedoes into a...a big tube...something like that. Whatever.

GEORGE: Or did you choose to *think* I did?

MARTA: Oh, no. I distinctly remember—

GEORGE: Because it sounded more glamorous?

CHRIS: You were on subs? Under all that water?

(GEORGE nods.)

I couldn't do that.

REGAN: *(to CHRIS)* He has medals. A row of them.

GEORGE: Enough. Enough.

Sudoku Fever

MARTA: And all the time I've thought of you as fixing things, repairing equipment.

REGAN: You were, Pops. Repairing sailors.

KATIE: Nurses don't do repairs. Doctors do that.

GEORGE: No doctor on a submarine.

KATIE: What if somebody needs surgery?

(GEORGE shrugs.)

You weren't licensed to wield a knife!

SHEILA: You had to do that?

GEORGE: Who else?

KATIE: You could've called in the ship's cook. Handy at cutting meat.

GEORGE: I don't want to talk about it.

REGAN: Oh, Pops: what if a sailor had a burst appendix?

KATIE: About to burst. Burst, it'd be too late.

SHEILA: Radio for a helicopter.

GEORGE: Not in a gale.

REGAN: You still had to do it, even in a gale?

GEORGE: Dove down a hundred feet. Calmer down there.

KATIE: You were in a submarine?

GEORGE: Hard to dive in a surface ship.

SHEILA: Did he survive?

GEORGE: As far as I know.

KATIE: As far as you know?

GEORGE: He waved to me from the stretcher the next day, as they hauled him up into a helicopter.

REGAN: After you'd taken out his appendix?

GEORGE: Uh-huh.

KATIE: Did you send it with him? Gift wrapped?

MARTA: How come you never— *(said anything about it before?)*

REGAN: Pops! That blue medal, in the box you showed me once… the one with a cross on it…is that for— *(doing the appendix operation?)*

GEORGE: Another time, Regan. Please.

MARTA: George: why're you telling us all this?

GEORGE: I didn't choose to. You dragged it out of me.

SHEILA: I think Marta means, about the certificate.

GEORGE: Ah! Yes. Well, I wanted you to see how, if I was able to do what normally is a woman's job—

SHEILA: And do it well.

KATIE: Yeah. Yeah.

GEORGE: If I could do that, is there any reason why Regan here couldn't do what some people still regard as a man's job? Become an engineer?

(Slight pause.)

CHRIS: Hear! Hear!

MARTA: George: That's not fair.

GEORGE: Think about it, Marta.

MARTA: I am!...I am.

(SHEILA places a sympathetic hand on MARTA's arm.)

GEORGE: You too, Regan.

REGAN: *(echoes her mother, but gently)* I am...I am.

(REGAN and MARTA exchange an understanding grin.)

GEORGE: Talk to Chris here. All of you. And *listen*!

KATIE: Talk about a pot calling a kettle black. When did you ever listen, George?

GEORGE: With four women in the house? All the time. It's expected.

SHEILA: Sometimes George does listen to me. About once a month.

GEORGE: *(to REGAN)* I won't deny, Regan, I shall miss you. But you must follow your intuition.

(REGAN places a hand on GEORGE's shoulder, pecks him on the cheek.)

(Sound of dog barking, stage right: two spaced yaps.)

MARTA: Rufus.

KATIE: Wants in.

SHEILA: *(starts toward upstage right)* I'll get the door.

REGAN: No, Gran. You don't have to. Just wait!

(Pause; they all face upstage right.)

He knows what to do.

KATIE: Ring the doorbell? *(laughs)*

(A single dog yap. SHEILA shakes her head, starts toward the door.)

REGAN: No! Wait, Gran. Please. I have been training him.
(A guffaw from KATIE.)
MARTA: Be fair, Katie.
GEORGE: *(to SHEILA)* He'll never learn if you keep answering the door.
(A single dog yap. Pause. Sound of scratching.)
REGAN: He's feeling for the button!
(Pause, then we hear the spring creaking and the door opening.)
MARTA: Well done!
GEORGE: *(looking at his watch)* Five...four...three...two...one.
(Sound of spring and door closing.)
CHRIS: You did it, Regan!
(Sound of painful yelps.)
Oops!
SHEILA: *(rushing toward door, to Regan)* What've you done! *(exits stage right)*
(MARTA, KATIE and REGAN follow and exit.)
GEORGE: Too bad.
CHRIS: She'll be fine.
GEORGE: His name is Rufus.
CHRIS: I meant Regan.
GEORGE: Ah...Yeah...Right.
(REGAN re-enters.)
REGAN: Just the tip of his tail. I'll increase the delay time to...um...twelve seconds.
GEORGE: Y'see, Chris! She should be an engineer.
(They laugh. GEORGE turns to REGAN.)
Sudoku time, I think.
REGAN: Right, Pops.
(Freeze.)

END

Seven Plays with a Light Touch

Character Descriptions

How Three Individual Dwellings Came Down to One

The house is owned by Marta. Katie owned her own house until ten years ago, when Marta's and Katie's husbands—who were brothers—abruptly pulled up stakes and left for Australia, leaving their wives without money (who subsequently divorced them in absentia, with no monetary gain). Katie was financially insecure and so sold her house, paid off the mortgage, and moved in with Marta.

George and Sheila also owned their own house, until eight years ago when George caused a motor vehicle accident which resulted in him and the other driver becoming paraplegics. He was sued by the other party and George lost his case. Sheila had to sell their house to make the payment. George then declared bankruptcy and they moved in with Marta, Katie and Regan.

George is permanently confined to a wheelchair.

Sheila

Sheila has firm although sometimes old-fashioned principles. She believes in a strong work ethic: that you give of your best and are paid to do so. She has worked primarily in the service trades, as a sales clerk, as a motel receptionist, as a server in a cafe, and even as a receptionist in a funeral home.

When her first husband left her for another woman, Sheila settled for the house they jointly owned as her divorce payment. A year later she married George. They have had a comfortable 20-year marriage.

When George was severely injured in a traffic accident (which he caused), she was considerably shaken. She was even more upset when he was sued by the other party, and vocally angry when she learned they would lose their house and the only escape was for them to declare bankruptcy.

She sees that Marta has done a good job in bringing up Regan. Although she doesn't always approve of Marta's methods, she has learned to 'hold her peace.' She is pleased to see that in some ways Regan is similar to herself, in her directness and ability to think past the ordinary to find a solution to a problem.

She is an intelligent woman and in a different setting could have seen a very different life. She reads newspaper editorials and watches political discussions with interest, and follows what is happening elsewhere in the world more than most people do.

Sometimes she creates the impression that she is a long-suffering, put-upon old lady, but when she sees it happening she makes an effort to shrug it off.

George

George is an enigma. One would expect him to be angry that life has taken his mobility away from him, permanently confining him to a wheelchair, and bankrupting him. Yet he seems to have accepted his state philosophically, refusing to see it as a burden. One could define him as a pragmatist and almost—but not quite—a fatalist. Perhaps his 31 years in the navy developed this trait.

He dislikes being a burden to those around him. So, except when bathroom calls are necessary—and everyone knows they are essential—he tries to limit his demands so they fit in with what others are doing.

He has a quirky sense of humor and uses it to lighten the day for those around him (although sometimes his remarks are so off-center the others don't understand them). He extends humor to his calls for bathroom attention, referring them as a need to play Sudoku, at which he is a whiz.

George's relationship with his wife Sheila is warm and friendly. They are good companions rather than deep lovers, as 20 years of marriage show. George respects her views but does not always agree with them, sometimes resulting in healthy but never vicious arguments.

His relationship with his step-daughter Marta and her sister-in-law Katie is rather like this:

"Okay, you're here, and I have to put up with you,
but I'm not going to make a scene about it."

He prefers Katie because she is a nurse who understands his condition better than Marta, and is practical and helpful in meeting his needs.

George has great affection for Regan, although he doesn't let it show other than by conversing and being with her comfortably and easily. He recognizes that, of the four women in the house, only

Regan has the potential to create a meaningful life, 'to take the tree and shake it from its roots up.'

George harbors a well-kept personal secret. He served in the navy for 31 years, and held both shore postings and sea postings in destroyers and submarines. He lets listeners imagine what his life must have been like, and the technical systems they assume he worked with. But he never lets on that the image they have created is incorrect. Why? Because he was trained as a registered nurse and was assigned to positions on shore and at sea as a male nurse. He was very good at it: hence, his long career with the navy.

Marta

Of the four women in the house, Marta probably faces the most disappointment: she has had a failed marriage and is unlikely to marry again. She has given over much of her life to ensure her daughter has a good start, and in no way regrets it. She knows that very soon she will have to part with Regan, and in some ways it's the factor that drives her to pressure Regan to give up the idea of going away to study engineering. She would prefer that Regan study business administration and sales at a local school and then join her in the small Realty business she owns (which she envisions Regan will eventually take over).

Marta is a great 'persuader,' which goes with her role as a realtor. Most of the time her persuasiveness is ethical, but on occasion she stretches the truth to help complete a sale. This willingness to distort the truth to make a point sometimes slips into her dealings with people who are associates and friends, and even within the family.

She also is a good organizer, planning events well and managing people to handle different tasks. This extends into her home life, which sometimes meets with resistance, particularly from Katie. She tends to take on more than she can manage, and because she complains about it with a 'poor me' whine, she has earned herself the nickname Marta the Martyr.

Most of the time she has a good relationship with her mother, but can be impatient with her when her mother demands too much (or grumbles because she feels Marta demands too much). She has sympathy for George, her step-father, but little patience with him because she (wrongly) feels he is using his condition to get attention.

She has strong affection for Katie, although they argue a lot. She has genuine affection for Regan, although again she can be impatient with her when she rebels against authority or wants to do things her way rather than the way her mother prescribes.

Katie

Katie is Irish and, traditionally, has inherited the gift of the gab. But her words come with a smile and, when she is teasing, a squarely planted tongue in the cheek. Her Irish accent normally doesn't show, but in moments of stress or when telling stories it tends to spring to the fore.

Katie is a registered nurse who works in the town's hospital, where she is liked by both staff and patients. Her smile and cheery demeanor are particularly appreciated.

She has affection for Marta and even more for Regan, although she doesn't always agree with how Marta has brought up her daughter; this causes problems because Katie can be vocal about it. When Regan was in her early teens she tended to be lippy and to talk back, which Katie was very critical about.

She tolerates Sheila and George, yet as a nurse she has sympathy for George's medical condition. Strangely, she is willing to cope with George's bathroom problems and need for a bottom-rub following too much sitting, a likely spin-off from her nursing capability. She thinks Sheila is too outspoken and strident in her opinions, forgetting sometimes that she can be the same.

She has no family locally. Her father is deceased and her mother is living with a nephew and niece in Ireland. Katie was an only child. She has a son, now 23, who on his 18th birthday chose to join his father in Australia. She rarely hears from him. Is she bitter about her husband's decision to pick up and go, and choose a divorce? At first she was, but now recognizes she is better off without him. She is not interested in a second marriage.

Regan

Regan knows how her parents chose her unusual name, but doesn't resent it: her mother wanted a boy and was adamant he should be called Reginald; her father also wanted a boy and was determined he should be called Anthony. When a girl was born to them, they settled on a compromise.

She is a competent student, achieving consistent A's in the sciences and mathematics, and B+ in the social subjects. Hence, her decision to become an engineer is well placed (although her grandmother keeps telling her she would do better to choose environmental studies.)

Why did Regan choose to go into mechanical engineering? Because she likes finding out how equipment works. She has frequently repaired the washing machine, broken deadlocks, damaged container hasps, hinges, and so on, without the family having to call in a service representative. (It was always a matter of chagrin to her mother, grandmother and aunt that she never paid attention to the dolls and stuffed toys they bestowed upon her.)

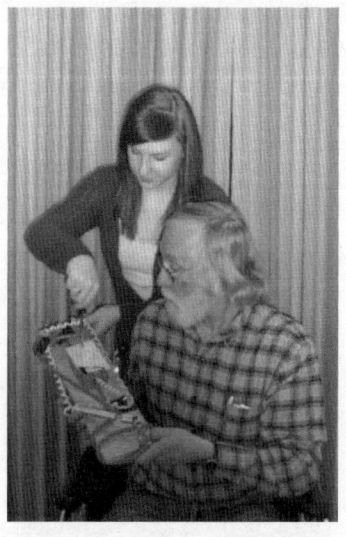

George (Ron Robinson) and Regan (Julie Seroy) discuss adjustments to be made to the hand-crafted door opener Regan is about to install.

Often, she consults with her step-grandfather George for advice, and they happily and knowledgeably discuss problems and how to go about fixing them or repairing damaged equipment. Theirs is a gentle, companionable relationship.

Most of the time her relationship with her grandmother is polite and accepting. She has been briefed by her mother that her grandmother has strong opinions and how it's often better to agree and say 'uh-huh' rather than be drawn into an interminable argument.

Regan is sharp enough to recognize that she is all her mother has worked for over the years. Yet she hesitates to let herself get too close, for fear that she will get drawn in to becoming what her mother wants her to become, rather than what she wants for herself. She knows she may have to fight to make her own path in life. She tolerates her aunt Katie but does not particularly like her.

Most of the time Regan seems equable and calm. She has a long fuse, but when someone pushes her beyond a certain point she erupts with a sudden blaze of temper. It dies quickly, then she feels guilty for letting her emotions get the better of her. She does have friends and associates, but few very close friends. Similarly with boyfriends: none have stayed the course. Frankly, she admits privately, the finds most of them are too parochial in their views of life and the world.

She works part-time in a fast-food restaurant, to earn money so she can buy clothes she feels are more appropriate for her age than those her mother or aunt would choose for her. She's a moderately competent soccer player in the summer, and hockey player in the winter, in both cases playing on mixed-sex teams.

All in all, Regan is a well-balanced young woman with a good head on her shoulders.

Chris

She has graduated as an electrical engineer and is employed by a major power utility. Her full name is Christina.

She is the middle of three children born to professional parents. Her father is an architect, her mother is a newspaper editor, and she has two brothers, age 32 and 17.

Chris is essentially highly intelligent, but proved to be a lazy student at school, achieving an average C to C+. She was bored by school and simply didn't put the effort in. She also resented how teachers compared her to her older brother, who was a high achiever (and her younger brother is demonstrating similar aptitudes).

Her parents were pragmatic and suggested she should seek out a trade or a course that would interest her at a community college. She chose to take a one-year electrical technician course, but liked it so much that half way through she opted to transfer into a two-year engineering technology course, at which she was very successful. Following graduation, she worked for an electrical contractor for a year, then took off to university where she earned a degree in Electrical Engineering. Since then she has been employed by the power utility and has completed the requirements to become a professional engineer.

As a person she is vocal, enthusiastic, well-spoken and pleased that she has found direction in her life. (Her parents are equally pleased.) Sometimes she argues a point for too long, and needs to know when to stop and listen.

She is a tennis player, skater, and swimmer, and has studied and performed in amateur dramatics.

Production Notes

For the printed version of the play, I have chosen a general location for the events that occur. For the Manitoba productions I chose a suitable-size town some 125 miles (200 km) west of the city of Winnipeg, and recommend that future directors also select a suitable location and make references to it in the script, to suit where the production will be performed.

The descriptions of the characters, and the situation in which they live, are a primary factor for helping the cast gain a feeling for the pace at which the play should be performed. The person playing George has a role with considerable humor, but which also comments on the quirks evident in other members of the family. The fact that he never talks about his role in the navy is not unusual among military men and women when they return to civilian life. Ideally, George has an infectious laugh.

The session in which various members of the family quote the expressions they use to describe various bathroom functions needs to be faced-paced, yet it has to be presented seriously. The effect tends to be lost if the actors overplay the humor.

The stage-left area of the set, with George's wheelchair and a laptop on a small side table. Furniture is Scandinavian, light and easy to move, which is essential for rapid set-up and removal. Often, the maximum set-up and tear-down time allowed at most Fringe Festivals and One-Act-Play Festivals is only 15 minutes.

Sudoku Fever

The contraption Regan has built to become an automatic door opener can be designed in any way the director or props manager chooses. Ideally, it will have a visible spring, plus an electrical cable and plug, to justify visually how the gadget will open the back door.

The adjudicator at the 2009 GADOC One-Act-Play Festival in Guernsey was Jan Palmer Bayer who, in her remarks following the performance, commented that:

> "I felt as if I was a fly on the wall watching this improbable family, and firmly believing in them."

I hope your audiences feel the same way.

Seven Plays with a Light Touch

Part 2

Plays for Adults

Seven Plays with a Light Touch

Play No. 4

A Touch of Gray

Synopsis

At age 26 Frankie is about to be launched on a promising career with a government agency, researching the lifestyles of people living in different parts of the world. Each research segment will mean living in a remote area for two years, where there will be few amenities.

When Frankie discovers she is pregnant, she decides to give her baby to her brother and his wife, who are childless. But when her ex-boyfriend hears of the plan he demands that, as he is the father, the child must come to him.

A Touch of Gray explores the conflict that occurs between the two parties: Frankie's brother and sister-in-law, and Frankie's ex-boyfriend and his new partner. Their demands influence Frankie as she works toward a decision that will set in motion the life her child will experience.

Rationale

A Touch of Gray pits the conflicting views expressed by the protagonists as they try to convince the primary character to make a decision that will favor them. Although I have made Frankie's sister-in-law severely vocal about the suitability of the baby going to Frankie's ex-boyfriend and his new partner, the play is not really exploring that issue. The real focus is on Frankie and how her character changes from being indefinite at the start of the play and then gradually becomes definite as she rationally and logically steps away from her previous indecisiveness.

The original name of the play was *Shades of Grey*, which unfortunately proved confusing to potential playgoers because an extremely popular novel with an erotic theme, and bearing exactly the same name, was published just weeks before the play was launched. Since then the name of the play has been changed to *A Touch of Gray*.

History

The first performances occurred at the Winnipeg, Fringe Theatre Festival, July 18th to 28th, 2012. Three further performances were presented August 10th to 12th, at the A-Spire Players Summer Theatre Program in Gimli, Manitoba.

Characters

The play has a cast of six, three male and three female:

Frankie (26)   **David** (37), Frankie's brother
Adrian (28), her ex-boyfriend   **Evie** (38), David's wife
Maisie (55), Frankie's mother   **Tyler** (36), Adrian's partner

A 'snapshot' description of each character follows. More detailed character descriptions start on page 190.

Frankie She is continually fighting the image (instilled into her by her mother) that she is inadequate and worthless. She is a dedicated, deeply involved worker/student, a good organizer, and a logical thinker when doing her research. But in her personal life she tends to be disorganized and is not a good decision-maker.

Adrian He is a Certified General Accountant (CGA) with a solid reputation at work. He is an alert, enquiring, thoughtful person who assesses a situation quickly and does not chase after ideas he has determined are not worth pursuing. He accepted that he is gay only five months ago.

> *Although Frankie and Adrian are no longer seeing each other, a solid and companionable friendship still exists between them. They have known each other since their high-school days.*

Maisie Maisie is brash, opinionated and forceful. She is divorced and has been affected by the loss of her favorite daughter, Marina, who died in an accident at nine-years old. Maisie continually compares Frankie (whom she considers weak and inadequate) against the imagined strengths and capabilities of Marina, strengths she is convinced Marina would have had if she had lived to be an adult.

David	He is a design engineer for a power utility: a methodical thinker who is satisfied with himself and so is viewed as being staid. He often lets his wife speak for both of them.
Evie	She is an efficient and competent Registered Nurse, working in a hospital. She tends to be definite and officious, which puts people off (particularly other nurses). She and David have a comfortable, not-very-exciting marriage in which he consistently defers to her wishes. Her full name is Evelyn.
Tyler	He is a career-oriented lawyer, well-respected by the firm where he has been appointed as a partner. He is a strong, confident individualist who expects to do things, and see them done, 'his way.' He is very articulate, as befits a lawyer, and uses language well.

The cast for the first production comprised:

Frankie	Kaeleigh Ayre
Adrian	John Mackenzie
Maisie	Kelley Hirst
David	David Wood
Evie	Heather Forgie
Tyler	Tony Porteous

The Set

The stage is divided into three areas. The primary set is the living room of Frankie's apartment, in which most of the action occurs. Secondary sets are Frankie's small kitchen, used in two scenes, and part of the living room of Tyler and Adrian's home, used for a single scene.

Frankie's Living Room *(center stage).* A simple apartment on the fifth floor of an older apartment block. Upstage center is the arched entrance to a hall leading to the kitchen at stage right and the front door at stage left. All entrances and exits are through the arched doorway.

Upstage right has a sofa or loveseat set at an angle facing downstage left. Upstage left has a bookcase set into the upstage wall with, in front of it, a small armchair facing downstage right. Mid-stage left is a small dining table with a laptop computer on it. The laptop is positioned so that when Frankie uses it she is facing downstage.

There are piles of books and papers on the table, on a coffee table, and on the floor, suited to someone carrying out an in-depth research project. There are two dining chairs beside the table. Downstage right is a small armchair facing stage left, with a coffee table beside it on which there are more papers.

There is a telephone on the dining/computer table, and a buzzer and speaker on the wall beside the entrance.

Frankie's Kitchen *(downstage right).* The kitchen is small with a counter and pantry shelves above it, and a table and chair.

Tyler and Adrian's Living Room *(downstage left).* Only part of the living room is visible. It is stylishly furnished, mostly with a Scandinavian décor. The main feature is a desk at which Tyler is working.

Notes about the first production start on page 195.

Approximate Length: 65 minutes

Some Script Guidelines

Throughout the script, two symbols are used occasionally at the end of a piece of dialogue to indicate how the sentence ends:

- ... An ellipsis at the end of a statement means that the speaker just trails off and leaves his or her thought hanging in the air (possibly accompanied by a shrug).
- – A dash at the end of a statement means that the speaker is interrupted by the next speaker and the first speaker's statement is incomplete. Sometimes there is an italicized continuation of the statement *(within brackets)* immediately following the dash, to help the actor sense where the sentence was going.

v.o. Means 'voice over' (i.e. the character speaks off stage).

Script: *A Touch of Gray*

© 2011, Ron Blicq

(At curtain up FRANKIE is sitting on a chair facing the small table at stage left. She is typing into her laptop, referring to handwritten notes on a pad beside it. She mouths the words as she types. Fade opening music.)

FRANKIE: In the mountain regions of Peru, five kilometers west of the village of Merinesti, population two hundred and eighty-seven, there are caves with scratched drawings on their walls, at least three thousand years old. My previous research shows— *(further evidence of migration from this area.)*

(Sound of wall buzzer. FRANKIE pushes her chair back, crosses to the speaker, holds down a button.)

Yes?

ADRIAN: *(telephone speaker voice)* Frankie, it's Adrian.

FRANKIE: Right. Come on up.

(FRANKIE pushes a door release button, returns to the computer and, standing, types in half a dozen more words. Then she straightens up, is thoughtful, looks toward the entrance. The doorbell rings and she exits into the hall, turning right (to stage left).)

FRANKIE: *(v.o.)* Hi, Come on in.

ADRIAN: *(v.o.)* Hi, Frankie. You okay?

FRANKIE: *(v.o.)* Yeah. Sure.

(FRANKIE and ADRIAN enter. He looks at the computer and papers.)

ADRIAN: Still at it? *(peers into computer screen)* Your thesis?

FRANKIE: No, a grant proposal.

(FRANKIE gestures for ADRIAN to sit in the chair downstage right; he doesn't.)

ADRIAN: *(reads)* "Strategies for Conducting Sociological Research in the Peruvian Mountains."

FRANKIE: Has to be in, in three weeks.

ADRIAN: Think you'll get funding?

FRANKIE: Pretty confident. They asked me to apply.

(Awkward pause. FRANKIE again indicates ADRIAN should sit. He does so.)

ADRIAN: You—um—you said you wanted to see me.

FRANKIE: Yeah...it's...um...there is something I need to... *(she takes a breath)* It's like this.

(FRANKIE stands in front of ADRIAN with her stomach pushed slightly forward, and points to it.)

Put your hand here.

ADRIAN: Frankie! We're not— *(seeing each other now)*

FRANKIE: Please, Adrian! Hold your palm against my stomach.

(ADRIAN hesitates. FRANKIE grabs his hand and holds it against her stomach.)

ADRIAN: Frankie: get real! We're not seeing each other.

FRANKIE: Feel anything?

(ADRIAN moves his hand slightly.)

ADRIAN: No. I don't think so. *(sudden concern)* You haven't got a lump or something, have you?

FRANKIE: No. Well...

ADRIAN: I don't want to seem impolite, but...uh...you do seem to have put on weight.

FRANKIE: Some.

ADRIAN: But why would you be showing me...? Oh! You can't be!

(FRANKIE nods.)

Why're you telling me this? It can't be mine.

FRANKIE: It is, Adrian.

ADRIAN: Not after four months; nearly five! The last time we...

FRANKIE: Slept together?

(ADRIAN paces, shakes his head.)

It's no one else's.

ADRIAN: It *can't* be mine! I can't believe that you—you, of all people—that you've been...

FRANKIE: Careless?

ADRIAN: No. Doing without.

FRANKIE: Ah! Celibate.

ADRIAN: Uh-huh.

FRANKIE: It hasn't been easy.

ADRIAN: I bet it hasn't!

FRANKIE: No, Adrian. The sickness. Every morning. I've never known anything like it. Till after noon. Day after day.

A Touch of Gray

ADRIAN: Couldn't you have arranged a...a termination?
FRANKIE: *No!* No. I cannot take a life. Ever.
   (Pause.)
ADRIAN: You should've told me.
FRANKIE: I couldn't.
ADRIAN: Why'd you wait so long? You must have known, before I left.
FRANKIE: I wasn't certain. I've always been irregular. You knew that.
ADRIAN: So, I am to be a father. Is that what you're saying?
FRANKIE: Uh-huh.
ADRIAN: And you're to be a mother?
FRANKIE: Yes, but...well...
ADRIAN: I don't understand you. Why you didn't call me. As soon as you knew for sure.
FRANKIE: No, Adrian. You'd've thought I was setting a trap. Like I was trying to drag you back.
   (Pause.)
ADRIAN: Frankie, if it is my child—
FRANKIE: It wouldn't've worked.
ADRIAN: But if—
FRANKIE: No, Adrian. It would be only a matter of time before we'd be at each other's throats.
ADRIAN: Then why've you asked me here? Tonight?
FRANKIE: We...we need to discuss...oh, it's so difficult.
ADRIAN: You want help, financially?
FRANKIE: No. Not that.
ADRIAN: I would expect to.
FRANKIE: I know you would.
ADRIAN: Then...?
   (FRANKIE raises her hand, palm vertical.)
FRANKIE: I don't want to keep it.
ADRIAN: Not keep it! You mean, put the baby up for adoption?
FRANKIE: I mustn't have children.
ADRIAN: Mustn't?
FRANKIE: Don't want to.
   (Slight pause.)

ADRIAN: Afraid you'd be like your mother?

FRANKIE: I wouldn't want any child of mine to experience what I've had to go through. Still face.

ADRIAN: But you're not like her.

FRANKIE: You know how she can be.

ADRIAN: You're too smart to let her influence you.

FRANKIE: Don't push it, Adrian. Please!

(FRANKIE points to the computer and her papers.)

This is what I *really* want to do. Must do. It's what I've been working toward, all this time.

ADRIAN: You *have* to go to Peru?

FRANKIE: It's where the research has to be done; what the funding's for.

ADRIAN: And a baby would— *(get in the way?)*

FRANKIE: I don't want to lose focus. I can't. Anyway, it's far too remote to take a baby. *(pause)* And the committee's already hinting they want me to do further research. In African countries: Tanzania; possibly Zimbabwe.

ADRIAN: Another two years?

FRANKIE: Each.

(The security door buzzer sounds.)

Shit! I'm not ready yet!

(FRANKIE crosses to the speaker.)

ADRIAN: Leave it. You don't have to answer.

FRANKIE: Yes. Yes I do.

(FRANKIE holds down the intercom button, speaks sharply into the mic.)

Yes?

EVIE: *(telephone voice)* It's us, Frankie. Me and David.

FRANKIE: You're early!…Alright, I'll let you in. But wait down below, will you. Just a couple of minutes. Then come up.

(FRANKIE pushes the door release button.)

EVIE: *(v.o.)* Oh. Well, see you in a minute.

(FRANKIE turns back to ADRIAN.)

FRANKIE: It's David and Evie.

ADRIAN: I could tell. You were expecting them?

A Touch of Gray

FRANKIE: They were supposed to be here fifteen minutes after you.

ADRIAN: After I'd left?

FRANKIE: No. I want all three of you here.

(Slight pause.)

ADRIAN: Do they know you're pregnant?

FRANKIE: Yes.

ADRIAN: So you told your brother, and his wife, before you told me! And I'm the father.

FRANKIE: I'm sorry, Adrian, but— *(I wanted everything to be in place before...)*

ADRIAN: This should be between us, Frankie. Just you and me.

FRANKIE: No, not any more.

ADRIAN: Oh, but it is...

(FRANKIE shakes her head 'no'.)

I suppose in another fifteen minutes your mother will be pushing the buzzer!

FRANKIE: You don't think I'd want *her* here, do you? You know what she's like.

ADRIAN: *(light laugh)* She knows you're pregnant?

FRANKIE: Yes.

ADRIAN: Another one! But brave you, just the same.

FRANKIE: She also knows about David and Evie.

ADRIAN: Evie's not pregnant, too?

FRANKIE: No. Nothing— *(like that)*

ADRIAN: No. Of course. They can't, can they?

FRANKIE: You're not supposed to know that.

ADRIAN: Sorry. Forgot.

FRANKIE: Which is why... *(she takes his hands)* they're going to take the baby.

ADRIAN: You're going to farm *our* child out to David and Evie?

FRANKIE: It's all arranged.

ADRIAN: Without even telling me?

FRANKIE: I am telling you.

ADRIAN: I don't mean now. Before.

FRANKIE: You weren't in the picture any more.

ADRIAN: But I am now!

(Pause.)

FRANKIE: I didn't want to take the final step without you knowing what I was planning to do.

ADRIAN: But you have taken it! It's a fait accompli. Isn't it?

(FRANKIE shrugs.)

Isn't it?

FRANKIE: They want to have children, and they can't. So it makes sense they should have the baby. It's logical.

ADRIAN: Logic doesn't come into it! This is our *child* we're talking about. Feelings come into it. Yours and mine. You should've told me so I could be— *(involved when you were making your decision)*

(The apartment doorbell rings.)

Oh, damn!

(Slight pause. ADRIAN gestures appealingly to FRANKIE. She turns away and exits, turning to stage left. We hear a door opened, exchange of "Hi's" and then whispered voices. Adrian paces, agitated.)

EVIE: *(v.o.)* Have you told him?

FRANKIE: *(v.o.)* Yes. He knows.

DAVID: *(v.o.)* It's all right, then?

FRANKIE: *(v.o.)* I think so.

(Enter EVIE, DAVID and FRANKIE. Greetings are awkward, stilted. FRANKIE watches the exchange uncomfortably.)

DAVID: Hello, Adrian.

ADRIAN: Oh, Hi.

EVIE: Hi, Adrian.

ADRIAN: Evie.

(Pause. FRANKIE indicates they should sit. EVIE and DAVID take the sofa. ADRIAN remains standing.)

FRANKIE: *(to DAVID and EVIE)* Thanks for waiting.

DAVID: S'alright.

FRANKIE: Gave me time to— *(tell Adrian you're taking the baby)*

ADRIAN: To put Adrian in the picture. Who just happens to be the father. And the last to know.

(Awkward pause.)

FRANKIE: I...er...I wanted you all here, so you'd all know what I'm planning to do.
ADRIAN: Who's 'all,' Frankie? Seems to be just me.
FRANKIE: Well, yes. But I...I just wanted... *(to be sure you'd know)*
DAVID: It makes sense, Adrian.
EVIE: Dave and I were already thinking of adopting— *(a child, a girl)*
ADRIAN: So Frankie conveniently does it for you.
FRANKIE: Adrian, don't!
ADRIAN: With my help, of course. She couldn't've done it on her own.
   (Awkward pause.)
DAVID: It'll keep the child in the family, Adrian.
ADRIAN: *Your* family?
DAVID: Well, yes.
ADRIAN: Aren't Frankie and I its immediate family?
   (DAVID gestures helplessly to EVIE. ADRIAN turns to FRANKIE.)
   Aren't we?...*Aren't we*?
FRANKIE: I guess, if you put it like that.
ADRIAN: *(to DAVID)* So, you and Evie are excluding me?
DAVID: No, I'm not saying that.
ADRIAN: Am I to have visiting rights?
DAVID: Of course. Any time.
EVIE: But only as a visitor.
ADRIAN: Which means?
EVIE: The child is not to know— *(who you really are)*
ADRIAN: That I'm his father?
DAVID: It would be too difficult to explain. Too upsetting.
ADRIAN: For whom?
EVIE: The child. Obviously.
ADRIAN: Or you?
   (EVIE shrugs.)
   You don't think perhaps *this* is upsetting? For me? Unreal?
EVIE: *(another shrug)* Those are my conditions.

ADRIAN: Conditions! You're making *conditions*? *(to* FRANKIE*)* You knew that?

FRANKIE: Not the right word, Evie. *(to* ADRIAN*)* Evie and David want the child to grow up…secure. Secure in its relationship with them.

ADRIAN: Which means?

EVIE: David will always be Daddy. And I'll be Mommy.

DAVID: There will never be any awkward questions to answer, as the child grows older.

ADRIAN: So, I'm being taken right out of the picture?

(Pause. ADRIAN *gestures an appeal to* FRANKIE.*)*

FRANKIE: It hasn't been easy, Adrian. Deciding— *(what I should do)*

ADRIAN: Without even talking to me about it?

EVIE: *(to* FRANKIE*)* I told you. You shouldn't have asked him here.

DAVID: You have to see it from Frankie's point of view, Adrian.

ADRIAN: But is it entirely Frankie's decision?

DAVID: Under the circumstances. I mean— *(you weren't here.)*

ADRIAN: Have any of you thought that perhaps I might want to take the baby?

EVIE: Oh, Adrian! Be realistic.

ADRIAN: Bring it up myself.

DAVID: No. What Frankie has arranged is much better.

ADRIAN: For whom?

EVIE: *(to* FRANKIE*)* Do we really have to put up with all this?

ADRIAN: *(to* DAVID*)* Better for whom?

DAVID: For everyone: Frankie. The baby. Evie.

ADRIAN: But not for me. *(to* FRANKIE*)* **But not for me!**

FRANKIE: I'm sorry, Adrian. I didn't want this evening— *(to be like this)*

ADRIAN: Then I'm no longer making a suggestion. I *will* take the baby.

EVIE: You're out of your mind!

FRANKIE: You can't be serious?

ADRIAN: *(to* FRANKIE*)* Can you give me one good reason why I shouldn't?

A Touch of Gray

FRANKIE: Yes, I can. *(slowly, definitely)* There is no way—absolutely no way—I am going to have *my* baby call the woman I imagine you've moved in with, that she's his mother. "Mommy!" Out...of...the...question!

ADRIAN: Oh.

(Pause. ADRIAN stands irresolute.)

But it's all right for the baby to call Evie its mother?

EVIE: Which is why Frankie has chosen us to have the baby.

(ADRIAN paces, mustering his thoughts. They watch apprehensively. He stands in front of Frankie, takes her hands.)

ADRIAN: Oh, Frankie. I really don't know how to tell you this. But you do have to know. *(pause)* I didn't leave you for another woman. *(pause)* His name is Tyler. Tyler Woodward.

(Stunned silence.)

DAVID: The lawyer? Andrews and Woodward?

(ADRIAN nods in DAVID's direction.)

EVIE: Does it matter, Dave, who he is? *(to ADRIAN)* So, suddenly you're gay?

ADRIAN: It's been coming...evolving...gradually.

EVIE: There's your answer, Frankie! Adrian clearly is not suitable to have your child.

ADRIAN: Our child, Evie. Frankie's and mine.

EVIE: But you're not together any more. If you were— *(I wouldn't want to interfere)*

(FRANKIE erupts into an almost hysterical laugh, mixed with tears. The others gape at her.)

FRANKIE: *(to ADRIAN, between outbursts)* You left me for a man? *(throaty giggle)*...and all the time, I thought...I was convinced you'd found a young blonde...some bitch out there, who... *(tears and giggles).* Oh, my God!

EVIE: Skip the hysterics, Frankie.

FRANKIE: Oh, Adrian! That explains...oh, so much... It wasn't another woman... Of course! Of course!... You were gay! Why didn't you say?

ADRIAN: How could I?

FRANKIE: I...I might have understood better. Your leaving...

ADRIAN: I had enough trouble living with it myself. Trying to find the courage to…to tell *anyone*.

FRANKIE: Not even your family?

(ADRIAN shakes his head 'no.')

They don't know?

ADRIAN: They do now. Oh, Frankie, it's been so difficult.

FRANKIE: Do they understand? Accept…what you are?

ADRIAN: I think my mother does. My father, not yet.

FRANKIE: Your sisters too?

ADRIAN: I think, maybe they'd guessed already.

FRANKIE: I wish I'd known. I wish you'd told me. I wouldn't've liked it any better. But…it would've been…easier.

(EVIE picks up her handbag, stands in front of FRANKIE.)

EVIE: That, my dear, settles it: your baby comes to me. Come, David. No point in staying now. Frankie has her answer.

DAVID: *(raising a hand to halt her)* Evie…

ADRIAN: *(to Evie)* Are you implying that I'm not suitable to be the father of Frankie's child? *(points to FRANKIE)* Our child?

EVIE: 'Our' in name only. Frankie should never have brought you here. *(to FRANKIE)* I told you it wouldn't work.

FRANKIE: Evie! Adrian *is* the biological father.

EVIE: Only because he chose not to use a condom!

DAVID: Easy, Eve.

ADRIAN: *(to Evie)* Do you think I deliberately tried to get Frankie pregnant?

EVIE: Why were you sleeping with her, anyway? When you were already seeing your male paramour.

FRANKIE: Evie! I was there too. And I wasn't resisting. *(to ADRIAN)* Was I?

ADRIAN: No…no.

(ADRIAN and FRANKIE exchange an understanding, almost complicit, glance. [This is the first indication of the depth of friendship that exists between them, which they both fear jeopardizing.])

EVIE: Hmph! Come, David. Time we went.

FRANKIE: No, Dave. Wait. Please.

(DAVID vacillates. EVIE walks to the archway.)
EVIE: Oh, come on, David!
FRANKIE: I'd rather you'd stay. *(to DAVID)* We need to talk.
EVIE: Do come on!
   (Awkward pause. DAVID hesitates. Front door buzzer sounds.)
FRANKIE: Oh, God!
ADRIAN: Just ignore it.
   (Pause. They look at each other uncertainly. The buzzer sounds again.)
EVIE: I'll get it.
FRANKIE: No, don't!
ADRIAN: Hold it, Evie!
   (EVIE holds down the button.)
EVIE: Who is it?
MAISIE: *(v.o. speaker voice)* Evelyn? You're still there. Good.
FRANKIE: *(to Adrian)* I don't need my mother here right now. I didn't ask her to come.
MAISIE: *(v.o.)* Let me in, will you.
FRANKIE: No!
   (EVIE pushes the door release button.)
MAISIE: *(v.o.)* I'll be right up.
FRANKIE: Shit! *(to DAVID)* Did you tell her? Ask her to come?
DAVID: I haven't seen her. Talked to her.
FRANKIE: Did you, Evie?
EVIE: Why would I do that?
   (EVIE exits, turning right, to stage left.)
ADRIAN: Well, that *does* put an interesting twist on the evening!
   (Doorbell sounds. DAVID follows EVIE, exits.)
   (ADRIAN crosses to FRANKIE, stands behind her, places a hand on each shoulder.)
   Are you angry with me?
FRANKIE: No. *(a little giggle)* Relieved, actually.
ADRIAN: That it's not another woman?
FRANKIE: Oh, Adrian, I don't know. I need to get my head around it.

(Enter MAISIE, followed by DAVID and EVIE.)
MAISIE: Oh, what a nice picture!
ADRIAN: Hi, Maisie.
MAISIE: You've decided to stay?
ADRIAN: *(lightly)* You mean right now? Or long term?
MAISIE: Whatever. *(to FRANKIE)* So, how's the mother to be?
FRANKIE: *(drily)* Hello, mother.
MAISIE: So, Adrian, what do you make of Frankie's little indiscretion?
DAVID: Mother!
ADRIAN: Surprised. But hardly an indiscretion.
MAISIE: No? And now it's indecision. If it had been— *(her older sister...)*
DAVID: Mother! Again.
MAISIE: If it had been her older sister—
ADRIAN: It would never have happened—
MAISIE: She'd've taken precautions—
ADRIAN: That's irrelevant. This is about Frankie: what happens to her. What happens to her baby.
MAISIE: Such a gentleman.
ADRIAN: *Our* baby.
MAISIE: Frankie's told you what she plans to do with her baby? Your baby.
ADRIAN: You mean, give it to...?
(ADRIAN points to DAVID and EVIE.)
MAISIE: Are you all right with that?
ADRIAN: No.
MAISIE: No?
ADRIAN: I wasn't asked.
MAISIE: Typical! And if you had been?
ADRIAN: I'd've said I'll take the baby. Bring it up.
MAISIE: *(to FRANKIE)* Did you even think of that?
FRANKIE: No. Well, yes. Now.
MAISIE: Should've been at the top of your mind.
DAVID: Mother, I don't think—
MAISIE: A perfectly reasonable suggestion.

EVIE: Maisie: If you had been here earlier, you'd know why.
DAVID: Leave it, Evie.
MAISIE: So? Tell me.
EVIE: Adrian's just not…suitable…to be a parent for the child.
MAISIE: Oh, come now!
ADRIAN: *(haltingly)* Maisie…what Evie is implying…trying to say…
MAISIE: That you're gay.
FRANKIE: You know, mother?
MAISIE: It was written all over him.
FRANKIE: You didn't say anything!
MAISIE: You wouldn't have listened.
FRANKIE: How long have you—?
MAISIE: Known he's living with that dishy lawyer?
ADRIAN: Oh, my God!
MAISIE: *(to ADRIAN)* Such a waste! *(to FRANKIE)* Longer than you'd think.
EVIE: That's precisely why he's not suitable—
MAISIE: On what grounds?
EVIE: Do you want your granddaughter…your grandson… *(to FRANKIE)* your child… *(to them both)* to be brought up by two men? No mother to nurture her?
MAISIE: Compared to you? You're a natural mother?
EVIE: More than he could ever be!
MAISIE: Hmph…How much do you know about Adrian?
EVIE: Enough. As much as you.
MAISIE: Oh, I don't think so.
FRANKIE: Don't listen to mother, Evie. She always takes Adrian's side.
ADRIAN: No. I don't think—
FRANKIE: Does it all the time.
MAISIE: If you had a firm head on your shoulders—
FRANKIE: Oh, mother! Look: do us a favor, will you. Go into the kitchen and put the kettle on. Make some coffee…or tea. I left a tray out.
MAISIE: Can't anyone else?

FRANKIE: *(gestures to DAVID, EVIE and ADRIAN)* We need to talk.

MAISIE: *(hesitates, then moves toward exit)* Alright. Alright.

FRANKIE: *(calls to MAISIE, now offstage)* And put an extra mug on the tray!

ADRIAN: *(to FRANKIE)* Can I ask a question?

EVIE: *(to FRANKIE)* Do we need to prolong— *(Adrian being here?)*

DAVID: *(raises his hand to stop her)* He deserves to be heard, my dear.

EVIE: Hmph!

ADRIAN: Look: I believe I could be an effective parent for our child. But I do need to know how you're judging me.

(Slight pause. he looks at each of them in turn)

Would you feel my suggestion was okay, if I was living on my own? Uninvolved?...David?

DAVID: *(hesitant shrug)* I'm the last person you should ask. *(slight pause)* It shouldn't make a difference, but I suspect it might.

ADRIAN: Does 'might' mean you wouldn't mind if it was a female partner?

DAVID: Oh, Adrian! Don't ask me that.

ADRIAN: I need to know.

DAVID: *(with difficulty)* It shouldn't, but it probably would.

(Pause. ADRIAN waits to see if DAVID will elaborate further.)

ADRIAN: Evie?

EVIE: Either on your own or living with someone else, you're definitely not suitable.

ADRIAN: That doesn't answer my question.

EVIE: It's clear enough.

ADRIAN: Please...?

EVIE: You know what I think!

ADRIAN: Yes. I think I do. Frankie?

FRANKIE: *(slowly)* Knowing a bit about your past...I think, perhaps, you could handle it, as a single parent.

(EVIE shows a shocked reaction.)

ADRIAN: Only if I'm on my own? Not living with someone else?

FRANKIE: Oh, I don't know!

EVIE: *(to FRANKIE)* What did you mean: "Knowing about his past?"

FRANKIE: Adrian has helped with young children. A baby even. Before.

EVIE: So it's not the first time. Who else did he get pregnant?

ADRIAN: Whoa! Can we get back to my question?

EVIE: What about mine?

FRANKIE: Later. Another time.

EVIE: I want to know!

FRANKIE: Oh, Evie, forget it! It has no relevance to what Adrian's asking.

EVIE: Oh, yes it has— *(if he's done this before...)*

DAVID: *(to Evie)* Easy...easy.

EVIE: No, Dave. I want to know.

(MAISIE enters, carrying a tray with mugs, milk, sugar, and a plate of cookies. She carries the tray to the coffee table.)

MAISIE: Adrian: be a dear, will you. Move all those papers.

(ADRIAN gathers papers, carries them to the computer table. During the following sequence, MAISIE pours and distributes the mugs and cookies.)

EVIE: *(after a pause, to DAVID)* Why are you and Frankie even considering an alternative?

MAISIE: David: two sugar.

EVIE: Frankie has agreed we'll take her baby. It's all arranged.

DAVID: Thanks. *(to EVIE)* In that sense, yes. *(to FRANKIE)* You actually asked Adrian to be here tonight?

FRANKIE: Yes.

DAVID: Then he's entitled to be heard.

EVIE: Oh, David!

MAISIE: *(irony)* No sugar for you, Evelyn.

EVIE: No. No cream, either.

MAISIE: Yes. I do remember.

EVIE: Thank you.

(MAISIE continues immediately, to prevent EVIE from speaking further.)

MAISIE: Adrian: Cream and one sugar.

ADRIAN: Yes. Please.
(Pause. MAISIE *hands a mug to* ADRIAN.*)*
Thanks.

MAISIE: Go on! Go on! Don't mind me.
(She hands a mug to FRANKIE.*)*

FRANKIE: Thanks.

EVIE: *(to* ADRIAN*)* So, you have a history?

ADRIAN: We all have.

EVIE: Not like that. *(pause)* Well, who's going to tell me?

FRANKIE: It's not relevant.

EVIE: Oh, it certainly is.

ADRIAN: Frankie's carrying the *only* child I've been responsible for. That's all.

EVIE: *(to* FRANKIE*)* Then why did you say...why did you imply— *(that it's happened before)*

FRANKIE: I didn't. I said—

MAISIE: You're backing the wrong horse, Evie.

FRANKIE: Adrian has two young sisters—

EVIE: I know. I know. Teen agers.

FRANKIE: They weren't always teen-agers.

EVIE: Obviously!

ADRIAN: Do we have to?

MAISIE: *(to* EVIE*)* Adrian doesn't like to talk about it. When his sisters were little—I mean *little,* no more than babies—his mother was taken ill—

FRANKIE: Chronic Fatigue Immune Dysfunction Syndrome.

EVIE: CFIDS. *(pronounced 'Siffids')* It's not yet defined properly as a real disease.

MAISIE: Five years, Evie. You're a nurse. You should know. Even Frankie understands—

FRANKIE: *(cautionary)* Mother!

MAISIE: So, who changed diapers? Dressed the children? Read them stories? Cooked and cleaned? Do I need to spell it out in three-letter words?

ADRIAN: Can we drop it, Maisie?

EVIE: You think that makes Adrian suitable?

A Touch of Gray

MAISIE: I'm not giving you an opinion. You wouldn't listen, anyway. None of you. Well, Adrian, maybe.

ADRIAN: *(to FRANKIE)* Is this to be an adoption, then? A true adoption?

FRANKIE: You mean legally?

(ADRIAN nods.)

DAVID: More like a transfer. Within the family.

ADRIAN: *(to FRANKIE)* Why didn't you ask me first, if I might want to take the baby, before talking to... *(gestures toward DAVID and EVIE)*

EVIE: Normally, men don't—

ADRIAN: *(to FRANKIE)* I'm the child's father!

EVIE: Courts rarely grant parental rights to the father.

ADRIAN: We're not in court, Evie.

EVIE: Adrian: be realistic.

FRANKIE: Evelyn: let me handle this. Please!

(EVIE throws her hands up, shrugs.)

Adrian: your idea is honorable, but a little altruistic I think. In the heat of the moment—

MAISIE: Alright! Alright! I've heard enough! Too many ideas, all at cross-purposes. Too many words.

FRANKIE: *(drily)* Rhetoric, mother.

MAISIE: Whatever. *(to everyone)* You're all different shades of gray. Aren't you? About Adrian's suitability to be father to Frankie's baby. Particularly you, David. And you, Frankie. You're both muddy gray. But Evie here: oh, a much darker shade of gray.

FRANKIE: This isn't getting us anywhere!

(Slight pause.)

EVIE: *(to ADRIAN)* Does your...partner...does he know what you have in mind?

FRANKIE: How could he?

EVIE: I was speaking to Adrian.

FRANKIE: I only told Adrian tonight.

EVIE: How can you even consider letting him take your baby? David and I *want* to have children. Don't we, David?

DAVID: Oh, yes. Definitely.

EVIE: And we're *married*. *(to* ADRIAN*)* Can you say that?

DAVID: Easy, Evie...

FRANKIE: Maybe we should give Adrian time to— *(discuss it with his partner)*

EVIE: You made your decision, Frankie. Stick to it.

ADRIAN: I would like to talk to Tyler.

EVIE: I can just imagine his answer!

ADRIAN: I think I can persuade him.

EVIE: This is ridiculous!

MAISIE: That's enough.

EVIE: Frankie decided three weeks ago—

MAISIE: I said that's enough! Just for once I agree with Frankie: Adrian does need to talk to his partner. Right now, it'd be better for everyone to go home and cool down. Agree, Frankie?

FRANKIE: Would I ever do otherwise?

MAISIE: Yes, well...Adrian?

ADRIAN: It would give me time...

MAISIE: Then go and do it!

(ADRIAN looks at FRANKIE, who nods. He turns toward the exit, then pauses.)

ADRIAN: Thanks, Frankie. And you, Maisie.

MAISIE: You owe me one!

(ADRIAN laughs, nods to DAVID and EVIE, and exits, turning to stage left. Frankie pauses a moment and then follows him. MAISIE collects mugs and places them on the tray, exits to stage right.)

EVIE: There was no need for Frankie to drag Adrian into this.

DAVID: In her view—

EVIE: Oh, Christ!

DAVID: It was the honorable thing to do.

EVIE: Honorable? *(laughs)* Do you believe that? Really believe it?

DAVID: Y-e-s. Frankie has strong principles.

EVIE: Come off it, David. You've heard how your mother speaks to her. Speaks of her.

DAVID: You think this is easy for Frankie?

EVIE: It's all of her own making.

A Touch of Gray

DAVID: *(shakes his head)* It's painful for her. No matter who the baby goes to.

EVIE: She got herself into this mess.

DAVID: Just think about it, Eve: she's giving up a baby. Something you'll never have to do.

EVIE: That's not fair!

DAVID: Sorry.

(EVIE *sniffles. Pause.*)

Sorry. I know how much you want— *(a baby)*

EVIE: *(sniffle)* It's just the luck of the draw, Dave, that your sperm count...

DAVID: Sorry.

(Pause. They lean into each other.)

EVIE: I've *got* to have Frankie's baby. There's no way I'm going back to that adoption agency. All those questions. The probing. Ugh!

(DAVID lays a hand over EVIE's. Pause. Both are trying to calm down.)

If only your mother would keep out of it!

(DAVID shrugs.)

Pushing her way in; confusing the whole issue. *(slight pause)* The worst thing is, deep down, I think she favors Adrian.

DAVID: Even though...?

EVIE: He's living in a homosexual relationship?

DAVID: This isn't like you, Evie...

(EVIE looks questioningly at DAVID.)

You've never been against...negative about...

EVIE: Lesbians? Homosexuals?

DAVID: Have you?

EVIE: No. I know. But this is different. It's the only weapon I've got—we've got—to convince Frankie, and your mother...particularly your mother...that the baby has to come to us.

DAVID: You're afraid my mother will work on Frankie?

EVIE: I don't trust her. You know that. But I can pull a rug right out from under her feet, without her even knowing it's happening.

(Slight pause. DAVID waits.)

EVIE: *(continuing)* Play on her maternal instincts. Or you can, Dave. I'll bet my bottom dollar she really, really wants to be a grandmother. Every woman her age does. But we've got to convince her the only way she'll be able to play at that game, is if *we* have Frankie's baby.

DAVID: You mean, if it goes to Adrian—

EVIE: She'll be shut right out. Now, if you were to whisper in her ear... make sure she realizes that, if Adrian gets the child, it's *his* mother who'll be playing at being grandma.

DAVID: You want *me* to tell her?

EVIE: She'll listen to you, David. Far more than she'll listen to me. Or Frankie.

(FRANKIE enters, hears her name.)

FRANKIE: Or me?

EVIE: Oh, yeah...I was telling David he should give your mother a hand. In the kitchen. Rather than you.

FRANKIE: *(aware Evie is prevaricating)* Oh?

EVIE: Go *on*, David!

DAVID: Uh...yeah! *(exits)*

(Awkward pause.)

EVIE: It's a shame, really, bringing Adrian into this.

FRANKIE: Please, Evie.

EVIE: It would have been so much simpler... *(shrugs)*

FRANKIE: That was *my* decision.

EVIE: But, in retrospect, not a wise one.

FRANKIE: *(raises her hand, palm vertical)* I've heard quite enough for one night!

(FRANKIE 'dismisses' EVIE by sitting at her computer and turning her back to her. EVIE shakes her head as the lights extinguish.)

(Lights come up stage right: the kitchen. MAISIE is drying mugs and placing them on the table. DAVID enters, carrying a mug, hands it to her, stands with his hands resting on the table between them.)

MAISIE: If that sister of yours had the guts to make a decision...

DAVID: She did, mother.

MAISIE: Yeah. The wrong one.

DAVID: You don't want Evie and me to have the baby?

MAISIE: Course I do. No. She shouldn't've opened the door to Adrian.

DAVID: I know, but she thought she was doing the right thing.

MAISIE: Should've done it before, if she was going to tell him. Then we wouldn't be having all this upset. *(shakes her head)* Her sister would've known better. Would've worked it out all before.

DAVID: Mother! There's no point in— *(bringing Marina into this)*

MAISIE: She'd've taken precautions. Never allowed herself to get pregnant.

DAVID: This isn't about Marina, mother.

MAISIE: She always thought things through properly. Never jumped to conclusions.

DAVID: How can you say that? Marina was only nine— *(when she died)*

MAISIE: She'd've never stepped out into the road, like Frankie did.

DAVID: They were at a crosswalk, mother!

MAISIE: Marina always took care to look both ways.

DAVID: You can't blame Frankie for Marina's death.

MAISIE: If Frankie had looked properly, she'd've seen that car coming.

DAVID: She was only five!

MAISIE: Seen he was going too fast.

DAVID: Mother: can we— *(drop the subject?)*

MAISIE: Had to swerve to avoid her.

DAVID: Mother: Stop it!

MAISIE: Up onto the sidewalk.

DAVID: *No!* No, no, no!

(MAISIE weeps.)

DAVID: *(continuing)* Mother...Mother! Somehow, somehow, you've just got to let up, stop comparing—

MAISIE: It isn't fair— *(sniff)*

DAVID: Give Frankie more credit.

MAISIE: To take her life away like that. So promising.

(DAVID walks around the table, puts an arm around MAISIE's shoulder. He has had to do this before.)

DAVID: That was twenty years ago, Ma.
MAISIE: Those lovely blonde curls. *(sniffs)*
(Slight pause.)
DAVID: Have you thought...have you thought that Frankie is *giving* you something.
MAISIE: Hmmm...?
DAVID: A grandchild.
MAISIE: A baby girl?
DAVID: Not to take Marina's place, mind. But to give you a fresh start, a new baby to be close to, to cuddle...help us bring up.
MAISIE: Hmmm. Yes...yes. In a way I had thought about that.
DAVID: You'll be very special to her. To the baby.
MAISIE: Hmmm. Grannie's *are* special. Telling bedtime stories—
DAVID: Taking her to the park—
MAISIE: Special treats, little secrets between us.
DAVID: That's why it's so important the baby comes to Evie and me. So *you* can be her grandmother.
MAISIE: You mean, if Adrian takes her...?
DAVID: It will be different. Very different. I mean, his mother, she'll be right there.
MAISIE: She'll be too close! *She'll* be the grandmother. Oh, no. We can't have that, can we?

(As MAISIE and DAVID turn toward the exit, lights fade stage right and come up on the living room, stage center. FRANKIE is hunched over her computer, working. EVIE is sitting stiffly upright on the sofa, her handbag standing upright beside her. She is ready to leave. MAISIE and DAVID enter.)

*(EVIE lifts the handbag onto her lap, looks at DAVID, inclines her head toward the door. DAVID nods.
FRANKIE remains unaware, continues typing.)*

MAISIE: There she is, as always: head over her computer. You'll get round shoulders, my girl.

(FRANKIE swings around on her chair, ready with a sharp retort, but is interrupted by EVIE, now standing.)

EVIE: You ready, David?
DAVID: Sure.

A Touch of Gray

(EVIE *raises a questioning eyebrow toward* DAVID, *who responds with a tiny nod.* EVIE *turns toward the exit.*)

EVIE: Well, we'll be on our way.

DAVID: *(to* FRANKIE*)* Let me know when, you know, what you...what you want to do.

FRANKIE: Sure.

EVIE: But make it *soon*!

FRANKIE: *(defensive)* I'll tell you when I'm ready.

EVIE: Don't wait for Adrian to say *he's* ready.

(FRANKIE *turns defiantly back to her computer.* DAVID, EVIE *and* MAISIE *exchange glances, shake heads.* MAISIE *ushers* DAVID *and* EVIE *out; all three exit.*)

(*Pause.* FRANKIE *continues typing.*)

(MAISIE *re-enters, pauses, tidies magazines and papers on the side table, looks around for more to do, leans over* FRANKIE'*s shoulder.* FRANKIE *hunches even further, makes an exasperated gesture with her arms, remains sitting in the chair, looking away.*)

MAISIE: We need to talk.

FRANKIE: I have work to do.

MAISIE: As always.

FRANKIE: Not now, mother!

MAISIE: No. Seriously.

(FRANKIE *gives another exasperated gesture. Pause.* MAISIE *subtly 'works' this scene, deviously leading Frankie to the point she wants to make: that the baby* ***must*** *go to David and Evie.*)

I know, you don't want to hear my opinion...what I think. *(pause)* But are you sure—completely sure—you really want to give up your baby?

FRANKIE: Mother! We've been over this. More than once. Can't you just drop it?

(*Pause.* MAISIE *points to Frankie's work.*)

MAISIE: You're not...you're not doing all this just to...get away? From us?...Me?

FRANKIE: Once, I might have.

163

MAISIE: No?

FRANKIE: I don't need to!

(Pause.)

MAISIE: I wouldn't want to be in your shoes.

FRANKIE: You've made that clear, often enough.

MAISIE: I mean, having to choose... *(slight pause)* You need to think, Frankie.

(FRANKIE shakes her head negatively.)

Just think! Would you want your baby—when she's five or six—waking at night and walking into her dad's room, wanting to climb into bed with him...but finds there's another man there, lying right up close to him? And they're both naked!

(Pause.)

FRANKIE: But it wouldn't be sprung on the child. It'll have been with them—them together—since it was a baby... *(FRANKIE shivers, turns away.)* But, no, the whole idea...

MAISIE: And, remember, you'll need to have access. When you get back from... *(shrugs)*

FRANKIE: Peru.

MAISIE: Yes, Peru. If you want to see, do things, with your baby—

FRANKIE: I'll cover that bridge— *(when I get back)*

MAISIE: I mean, how stable will they be? Adrian and that Tyler? Will they stay here? Always be accessible to you?

(Pause.).

David and Evie...they're not likely to move away.

FRANKIE: No... No, David's made himself too comfortable. He's 'married' to that power company. He'll retire from it!

MAISIE: That young lawyer, he's sharp. He's going to be in demand. Other companies, they'll make attractive offers. And off he'll go.

FRANKIE: With Adrian?

MAISIE: Depends, doesn't it? Makes David and Evie look a lot safer.

(Lights fade rapidly stage center, come up stage left on a corner of Tyler and Adrian's living room. TYLER is sitting at the table referring to heavy tomes. Light classical music in the background. ADRIAN enters.)

TYLER: Took you a while.

A Touch of Gray

ADRIAN: Yeah.
  (Pause.)
TYLER: Problem?
ADRIAN: Whole family was there.
TYLER: Confrontation?
ADRIAN: Sort of... She says she's pregnant.
TYLER: Pregnant!
  (ADRIAN nods. TYLER switches off the music.)
  She says she's pregnant?
ADRIAN: Oh, she is.
TYLER: But she only *says* it?
ADRIAN: Oh, no. You can see it. Feel it.
TYLER: *(lightly; with humor, but...)* So! You've been going back to her!
ADRIAN: No!
TYLER: Behind my back!
ADRIAN: No! I haven't seen her, Ty. It's— *(not like that)*
TYLER: Alright, alright! I was just having you on!
ADRIAN: I haven't even talked to her, since we... *(moved in together)*
TYLER: Then it can't be yours.
ADRIAN: She says it is.
TYLER: Says? Says?
  (ADRIAN nods, glumly.)
  It's someone else's, man, and she's trying to slap paternity on you.
ADRIAN: No, Ty. It isn't like that. She just wants— *(me to know what she plans to do)*
TYLER: Oh, I could wreak havoc with that, in court. Just give me the chance.
ADRIAN: No. No. Frankie's not like that.
TYLER: Uh-uh. They all are. You're too gullible, man. She's pulled all the family in, like witnesses, to provide her with a united front.
ADRIAN: It's five months.
TYLER: Them against you. On your own.

ADRIAN: It's...five...months. She's been pregnant for five months.

TYLER: That scheming bitch! She set you up! She wants to drag you back.

ADRIAN: No, Ty. She doesn't want me back.

TYLER: Don't you see it? You're blind, man!

ADRIAN: No. She has— *(plans for the baby)*

TYLER: Oh, if only I could have been there!

ADRIAN: It wouldn't have changed— *(anything)*

TYLER: You wouldn't be standing here right now, all worked up about it. I can guarantee you that.

ADRIAN: *(raises his hand, spaces the words)* Ty: She's going away. As soon as she can, after the baby's born.

(Pause.)

TYLER: You're sure you didn't know this—about the baby—before you moved in with me?

ADRIAN: No. Tonight's the first time I've seen her, since—

TYLER: But you could have known.

ADRIAN: No. No.

TYLER: And chose not to say anything.

ADRIAN: I *didn't know*.

TYLER: Hoping it would just blow away.

ADRIAN: I..did..not..know! *(drops onto his haunches beside or in front of* TYLER, *if Tyler is still sitting)* I would have told you before—before I moved in—if I'd known.

(Pause. TYLER *nods [he knows it's true].)*

TYLER: But why has she waited so long? Why's she demanding support now?

ADRIAN: She's not *demanding* anything.

TYLER: There I *can* help you.

ADRIAN: No, Ty. I wouldn't expect— *(you to help pay support)*

TYLER: Legally, I mean.

ADRIAN: Ah! There's no need.

TYLER: You're not listening.

ADRIAN: Yes. I am. She's not demanding anything.

TYLER: There'll be a hidden agenda, secreted like shadows among all those family members. Mark my words.

ADRIAN: She's not like that. You don't know her.

A Touch of Gray

TYLER: I know the type.

ADRIAN: Do you?

(Pause.)

TYLER: She's thrown a spike between us, hasn't she?

ADRIAN: No. Not intentionally.

TYLER: Can't you *see* what she's up to?

(Pause.)

ADRIAN: Ty: she's not keeping the baby.

(TYLER looks questioningly at ADRIAN.)

She's giving it to her brother. And his wife, Evie.

TYLER: So?

ADRIAN: They're childless. Can't have— *(children)*

TYLER: So it's them. They're after money.

ADRIAN: Don't need to.

(TYLER shakes his head.)

Frankie's not staying here, Ty. She's giving the child up, for good.

TYLER: She doesn't *want* the kid?

ADRIAN: It's her research. She's dedicated to it. It's her life.

TYLER: So, the child will neither affect nor intrude on us?

ADRIAN: No, not in that way.

(Pause.)

But...there is one thing...

TYLER: I knew it!

ADRIAN: I want to take the baby.

TYLER: You...what!

ADRIAN: Bring it up myself.

TYLER: I can't believe what I'm hearing.

ADRIAN: I...I... *(shrugs)*

TYLER: You want to be a single parent?

ADRIAN: No.

TYLER: Without even consulting me?

ADRIAN: I am consulting you. Right now. *(pause)* I want to bring him here.

TYLER: Here?

ADRIAN: For us. To be his parents.

TYLER: Are you out of your mind?

ADRIAN: Male partners are allowed to adopt. It's being done.

TYLER: You want to bring a smelly, squally brat into my home, to—

ADRIAN: *Your* home?

TYLER: To drag sticky fingers over my teak furniture and—

ADRIAN: I thought this is *our* home.

TYLER: And scratch it up, rolling metal wind-up cars and trucks—

ADRIAN: It will be more than a year before— *(he's mobile)*

TYLER: Absolutely not!

(Long pause.)

ADRIAN: Will I ever have another opportunity to bring up a child that is of my own flesh and blood?

TYLER: But not mine.

ADRIAN: True. *(pause)* Oh, Ty. You could bring so much to the child. Your knowledge; your approach to learning; your determination; your self-confidence. *(slight pause)* I don't want to have to choose between you—who I know, and love—and a baby who I do not yet know, but will grow to love.

(Pause. TYLER, affected, reaches a hand out to ADRIAN.)

TYLER: You don't have to. Just take a step back. Tell her to leave things as they are: keep the original arrangements. Maintain the status quo.

ADRIAN: *(slight pause, then slowly)* I can't do that.

TYLER: Then it's him or me?

ADRIAN: Only if you're so set on my not bringing the child here.

TYLER: My God, Adrian. You're pointing a gun at my head!

(Fade lights on scene, hold low light. Brief music bridge [the same music Tyler was listening to earlier], then gradually fade in lights on Frankie's living room. Fade music.)

(It's two months later. FRANKIE and MAISIE are seated. FRANKIE, who clearly is in advanced pregnancy—only seven weeks to delivery—is in an upright chair beside the table. MAISIE sits in an armchair.)

A Touch of Gray

(EVIE *and* DAVID *are entering, both carrying bulging shopping bags from baby clothing and toy stores.* EVIE *lays her bags on the side table.* DAVID *places his on the floor beside a chair, then sits on it.*)

(MAISIE *watches, has guessed that* EVIE *has brought the kids clothes and toys as a strategy, to convince* FRANKIE *of her seriousness, her dedication, and her expectation.*)

MAISIE: Well, well! You two have been busy.

EVIE: Only seven weeks now, Maisie.

MAISIE: You're assuming— *(the baby is coming to you?)*

EVIE: I'm not assuming anything. We can't just wait and wonder.

DAVID: What Evie means is: what if Frankie delivers early? We don't want to be caught short. Unready.

MAISIE: Hmmph.

(EVIE *pulls items out of the bags, holds them up for* MAISIE *and* FRANKIE *to see. She holds up a yellow bodysuit.*)

EVIE: Cute, eh?

FRANKIE: *(with irony)* Adorable.

MAISIE: How come it's not pink?

DAVID: That would be a bit premature, Mum.

MAISIE: You don't think all this is premature?

EVIE: We can't leave everything to the last minute, can we? *(holds up a white dress on a hanger)* I couldn't resist this.

MAISIE: Boys love wearing dresses.

DAVID: *(quickly, holding up a checked blanket)* My choice: multi-colored. No risk there.

FRANKIE: Nice try, David.

DAVID: *(holds up a teddy bear)* And teddies are always brown.

EVIE: My mother's hooking an afghan.

MAISIE: Multi-colored?

EVIE: With the alphabet spelled out, all the way around the edge.

DAVID: And she's hooking a picture of an animal next to each letter.

MAISIE: Like an elephant beside the 'E'?

DAVID: Right!

MAISIE: Quite the happy hooker.

EVIE: It'll be a learning experience for the baby. As she grows older.

FRANKIE: *(with irony)* Very original.

(Door buzzer sounds. FRANKIE rises and goes to the speaker box, presses a button, speaks into it.)

FRANKIE: Adrian?

ADRIAN: *(v.o. from speaker)* Yes.

FRANKIE: Come on up.

(FRANKIE pushes the button, turns to EVIE.)
Pack all that up, will you?

(She exits and turns right [to stage left]. Slight pause.)

MAISIE: *(to EVIE, inclining her head towards clothes)* Well?

EVIE: No.

MAISIE: Frankie asked you to—

EVIE: No. It'll convey a message to him.

DAVID: In all fairness— *(I think we should)*

EVIE: Let him see that we—the family—*expect* the baby will be coming to us.

(Sound of door opening.)

ADRIAN: *(v.o.)* Hi.

FRANKIE: *(v.o.)* Hi. David and Evie are already here.

ADRIAN: *(v.o.)* I saw their car.

FRANKIE: *(v.o.)* Mother, too.

ADRIAN: *(v.o.)* Good... *(sotto voce)* Look: I...I haven't come alone.

FRANKIE: *(v.o.)* You brought him with you? Tyler?

(Everyone in the room turns toward the door, listens.)

ADRIAN: *(v.o.)* Yes. He's waiting down below. *(pause)* Is it all right? To have him come up? He wants to ask some...questions.

FRANKIE: *(v.o.)* Like a security check?

ADRIAN: *(v.o.)* He's a lawyer.

FRANKIE: *(v.o.)* I know. *(slight pause)* Yes, Adrian, tell him to come up. I'll wedge the door.

(Concern on listeners' faces. FRANKIE enters.)

A Touch of Gray

EVIE: You're not letting Adrian bring that man up here?

FRANKIE: Evie: that's my decision. Adrian and his friend need to be heard.

MAISIE: So they should!

(Pause.)

FRANKIE: *(to* EVIE*)* I thought I asked you to... *(points to child's clothes)*

EVIE: All the more reason now, to leave them out, for them both to see.

*(*FRANKIE *goes to pick up clothes, put them in a bag.* EVIE *pulls them away from her. They stop when they hear voices in the front hall.)*

ADRIAN: *(v.o.)* I'll introduce you.

TYLER: *(v.o.)* No. Let me do it my way.

*(*TYLER *enters, followed by* ADRIAN. TYLER *is confident and definite without being overwhelming. He pauses slightly on entering, scans the room, strides over to* MAISIE, *right hand outstretched toward her.)*

TYLER: Ms. Warburton: the grandmother-to-be, I'm told. So glad to meet you.

MAISIE: Oh! How do you do, sir.

TYLER: Oh, 'Tyler,' Please. And is it acceptable for me to address you as 'Maisie'?

MAISIE: Of course.

*(*MAISIE *is a little a-flutter.)*

TYLER: *(turning to* FRANKIE*)* Ah! You must be Frankie.

(They shake hands)

FRANKIE: How do you do? Is it acceptable for me to address you as 'Tyler'?

TYLER: Touché! *(turns toward* EVIE, *holds hand out)* Evelyn, I assume.

EVIE: Mrs. Warburton.

TYLER: True. Forgive me. *(points toward baby clothing)* I see you are prepared for the event, Mrs. Warburton. *(turns toward David)* And you, of course, must be Mr. Warburton. How do you do?

(They shake hands.)

DAVID: Good to meet you, Tyler. And I think 'David' would be more appropriate, given the circumstances.

(EVIE *shakes her head in disapproval.*)

TYLER: Glad to hear it. *(turns to all the family)* It's a pleasure for me to meet the family Adrian has told me about.

(Pause.)

FRANKIE: *(to* EVIE*)* Clear all that up, will you. Make space.

(Pause. DAVID *rises, pushes some clothing aside, indicates for* TYLER *to sit on the seat he has vacated.)*

DAVID: There! Do sit, Tyler.

TYLER: Thank you. *(he sits)*

DAVID: You too, Adrian.

(ADRIAN *sits beside Tyler, on the arm of the sofa.)*
(DAVID *pulls a chair out from the table, sits on it.)*

TYLER: I think I should explain that I am here only as an observer. *(pause)* And to give Adrian support. *(pause)* So he'll feel a little less alone. Like he's an outsider.

MAISIE: Oh, we've never thought of Adrian as an outsider. *(to the others)* Have we? *(no response)* Have we ever made you feel like an outsider, Adrian?

ADRIAN: No. No. None of you have.

*(*EVIE *'harrumphs.' Pause.)*

MAISIE: Shall we start, then? Frankie?

FRANKIE: Well, uh…I think I'd like to talk to Tyler first.

*(*DAVID*'s,* EVIE*'s,* ADRIAN*'s and* MAISIE*'s heads come up.)*

TYLER: Me?

FRANKIE: Yes.

TYLER: Here?

FRANKIE: No, in private.

*(*FRANKIE *inclines her head toward the door, rises.* TYLER *looks at* ADRIAN*, who indicates for Tyler to follow Frankie.* TYLER *and* FRANKIE *exit.)*
(As lights fade on the living room, EVIE *and* DAVID *exchange looks of consternation.)*
(Lights come up on the kitchen. FRANKIE *enters, followed by* TYLER. *She leans against the table. For once we sense* TYLER *is a little unsure of himself.)*

A Touch of Gray

FRANKIE: Do sit.
TYLER: If you will.
FRANKIE: I prefer to stand.
TYLER: Then I shall too.
 (Pause.)
FRANKIE: This is one for the book, isn't it?
 (She senses that Tyler does not comprehend.)
 You and me. Meeting like this.
TYLER: It was not my intention for my presence to make this evening more difficult for you. My coming with Adrian.
FRANKIE: Cut the crap. That's not why I wanted to speak to you. *(pause)* How much do you know?
TYLER: Know?
FRANKIE: About...*(gestures toward the living room)* all this?
TYLER: Well, I know you're pregnant. I can see you're pregnant.
 (FRANKIE responds with a slight smile.)
 You've chosen not to keep the baby. You have even chosen to whom the baby should go. And I know Adrian is it's male parent. And as such he has indicated that he would like you to reverse your decision and let him have the baby.
FRANKIE: What do you think about that?
TYLER: It's a very brave suggestion.
FRANKIE: Brave? That tells me very little. About you. What you think.
TYLER: I am not a partisan. I am here solely as an observer.
FRANKIE: But you can tell me how you feel about Adrian bringing a baby into...your space.
TYLER: It's not my preference.
FRANKIE: What was your reaction, two months ago, when Adrian told you what he wanted to do?
TYLER: I admit it came as a...a surprise.
FRANKIE: Can you be more precise? In one word. Please.
TYLER: *(slight pause as he considers)* Hmm...then 'outraged.'
FRANKIE: Are you still? Outraged?
TYLER: Not so much. *(pause)* We've talked.
FRANKIE: Enough, to accept...?
TYLER: Perhaps. I need more time to— *(think what it all implies).*

FRANKIE: There is no time. It has to be tonight: my decision. *(pause)* If I should choose that Adrian is to have the baby, would it harm your relationship? With Adrian?

TYLER: It's bound to.

FRANKIE: Irreparably?

TYLER: *(pause)* Not necessarily.

FRANKIE: But it might?

TYLER: I'd try not to let that happen.

FRANKIE: At least you're honest. About how you feel.

TYLER: No point in being otherwise.

(Pause.)

FRANKIE: Did Adrian ask you to accompany him tonight?

TYLER: No. I chose to.

FRANKIE: Did he prepare you? Prime you?

TYLER: No. It wouldn't have worked if he had. He knows better than that.

FRANKIE: Yes. He would. So what prompted you?

TYLER: So you could see—and your mother and brother and his wife—that... *(shrugs)*

FRANKIE: You're not a monster?

TYLER: That I'm just Adrian's partner.

FRANKIE: Fair enough. Let's join the others.

(FRANKIE moves toward the door.)

TYLER: Wait...please. Am I allowed a question?

FRANKIE: If you insist.

TYLER: I don't

(FRANKIE inclines her head 'yes'.)

Why did you feel you had to tell Adrian you were pregnant? That it was his child?

FRANKIE: Because it is.

TYLER: That doesn't answer my question.

FRANKIE: *(slowly)* I just felt I had to. No: I wanted to. Adrian's a very honest person.

TYLER: True. No more questions.

FRANKIE: Is that the lawyer talking?

(They exchange a light laugh and turn toward the exit. TYLER stands back, gestures for FRANKIE to go first.)

A Touch of Gray

(Lights fade on the kitchen and come up on the living room, where the children's goods have been packed away. The bear, however, has been left on the sofa, sitting there incongruously. DAVID *is showing a brochure to* MAISIE.*)*

(As FRANKIE *enters, she pauses, gestures to* TYLER *to wait a moment. He stands in the doorway, slightly behind her).*

EVIE: *(to* MAISIE*) I* keep telling Frankie: it would have been so much better if she'd had a scan, so she'd know whether it's a boy or a girl.

FRANKIE: *(stepping into the room)* You know why not!

MAISIE: That was Frankie's decision, Evie. Respect it.

FRANKIE: Can you imagine…? Can you see what it'd be like…? To take a picture of your child—then look at it, even in its unborn form, its shape—then coldly push it aside? Say: "No. I don't want it. I don't like it; take it away." *(pause)* Can you?

MAISIE: As the only one here who has carried a child, except Frankie of course, no. Never.

(Pause. ADRIAN *glances up at* TYLER*, his expression questioning if his meeting with Frankie was ok.* TYLER *refuses to be drawn.)*

*(*TYLER *sits on the sofa, beside* ADRIAN. FRANKIE *sits on the chair beside the desk, starts to tap into the laptop.)*

EVIE: Mr. Woodward. Don't you agree: it would've been better if Frankie had had a scan?

TYLER: Normally I choose for myself, what I should or should not agree to.

EVIE: But, in this case…

TYLER: I am here solely as an observer.

EVIE: Then, is there any point in your staying?

TYLER: It's not for me to choose: Frankie and Adrian made that decision.

(Awkward pause.)

MAISIE: Well then, I suggest we begin.

(Pause.)

Frankie?

FRANKIE: Yes… Right.

(Pause: FRANKIE continues making notes.)

MAISIE: Frankie!

FRANKIE: *(with irritation)* Oh! Alright!

(FRANKIE swings her chair around, turns the laptop screen toward herself.)

Collecting my thoughts.

EVIE: Emulating a lawyer?

MAISIE: Fair enough, Evie. She's got to do it right.

FRANKIE: Mother! Will you let me handle this?

MAISIE: Alright, alright! *(to TYLER and ADRIAN)* I'm about to be banished to the kitchen.

ADRIAN: Understood!

MAISIE: *(to FRANKIE)* Shall I put the kettle on?

FRANKIE: If you must.

MAISIE: Or hunt up something stronger?

FRANKIE: Oh, do what you want!

(ADRIAN accompanies MAISIE to the door. She exits.)

EVIE: Very elegant.

(ADRIAN re-sits. EVIE addresses him.)

We plan to send the baby to a private school, so she can get a better education. Would you be able to do that?

ADRIAN: No. I'd want him—or her—to see life the way most children see it.

FRANKIE: You wouldn't want our child to have a good education? A better chance to get a good job?

ADRIAN: Technically, yes, of course. But I feel a broader base, followed by good coaching at home, would be better.

EVIE: Are you implying that David and I won't— *(be giving good coaching?)*

FRANKIE: I'm asking the questions, Evie. *(slight pause)* What about you, Tyler?

TYLER: I'm not supposed to have an opinion.

FRANKIE: Tell us whether you personally think a private school is better than a public school when it comes to giving a child a rounded education. You can still be objective.

TYLER: I went to a private school. But now, let's say I side with Adrian.

(Pause. FRANKIE studies her notes.)

A Touch of Gray

FRANKIE: Evie: as private schools go, which do you prefer: Linton or Shawcross?

EVIE: Oh, Linton. Definitely.

FRANKIE: The school for aspiring girls.

ADRIAN: Aspiring parents, more likely!

TYLER: *(to FRANKIE)* If Linton is a girls' school, Shawcross is...?

FRANKIE: Both: girls and boys.

ADRIAN: Predominantly boys.

FRANKIE: *(to EVIE)* So, would you rather I gave birth to a girl or a boy?

(Slight pause.)

DAVID: Really, Frankie, we don't mind.

FRANKIE: I think Evie does. *(to EVIE)* Don't you? *(pats her stomach)* Are you listening in there, young one? *(turns to ADRIAN)* Adrian: what about you?

ADRIAN: Whichever. *(shrugs)* I'm the father. I just want to have my child.

FRANKIE: *(to DAVID and EVIE)* Then how would you feel if I were to say: "If it's a girl, it goes to you"? *(to ADRIAN)* "But if it's a boy, it goes to you"?

ADRIAN: I couldn't agree to that.

FRANKIE: *(to EVIE)* What about you?

EVIE: No, not really.

DAVID: No.

EVIE: I mean, I guess in unusual circumstances a case could be made for a man to have it. But only if it's a boy.

FRANKIE: So, if it's a girl, you're saying it's not okay for a man to have it?

EVIE: Think about it.

(TYLER half rises to remonstrate, but ADRIAN places a hand on his shoulder to restrain him.)

ADRIAN: Evie: Are you implying that it would be suitable for me to bring up a boy, but not a girl?

EVIE: I repeat: think about it.

TYLER: H-m-m...That's an interesting point, Mrs. Warburton. *(slight pause; he stands and approaches her)* Let's make sure we all understand you correctly.

EVIE: You said you were here only as an observer.

TYLER: Were you not, in fact, saying that it would *not* be suitable for Adrian to adopt and bring up a girl?

EVIE: I repeat: you're only an observer.

TYLER: True. But if someone makes a remark that casts a slur on Adrian, and so by implication also on me, then I believe I have the right to respond.

EVIE: I wasn't talking about you. Or to you.

TYLER: But you were talking about Adrian?

EVIE: Only in a manner of speaking.

TYLER: Oh. But it was more than just a thought?

EVIE: I was just...thinking out loud.

(ADRIAN attempts to pull TYLER away from the confrontation, but TYLER shakes him off.)

TYLER: H-m-m. You were thinking out loud. *(pause)* Could it be construed that, in thinking out loud, you were implying that the child—if it's a girl—would be 'at risk' if placed under Adrian's care?

EVIE: That's not what I was saying.

TYLER: But was it not implied?

EVIE: You said 'at risk.' I didn't.

TYLER: Then perhaps you could define for us just what you did mean.

EVIE: I didn't *mean* anything. I was just... I was just offering an opinion.

TYLER: An opinion. As you and your husband are contenders for the choice your sister-in-law has to make, I suggest it's important for her to know exactly to what extent you believe in that opinion.

EVIE: You're a contender, too!

TYLER: I am?

EVIE: You're here with Adrian.

ADRIAN: Tyler and I live together, Evie. Just like you and David.

EVIE: But we're married.

TYLER: And we're equal partners.

EVIE: Yes, but you're not married.

ADRIAN: The equivalent of.

EVIE: No way.

A Touch of Gray

FRANKIE: Evie: You and David lived together for—how long was it?—two years, before you decided to get married.

EVIE: That was different.

FRANKIE: In what way?

EVIE: We weren't... We were a normal couple.

ADRIAN: Are you saying that Tyler and I are an abnormal couple?

EVIE: It's just that you are...*(pause)*

FRANKIE? They are what?

EVIE: You know what I mean.

(Pause.)

TYLER: If Adrian and I were married, legally—and in a growing number of countries it is legal for two men, or two women, to marry—would that in your eyes put us on an equal footing, as 'contenders,' with you and your husband?

EVIE: No. I could not agree.

TYLER: David?

DAVID: *(slowly)* No. I have to say the same as my wife.

TYLER: Frankie?

FRANKIE: *(slight pause)* I don't see why not.

EVIE: Frankie!

FRANKIE: I gave my opinion, just as you gave yours.

EVIE: But...?

(FRANKIE shrugs, turns away. TYLER sits, as though he is 'resting his case.' Pause.)

FRANKIE: *(slowly)* Before I decide, I need to ask Evie and Adrian a question. Two questions. So, please, when they answer, can you all refrain from interrupting? Making comments or offering advice? *(slight pause)* Can you?

(EVIE shrugs her acknowledgment; ADRIAN says 'Sure'; DAVID nods; TYLER says 'Understood.')

(FRANKIE turns to EVIE and ADRIAN.)

FRANKIE: I want to know why you—you, personally—think your proposal for my baby is the better plan. But from the *baby's* point of view. Not yours. Or mine.

(Pause. She looks first at ADRIAN and then at EVIE.)

Evie?

EVIE: Why me? First?

FRANKIE: Because you were my original choice for the baby.
(EVIE hesitates, looks at DAVID, who shrugs.)
EVIE: Well, really... I mean, I've said it all. You know how David and I feel.
FRANKIE: Is that from the *baby's* point of view?
EVIE: Well, it's obvious, isn't it? The baby—the child—will grow up secure, knowing she's living in a natural family—a God-given family. She'll have two loving parents: a father *and* a mother. Many children don't have that today. And she'll know her home is a secure home; a *complete* home. It will always be there for her. Like when she comes home from school, there'll be a mother waiting to greet her. Always. Every day.
FRANKIE: You work shifts.
EVIE: It can be arranged. I'll *be* there.
DAVID: Or I will.
EVIE: Right.
DAVID: And money won't be a problem.
(FRANKIE raises a restraining hand toward DAVID.)
EVIE: So she'll always eat well. No junk food! And she'll be dressed well, in up-to-date fashions that other girls will accept, recognize. Envy her for.
DAVID: She'll never have to want, for anything.
EVIE: It's as simple as that.
(Slight pause.)
FRANKIE: Is that it?
EVIE: Yes. We don't need to say anything more. Do we, Dave?
DAVID: *(slowly)* No. I think you've said it well enough.
FRANKIE: I will have another question for you. But first, it's Adrian's turn.
ADRIAN: Ah, yes...hmm...from the baby's point of view...
(Slight pause. ADRIAN arranges his thoughts, stands.)
Frankly, I don't think one plan is better than the other. I will be able to provide the baby with an equally secure environment, either as a single parent or living with a partner. *(slight pause)* He—the child—will know right from the beginning that he has a real father and a real mother, even if he doesn't see or hear much from her. And he'll know that both are his birth parents. And that he was conceived in a caring relationship.

ADRIAN: *(continuing)* That his parents, even though they aren't married or living together, still have affection for each other.

(ADRIAN pauses. FRANKIE gives a slight nod in agreement.)

And he'll know the person I'm living with is *my* chosen partner. And that you—if you are living with or have married someone else—that he or she is *your* chosen partner. I think the key here is that he will know that each of his parents is living in a loving relationship, and he will feel the benefit from knowing that.

(FRANKIE waits to see if ADRIAN wants to say more, then turns to TYLER.)

FRANKIE: Is there anything you might like to add, Tyler?

TYLER: At this point, no.

(FRANKIE considers her notes.)

FRANKIE: Another question. *(to ADRIAN)* And you first, this time.

ADRIAN: Fair enough.

FRANKIE: What issues do you foresee, that the baby will have to face, as a child growing up with you?

ADRIAN: H-m-m. As a single parent, male? Or as two parents, both male?

FRANKIE: Both ways.

ADRIAN: Well, as a single parent, it would be no different than for any other child living with a single parent; and there are many of them.

EVIE: No, not male.

(FRANKIE raises a restraining hand toward EVIE.)

FRANKIE: *(to ADRIAN)* Continue.

ADRIAN: I would do as any single parent does: make arrangements for day care, all day at first, and then after school later, until I come home from work.

FRANKIE: That's from the child's point of view?

ADRIAN: Y-e-s, I think so. The child will experience daily day care, much as many do now—whether they are living in a single or a two-parent family. *(slight pause)* In a day care he will learn socializing skills, more than a single child always kept at home. In that way he will feel little different from other kids.

FRANKIE: What happens if he's too sick to go to day care?

ADRIAN: I'll take time off. Or work at home. In my job I can do that. So he'll know I'm there when he specially needs me. *(slight pause)* And I'm sure that, if necessary, I could call on one of his grandmas to come in, either of them. My mother or yours: Maisie.

FRANKIE: My mother?

ADRIAN: Why not?

FRANKIE: Alright. *(turns to* TYLER*)* What is your view, Tyler?

TYLER: If the child were to sense that I have developed sufficient nurturing skills, and would feel comfortable having a crusty lawyer peering over the edge of his crib or bed, then I could give his father a break.

FRANKIE: Does that imply you will stay, if I say Adrian is to have the baby?

TYLER: If I remember correctly, you insisted that any response to your questions should be from the child's point of view.

FRANKIE: *(slight smile)* A-a-h. *(to* DAVID *and* EVIE*)* So, how would you handle sick days?

DAVID: There are two of us. One of us will take time off.

EVIE: So the baby would always see one of her parents is there. No being carted off to day care when she's borderline sick. And, although she will love her grandma, when you're sick it's your parents you really want to know are there.

FRANKIE: *(slowly)* You're so sure of yourselves, aren't you? All of you. David and Evie call the baby 'she', and Adrian and Tyler say 'he'. And I'm the mother and even I don't know! *(pause)* I think mother should be here now. Fetch her, will you Dave?

DAVID: Are you sure?

FRANKIE: Definitely. Go on!

*(*DAVID *exits.* FRANKIE *paces slowly, pondering. As she passes* ADRIAN, *she briefly—absent-mindedly—rests a hand on his shoulder. He looks at it, reaches up to touch it, but doesn't.* TYLER *notices, gives a slight nod.)*

*(*FRANKIE *crosses to* EVIE, *looks down at her, goes to speak, then changes her mind. She turns away as* DAVID *and* MAISIE *enter.* DAVID *reseats himself beside* EVIE. MAISIE *is carrying a glass with what could be Scotch and ice in it. She hesitates in the doorway.)*

MAISIE: *(to* FRANKIE*)* You *want* me here? David said...
FRANKIE: I want you to see me choose. *How* I choose.
   (Slight pause. FRANKIE *waits, expects* MAISIE *to react.* MAISIE *remains silent.)*
   Do you want a seat?
MAISIE: No. I'll watch from here.
   *(*FRANKIE *looks quizzically at* MAISIE, *then turns to* ADRIAN.*)*
FRANKIE: What's your main reason for saying the baby should come to you, and not David and Evie?
ADRIAN: *(resigned)* Frankly, I can't find a valid reason why the baby shouldn't go to them.
   (Slight pause.)
FRANKIE: Is that it?
ADRIAN: I think so.
FRANKIE: David, Evie: Your reason?
EVIE: It's obvious, isn't it?
FRANKIE: To whom?
EVIE: To everyone. It doesn't need to be put into words.
DAVID: What Evie is trying to say...she'd feel more comfortable seeing your baby growing up in a natural family.
   *(*ADRIAN *goes to speak, but* FRANKIE *gestures to him not to.)*
EVIE: Even if Adrian was on his own, we would still say that.
FRANKIE: Why?
DAVID: Because of the...potential...that eventually he'd enter into another relationship. Like he has now.
TYLER: *(to* FRANKIE*)* May I?
   *(*FRANKIE *hesitates, looks questioningly at* TYLER.*)*
FRANKIE: Providing it's relevant...
TYLER: Oh, it is. Just remove the word 'potential.' You may assume that Adrian's and my relationship is firm.
   *(*TYLER *places a hand on* ADRIAN's *shoulder.)*
FRANKIE: *(a quick interjection, to prevent interruption)* Next question, then. What are your views on access to the child? For my family. *Continuing* access. Let's start with access for my mother. Adrian?

ADRIAN: Not a problem. Maisie will be the child's grandmother—just as my mother will—a direct blood relation—and her presence in his life, his upbringing, will be welcome.

FRANKIE: David?

DAVID: The same.

FRANKIE: Evie?

EVIE: Same as David.

FRANKIE: What about access for Adrian?

DAVID: Adrian will be welcome to see the child. At any time.

EVIE: But only as a visitor, with no personal connection.

FRANKIE: *(to ADRIAN)* How do you feel about that?

ADRIAN: Not good. Unsatisfactory. But, really, do I have a choice?

FRANKIE: Let's turn it around. If you have the baby, will that eliminate access for David and Evie?

ADRIAN: Of course not. They'll still be his uncle and aunt.

FRANKIE: *(to TYLER)* Do you agree?

TYLER: It's legally valid.

FRANKIE: But do you *agree?*

TYLER: Absolutely.

FRANKIE: *(thinks for a moment)* Now...what about me, then? What access will I have to my baby, once I part with it? Evie? David?

EVIE: Any time. You know that.

DAVID: Agree.

FRANKIE: *(to ADRIAN)* And if you have the baby? What access will I have?

ADRIAN: Also any time. Just like a couple who've separated but have agreed on joint support.

MAISIE: All very nice. *(to FRANKIE)* Can I ask a question?

(FRANKIE hesitates.).

Then I'll shut up.

FRANKIE: *(slight pause)* Oh, just do it!

MAISIE: *(to ADRIAN)* When the child is three, or five, or eight, will it know who Frankie is?

ADRIAN: Of course.

MAISIE: How will it refer to her?

ADRIAN: As his or her mother. Mommy, I suppose. "Mom."

A Touch of Gray

ADRIAN: *(continuing)* Even if he rarely sees her.

MAISIE: *(to EVIE and DAVID)* And you two? How will the baby know—refer to—Frankie?

EVIE: As her aunt: She'll be Auntie Frankie.

MAISIE: David: do you agree with that?

DAVID: Of course. And Frankie will be able to see the baby whenever she wants.

EVIE: When she's in town. But she'll be able to write to her—and send her gifts—when she's not.

MAISIE: Hmmm... *(to FRANKIE)* That's it. It has to be a decision, mind.

FRANKIE: *(resigned irony)* Yes, mother.

(MAISIE sits in the chair by the desk, half turns away, makes it clear she does not intend to interfere. Pause.)

I can't help thinking...is it right, for me to be choosing a life for an unborn child who has no input whatever into my choice? I mean, how do I *know* what kind of life she—or he—would want to have?

EVIE: You have to speak for yourself, Frankie. And the child. Doesn't she, David?

DAVID: Indubitably. Definitely. *(to FRANKIE)* It's your child.

FRANKIE: And Adrian's.

DAVID: But you're carrying it.

FRANKIE: Let me think about that. See if it bears any weight.

(FRANKIE pats her stomach, smiles.)

Hmmm...coming along.

(Slight pause, then she turns to all five.)

Will you give me time to follow my thinking—aloud—right through to a logical...a realistic...conclusion? Without any distractions? Will you? Please?

(FRANKIE looks at EVIE, DAVID, ADRIAN and TYLER in turn and waits for a response from each.)

EVIE: *(slight pause)* If you wish.

(EVIE picks up the bear as an outlet for her pent-up emotions. She holds it until the very last scene.)

DAVID: Yes. For sure.

ADRIAN: Definitely.

TYLER: Like Adrian.

FRANKIE: *(to* MAISIE*)* Mother?

MAISIE: Me?

FRANKIE: You won't interrupt?

MAISIE: Not without your approval.

>   *(*FRANKIE *gestures, frustrated. She continues slowly, thoughtfully, with brief pauses.)*

FRANKIE: Have you any idea how unnatural it feels, saying I don't want to keep my baby? *(pause)* And how I will feel if, when my research is done, I suddenly develop a motherly streak? *(pause)* Will I regret I can't do things with her: play and read stories, tuck her in her bed at night? *(pause, she paces)* But that's all from *my* point of view, isn't it?

*(*FRANKIE *shakes her head.)*

No, like you, I've got to look at it from the baby's point of view.

*(*FRAKIE *paces, growing firmer in her delivery)*

She must *never* know how her mother made a critical choice for her, seven weeks before she was born. She must *never* know what her life might have been like, how different it might have been...

(She looks piercingly at each listener, in turn.)

Oh, we're going to have to be so careful, aren't we? About keeping all this—this evening—my decision—a secret.

*(*FRANKIE *scrutinizes each of them, quizzically.)*

So, still from the baby's point of view....

(She stands in front of DAVID *and* EVIE*, looks down at them.)*

Living with you—David, Evie—she'll have a secure, serene, very traditional life. And I *like* that. She'll like that.

(She crosses to ADRIAN*, stands in front of him.)*

With you, Adrian, he would have a much less predictable life. He'd feel secure with you, that I know. But as he grows, he'd have to face living in a much less traditional home; a lifestyle that sometimes may cause him pain... particularly among friends at school. And that has planted a question in all of our minds.

(Pause. FRANKIE *returns to the center of the room and peers at each of them in turn. Her confidence is now evident, through her definiteness.)*

A Touch of Gray

FRANKIE: *(continuing)* Adrian: Can you accept—without argument or interference, now or in the future—the decision I make tonight?

ADRIAN: Y-e-s. Yes, of course.

FRANKIE: Thank you. *(to* TYLER*)* And will you hold your peace, no matter what I choose to say? To do?

TYLER: Certainly.

*(*FRANKIE *turns and faces* DAVID *and* EVIE.*)*

FRANKIE: David: can you? Will you accept my decision? Unequivocally?

*(*DAVID *and* EVIE *exchange slow glances, ensuring they have a common understanding.).*

DAVID: Sure.

FRANKIE: Evie?

EVIE: Yes. If you're sure it's what you want.

FRANKIE: It has to be.

*(*FRANKIE *stands in front of* MAISIE*)*

Mother: Will you?

MAISIE: It's your decision, Frankie.

FRANKIE: Right, then.

(She takes a central position, speaks slowly and confidently)

I want my baby to have a life in which there will be no subterfuge, no unanswered questions. No hidden agenda. A life in which there can be no chance that, at some point—either as a child or as an adult—he or she will discover something about her parents' heritage that contradicts what she—or he—has always been led to believe.

(Slight pause)

Can you all guarantee that?

(They all give slow, silent nods. FRANKIE *turns, paces, still thoughtful, but with a definiteness, a confidence about her, that we have not seen before.)*

But will I? Will I be content to sit on the sidelines? Ignore my maternal instincts, if they erupt? Can I be *sure*? Absolutely sure?

(Slight pause.)

FRANKIE: *(continuing)* No…no…

    (FRANKIE takes ADRIAN's hand.)

    Which means, Adrian, that—regardless of your personal lifestyle—if I am to have access, as the child's *mother,* I want our baby to live with you.

    (There is a gasp and a muted "No!" from EVIE. She half stands. DAVID takes her hand to restrain her. She sits slowly, holding his hand like a lifeline.)

    (For the moment, EVIE's anger is probably more from being thwarted than from hearing the 'wrong' decision. DAVID is frankly surprised at FRANKIE's choice, unsure of his personal feelings but concerned for the effect on EVIE. In still another sense, he suddenly admires FRANKIE, for he has seen his sister in a new, much stronger light.)

    (ADRIAN clearly was not expecting FRANKIE to assign the child to him. Almost in tears, he clings to FRANKIE's hand.)

    (FRANKIE looks over ADRIAN's shoulder, searching for TYLER.)

    And with you, Tyler, if you can accept being a third parent.

TYLER: If you can accept me, then…yes. Thank you.

FRANKIE: I hope, Adrian, that in time I'll want to take an active part, even if sometimes from a distance, so I can help our child have a life that's complete.

    (Slight pause. DAVID and EVIE look askance at one another. ADRIAN clings to FRANKIE's hand. TYLER resists a pent-up urge to go to ADRIAN and physically show his support for him, but recognizes that for the moment he must not breach the connection between ADRIAN and FRANKIE. MAISIE watches for a moment, then makes a loud announcement.)

MAISIE: Well, well, Frankie. Not even a hint of gray there!

    (EVIE stands up abruptly, the bear still in her hand, and steps up to ADRIAN and FRANKIE. There is a brief pause and then ADRIAN, fearing some action EVIE may take, stands, raises his hands in a 'don't' gesture, partly shielding FRANKIE.)

A Touch of Gray

(EVIE *shakes her head slowly from side to side, then lifts the bear, which is facing toward her, and for a moment holds it out in front of herself. Then, just as abruptly, she turns the bear around so it faces* ADRIAN *and thrusts it at him. He, unsure what is expected of him, stands motionless.* EVIE *shakes the bear in front of him, signifying "Take it!"* ADRIAN *slowly reaches for the bear.* EVIE *let's go and turns to* DAVID, *who has moved up beside her, burying her face in his chest.* ADRIAN *is almost in tears as he holds the bear and the lights dim to blackout.)*

(Closing music up.)

END

Seven Plays with a Light Touch

Character Descriptions

Although she is not the primary character in the play, I am describing Maisie first because she has strongly influenced Frankie's character and, to a lesser extent, David's.

Maisie

Maisie's brashness evolves from a basic and intrinsic insecurity. She had a mother who continually dwelt on her inadequacy, implying that she was never as good as she could be—at school, in the home, at making friends—and she has carried this insecurity into adulthood. She presents herself strongly to mask the label.

As a teen-ager Maisie became uncontrollable and had a series of undesirable boyfriends. At age 18 she met Roger, a well-educated successful businessman 12 years her senior, with whom she became pregnant, refused to have an abortion, and convinced him he should leave his partner and marry her. After their third child (Frankie) was born, Roger pulled out of the marriage but left Maisie sufficiently stable financially. She is still bitter about him abandoning her and has even allowed herself to feel that the arrival of their third child triggered Roger's departure. This has become another element to fuel her negative feelings about Frankie.

Maisie has carried her mother's negativity into bringing up her own children. This particularly affected Frankie, who has been—and still is—extremely sensitive to her mother's comments and implications that she is not as capable as her deceased older sister Marina, who Maisie has idolized and won't let the memory go.

What is Maisie's view of the four protagonists? She thinks her son David is clever but dull. Deep down she recognizes that her daughter Frankie is cleverer and sharper than she has given Frankie credit for, but has difficulty admitting it. She has never really accepted Evie as a suitable mate for her son, thinks she is too opinionated and controlling, and cannot accept that David allows Evie to 'run' him.

She likes Adrian and has even had the errant thought that, if Adrian's and Frankie's relationship had evolved into marriage, she might have felt that Frankie would not have been good enough for him.

She has no opinion about Tyler, except a mild sense of awe.

Frankie

Frankie's real name is *Francine* but in her teens she defied her mother by choosing only to be known as *Frankie*. She is continually fighting the image that her mother has created: that she is inadequate and worthless. To erase it she is determined to 'be the very best' at whatever she does. This evolved from a deep-seated awareness that she could either give in and become the incompetent person her mother makes her out to be, or knuckle down and become the high achiever she knows she is capable of being.

Currently she is pursuing a Ph.D. in Sociology with a major in Anthropology. For her research she will be travelling to Peru to live in a remote, mountainous area for a two-year study of Peruvian social and hierarchical issues.

She is a good organizer and a clear, logical thinker, *when she is doing her research*, yet she tends to be scatter-brained and forgetful when it comes to remembering details and appointments outside her primary interest. She is a dedicated, deeply involved student who writes well and commands respect from her advisers. She is reasonably tolerant of others, but tends to react sharply if they impinge on or interfere with the work she wants to get done.

Her relationship with her mother (Maisie) is restrained. She is polite to her, permits herself to engage with her only on innocuous topics, and has learned never to share information with her (because her mother will inevitably find a way to downgrade it). She understands her mother's basic insecurity better than her brother David does. She and her brother have never been close, partly because of their 11-year age difference and partly by his self-contained remoteness. She is ambivalent about David's wife Evie, who she does not know well. She knows David is happy with Evie, but she resents the way David lets Evie run his life.

She freely admits (to herself) that she has been the driving force in her relationship with Adrian. They have always been affectionate with each other, but theirs has never been an outstanding love affair—just a sound, caring friendship.

David

David is a design engineer employed by the local power utility. He is methodical, a thinker, and tends to be staid. He speaks slowly, thoughtfully, and only after considering a point in depth before delivering it.

He loves Evie in a quiet, restrained way, and is perfectly happy that she organizes him and their life. His life is comfortable and (privately) he admits to himself that he does not have a real urge to have children.

He recognizes the qualities that Frankie exhibits and is aware she is cleverer and more intelligent than he is. He does not like the way their mother has always downgraded Frankie's efforts but does not know how to correct it (he has been less affected by their mother's negativity, because he has always hidden behind his books and ignored it). His relationship with his mother is essentially casual and protective—mainly protecting her from herself.

David leaves most contentious issues to Evie to deal with. Even in the proposed adoption of Frankie's child—which basically he would prefer not to do—he has allowed Evie to be the speaker and decision-maker.

Evie

Evie is a Registered Nurse who is recognized as efficient and extremely competent. The hospital administrators love her, because she runs a tight ship on the wards she supervises, but the nurses she works with respect her but do not like her. She tends to be officious, overbearing, and sharp-tongued, and has little patience with people who do not respond readily to her views. She *expects* those she works with, and interacts with, to respond positively and quickly to her requirements. She tends to have a short fuse.

She and David have a comfortable marriage with few conflicts. Although they have strong affection for one-another, theirs is not an ardent love affair. Evie is disappointed they are unable to conceive children, but it's more because it's a reflection on her womanhood than a deep-down sadness. She is willing to take over Frankie's baby, but it's not an urgent need. She does not, however, intend to 'share' the child with Frankie (and particularly Adrian); she is determined that she and David are always to be known as its 'real' parents.

Evie does not have much time for Maisie, whom she regards as coarse and really unsuitable as a parent for her professional husband. She also is on a light conversational basis with Frankie, and is a little in awe of her intelligence and dedication to her studies. At the same time she cannot understand why Frankie lets her mother put her down so consistently. She has met Adrian occasionally over the past two years, but does not know him other than cursorily.

Adrian

Adrian is a Certified General Accountant (CGA) with the Department of Agriculture, where he is regarded as being very competent. He was well liked at school and respected for his prowess as a member of both the swim team and the chess club (he has a sharp, analytical mind, which has contributed to his skill). He is a certified swimming instructor and the coach for an advanced swim team. It was in the shower and locker rooms that Adrian first began to be aware that he is attracted to male bodies.

His father is a long-distance coach driver who frequently is absent from home; his mother is a clerk for an insurance agency, but suffers from ill-health that has occasionally inhibited her from working and even looking after the family and home. He has two sisters, both younger by 10 and 12 years, for whom, because of his mother's recurring illness, he learned early to cook, do housekeeping, and help them when they were infants through to their early teens.

Adrian is an alert, enquiring, thoughtful person, who assesses a situation quickly and does not chase after ideas that he determines are not worth pursuing. His strengths lie in his reasonableness, acceptance and understanding of another's point of view, clarity of thought, good judgment, and a tough doggedness. His weaknesses are his fear of conflict (often, he will rather give in than face a protagonist's forceful argument, particularly if the protagonist tends to be dogmatic and overbearing), his unwillingness to say anything that might hurt another (why he hesitated for so long before informing Frankie that he was breaking off their relationship), and a tendency to procrastinate. He is very fond of Frankie, yet has never deeply loved her.

Tyler

Tyler is a very career-oriented lawyer who is gay, a competitive polo and tennis player, and always likes to win—in sport, as a lawyer, and in his life generally. Both his parents are doctors who expected him to follow in their footsteps and were disappointed when he chose not to.

He was an only child, somewhat spoiled, and left on his own or in the care of a housekeeper much of the time, because his parents worked long hours. He went to a private boys-only school until he was 13, and then to a residential school, also boys-only.

Two things happened that led him to his present occupation and life-style. First, Tyler became enamored with learning accompanied by an inbuilt need to show his parents he was a success, and so became a highly respected 'A' student. He also became a member of the school's debating society, discovered he had excellent skills when arguing a point, challenging an assumption, and defending an issue.

This led him into studying law, and now he has embarked on a solid career with clients who have contentious issues lining up to procure his services. His voice is heard both in the courtroom and publicly, where he is not afraid to speak out on difficult issues. Consequently his firm considers him a very positive asset, pays him well, and has brought him in as a partner.

Tyler has bought a condominium in an upscale area of the city, employs a part-time cleaner/cook, and lives very comfortably. He has furnished his home primarily with Scandinavian furniture and has purchased some contemporary art originals. He is *proud* of his home.

His homosexuality evolved when he was at the residential school. Unlike Adrian, throughout his life Tyler has been solidly male-oriented in his affections. He has been the driver in developing a long-term relationship with Adrian.

Tyler is a strong individualist who expects to do things, and to see things done, 'his way.' He is outspoken, articulate, confident he is right, and resents anyone challenging or trying to change his point of view.

A Touch of Gray

Production Notes

The immediate difficulty when performing this play is ensuring the audience achieves the correct focus. It's a matter of perception. Frankie's dilemma seems logical and reasonably straightforward: she has to decide whether her baby should go to her brother David and his wife Evie, or to her ex-boyfriend Adrian (who is the child's father) and his partner Tyler.

Yet the focus can easily be misplaced by an audience, who may *assume* the play is really questioning whether it's suitable for the child to go to two men living in a homosexual relationship. (Or the actors may even make that assumption and build it into their portrayal of the situation.) There is a historical parallel here: when Henrik Ibsen's play *A Doll's House* was first produced in 1879, it was generally thought Ibsen was making a rousing proclamation for women's emancipation. His intention, however, really was to show how men and women can hide behind the word 'respectability' to conceal their personal struggle for power over another person.

Consequently, in this version of *A Touch of Gray* I have made some minor changes which I hope will lessen the likelihood an audience may view Evie as too cold, too severe and too opinionated to be chosen as the 'mother' for Frankie's unborn child. Yet, although she is outspoken about Adrian's and Tyler's homosexual relationship, this does not mean she is against such an arrangement; she is simply using it as a convenient weapon in her argument that the child should come to her and David.

The confrontation between Tyler and Evie (pages 178 and 179) is there to encourage the audience to have sympathy for Evie as he exerts a court-like pressure on her.

I have included detailed character descriptions to help the actors better understand their relationships with one-another, to which the director may introduce further interpretations. The actor playing Maisie probably has the most difficult task, in that she has to be brash and outspoken without overplaying the role. Similarly, Evie can be shown as a cold, demanding person, yet not to the extent that she turns the audience against her as a suitable candidate for the baby.

The relationship between Adrian and Frankie also has to be handled adroitly so that their comfortable affection for each other, even though they are separated, seems natural. To some extent, it's a relief for Frankie when she discovers that Adrian left her for a man and not another woman; it's something she can understand and more readily accept. Their continuing friendship also may seem unusual to some people, yet in today's more 'accepting' environment it is likely to be understood.

Frankie's early indecision has to evolve into a confidence in herself when, during the closing moments, she has to present her decision. She also has to accept, even though her acceptance is not articulated in the play, her mother's question to Evie, David and Adrian on how they perceive Frankie's relationship to the growing child. Their individual responses become a major factor as she reaches for a decision. Although perhaps unexpected, it makes Frankie's choice more than simply 'logical'. In human terms, it is the 'right' choice.

I found the closing moments following Frankie's decision difficult to achieve. Should Evie storm out in high dudgeon? Should she have a major breakdown? Should David show his displeasure? Should Tyler congratulate Adrian? What would Frankie do next? And how should Adrian react?

My feeling as a story-teller was that I should show the impact that Frankie's decision has on each person; that is, 'tie up the loose ends.' Yet a contrary emotion kept emerging: would it not be better if, when Frankie makes her decision, I consider the story as complete and end the play quickly?

Bringing a cuddly 14-inch brown bear into the picture not only provided a solution for the closing moment, but also offered a way to imbue the audience with some sympathy for Evie (rather than leave the theater with a 'you got what you deserved' attitude about her).

It took a lot of fiddling, but at last I feel the ending is 'tight.'

Play No. 5

The Sicilian Wine Test

Synopsis

Barry is a 37-year-old bachelor who would like to find the right woman to marry, but each time he finds a promising candidate he has backed away, fearing what she might be like in 20 years' time. Now he has discovered a Sicilian wine which has a unique trait: it tends to loosen the drinker's tongue and so display hidden characteristics that Barry might find distasteful. He uses the wine to test the delightful women he meets.

He invites them to dinner, plies them with the Sicilian wine, and is saddened to discover that each has displayed some unhappy traits. Then he meets Lorraine, who passes his test with flying colors! Now he is ready to propose, but is surprised to encounter an unexpected and seemingly intractable obstacle.

Rationale

I wrote the first draft of *The Sicilian Wine Test* as a television comedy, using 'flash-forwards' for Barry to see what each potential wife would be like in 20 years' time. Later, I recognized it would be better as a stage play, where the actors would perform before a live audience and *hear* their reaction to what was happening during the two meals. The laughter I have observed at the locations where the play has been performed has reinforced my belief.

History

A public reading of *The Sicilian Wine Test* was held in the Prairie Theatre Exchange, Winnipeg, as part of the Carol Shields Festival of New Works in May 2006. The first performance was at the GADOC One-Act-Play Festival in Guernsey, UK, May, 2007, where it won the Burns Trophy for the best original unpublished play. The next performance was as part of a double bill at the Summer Theatre Festival in Gimli, Manitoba, in August 2008.

Characters

The play has a cast of three:
 Barry, dark haired and dark eyed, age 37
 Shelley, a blonde with blue eyes, age 32
 Lorraine, dark haired and dark eyed, age 36

At the reading and the following regular stage performances, the three roles were played by:

Role	2006	2007	2008
Barry	Darcy Fehr	Andrew McCutcheon	Jeff Wahl
Shelley	Rea Kavanagh	Claire Ozanne	Erica Châtelain
Lorraine	Talia Pura	Rachael Fairbairn	Holly Steele
Director	*The author*	*Jane Blower*	*The author*

Character descriptions start on page 225.

The Set

The stage can be set up in two ways:

- Into three sections, each lit separately. At stage left is Barry's dining area; at stage right is Lorraine's dining area; at stage center is a narrow piece that represents a small washroom.

- As a single dining area that represents Barry's dining table for the first scene and Lorraine's dining table for the second scene. To one side is the small washroom used in both scenes.

Barry's dining area has a playing-card-size table downstage with a colored cloth and china and cutlery set for a dinner; off-stage left is presumed to be the kitchen, from which Barry will progressively bring in the meal. Lorraine's dining area is more-or-less a mirror image of Barry's, with a kitchen supposedly off-stage right. Each table has two chairs, one on each side.

The dining cloth in Lorraine's area is a light cream in color. If there are other furnishings, in Lorraine's area they will tend to be of better quality, possibly of Scandinavian origin; in Barry's area they tend to be more traditional.

Between the two dining areas, or to one side, is a narrow bathroom with a counter-top downstage which supposedly has a wash-hand basin in it, and a soap dish, toothbrush holder, box of facial tissues, etc, along its downstage edge. On the audience's side of the counter there is supposedly a mirror, so that when Shelley and Barry look into it they are directly facing the audience.

There are notes about previous productions on page 228.

A happy moment during a rehearsal for the 2008 production of The Sicilian Wine Test, *performed in Winnipeg and Gimli, Manitoba.*

From the left: Holly Steele as Lorraine, Jeff Wahl as Barry, and Erica Châtelain as Shelley.

There are notes about previous productions on page 227.

Approximate Length: 35 minutes:

Some Script Guidelines

Throughout the script, two symbols are used occasionally at the end of a piece of dialogue to indicate how the sentence ends:

> ... An ellipsis at the end of a statement means the speaker just trails off and leaves his or her thought hanging in the air (possibly accompanied by a shrug).

> — A dash at the end of a statement means the speaker is interrupted by the next speaker, so that the first speaker's statement is incomplete. Sometimes there is an italicized continuation of the statement *(within brackets)* immediately following the dash, to help the actor sense where the sentence was going.

> v.o. Means that the words are spoken by someone off-stage.

Seven Plays with a Light Touch

Script: The Sicilian Wine Test
© 2005, Ron Blicq

Although both Shelley and Barry drink a fair amount of wine when each is the guest at a meal, at no time should they appear to be drunk or inebriated. The effect of the wine is to loosen the tongue and so display a different side to their character. We are intended to be aware of their foibles, and to empathize with each character, but not to dislike them for having them. Shelley should be blonde and have blue eyes. Barry will have dark hair (i.e. not be blonde) and must not have blue eyes.

Curtain Up

(The dining area in Barry's apartment. SHELLEY *and* BARRY *are in the middle of a lasagna-and-salad dinner he has served up. There is a wine cooler with a single bottle of white wine in it.* SHELLEY *sits stage right and* BARRY *stage left of the table.)*

*(*SHELLEY *holds up a food-laden fork.)*

SHELLEY: From T.G.T? The Governor's Table?

BARRY: Good lord, no.

SHELLEY: Tastes like it.

BARRY: Is that a compliment?

SHELLEY: Whitlaw's then?

BARRY: Now, I am offended.

SHELLEY: My mother says Whitlaw's Christmas pudding is just as good as the ones she makes. And she's an expert.

BARRY: Can *you* tell the difference?

SHELLEY: Nah. Can't stand the stuff. All those currants and bits of peel. And swimming in suet. Ugh. Puts me right off. *(points her fork to her plate)* Then it must be from Montrose Food Market.

BARRY: Oh, for Pete's sake!

SHELLEY: You don't mean...? *(points her fork at him)*

BARRY: Give me some credit.

SHELLEY: *You* made it?

BARRY: Any reason why I shouldn't?

SHELLEY: You're not going to tell me you made the lobster bisque, too?

The Sicilian Wine Test

BARRY: Went out and trapped the lobster myself.
SHELLEY: Oh, Barry!
  (BARRY pours more wine into SHELLEY's glass; none into his.)
  Where'd you learn to cook...thanks...I mean, like this?
BARRY: Just a hobby.
SHELLEY: With your heavy work schedule, you have time?
BARRY: Relaxing, really. Takes my mind off all those figures.
SHELLEY: Except mine, I hope.
BARRY: Quite.
  (SHELLEY drinks—not sips—more wine, reaches for the bottle.)
SHELLEY: Mmmm. *(reads)* "Product of Sicily. Creative Amontillado." Where'd you get it?
BARRY: Hard to find.
SHELLEY: Yes, but where?
BARRY: I know a place.
SHELLEY: The wine shop in Grandview Mall?
BARRY: No.
SHELLEY: You're being cagey.
BARRY: They bring in just one case at a time.
  (BARRY stands, starts toward the kitchen, pauses as Shelley speaks.)
SHELLEY: You're still being cagey.
BARRY: True.
SHELLEY: But why?
BARRY: I don't want word to get around.
  (BARRY exits. SHELLEY calls after him.)
SHELLEY: You want to keep it all for yourself?
BARRY: *(v.o.)* And you. Especially you.
  (BARRY steps downstage left and addresses the audience.)
BARRY: That's Shelley in there, at my dining table. We've been...well, an item, I suppose...for several months now.
  (BARRY looks right to ensure Shelley can't hear; he speaks confidentially.)

BARRY: *(continuing)* Actually, Shelley doesn't know it but she's taking a test—the Sicilian Wine Test.

SHELLEY: *(calls)* You can tell me, surely?

BARRY: *(calls back)* Uh-uh! *(to the audience)* Sorry about that. I'll tell you about the test later.

(BARRY enters the dining area carrying a basket of rolls covered by a light cloth.)

SHELLEY: You are a dark horse! In all the months we've been going out, I've never seen you keep something like this to yourself.

BARRY: Don't look a gift horse in the mouth! Especially a dark one.

(SHELLEY sips wine. BARRY holds the basket of bread out to her.)

Another roll?...Easy! They're hot.

SHELLEY: And you baked them, too!

BARRY: I admit, from a prepared dough.

SHELLEY: Thanks. You mean you didn't roll the dough out, like on a pastry board?

BARRY: No. I just shaped it.

(BARRY places a roll on his plate, carries the basket back to the kitchen.)

SHELLEY: *(calls)* Oh, Barry. Think of all the angst you could be working out. Get rid of all that tension.

BARRY: *(v.o.)* You think I'm tense?

SHELLEY: *(calls, demonstrates with her hands)* All that squeezing, rolling...You're nothing like my father.

BARRY: *(v.o.)* I should hope not.

SHELLEY: No, I mean...he wouldn't know how to bake...*anything*. Your father's not like that, is he?

BARRY: *(re-entering)* Huh?

SHELLEY: I said your father's not like that.

BARRY: Oh...no. I don't think so.

SHELLEY: Of course he's not.

BARRY: Uh...yes. Quite.

SHELLEY: It's all my mother's fault. She just won't stand up to him. Lets him boss her about, like she's an unpaid skivvy. You've seen what she can be like.

The Sicilian Wine Test

BARRY: I can't say I've noticed— *(anything that would...)*

SHELLEY: Oh, Barry, you must have. Last time we were over for dinner. The Smithsons were there too, remember? We'd finished the main course. My mother gets up to clear the table and you move to get up, to help.

BARRY: And she said: "No. I'll look after it. You talk to Dad and Harvey."

SHELLEY: And she pushed down on your shoulders, to keep you in your seat.

BARRY: She did?

SHELLEY: Then she says: "Shelley will help, won't you love?"

BARRY: And you jumped right up!

SHELLEY: I certainly did not.

BARRY: No. But you signaled to your father... *(emulates by inclining his head)* that he should do something.

SHELLEY: Which he chose to ignore.

BARRY: No. Not true. He did push his chair back— *(as though he intended to get up)*

SHELLEY: He always does that when he's finished eating.

BARRY: But your mother signaled to him that he should stay where he was.

(BARRY demonstrates how she signaled.)

SHELLEY: He started into a lengthy discussion—

BARRY: The smoking ban in public buildings.

SHELLEY: Controversial enough to keep him occupied until the sweet was on the table. Typical!

BARRY: You'd think your family was in in the secret service. All that underhand signaling!

(They laugh. Fade lighting to 20%.)

(The lights come up as BARRY *clears the main course from the table and prepares to bring in the sweet.*
SHELLEY *helps, speaking continually.)*

SHELLEY: She does, you know. She leaves me to do everything.

BARRY: This is still about your mother?

SHELLEY: Goes without saying! No, silly. Marjorie Hammond.

BARRY: Ah! President of your Condo Owners' Association.

SHELLEY: You know her?

BARRY: No. You told me about her. Before.

SHELLEY: I did?

BARRY: No matter. Do go on.

SHELLEY: You'd think, when she wants to announce another of her interminable meetings, *she'd* prepare the agenda. But no. Not that woman! Drops scraps of paper into my mail box, each an item for me to put in— *(to make up the agenda)*

BARRY: Well, as you're the secretary—

SHELLEY: Then when I do, and send it for her to check, she moves everything around. All her stuff goes to the top—to be dealt with first.

BARRY: Well, as president, she does have the prerogative to—

SHELLEY: Prerogative? That woman? Pig-headed and self-centered, that's her.

(SHELLEY stands by the table, drinks more wine.)

You'd think she'd know how to run a meeting. Not her! No idea. Well, I guess she does run it, if you consider *controlling* it the same as running it. Everything goes in the direction *she* wants; every decision. And no one—not one of those chicken-hearted condo owners—particularly the men—not *one* of them has the guts to challenge her.

(She sips more wine.)

BARRY: Surely, you could— *(as secretary, ask...)*

SHELLEY: Are you telling me what I should do?

BARRY: No, I just thought you might—

SHELLEY: You're always interrupting.

BARRY: Not intentional, I assure you.

SHELLEY: You and your half-baked opinions!

BARRY: I was only trying to help.

SHELLEY: You know what the trouble is? You don't listen.

BARRY: I hardly think—

SHELLEY: There! You see: you don't think, either!

BARRY: I try my best to—

SHELLEY: You're just like my mother!

BARRY: Your *mother*?

SHELLEY: She never listens. Only when she wants to. The rest of the time she keeps nodding her head and mumbling "uh-huh,"

The Sicilian Wine Test

SHELLEY: *(continuing)* as though she's taking it all in. Just like a machine. Every time I ask her if she remembers... *(what I said to her...)*
BARRY: When have I ever said "uh-huh" to you?
SHELLEY: There! You're doing it again!
BARRY: Doing what?
SHELLEY: Interrupting!
   *(*Slight pause. BARRY *takes a deep breath.)*
BARRY: Can we, perhaps, get back to Marjorie Hammond?
SHELLEY: What's she got to do with it?
BARRY: You were going to tell me—
SHELLEY: She never listens either.
BARRY: *(slight pause)* Ah, I see...
SHELLEY: No, you don't.
   *(*SHELLEY *waits for him to respond;* BARRY *doesn't.)*
   I was going to tell you about Mary Boyce.
BARRY: Mary Boyce?
SHELLEY: You really weren't listening, were you?
BARRY: Uh...sorry. About Mary Boyce...
SHELLEY: The one whose husband sneaked off to South America—Brazil, I think—with that bimbo from number twenty-two. Lives at number fourteen; has an eighteen-month-old baby. Well, at the last meeting she wanted to change the by-laws so she could run a crèche—like a mini-day care—for condo owners with wee kiddies. Wouldn't affect me, of course. Well it might one day, if I get lucky; you never know, do you? *(giggles)* You know what I'd really like? Twins. One of each. Blonde, blue-eyed, like me. Have you got blue eyes?
BARRY: No, not today.
SHELLEY: Oh, Barry! *(giggles)* A complete family in just one go. Just one pregnancy. Get my figure back quickly, and keep it like that. No stretch marks, either. Oh, you should see my sister's stretch marks—Nancy's—she'll never be able to wear a bikini. I wouldn't be seen dead in a one-piece. I mean, with my figure, it wouldn't make sense...
BARRY: To hide it?
SHELLEY: Oh, Barry! You should know! *(giggles)* Oh, I need the washroom. Will you excuse me?

BARRY: Certainly. I'll put out the sweet.
SHELLEY: Which you made yourself!
BARRY: You'll see.
>(SHELLEY *exits. As* BARRY *continues clearing the table and setting new pieces on it, he occasionally stops and speaks to the audience, sometimes crossing to a chair downstage, placing his hands on its back and leaning forward.)*

The Sicilian Wine Test: I doubt you've heard of it. *(holds up the bottle)* I discovered this wine three years ago, purely by accident. I bought a bottle to share with my girlfriend at the time—Freda. Number five, if I remember correctly. The effect was amazing.

(Pause.)

We were having a picnic at the far end of Watrous Beach—a secluded spot on Lake Catrona, Then half way through the afternoon—just at the moment when I thought we'd be getting amorous—Freda's character changed completely. In place of the demure, composed, thoughtful woman I'd been dating for four months, I was besieged by a deluge of words—like a succession of waves breaking on the shore. Freda seemed to have become an opinionated, belligerent woman with a major chip on her shoulder. Full of complaints, just like her father!

(Sound of toilet flushing, offstage.)

That's when I got to thinking. Is this what Freda's going to be like, twenty years down the road? If we were to marry, would I want to be held captive to a woman like that?

(Lights come up on washroom area. SHELLEY *is primping in front of an imaginary mirror—applying lipstick, brushing her hair, etc—facing the audience.* BARRY *continues setting the sweet and coffee cups on the table.)*

(Shelley turns right, looks at her profile in the mirror, places her hands under her breasts, pushes them up slightly, lets them drop [they drop very little], giggles.)

SHELLEY: Not bad. For twenty-nine!
BARRY: *(to audience)* I've used the Sicilian wine test ever since, with singular success. If you can call it success: I'm still single. I've yet to find a partner who can pass the test.

The Sicilian Wine Test

BARRY: *(continuing)* And there've been some delightful women in my life.

SHELLEY: That Barry! *(giggles)* All those women he's had before. None of them could cut the mustard. But this time... That Freda, with her superior airs! Barry doesn't know I knew her. And some of the others. Made a point of finding out about each of them. Just biding my time.

BARRY: For the first four or five months, they'd seem ideal. Reasonably intelligent. Good conversationalists. Good company. And fun, in a comfortable sort of way. Then, just as I began to think "maybe this is the one," annoying habits would start creeping in.

SHELLEY: I think Barry has a fetish about the letter 'A.' All his previous girlfriends, their names ended in 'A.' At least, the ones I know about: Freda, Georgina, Katerina, Miranda. They even turned up in alphabetical order! But I've broken the pattern: Shelley! Hah!

BARRY: Katerina was fine until she decided she wanted to call me "Bar." Said it was short for Barry. Bar? Not in my book. I mean, if a person's got a perfectly good name, then one should use it properly. I remonstrated. Even tried calling her "Kat."

(He holds his hands up in front of him, like cat's paws.)

"Miaow!" But she loved it! Started telling everyone we were "Kat and Bar," like we'd been made by Hershey's.

SHELLEY: Never did get to know much about Marina, except she worked in a milk bar. She didn't last long.

BARRY: Pity about Marina—she was a stunner! But all she wanted to talk about was how she coped with her pets. Cows! Turned out she was a dairy maid, sitting on a three-legged stool, milking by hand! *(he demonstrates)* She insisted on telling me all about mastitis. And milk fever. And how she'd impregnate fertile cows by thrusting her arm in right up to the shoulder. Not much fun for the cow. Or me, for that matter. Put me off my dinner! But, oh, those hands: rough, calloused maybe, but oh so tough, so pliable. Pity.

SHELLEY: *(giggles)* Yeah, I'd like to go one better than my mother: give her something to think about. She only had twin girls—six years before she had me—I'm going to have one of each: a boy and a girl.

SHELLEY: *(continuing)* That'll show her. A complete family all in one go. Yeah, that's what I want: identical twins.

BARRY: *(to audience)* Shelley goes on and on about wanting to have twins. One child would be too many! And just think of the mess that would erupt in the back of my Mini-Cooper. Curled up bits of orange peel. Sticky cookie crumbs. Spilled apple juice. Ugh!

SHELLEY: Barry's car would be too small. So would mine. But we could trade the two of them in for a Volvo. A station wagon. Volvos are safe. Specially for twins. A light blue Volvo, to match their blue eyes. *(giggles)*

(BARRY pulls out his cell phone.)

BARRY: *(talking to himself)* I guess I'd better do it.

(He taps in eight numbers, listens.)

Number four, I think.

(He taps eleven more numbers, looks at his watch, calculates.)

Nine minutes should be about right.

(He taps two more numbers, switches off the cell phone, addresses the audience.)

I hate having to do this. Makes me feel like I'm being brutal. And Shelley'll be *expecting* to stay over. But that's the danger: when I wake up in the morning, after a good night's...sleep...my resolve could well have evaporated. Too risky.

(Slight pause. BARRY puts finishing touches to the table, plus two theater tickets beside Shelley's place. SHELLEY enters, approaches the table.)

Ready for the sweet?

SHELLEY: From T.G.T?

BARRY: Well, I must confess, the meringue shells are. They're too tricky to bake myself. But the peaches are real, not from tins.

SHELLEY: *(sits)* Looks pretty.

BARRY: And I whipped the cream myself.

SHELLEY: From Marina's dairy? Oops! Not appropriate, Shel.

(SHELLEY sees the tickets, picks them up, continues speaking to cover her gaffe.)

What are these?

The Sicilian Wine Test

BARRY: Went down to the Royal today. Picked up two tickets for H.M.S. Pinafore. On the eighth.

SHELLEY: *(examining tickets)* Gilbert and Sullivan?

BARRY: Interested?

SHELLEY: But you like action movies, not old-fashioned stuff like this.

BARRY: It's not a movie, Shelley. You're thinking of Taranta-Ra, Taranta-Ra.

SHELLEY: You *like* Gilbert and Sullivan?

BARRY: Grew to appreciate them. Had to write a paper about them and their strange relationship, at university. They weren't a happy couple. Didn't really get on.

SHELLEY: You mean they were gay?

BARRY: Lord, no. They just didn't always agree. It's a wonder how they came to write all those happy pieces.

SHELLEY: *(mimes, tapping on table with her hand)* Can't stand all that di-da-di-da-di-da-di-da...

*(*BARRY *picks up the rhythm, sings from* H.M.S. Pinafore.*)*

BARRY: When I was a lad I served a term
As office boy to an attorney's firm.

(He pulls SHELLEY *to her feet and swings her around in time with the song.)*

I cleaned the windows and I swept the floor,
And I polished up the handle of the big front door.
I polished up that handle so carefullee
That now I am the Ruler of the Queen's Navee!

SHELLEY: Oh, Barry!

BARRY: Or what about this? *(sings)*

For you're called Little Buttercup, dear Little Buttercup,
Though I could never tell why,
But still you're called Buttercup, poor Little Buttercup,
Sweet Little Buttercup, I ... You!

(Slight pause.)

Not for you?

SHELLEY: Buttercup? Makes me sound yellow. All over yellow!

BARRY: Understood. I'll find a use for them.

(BARRY takes the tickets from SHELLEY, puts them in his shirt pocket.)

BARRY: *(continuing)* Come on, time for the sweet.

(They sit, start the sweet.)

SHELLEY: Very nice.

BARRY: One of my favorites.

(The cell phone rings.)

Excuse me.

(BARRY steps away from the table, opens the phone, looks at the number.)

It's the office. *(into the phone)* Three seven one, six four two eight.

(A male voice can be heard, unintelligible.)

Who?...Oh, security...The alarm's gone off? Can't you switch it off?...Won't stop? Isn't there anyone else you can call?...Philip Hanson?...No answer...Oh...Alright, I'll be there. About thirty minutes...Right.

(He closes the phone, pockets it.)

(to SHELLEY*)* Sorry about that.

SHELLEY: You've got to go?

BARRY: 'Fraid so. Security problem.

(SHELLEY starts gathering her things together.)

No, have your sweet first. And I've made some coffee. Then I'll drive you home. It's on the way.

(Lights dim to 20%, with musical bridge.)

(Lights come up stage right, on Lorraine's dining room. LORRAINE is setting the table, moving things around. There is a small vase of short-stemmed flowers on the table. She is smartly dressed for a home dinner evening: clearly she wants to create a positive impression. She speaks to herself.)

LORRAINE: Dinner's got to be just right.

(She checks off on her fingers.)

Crusty rolls. Local butter—now that's a treat in itself! Avocado half with lemon and paprika. No soup. Then grilled filet mignon. Baked potatoes. Asparagus. Baby carrots. For wine...

The Sicilian Wine Test

(LORRAINE turns to a side table where there are three different red wines. She examines the labels, then selects one.)

LORRAINE: *(continuing)* This one, I think. It will go nicely with the filet. Cap the meal with crème brûlée and cappuccino. Not bad. He'll approve, I'm sure.

(She starts rearranging the flowers, hums.)

(Lights come up on stage left, where BARRY is dressing in a comfortable but stylish outfit. His jacket is hanging over the back of a dining chair downstage, with the seat facing upstage. When he talks to the audience, he straddles the chair and leans forward, over its back, to address them. Between his 'audience-talks' he gradually finishes dressing. LORRAINE continues arranging the table.)

(BARRY glances across at LORRAINE, turns to the audience.)

BARRY: That's Lorraine, in her little house on Oak Street. Tonight she's doing the cooking.

(He leans over and pats his jacket pocket.)

And it's going to be a special occasion. Lorraine and I, we've been seeing each other for four months now. We get on really well.

(LORRAINE stands, one hand to her chin, the other cupping the first hand's elbow, studies the table, shakes her head doubtfully.)

LORRAINE: N-o-o. Too formal. Needs to be a little more subtle. More laid-back.

(She refolds the napkins, moves the flowers to one side of the table.)

BARRY: *(to the audience)* Look: I don't want you to think I just ditched Shelley. Not at all. I just eased back gently, saw her less. I'd phone her and suggest we'd meet for dinner or a movie, but I'd set it for a night when she already had something else on— used my network to find out—until she began to think she was the one who was pulling away.

LORRAINE: *(studies table)* Yes. That's better.

(LORRAINE adjust the napkins. Fade lights on her room.)

(BARRY's cell phone rings.)

BARRY: Barry here.

(Lights come up far stage right. SHELLEY *steps in front of the curtain and speaks animatedly into her cell phone.)*

SHELLEY: Hi, Barry.

BARRY: Oh! Shelley?

SHELLEY: How're you doing?

BARRY: *(disconcerted)* Oh, fine. Fine. How about you?

SHELLEY: Lorraine, too?

BARRY: How did you know about—

SHELLEY: Oh, Barry. You're so predictable! *(bubbling with excitement)* I've got such a surprise for you!

BARRY: *(cautious)* You have?

SHELLEY: You know I'm married now?

BARRY: Yes. I'd heard.

SHELLEY: To Martin. The accountant. You introduced me to him.

BARRY: Blonde, blue-eyed Martin?

SHELLEY: Right!

BARRY: Made to order, I should think.

SHELLEY: Oh, Barry! I've just come back from the clinic.

BARRY: Martin's sick?

SHELLEY: Oh, no. Nothing like that.

BARRY: It's you, then?

SHELLEY: Well, in a way. *(giggles)* I wanted you to be the first to know.

BARRY: To know? To know what?

SHELLEY: Would you believe…already I'm pregnant!

BARRY: O-o-h!

SHELLEY: They did a scan of some sort. Looks like it's twins!

BARRY: Oh, my lord. Does Martin know?

SHELLEY: I'll tell him when he gets home. But first I wanted you to know. And my mother. I'll phone her next. She'll have kittens! Bye….

(Lights fade out on SHELLEY. BARRY *closes his phone.)*

BARRY: Whew! They'd just better be blonde. And blue-eyed.

The Sicilian Wine Test

(BARRY sits, straddles chair, turns to the audience.)

With Lorraine, it's been so different. She has much more refined tastes. She *liked* H.M.S. Pinafore. Likes the ballet. Opera too. And having a conversation with her, she talks with knowledge and authority. We're a good match. There's so much she knows, can talk about. Well, I mean, she's a lawyer. A corporate lawyer.

(He looks at his watch.)

Time, I think...

(He pulls on his jacket, reaches into the pocket, pulls out and opens a ring box, gazes at it, turns to the audience.)

Have you guessed? Lorraine actually *passed* the Sicilian wine test. Not once, but twice! Just in case the first bottle wasn't fully potent. Not a step wrong; not a word out of place. Both times. What a woman!

(He pockets the ring box, exits. Fade to blackout stage left.)

(Sound of doorbell or buzzer. Lights up on Lorraine's dining area. LORRAINE is inserting an ear ring.)

LORRAINE: *(calls)* Barry?

BARRY: *(v.o.)* It's me!

LORRAINE: Should be "I," I think. "It is I." Have you got your key?

BARRY: *(v.o.)* Yes.

LORRAINE: Let yourself in, will you.

(Sound of key in lock as LORRAINE puts in the second ear ring. Enter BARRY carrying a large, elegant bunch of long-stemmed flowers. He holds them out to Lorraine with a mock bow.)

Oh, Barry. Thank you. Really, you shouldn't.

BARRY: You always say that.

LORRAINE: Oh, they're lovely.

(They exchange a kiss.)

I'll put them in water.

(LORRAINE exits to kitchen. BARRY picks up a leather photograph holder.)

BARRY: *(calls)* You've framed the pictures from our holiday at Falcon Lake.

LORRAINE: *(v.o.)* Yes. The four I like best.

BARRY: You splashing me on the beach!

LORRAINE: *(v.o.)* You looked like a wet spaniel!

BARRY: That water was bloody cold!

LORRAINE: *(v.o.)* You were determined not to let it show.

(LORRAINE enters and places the flowers on the table; they are now in a tall vase. She removes the small vase and places it on a side table. She stands beside BARRY, an arm around his waist, looks at the pictures.)

LORRAINE: *(continuing)* You weren't all that keen, were you, on going up there?

BARRY: I admit, three days beside what I considered to be a really remote lake, with little or no amenities…

LORRAINE: But you did enjoy it?

BARRY: Oh, yes. Very much.

(They kiss.)

LORRAINE: Take off your jacket. Throw it on my bed.

BARRY: No. *(pats ring pocket)* I'll just hang it over the back of my chair. *(looks at the table)* Which is mine?

LORRAINE: The one with an envelope beside the place setting.

BARRY: *(hangs up his jacket)* What's in the envelope?

LORRAINE: Open it.

(LORRAINE indicates he should sit. He does so and she follows suit.)

(BARRY opens the envelope.)

BARRY: Oh, you are a dear! Tickets for Pirates of Penzance. Next month. Row F, seats 18 and 19.

LORRAINE: Dead center.

BARRY: The box office only opened today.

LORRAINE: I wanted to surprise you.

(BARRY reaches across the table, around the vase, takes her hand; they exchange affectionate smiles.)

BARRY: That was so thoughtful.

LORRAINE: Glad you like it. *(slight pause)* Dig in. Bon appetit!

(As they talk, they have to look around the flowers, or crane upwards to see each other.)

The Sicilian Wine Test

BARRY: I can't remember anyone—ever—doing anything like that. Buying tickets for me.

LORRAINE: Then we'll have to do it again. *(slight pause, as they eat)* They're doing Yeoman of the Guard in November. I saw a poster in the lobby.

BARRY: Yeoman? No, I'd rather not.

LORRAINE: It's the best they did!

BARRY: Too depressing.

LORRAINE: The nearest they came to grand opera.

BARRY: Exactly! *(recites harshly)*
> The screw may twist and the rack may turn,
> And men may bleed and men may burn.

LORRAINE: Dame Carruthers. See, you do know the lines!

BARRY: I had to study it. At university. Write a paper about it. That was enough.

LORRAINE: Before the curtain goes up, you can *hear* the sound of a spinning wheel, right in the music. Then, as the curtain rises, there the wheel is, center stage, with Phoebe Merryll sitting beside it, singing: *(recites)*
> When maiden loves, she sits and sighs,
> She wanders to and fro;
> Unbidden tear-drops fill her eyes,
> And to all questions she replies
> With a sad 'heigh-ho!'

BARRY: Too plaintive for me.

LORRAINE: And Yeoman has the finest ballad in all of the operettas. It's sung by Colonel Fairfax, after he's been sentenced to death.

BARRY: Morbid.

LORRAINE: *(recites)*
> Is life a boon?
> If so, it must befall
> That death, whene'er he call,
> Must call too soon.

BARRY: Hardly a *comic* opera!

LORRAINE: It's the only G & S operetta with a real heart.

BARRY: Yeah, Jack Point's. And his girlfriend breaks it for him.
LORRAINE: Give me time. I'll persuade you.
(BARRY quickly changes the subject; refers to the meal they are eating.)
BARRY: Interesting flavor.
LORRAINE: Thank you. My grandmother's recipe.
BARRY: Which you're not about to share?
LORRAINE: Right. Will you pour more wine?
BARRY: Be happy to!
(BARRY pours.)
LORRAINE: Easy for me. I've got an early start tomorrow.
BARRY: In court?
LORRAINE: In Brandon.
BARRY: But you can't talk about it.
LORRAINE: No.
BARRY: You're driving?
LORRAINE: Start at six.
BARRY: Back the same day?
LORRAINE: Depends. More likely two or three days.
BARRY: Pity. There's a reception I'd like to take you to on Saturday.
(Fade to 20%. When lights come up, LORRAINE is placing plates with vegetables on the table. Her wine glass is half full, Barry's is nearly empty. BARRY enters, carrying a platter with two small, deep steaks and two baked potatoes on it; he holds a spatula and an oven mitt in the other hand. He uses the spatula to place the steaks on their plates and the mitt to place the potatoes.)
LORRAINE: The smaller one for me.
BARRY: Well done, right?
LORRAINE: Thanks.
BARRY: *(lifting a steak onto his plate)* And one medium rare.
(BARRY carries the platter and utensils into the kitchen. He returns as LORRAINE cuts into her steak and holds up a piece on her fork.)
LORRAINE: Just right.
BARRY: Oh, good. *(he cuts into his steak)* From T.G.T.?

The Sicilian Wine Test

LORRAINE: *(laughs, echoes Barry)* You always say that! But, yes.

BARRY: I thought as much. *(slight pause)* Have you thought about...oh, these flowers. I wish I could see you better.

LORRAINE: It's like looking through an Amazonian jungle.

BARRY: Here, I'll move them.

(While still seated, BARRY lifts the vase to the upstage side of the table; it's top-heavy, waves about, knocks over his wine glass.)

Ouch!

(They both jump up. LORRAINE runs into the kitchen, returns with a cloth, dabs at the table. BARRY is still holding the vase.)

LORRAINE: No harm done. Good thing your glass was nearly empty.

BARRY: Red wine on a cream table cloth...

LORRAINE: Oh, put them down, Barry!

(BARRY places the vase on the upstage edge of the table. They re-sit, but still have to peer around the flowers.)

BARRY: Some stain you'll have. Sorry.

LORRAINE: Don't fuss about it. I've got a better idea.

(LORRAINE hands BARRY the wine bottle, then lifts the vase onto the floor, beside the table. He refills his glass.)

I hate to hide your flowers, but at the moment I prefer to see you.

BARRY: *(raising his glass in a toast)* And me, you!

(Pause while they eat. During the ensuing conversation, BARRY drinks and again refills his glass.)

Have you recorded your fuel consumption yet? On your Porsche?

LORRAINE: I've only had to fill it twice. It's too soon.

BARRY: You know how to make the calculation?

LORRAINE: Of course.

BARRY: You divide the distance you've travelled since the last fill, into the amount of gas you've just put in. Make sure the tank is completely full each time. Then—

LORRAINE: Barry, I—

BARRY: Then multiply by one hundred. For example, if you've driven 372 miles, or kilometers, since your last fill—
LORRAINE: *Barry!*
BARRY: Huh?
LORRAINE: I don't really care what mileage I'm getting.
BARRY: Oh, you should.
LORRAINE: I just want to enjoy driving my car, not turn it into a mathematical exercise.
BARRY: But that's half the fun of driving. Knowing how well you're achieving a good R.O.I...Return on investment.
LORRAINE: I know what R.O.I. means.
BARRY: Yes. Of course...The R.O.I. on the gas you're buying.
LORRAINE: Barry! It's all right for you, calculating the fuel consumption you get with your Mini-Cooper. It just goes with the territory.
BARRY: But, as a lawyer, don't you need factual evidence to support the case you're presenting?
LORRAINE: When will I ever have my car in court?
BARRY: Oh, I can see it:
(BARRY jumps up, acts the following out.)
You drive in through those big double doors and brake to a stop. Right in the center of the court, in that triangle between the judge, the prosecution and the defense. Then you push the button on the dash—the one that automatically opens the trunk and swallows up the folding roof.
(With his hands he demonstrates the trunk opening. He re-sits.)
When you appear, sitting elegantly, intelligently, upright in the driver's seat—fully in control of the situation—you turn to the judge, and the jury, and you announce: "I just want to demonstrate, your honor, that in presenting my client's case, I am in no way concealing any of the information I have gathered. In fact, it's an open-and-shut case!"
LORRAINE: *(laughs)* Barry! You have such a warped sense of humor.
BARRY: It'd confound the opposition. Create quite an impression.
LORRAINE: But hardly have the right effect.

The Sicilian Wine Test

BARRY: *(laughs)* True. *(slight pause)* But I know a better use for your Porsche.

LORRAINE: I need a better use?

BARRY: We could enter it in the next car rally.

LORRAINE: I've never taken part in a—

BARRY: Oh, I can show you.

LORRAINE: *(half rises)* I'll get a map.

BARRY: No. That'll come later. You don't know where you're going before you get there. Just the starting point. Usually it's at Southport.

LORRAINE: Clear, so far.

BARRY: Then, at the appointed start time, you're given a folder that identifies your finishing point—let's say it's the Yacht Club at Brooks Beach—and the time you're supposed to get there. To the second. In ten-second increments.

LORRAINE: Sounds straightforward enough.

BARRY: Oh, no. You haven't got the picture yet. There are three or four intermediary check points, each with a set arrival time—like the Marine Museum at Weybridge and the Motorways station at Confusion Corner. And there's a time-keeper at each, recording your arrival time.

LORRAINE: How many of you take part? I mean, how many cars?

BARRY: Usually between twenty and thirty.

LORRAINE: Isn't that dangerous? All those drivers fighting to get to each check point—and Brooks Beach—at exactly the same time?

BARRY: Oh, no, no, no. *(he sounds as though he is 'putting her down')* We each start at a different time, at three-minute intervals.

LORRAINE: Then how can it be a race?

BARRY: It's not *meant* to be a race! Just a test of skill. Each car's schedule is worked out as elapsed time from the time the car rolls away from Southport. It's part of the navigator's job. Does *that* make sense to you?

LORRAINE: Yes, Now it does.

BARRY: Are you game?

LORRAINE: Huh?

BARRY: *(slowly)* Do you want to take part?

LORRAINE: Depends when.

BARRY: About three weeks, Sunday the twenty-fourth.

LORRAINE: I wouldn't mind.

BARRY: We'll use your Porsche, with its built-in computerized distance and speed calculator. It would make navigation and timing so much simpler for you, than in my car. And there's more room for—

LORRAINE: Do I have to navigate *and* drive? Won't you do the navigating?

BARRY: Oh, no. I'll be doing the driving.

LORRAINE: You'll be doing the driving?

BARRY: Of course.

LORRAINE: In my car?

BARRY: It's traditional: the man always drives. You'll see.

(Slight pause.)

LORRAINE: Really? *(slight pause)* What if two women choose to enter as a team, in the same car?

BARRY: Well...one of them has to drive. Doesn't happen often.

LORRAINE: Then why can't I?

BARRY: I don't want to break with tradition.

LORRAINE: What you mean is, you don't want to be seen sitting in the passenger seat, beside a woman doing the driving!

BARRY: No, it's not that. It's just that I'm the better driver.

LORRAINE: On what grounds?

BARRY: I've got rally experience. You haven't.

LORRAINE: But, really, isn't accurate navigation the key? So you get the timing right?

BARRY: Nothing to it.

LORRAINE: Because you work with numbers every day. I work with words.

BARRY: We've got three weeks. We'll do a practice run. Two if necessary.

LORRAINE: In my car?

(BARRY is blithely unaware of the irony in LORRAINE's voice.)

BARRY: Preferably.

LORRAINE: And you driving.

BARRY: Of course. *(slight pause)* You will come?

LORRAINE: I'll think about it. *(glances at his plate)* Finished?

BARRY: Oh, yes! Thank you. Excellent filet.

LORRAINE: Glad you liked it. *(piles the two big plates together)* I'll bring out the dessert.

(LORRAINE starts gathering up the side plates and vegetable dishes.)

BARRY: Here, I'll help you.

LORRAINE: *(a little cool)* No, Barry, thank you. I can manage.

(Awkward pause.)

BARRY: Then, if you'll excuse me, I'll just use your washroom.

LORRAINE: Right...

(LORRAINE carries the dishes toward the kitchen. BARRY calls after her.)

BARRY: Umm...I've got a little...umm...surprise for you.

(LORRAINE turns back, faces him.)

LORRAINE: Oh?

BARRY: Would you like it before or after the dessert?

LORRAINE: Barry, that's up to you.

BARRY: No, no. Your choice.

LORRAINE: *(slight exasperated sigh)* Before, I should think. Now you've sparked my interest.

(LORRAINE exits into the kitchen. BARRY picks up his jacket, lays it over his shoulder, exits.)

(NOTE: Although the remainder of the scene has much humor integrated into it, it's important for the actors to play it with empathy and sympathy for each other.)

(LORRAINE returns with a tray, places more things on it, carries it out, brings in a change of items, brushes the table. As she does this she occasionally pauses to talk to the audience.)

He thinks I don't know what the surprise is.

(She holds her hand up with thumb and forefinger spaced the size of the box.)

I saw the bulge in his jacket pocket. *(shrugs, laughs)* And I can tell by his manner. Sometimes he can be so transparent.

(She carries dishes out, returns, spruces up the table.)

LORRAINE: *(continuing)* So, what are my options? Say "Yes?"...Say "No?"...Well, "No thanks" would be nicer. Or: "Thank you, but give me time to think about it." *(shakes her head.)* No. A verdict should come immediately after all the evidence has been presented. Never keep the accused on tenterhooks. *(light laugh)* The Accused? Hardly!...The Appellant. That's more like it.

(Sound of toilet flushing.)

Oh, dear. Now I *have* to make a decision. Before he comes back in.

(BARRY enters the washroom downstage center, his jacket now on. He stands in front of an imaginary mirror, facing the audience. He mimes washing his hands, then reaches into an inside pocket of his jacket, pulls out a comb and carefully combs his hair.)

My heart says "Yes, go ahead."...We would make a good couple. But my legal mind seems to be ringing a warning bell: "Hold it now! Think of the consequences. Does what you've just seen constitute a good basis on which to...?" *(shakes her head; pause)*

I wonder how he'll do it? *(chuckles)* Bow? Then take my hand and advance the ring toward it?

(BARRY has pulled the ring box out, opens it, steps back, faces stage right, holds it forward with his right hand, makes a small bow.)

BARRY: Lorraine: Will you marry me?

(BARRY looks at himself in the mirror, shakes his head in a negative gesture.)

LORRAINE: Or will he go down on bended knee? *(laughs)* No, not Barry.

(BARRY goes down on one knee facing stage right, holds the ring box out in front of him.)

BARRY: Lorraine Will you do me the honor of joining me in marriage?

LORRAINE: *(musing, to herself)* "Damn!, Damn!, Damn!, Damn!" *(laughs)* Just like 'Enry 'Iggins! *(sings quietly)*

"I've grown accustomed to his face...
    his smile, his frowns,

The Sicilian Wine Test

LORRAINE: *(continues singing)*
    his ups, his downs, are second nature to me now."
Oh, dear.
(BARRY dusts off his clothes, re-combs his hair, takes a last look in the mirror and exits. Lights fade on the washroom area.)
(LORRAINE picks up the wine bottle, inspects its label, speaks to the bottle.)
You've done your work well, my friend. Too well, I fear.
(LORRAINE holds the bottle close to her chest.)
(Enter BARRY, ring box semi-concealed in his hand. He stands in front of her.)
BARRY: Are you ready, Lorraine? For the surprise?
LORRAINE: Oh, Barry. Are you?
(Slight pause. LORRAINE hands the bottle to him.)
BARRY: What's this? *(reads)* "Sicilian Creative Rosé." *(brief pause)* Have you been…? Did you…?
LORRAINE: *(nods)* Just as you did.
BARRY: You mean… We *both* did it?
(LORRAINE nods again.)
And I thought I was…you're not saying I didn't pass?
(Another nod from LORRAINE.)
Oh, how could you?
(He thrusts the bottle back at her, mildly angered.)
That's not playing fair!
LORRAINE: Fair? *I'm* not playing fair?
BARRY: I thought tonight… *(holds up the ring box)* What a caper!
LORRAINE: I'm sorry, Barry. I didn't— *(want to hurt you)*
BARRY: Oh, how could you! Just when I was about to…
(He trails off, now sharply angry)
LORRAINE: Propose?
BARRY: What does it look like?
(He thrusts the ring box into his pocket.)
LORRAINE: I would rather— *(not have had to do this)*
BARRY: Oh, forget it!
(BARRY moves toward the door.)

LORRAINE: Barry!
> (BARRY *stops, slowly turns back to face* LORRAINE. *There is the equivalent of 'a pregnant pause,' then* BARRY *erupts into an uncontrolled giggle.)*
> I didn't want to hurt you.

BARRY: You didn't want to….
> (BARRY'S *giggle erupts into an outright laugh.)*
> You didn't want to…?
> (BARRY*'s laughter is now uncontrolled.* LORRAINE *looks at him in amazement. Pause. Then she, too, starts to laugh.)*
> *(They step toward each other, their laughter prolonged and hearty, cling to each other laughing helplessly, the bottle squeezed between them. They pull apart, hold each other at arm's length, still erupting into bursts of milder laughter. Lorraine places the bottle on the table, reaches around* BARRY *and pulls the ring box from his jacket pocket.)*

LORRAINE: This is the surprise?
> (BARRY *nods, but with a laugh.)*
> Show it to me.

BARRY: Now? After you've…

LORRAINE: *(with a laugh)* Oh, go on!
> *(He lifts out the ring, holds it toward her.)*

BARRY: Lorraine: will you…? *(he waits)*
> (LORRAINE *steps slightly back, nods, smiles.)*
> You will?
> (LORRAINE *gives another nod [a slow one], then crosses her arms in front of her chest.)*

LORRAINE: But only if I do the driving!
> *(Slight pause.* BARRY *nods resignedly. They both laugh.)*
> *(Freeze for two seconds, then blackout.)*

CURTAIN

The Sicilian Wine Test

Character Descriptions

Barry

At age 37, Barry is senior accountant with a small chain of retail bookshops/stationers. He oversees all accounting operations and is highly regarded for his strong, intuitive financial control and ability to foresee trends and opportunities.

Is Barry attracted to the Arts? He thinks he is—it goes with his image—but in effect his view is narrow. He has done some research into the history of the Gilbert and Sullivan operettas as part of a language arts course he took at university, and now considers himself a qualified and knowledgeable adviser. Yet in reality his view is limited.

Although essentially a shy man who values his personal privacy, Barry intentionally presents a mildly gregarious front to his friends and acquaintances, retreating behind it—and the wheel of his Mini-Cooper—when he feels he needs his own space.

He is not yet married, partly because he values that space. When he marries, he rationalizes, it must be with someone who can relate to him long-term and in a way that suits *him* as the years lengthen. So he has stepped carefully, not letting his guard down.

He allows each relationship to evolve slowly, being genuine about his liking for each woman, yet taking the steps gradually, watching and waiting to see if the woman displays any traits that might forecast a person he would not want to live with permanently. He has come close several times, but not once has he found the right woman for him, until Lorraine appears on his horizon.

Lorraine

Lorraine is a lawyer, age 36. Well groomed, is polished in her manner, confident in her actions, and very much 'aware' of herself, the people around her, and where and how she fits into the society in which she works and lives.

She likes Barry very much, yet she won't yet permit herself to seriously consider letting their affair develop into a long-term permanent relationship. (She would admit that 'likes' probably isn't strong enough: it could well be 'loves.') She admires his confidence, his seeming lack of 'pushiness,' the ease and gentleness with which he has allowed their friendship to evolve. But, like

Barry himself, she hesitates to commit herself: the lawyer in her makeup encourages her to look at all angles, to consider all possibilities, before making a firm judgment.

Her academic strengths, apart from her strong degrees in law, are in history and language studies: she is fluent in French and Italian, and is currently studying Spanish. She likes to travel but has done less than she would like.

Lorraine has had only one in-depth previous relationship, when she first graduated, with an electrician who also was a rugby player. She pulled out when she grew tired of the stream of rugby players Robert brought home for a meal and then invited them to stay on for the weekend.

Lorraine loves an eclectic range of music from Mendelssohn to Gershwin, and also has a penchant for watching good drama, on stage, on film, or on television. She hates action movies loaded with shooting and chase scenes, and isn't particularly interested in musicals (with the exception of *Les Miserables*, in which she feels the characters develop well as the play progresses).

She enjoys cooking, particularly creating Italian and Greek dishes. She does not have time to read a lot, but when she chooses fiction it's by authors such as A. S. Byatt, Alice Munro, and Margaret Atwood.

Shelley

On first appearance people tend to think of 32-year-old Shelley as a 'dumb blonde', for she is naturally very blonde and voluptuously built. Yet Barry knows that her outside appearance conceals a composed, efficient person who is fun to be with. She is a customer accounts supervisor for a telephone company.

Shelley likes Barry, partly because of the kind of person he is and partly because he intrigues her: whereas most men are drawn to her like a moth to a candle and soon burn their wings, in their early days Barry consistently treated her with respect, almost in a friendly but businesslike way. Now that they are more intimate, she likes the warm way in which he relates to her.

Her relationship with her older twin sisters is pleasant, although she is not particularly close to them. That they were a twin has created a strong bond between them that Shelley has always felt she could never breach. They have both married successful professional people and have settled into what Shelley considers rather a dull routine life.

Shelley holds strong opinions about her family, about herself, and about other people. When incensed or outraged, she can be headstrong, forthright and vocal, although sometimes her opinions are based on inadequate research. When challenged, she can argue dogmatically that her view is correct.

She has not married previously, but has had several close relationships each of which, although she does not admit it, foundered when her expectations about her partner were too high or her partner tired of hearing her defend some inaccurate opinions. In that sense she could be a social embarrassment, particularly when she has had too much to drink.

Production Notes

The three characters in this play may have strange ideas, or display traits we personally dislike, yet they still are essentially likeable. This is particularly true of Barry who, although he may have an unusual approach to finding the 'right' woman, is still believable.

We see Shelley as a happy person who initially makes us feel she would be a good mate for Barry. Even when she displays traits we suspect will cause him to turn away from her, we tend to feel sorrier for her than for him.

Although Lorraine's efficiency and seeming professional level may make us feel she is a less suitable choice for Barry, we accept her more readily when Barry becomes officious and over-opinionated.

At the closing moments of the play, the ability for Barry and Lorraine to laugh at—and with—each other in an infectious way becomes an essential component. The audience giggles in empathy with them, and then laughs outright when Lorraine crosses her arms across her chest and in the very last line announces that, yes, she will marry him, "but only if I do the driving."

The reference at the start of the play to 'T.G.T.' (a purveyor of high-quality foods known as The Governor's Table), can be changed to a local food purveyor that fits the same category, with which the audience will readily identify. Similarly, the start, intermediary, and finish locations of the car rally that Barry describes to Lorraine can be changed to locations within a suitable range of the production site.

From personal experience I recommend having two stage managers, not only to enable a quick change between the two sets (Barry's and Lorraine's dining areas), but also to hand out the different parts of each meal as the two scenes progress.

Play No. 6

Just a Two-cent Stamp

Synopsis

Gareth wants to buy a two-cent stamp, but confuses the salesperson and annoys the next customer by insisting that a government-imposed technicality means he is not obliged to pay.

Rationale

In February 2013, the Canadian Government abolished the penny coin, so that now the five-cent coin (the nickel) is the lowest denomination in the country's coinage.

Because add-on federal and provincial taxes create purchase prices that can still end with a penny, such as 27 or 53 cents, the Government concurrently established a guideline to fit in with the non-penny coinage:

- If the final cost ends in 1, 2, 6 or 7 cents, the purchase price is *reduced* so that it ends in 0 or 5 cents (in other words, the seller absorbs the difference).

- If the final cost ends in 3, 4, 8 or 9 cents, the purchase price is *increased* so that it ends in 5 or 0, and the purchaser pays the slightly higher difference.

I realized this new way of paying had created the potential for a humorous play, particularly as the lowest-denomination coin is being dropped from circulation by more and more countries. But first I had to test the idea. So I ventured into my local post office, asked for a two-cent stamp, then surprised the clerk by asking whether I really had to pay for it.

When I explained about the play, she—now intrigued—searched the postal handbook. She found the situation simply had not been addressed. (It since has: one has to pay five cents to buy even a one-cent stamp!)

History

I wrote the play as an entry into the 2013 Pint-size Play competition in the UK. Pint-size Plays are intended primarily for presentation as brief and usually light entertainment in an informal setting such as a pub or community club, where a table and a few chairs are moved aside to provide a small performance area. Normally there is no platform or special lighting.

Consequently, the primary guidelines for writers who venture into this relatively new domain comprise
- a maximum length of 10 minutes,
- no more than 3 characters, and
- a very basic set.

Characters

There are three members in the cast:

Gareth, 50, an impatient customer.

Lee-Anne, 25, a postal clerk.

Dan, 35, a patient customer.

There is more information about the characters on page 238.

The Set

A table representing a post office counter in a retail outlet faces stage left. On it there is an iPad or laptop computer to simulate the screen of a cash register. On the downstage end of the counter there is a 12 x 10 inch (30 x 25 millimeters) raised platform representing a weigh scale; on the upstage end there is a folder with stamps in it.

Lee-Anne is behind the counter and faces stage left when addressing customers. Customers approach from stage left and face stage right when addressing Lee-Anne. It is exactly 12:02 p.m.

The Props

Each character has several props:
- In his pockets, Gareth has a pocket watch on a strap or chain, a five-cent coin, a credit card, and an approximately 8-inch wide by 6-inch high envelope (20 x 15 millimeters) with a thick birthday card in it. The envelope has been covered on front and back with 92 two-cent stamps, with a space in the

middle of the front on which an address has been written. (The envelope, card and affixed stamps together weigh just over 30 grams.) There is an open space for just one more stamp.

- Lee-Anne has a two-cent stamp, a 5-cent stamp, and two 50-stamp sheets of 2-cent stamps in a folder on the counter.
- Dan is carrying a 9 x 12 inch envelope with several sheets of paper inside it; the envelope is addressed but does not carry a stamp. In his pocket he carries change and, particularly, a five-cent coin.

The Production Notes on page 238 present further ideas on preparing the envelope Gareth carries.

Approximate Length: 9 to 10 minutes

Some Script Guidelines

Throughout the script, two symbols are used occasionally at the end of a piece of dialogue to indicate how the sentence ends:

- ... An ellipsis at the end of a statement means the speaker just trails off and leaves his or her thought hanging in the air (possibly accompanied by a shrug).
- — A dash at the end of a statement means the speaker is interrupted by the next speaker, so that the first speaker's statement is incomplete. Sometimes there is an italicized continuation of the statement *(within brackets)* immediately following the dash, to help the actor sense where the sentence was going.

v.o. Means that the words are spoken by someone off-stage.

Script: *Just a Two-cent Stamp*

© 2013, Ron Blicq

(At rise, LEE-ANNE is punching numbers into the cash register screen. GARETH enters stage left and approaches the counter. LEE-ANNE does not hear or see him, so he taps on the counter. She looks up, slightly startled.)

LEE-ANNE: Oh!...Hi.

(GARETH raises a caustic eyebrow.)

Uh...well, good morning, then.

GARETH: Afternoon, I think.

(GARETH reaches into his pocket and pulls out a pocket watch on a cord or chain, consults it.)

Twelve - O - Two, exactly. Atomic watch. Always correct. To the nanosecond.

LEE-ANNE: *(irony)* Cool.

GARETH: Very expensive.

LEE-ANNE: Which is why you keep it on a chain?

GARETH: *(irony)* Sharp, eh? *(pockets the watch)*

LEE-ANNE: So...how can I help you? *(giggles)* In atomic time.

GARETH: One two-cent stamp, please.

LEE-ANNE: One? Just one?

GARETH: That's what I asked for.

(LEE-ANNE searches the handbook for the stamp.)

(DAN enters hurriedly from stage left, crosses to the counter, stands behind GARETH, and waves an envelope toward LEE-ANNE.)

DAN: Has the noon pick-up gone yet, Lee?

LEE-ANNE: Oh, hi Dan.

(She steps back from the counter, looks toward upstage.)

No, you're still in time. The usual?

DAN: Sure.

GARETH: *(to DAN)* Would you mind?

DAN: Got to get this away. *(waves the envelope in front of Gareth)*

GARETH: All in good time. *(to LEE-ANNE)* Well...?

(LEE-ANNE continues searching.)

Just a Two-cent Stamp

One two-cent stamp shouldn't be all that difficult— *(to find)*
LEE-ANNE: I don't often get asked for...Ah: here's one!
(LEE-ANNE holds up the stamp and hands it to GARETH, who inspects it. He then starts walking away, to downstage left.)
GARETH: *(to DAN, with irony)* Now you two can get on.
(As GARETH nears the exit, LEE-ANNE shouts after him.)
LEE-ANNE: Hey, sir! You haven't paid!
GARETH: *(turning back, but not approaching)* I don't have to pay.
LEE-ANNE: I don't give out free stamps!
GARETH: You can't charge me for a one-cent or a two-cent stamp, purchased on its own.
LEE-ANNE: Of course I can: I have to.
GARETH: No, you're wrong there. Not paying is perfectly legal.
LEE-ANNE: You have to pay for every stamp you buy.
GARETH: You haven't read the guidelines, have you?
LEE-ANNE: I know my job. I've been trained.
GARETH: The government has mandated that—
LEE-ANNE: I don't know what you're talking about!
(GARETH approaches the counter; DAN steps back.)
GARETH: Look, young lady: there aren't any more pennies in circulation in Canada. Right?
LEE-ANNE: Y-e-s...I mean no, there aren't.
GARETH: So the smallest coin in our currency is the nickel: the five-cent piece. *(he holds a five-cent coin up in front of her)*
LEE-ANNE: Yes, I know.
GARETH: Which means you can only sell something for a price that ends in a zero or five cents.
DAN: Oh, get on with it man!
GARETH: So if the price of an item ends in a three or a four...
LEE-ANNE: You move the price *up,* to end as five.
GARETH: Sharp! So if I were to buy a 23-cent stamp, I would have to pay 25 cents.
LEE-ANNE: That's the rule.
GARETH: Ah...the rule!
DAN: And if you buy a 22-cent stamp, you pay only 20 cents.

LEE-ANNE: Yeah, yeah...I know.

GARETH: Which means, if I buy a 2-cent stamp, I don't have to pay.

LEE-ANNE: No, no. It doesn't work like that!

GARETH: Then how does it work?

DAN: I think he's got you there, Lee.

LEE-ANNE: *(flustered)* No. It can't be...The book doesn't say—

GARETH: Alright...alright! Let's change the premise—

DAN: N-o-o! *(waves his envelope)* Not now, please!

GARETH: *(to* LEE-ANNE*)* I'll change my order. I'll have a seven-cent stamp.

LEE-ANNE: *Seven* cents?

GARETH: That's what I said.

LEE-ANNE: There isn't a seven-cent stamp.

GARETH: Then give me a five and a two.

LEE-ANNE: You already have a two-cent stamp.

GARETH: Absolutely.

*(*LEE-ANNE *searches for a five-cent stamp and pushes it toward* GARETH.*)*

Ring it up then.

*(*LEE-ANNE *touches the computer screen.)*

LEE-ANNE: Okay...that's seven cents, which moves down to five cents.

GARETH: Quite correct. I pay five cents

LEE-ANNE: Yes.

GARETH: Which means my two-cent stamp is free!

LEE-ANNE: In that sense, I guess...

GARETH: There is no other sense.

DAN: Oh, get on with it! Just give her the money!

GARETH: Ah...yes...

*(*GARETH *takes out his wallet, extracts a credit card, and holds the card up for* LEE-ANNE *to take. She does not take it.)*

LEE-ANNE: A credit card! You can't pay with that!

GARETH: Of course I can.

LEE-ANNE: Not for five cents!

GARETH: It's legal tender.

Just a Two-cent Stamp

LEE-ANNE: Not for such a small amount.

GARETH: I beg to differ.

DAN: Oh, for God's sake...!

GARETH: *(to* DAN*)* I want to make a point. This young lady doesn't seem to understand—

*(*DAN *has pulled coins from his pocket and holds a five cent coin out to* LEE-ANNE.*)*

DAN: Take it, Lee!

GARETH: *(brushes* DAN*'s hand aside)* I'm perfectly capable of paying—

DAN: Then *do* it!

GARETH: Without your interruptions, this young lady and I would have finished our transaction by now.

*(*DAN *throws his hands up in exasperation and tosses his five-cent coin onto the counter.* GARETH *holds his hand up toward* LEE-ANNE.*)*

Just ignore that!

*(*GARETH *reaches into his pocket, pulls out a five-cent coin, and places it on the counter.)*

Paid in full, I believe.

*(*GARETH *takes a heavily over-stamped envelope from his pocket, sticks the two-cent stamp on the one remaining space.* LEE-ANNE *looks at it with an amazed expression.)*

I assume this will now catch the noon post?

LEE-ANNE: What is it?

GARETH: A letter.

LEE-ANNE: All those stamps...!

GARETH: It's the correct amount. I've counted them. Twice.

LEE-ANNE: How much is it?

GARETH: There are 93 two-cent stamps, which is the correct amount for international mail: one dollar and eighty-five cents. In fact, it's a penny over.

DAN: You mean, you've been going from post office to post office—

GARETH: Took me five days!

DAN: And you didn't pay for any of those stamps?

GARETH: Not one!

LEE-ANNE: But why?

GARETH: I'm making a point.

LEE-ANNE: *But why?*

GARETH: I have a bet with my brother, in England.

LEE-ANNE: A bet?

GARETH: We were on Skype. I said I would send him a card for his birthday—the week after next— and I wouldn't pay a penny postage.

DAN: So now you've won the bet?

GARETH: Absolutely!

DAN: For how much? I mean, the bet.

GARETH: A dinner out at The Hargrove Inn, in Shrewsbury. A very expensive restaurant. I'll be over there next month.

DAN: And you're convinced your brother will understand he has to pay?

GARETH: Damn right he will. *(laughs)* He won't be happy about it.

DAN: But you will?

GARETH: Absolutely!

(GARETH holds the envelope out to LEE-ANNE, who takes it, examines it, then throws it onto the scale.)

DAN: So, you've been doing all this just to 'make a point'?

GARETH: Exactly. And I have.

(LEE-ANNE giggles, grins at DAN, turns back to GARETH.)

LEE-ANNE: Umm…you still owe me eighty-three cents. Eighty-five cents, with tax.

GARETH: No, no. It's all there. Just count the stamps.

LEE-ANNE: No need: I believe you.

GARETH: Of course.

LEE-ANNE: But you still owe me eighty-five cents.

GARETH: Out of the question!

LEE-ANNE: Your letter's overweight: thirty-two-point-three grams.

GARETH: It can't be!

LEE-ANNE: Oh, it is. *(points to screen)* You can see for yourself.

(GARETH peers at the screen.)

GARETH: Must be something wrong with your scale.

Just a Two-cent Stamp

LEE-ANNE: No. No, it was checked—inspected—just last week.

GARETH: But I had the envelope weighed, with the card in it, when I bought the card. Twenty-eight grams. Exactly.

LEE-ANNE: Uh-huh.

GARETH: So your scale *must* be out of order.

LEE-ANNE: No. The scale's always right. *(with a smile, a little triumphant)* You didn't allow for the weight of all those stamps.

GARETH: Oh, come now! Stamps weigh hardly anything.

(LEE-ANNE *takes two full sheets from the folder, each holding 50 two-cent stamps, and places them on the scale.)*

LEE-ANNE: There you are: one hundred two-cent stamps weigh five-point-eight grams.

GARETH: Oh, no! The envelope has only—

LEE-ANNE: Ninety-three stamps. You told me. So if I take off ten percent, it still weighs five-point-two grams.

DAN: *(to* GARETH*)* Are you going to pay the difference?

GARETH: Certainly not!

DAN: Anyway, where would you put the stamps? You don't have room for any more!

GARETH: *(to* LEE-ANNE*)* You know what you've done, don't you?

LEE-ANNE: Yeah. Sold you two stamps.

DAN: One stamp!

GARETH: You've made me lose my bet. And that dinner is going to cost me a fortune!

*(*GARETH *takes the envelope from* LEE-ANNE*, turns to stage left, exits.* DAN *and* LEE-ANNE *burst into laughter.)*

END

Character Descriptions

Gareth

He is a well-dressed man of about 50, very opinionated, who expects always to be 'right.' He tends to look down on those who don't understand him or don't agree with him.

Lee-Anne

She is a postal clerk of about 25 who is fairly new to the job. Generally she is efficient but is disoriented by Gareth's abrupt and imperious manner.

Dan

He is about 35. Normally a patient man, yet he is in a hurry to buy a stamp for a letter he must get into the post before the noon pickup.

Production Notes

At the time of writing, there has not yet been a performance to describe. However, the following notes may be useful.

The play is particularly suitable for countries in which the penny has been removed from circulation. In each case the script may have to be adjusted to fit the names used for each level of coinage, and what has been set as the lowest level of currency in circulation. In New Zealand, for example, both the penny and the five-cent coin have been abolished, which means that the seller bears the cost if the total price ends in one to four cents, and the buyer bears the cost from five to nine cents. Similarly, the cost of mailing an international letter will have to be adjusted as prices increase.

Ideally, it's best to stick the correct number of stamps to fill both front and back of just one envelope (except for two empty spaces: one for the address of the recipient and one for the final stamp to be affixed as the play is performed). Then you can print copies of both sides, trim them to the correct size, and glue them onto a blank envelope for each performance.

Play No. 7

Chords, Accords and Discords

A musically accompanied account of the collaboration between W. S. Gilbert and Arthur Sullivan, who together wrote and produced the Savoy Comic Operas.

Synopsis

Chords, Accords and Discords dramatizes the collaboration that existed during Gilbert and Sullivan's most productive years. It traces their accords and discords as they met, wrote, composed, rehearsed, and produced what became known as the Savoy Comic Operas.

Act 1 demonstrates the accord that existed between them from 1875 to 1883. Richard D'Oyly Carte approaches Gilbert and asks him to write the libretto for a 50-minute operetta, and suggests Sullivan as the composer. The result is *Trial by Jury*. In the ensuing years they write and produce *The Sorcerer, H.M.S. Pinafore, The Pirates of Penzance* and *Iolanthe*. To establish US copyright, they travel to New York for the first—secret/surprise—production of *Pirates*. The act closes with Sullivan being knighted by Queen Victoria.

Act 2 reflects the discords that develop between them between 1884 and 1890—discords that culminate in their writing two of their most popular operetta, *The Mikado* and *The Gondoliers,* and their most serious operetta *The Yeomen of the Guard.* A major argument in 1891 over the costs incurred during production of *The Gondoliers* results in Gilbert taking court action against Sullivan and Carte. Sullivan's health is waning and he and D'Oyly Carte die within six months of each other. Helen Carte takes over the business and, to maintain the quality of the productions, establishes what becomes the D'Oyly Carte Opera Company. The play closes with Gilbert being knighted in 1907, 24 years after Sullivan.

Rationale

The play does not contain a plot in the normal sense, since it traces real events over a 25-year period. It does, however, show the marked differences between the two principal characters: W. S. Gilbert as a volatile person whose occasional irrational actions are driven by an inexplicable inner force; and Arthur Sullivan as a suave, likable person carrying the burden of increasingly painful ill-health. He also faces an internal conflict created by his intense desire to compose great works, which is tempered by his financial need to write comic operas with Gilbert.

The action is intended to be continuous within each act. Hence, the individual scenes are designed mostly to flow from one to the next without interruption. Some of the best-known G & S songs are integrated into the storyline.

History

The play has not yet been produced. The first draft was written in 2000, but no further work was done on it until 2014, when I refreshed and updated the original script, in particular providing opportunities to integrate audio-visual technology into the production.

Characters

The Principals (non-singing roles)

There are five principals, who age about 15 to 30 years over the length of the play:

WS Gilbert, 38-71
Arthur Sullivan, 32-58
Richard D'Oyly Carte, 31-56
Helen Carte, 35-40
Lucy Gilbert, 25-57

Character descriptions for the Principals start on page 316.

Chords, Accords and Discords

Principal Singing Roles

These were real people. They are presented here in order of appearance, with their age shown when each is first seen:

Fred Sullivan, 30
George Grossmith, 28
Rosina Brandram (a large woman), 40
Leonara Braham, 25
Rutland Barrington (rather heavy), 30
Jessie Bond, 23
Richard Temple, 35
Geraldine Ulmar, 22
Courtice Pounds, 26

Other Characters

These are non-singing roles:

Harry Schacter (newspaper reporter, New York)
Fred O'Leary (newspaper reporter, New York)
Hosts and two lady guests (at NY reception)
Lord Cranmore
Lady Frederic
Prince of Wales (later, King Edward VII)
Queen Victoria
Martin (Sullivan's manservant)
1 man and 2 women in a London street
Guests at NY reception and people in street
(There is room for doubling up some of the non-singing roles.)

The Set

Center stage becomes the bare stages of the Royalty, Opera Comique and Savoy theatres in London, and the Fifth Avenue Theatre in New York. Here, rehearsals are held and performances are given throughout the action of the play. (Possibly, the stage center rotates so that the actors may on occasion be seen playing to an imaginary audience at stage left.) A piano is used on stage during the rehearsals.

Seven Plays with a Light Touch

Downstage right is W. S. Gilbert's study with a desk facing upstage; there is a large armchair with a footstool and a Japanese sword hangs prominently featured above the door on the rear wall. Downstage left is Arthur Sullivan's study, which is more economically furnished than Gilbert's. Other locations are Richard D'Oyly Carte's office, Sullivan's living room in London, a backdrop of the ticket office and part of the platform at Uxbridge railway station, a small portion of the front of the Savoy theatre, the dais on which Queen Victoria and King Edward VII knight the two men in Buckingham Palace, and a London street.

Approximate Length: 2 hours and 30 minutes (plus interval)

Some Script Guidelines

Throughout the script, two symbols are used occasionally at the end of a piece of dialogue to indicate how the sentence ends:

- ... An ellipsis at the end of a statement means the speaker just trails off and leaves his or her thought hanging in the air (possibly accompanied by a shrug).

- — A dash at the end of a statement means the speaker is interrupted by the next speaker, so that the first speaker's statement is incomplete. Sometimes there is an italicized continuation of the statement *(within brackets)* immediately following the dash, to help the actor sense where the sentence was going.

    v.o. Means that the words are spoken by someone off-stage.

Script: *Chords, Accords and Discords*
A Musical Play in Two Acts
© 2000, 2014, Ron Blicq

Act 1 – Accords

*(**Introductory music:** Excerpts from one or more of the songs from the operettas in Act One*: Trial by Jury, The Sorcerer, H.M.S. Pinafore, *T*he Pirates of Penzance, *and* Iolanthe.*)*

> ***Video Option****: As the songs are played, a horse-drawn coach pulls up at steps leading to a front door. D'Oyly Carte steps out and knocks on the door. The door opens, he steps in. The words 'London 1875' are superimposed.*

(W. S. Gilbert's study, downstage right. GILBERT *is alone, sitting in an armchair, a sheaf of papers in one hand [a manuscript] and a pen in the other. He makes changes to the manuscript as he recites what he has written.)*

GILBERT: There was a young lady from Malta
             Who strung up her aunt with a halter.
             She said: "I won't bury her…

(He thinks momentarily, working out the remaining words. He then recites them, simultaneously tapping out the meter with his pen on the chair arm.)

             She'll feed my fox terrier,
             And keep for a month if I salt her."

(He nods, pleased with the last two lines, and starts to write them down. LUCY *peers around the door, a visiting card in her hand.)*

LUCY: William…?

GILBERT: One minute, Kitten.

(He finishes writing the line, looks up quizzically. She enters and crosses to him.)

LUCY: There's a gentleman to see you. I didn't know if I should disturb you…

GILBERT: Depends who it is!

LUCY: It's a Mr. Carte. *(reads card)* Richard D'Oyly Carte.

GILBERT: Oh, that rogue!

LUCY: You would rather not…?

GILBERT: No, no, Kitten. Bring him in. He wouldn't be here if he didn't have some sharp scheme in mind.

(LUCY exits. GILBERT pulls himself up from his chair, searches for something on his desk, pauses when he hears voices; CARTE and LUCY enter.)

CARTE: *(as he enters, to LUCY)* It was produced in 1868 at the Gaiety Theatre. Am I not correct?

GILBERT: *(interposing)* If you are referring to 'Robert Le Diable', sir, then you are quite correct. *(extends his hand)* You have a good memory, Mr. Carte.

CARTE: *(Shaking hands)* My pleasure, Mr. Gilbert.

LUCY: We will be having tea shortly, Mr. Carte. Will you stay?

CARTE: Indeed I will, Mrs. Gilbert. Thank you.

(LUCY exits. GILBERT indicates CARTE should sit, sits himself. As he sits, CARTE points to papers in GILBERT's hand.)

You are writing a new play?

GILBERT: It would be more accurate to say I am indulging in an eccentric hobby.

CARTE: For the Haymarket? When 'Sweethearts' closes?

GILBERT: A mere frivolity, in its present form. *(peers at Carte's card)* You are a theatrical manager, Mr. Carte?

CARTE: The Royalty Theatre, sir. In Soho. I manage it for Madame Dolaro.

GILBERT: Exactly!

CARTE: She is presenting a series of operettas. Works by Jacques Offenbach, for the most part.

GILBERT: That foreigner!

(CARTE shrugs.)

Are there no British composers?

CARTE: There is one, I believe, who—

Chords, Accords and Discords

GILBERT: I have no ear for music. But even I find British choral work more fitting for a funeral than a public presentation.

CARTE: I have a proposal, Mr. Gilbert, which I hope will correct that.

(He pauses. GILBERT *signals for him to continue.)*
In March I plan to open with Offenbach's 'La Périchole.' It's only a short piece, and I'm looking for a second operetta to support it. About forty-five minutes. Perhaps an hour. Would you be willing to write a libretto?

GILBERT: Humph! You allow me very little time, Mr. Carte.

CARTE: Well...perhaps the play you are working on now. Could you adapt it? Keep it down to one hour?

GILBERT: My dear fellow! One does not trim a manuscript as one does one's beard! If a story is to be told properly, it requires exactly so many words. No less and no more.

CARTE: Forgive me if—

GILBERT: Nevertheless, there is a possibility...*(crosses to his desk, rummages through a drawer)* About seven years ago...I wrote a ballad...for the magazine 'Fun'...recently expanded it into a libretto. Ah! Here it is. A mock trial...

(GILBERT hands the script to CARTE.)
It still has to be set to music.

CARTE: *(riffling through the pages)* How long would you say it is?

GILBERT: If you take the time to glance more closely at the pages, Mr. Carte, you will see they are numbered.

CARTE: Ah, no. I was enquiring about its length of performance.

GILBERT: To read aloud, twenty minutes. With musical accompaniment, I'd venture forty minutes. Perhaps fifty.

CARTE: Would you consider Arthur Sullivan, to compose the music?

GILBERT: Sullivan? *(deprecatory)* The man who wrote 'Onward, Christian Soldiers'?

CARTE: He's the only British composer who can stand up against Offenbach. He's written a symphony. And the music for two of Shakespeare's plays.

GILBERT: I am not entirely unaware of his renown, Mr. Carte.

CARTE: Then you will speak to him?

GILBERT: It's an interesting idea. Hmmm...

(The music of Onward Christian Soldiers *can be heard.* GILBERT *rises, takes the manuscript from* CARTE, *and steps toward center stage. The lights fade on his study as he marches resolutely stage left and seats himself in Sullivan's study, where the lights come up.* SULLIVAN *leans back in an armchair, listening as* GILBERT *reads from his manuscript.* SULLIVAN *is amused by the piece, but* GILBERT *thinks he dislikes the plot.)*

GILBERT: The scene takes place in the Court of the Exchequer.

SULLIVAN: You are drawing on your legal experience?

GILBERT: Not the most effective period of my life, Mr. Sullivan. It provided an income but I can hardly describe it as important. Now! Trial by Jury is simple, really: the plaintiff—Angelina—is suing a young man—Edwin—for breach of promise. Picture a bride and her bridesmaids, all in their wedding finery, sweeping into a London court!

SULLIVAN: Not very likely!

GILBERT: That's the whole point! The inappropriateness of the situation underscores its humor.

SULLIVAN: Quite.

GILBERT: *(abruptly folding the manuscript)* I realize, Mr. Sullivan, that a libretto of this nature hardly measures up to the serious work you write. *(standing)* Now, if you'll kindly ask your valet to fetch my coat...

SULLIVAN: Oh, do sit down, Mr. Gilbert. Your plot is intriguing. I'll gladly set it to music for you. But first let me pour each of us a glass of sherry. *(goes to side cabinet)* Now! Tell me more.

GILBERT: *(sits)* Yes. Well...the judge's role is especially important. Mind you, he's not exactly a paragon of virtue.

(A spotlight picks out FRED Sullivan, *in street clothes, singing the Judge's song from* Trial by Jury. *Lights fade on Sullivan's study.)*

JUDGE: *(sings)* When I, good friends, was called to the bar,
    I'd an appetite fresh and hearty,
  But I was, as many young barristers are,
    An impecunious party.

  I'd a swallow-tail coat of a beautiful blue—
    A brief which I bought of a booby—

> A couple of shirts and a collar or two,
> And a ring that looked like a ruby!

(During the song the lights have come up around FRED *on a bare stage used for rehearsal. He is surrounded by cast members in their street clothes.* SULLIVAN *and* CARTE *watch from the edge of the group.* GILBERT *has stepped off-stage and stands in an aisle near the front of the stalls.)*

GILBERT: **Show** the ruby, Fred!

*(*FRED *holds his hand forward.)*

And let's hear you say 'impecunious.'

FRED: Impecunuss

GILBERT: No! No! No! Im-pe-cu-nious. Articulate it, man!

FRED: Im-pe-cu-nious.

GILBERT: Again.

FRED: Im-pe-cu-nious

GILBERT: Better! Just remember that the irony of the whole play hinges on what the judge sings about himself. And remember: the audience has to hear *every* word. Even in the back row! Continue.

(As FRED *sings the next verse,* GILBERT *backs toward the rear of the stalls)*

JUDGE:
> In Westminster Hall I danced a dance,
> Like a semi-despondent fury;
> For I thought I should never hit on a chance
> Of addressing a British jury—
>
> But I soon got tired of third-class journeys,
> And dinners of bread and water;
> So I fell in love with a rich attorney's
> Elderly, ugly daughter.

CHORUS:
> So he fell in love with a rich attorney's
> Elderly, ugly daughter.

GILBERT: *(mid-theatre)* Good. Good. Continue.

(As he continues to sing, FRED *dons a judge's gown and wig.)*

JUDGE:
> The rich attorney, he jumped with joy,
> And replied to my fond professions:

JUDGE: *(continues singing)*
"You shall reap the reward of your pluck, my boy
At the Bailey and Middlesex Sessions.

You'll soon get used to her looks," said he,
"And a very nice girl you'll find her!
She may very well pass for forty-three
In the dusk, with a light behind her!"

CHORUS: She may very well pass for forty-three
In the dusk, with a light behind her.

(As they sing, CARTE, SULLIVAN *and* GILBERT *exit unobtrusively.* FRED *is spotlighted: he is now playing to the first-night audience.)*

JUDGE: The rich attorney was as good as his word;
The briefs came trooping gaily,
And every day my voice was heard
At the Sessions or Ancient Bailey.

All thieves who could my fees afford
Relied on my orations,
And many a burglar I've restored
To his friends and his relations.

CHORUS: And many a burglar he's restored
To his friends and his relations.

JUDGE: At length I became as rich as the Gurneys—
An incubus then I thought her,
So I threw over that rich attorney's
Elderly, ugly daughter.

The rich attorney my character high
Tried vainly to disparage—
And now, if you please, I'm ready to try
This Breach of Promise of Marriage!

CHORUS: And now, if you please, he's ready to try
This Breach of Promise of Marriage!

(There is resounding applause [recorded? real?] and FRED *bows. The lights fade and come up on both Gilbert's and Sullivan's studies.* LUCY *is with* GILBERT; CARTE *is with* SULLIVAN. *They are reading the following morning's newspapers.)*

CARTE: This one has done you proud! *(reads)* "Trial by Jury, the joint production of Messrs. W. S. Gilbert and Arthur Sullivan"—

SULLIVAN: Gilbert will be pleased with that!

(CARTE looks questioningly at him.)

His name appearing first.

CARTE: Is he that sensitive?

SULLIVAN: I'd rather say...well...he likes his name to be seen at the front, in the program, on posters,,,

CARTE: That's his legal mind at work! *(reads)* "Trial by Jury is a pleasant addition to the bill of fare at Madam Selina Dolaro's pretty theatre in Soho."

GILBERT: *(reads to* LUCY*)* "It is to be gathered from the public prints that Mr. Arthur Sullivan, the versatile composer of the Light of the World, has turned his attention lately to musical burlesque." That's meant to be a slap in the face for Sullivan: that in composing the music for Trial by Jury he has stooped beneath himself. To *my* level, presumably.

CARTE: *(reads)* "Two more expert practitioners than Messrs. Gilbert and Sullivan could hardly have been invited to combine in so odd a piece of work."

SULLIVAN: Odd? Who finds it odd?

CARTE: The Times. A good review in The Times often predicts a long run.

LUCY: *(reads from another newspaper)* "This reviewer found the harmonies of Trial by Jury unexpectedly churchy after Offenbach..."

GILBERT: Only Corno di Bossetto writes like that.

LUCY: An Italian? Writing in The Star?

GILBERT: Oh, no! He's from Ireland. Cheeky young fellow, writes under a pseudonym. Real name's Shaw. George Bernard Shaw.

(As the lights fade on both studies, SULLIVAN *rises and, still lit, crosses to Gilbert's study.* CARTE *and* LUCY *have exited.)*

GILBERT: Have you heard from D'Oyly Carte?

SULLIVAN: From time to time. I gather he wants us to introduce full-length comic opera to the British public.

GILBERT: Exactly.

SULLIVAN: *(shakes head)* There is too much else I have to do.

GILBERT: Now you're principal of the Royal College of Music?

SULLIVAN: *(shrugs)* When the Prince of Wales commands...

GILBERT: Oh, come now. There's no better man for the post.

*(*SULLIVAN *smiles deprecatingly; slight pause.)*
Carte wants to buy a permanent theater for our productions. He's looking at the Opera Comique, in Wych Street.

SULLIVAN: Rather small, isn't it?

GILBERT: For grand opera, I agree. But ours would be *comic* opera. With the right opening piece—if it's on the lines of Trial by Jury—Carte says we're bound to have a success.

SULLIVAN: I'm not convinced. Yet you are?

GILBERT: Definitely. But only if you agree to compose the music.

SULLIVAN: And if I decline?

GILBERT: Then... *(shrugs)* I'll just go on writing plays.

SULLIVAN: With your usual success!

GILBERT: British audiences do seem to have an uneducated taste.

SULLIVAN: *(laughs lightly, then becomes earnest)* You realize, Gilbert, that for any other author I would not even consider the idea. Not for one moment. *(thoughtfully)* My mind says: "Be reasonable. You know you have not the time. Comic opera is not a path you should pursue." But my heart says: "Yes. It could be fun. And it might even pay well."

GILBERT: It might at that. But we'll have to draw up an agreement.

SULLIVAN: My word is not good enough for you?

GILBERT: Oh, good lord, man! Of course it is! We have but to shake hands...*(they stand and shake)* and the agreement is made. *(they re-sit)* I have a plot, an outline: Imagine a sorcerer—a dealer in magic and spells—who agrees to make up a love potion, an elixir, for everyone in a certain village... particularly for two young people. But when the elixir is drunk by the villagers, they fall in love with the most unlikely mates. And a less-than-pretty middle-aged woman falls for the sorcerer!

*(*SULLIVAN *laughs.)*

GILBERT: *(continuing)* I've found the ideal man to play the part. Name of Grossmith. Virtually unknown in the theatre.

(The lights dim on Gilbert's study, come up on the stage area. GROSSMITH, *dressed in a black cloak and tall black top hat, carries a teapot shaped like a kettle, from which fumes escape. He dashes about waving the teapot at any* VILLAGERS *who come into the area. They recoil from him.)*

GROSSMITH:

    Oh! My name is John Wellington Wells,
    I'm a dealer in magic and spells,
      In blessings and curses
      And ever-filled purses,
    In prophecies, witches, and knells.

    If you want a proud foe to 'make tracks' –
    If you'd melt a rich uncle in wax –
      You've but to look in
      On our resident Djinn,
    Number seventy, Simmery Axe!

    We've a first-class assortment of magic;
      And for raising a posthumous shade
    With effects that are comic or tragic,
      There's no cheaper house in the trade.

    Love-philtre—we've quantities of it;
      And for knowledge if any one burns,
    We keep an extremely small prophet, a prophet
      Who brings us unbounded returns:

        For he can prophesy
        With a wink of his eye,
        Peep with security
        Into futurity,
        Clear up a mystery,
        Humour proclivity
        For a nativity—for a nativity,
        With mirrors so magical,
        Tetrapods tragical,
        Bogies spectacular,
        Answers oracular,

GROSSMITH: *(continues singing)*

> Facts astronomical,
> Solemn or comical,
> And if you want it, he
> Makes a reduction on taking a quantity!
> Oh!...

If anyone anything lacks,
He'll find it all ready in stacks,
If he'll only look in
On the resident Djinn,
Number seventy, Simmery Axe!

(The lights fade on GROSSMITH and come up on Sullivan's lodgings. SULLIVAN sits in a large upright chair with a blanket over his legs. He is reading a book. MARTIN—his valet—enters carrying a letter.)

MARTIN: Mr. Sullivan.

SULLIVAN: Oh...Martin.

MARTIN: There is a letter for you.

(MARTIN hands the letter to SULLIVAN, who tears the envelope open and extracts several pages.)

SULLIVAN: Thank you.

(MARTIN exits. SULLIVAN opens and reads the letter. A spotlight comes up on GILBERT as he writes the letter.)

> **Video Option:** Gilbert, sitting at the desk in his study, writing the letter.

GILBERT: *(v.o.)* My dear Sullivan. D'Oyly Carte has been to see me. He says The Sorcerer is still running to good houses and predicts it will continue for about three more months. So I am sending you a sketch plot of the proposed opera, which takes place on a naval ship. I call it H.M.S. Pinafore.

(SULLIVAN separates the plot outline from the letter. He studies it as GILBERT continues.)

I want to go to Portsmouth, to tour some naval ships. It's essential to get the details right. If you are in accord with my plans, I deem it of the utmost importance that you accompany me. Would you be willing to go with me? Are you in sufficiently good health?

Chords, Accords and Discords

(The overture to H.M.S. Pinafore *can be heard quietly, and continues into the start of the next scene.* SULLIVAN *turns over a page, laughs)*

SULLIVAN: Marvelous!

(The lights extinguish on Sullivan's room and come up fully on Gilbert's study. A model of the stage at the Opera Comique, built to half-inch [1/24th] scale, is prominently visible on a table. In it is a backdrop and construction of the Pinafore's deck, exactly as it will be on stage. Little blocks of wood, some 2.5 to 3 inches (7 centimeters) high, are set on the stage and table. Each is painted in different striped colors. CARTE *and* GILBERT *peer into the miniature stage. The music ceases.)*

CARTE: I was down at the scene dock only this morning. Looks just like this!

GILBERT: Exactly! So it should. This is an exact replica of the set you are building. Sullivan and I went to Portsmouth. Aboard the Victory and two other warships. I took exact measurements, made sketches.

*(*GILBERT *pulls* CARTE *about two paces back, then gestures toward the miniature stage.)*

This is what the audience will see from the dress circle.

*(*GILBERT *squats and pulls* CARTE *down beside him, so their heads are level with the floor of the miniature stage.)*

Now, from the twelfth row of the orchestra stalls.

CARTE: Ingenious!

*(*GILBERT *points into the stage.)*

GILBERT: I use colored blocks to plan every move. One for each principal member of the cast. Then I make a sketch. At rehearsal I know exactly where each should be at a particular moment.

CARTE: So you mastermind the whole production?

GILBERT: Exactly! Tomorrow we will rehearse the opening scene. The sailors will be gathered around the quarterdeck—here *(points into stage)*. They'll be setting the rigging, cleaning brass. The boatswain will be here *(points)*. Little Buttercup will enter after the opening chorus *(he picks up a block, moves it into stage area)*.

GILBERT: *(continuing)* She's a Bumboat woman. Goes from ship to ship, pedals small goods to the sailors. She'll move downstage, like this...

(On the words 'She's a Bumboat woman' a spotlight comes up on Rosina BRANDRAM moving downstage. She is a large woman of about 40, dressed in her own clothes but carrying a basket bearing the wares Little Buttercup is pedaling. GILBERT moves the block downstage in his model and continues to gesture and silently describe the scene to CARTE. Part way through Buttercup's song the lights come up around her and we see that this is a rehearsal. SULLIVAN is coaching her by semi-conducting. Other CAST members are in their appropriate positions.)

BUTTERCUP: *(sings)*

> I'm called Little Buttercup—dear Little Buttercup,
> Though I could never tell why,
> But still I'm called Buttercup—dear Little Buttercup,
> Sweet Little Buttercup, I!
>
> I've snuffy and tobaccy, and excellent jacky,
> I've scissors, and watches, and knives;
> I've ribbons and laces to set off the faces
> Of pretty young sweethearts and wives.

(The lights fade and extinguish in Gilbert's *study.* GILBERT *and* CARTE *walk into the stage area and watch the song.)*

(In the previous and the next verse, BUTTERCUP *pronounces 'excellent' as though it has only two syllables: 'exclent'. This should be done naturally, unobtrusively.)*

BUTTERCUP:

> I've treacle and toffee, I've tea and I've coffee,
> Soft tommy and succulent chops;
> I've chicken and conies, and pretty polonies,
> And excellent peppermint drops.
>
> Then buy of your Buttercup—dear Little Buttercup;
> Sailors should never be shy;
> So buy of your Buttercup—poor Little Buttercup;
> Come, of your Buttercup buy!

Chords, Accords and Discords

(The CAST *applaud.)*

SULLIVAN: That was delightful, Miss Brandram. How could the sailors resist you?

(The CAST *laugh.)*

BRANDRAM: Thank you, Mr. Sullivan. I hope you don't mind that I dropped a word from the first line.

SULLIVAN: You know, I didn't notice.

GILBERT: But I certainly did!

BRANDRAM: I had to, to keep the meter the same as— *(in the third line)*

GILBERT: Yes! Yes! I see that! But, Miss Brandram, ask me first, if you must change my words.

BRANDRAM: I'm sorry, Mr. Gilbert.

*(*BRANDRAM *turns away, as if to sit down.)*

GILBERT: And Miss Brandram!

(She turns and faces him.)

You are aware, I assume, that the word "excellent" has three syllables? Ex-cel-lent.

*(*BRANDRAM *nods.)*

Well, it is not excellent to say 'exclent', as you did in the second and the third verses!

*(*BRANDRAM *sits and sighs.* GILBERT *steps forward and addresses the* CAST.*)*

I have said this before and I'll say it again. Your articulation is of the utmost importance. Slurred words imply that we have a careless production; a production that deserves only a short run. I assume you wish to serve on H.M.S. Pinafore for a reasonable length of time? *(he looks around for nods of agreement)* Then do not let me hear you short-change your audience. You have to give them the full measure of the words I have written for them. *(looks around)* Mr. Sullivan! You will conduct the first night?

SULLIVAN: Yes. I plan to.

GILBERT: Then I'll ask you to remind your musicians that a comic opera is *not* an invitation for them to indulge in a contest with my singers to see who can be heard better.

SULLIVAN: *(with a twinkle)* Mr. Gilbert: I will take great care that my inconsiderate players will not drown out a single word!

GILBERT: *(taken aback by Sullivan's levity)* Yes. Well. I'm sure you will.

(BARRINGTON and GROSSMITH enter. GROSSMITH wears the uniform of the First Sea Lord. BARRINGTON is in the uniform of a ship's captain. During the following sequence SULLIVAN and CARTE mime talking then exit stage right.)

All right, you naval officers. Step forward!

(BARRINGTON and GROSSMITH stand in from of him. GILBERT straightens the trim of their uniforms and levels their hats as he speaks, first to GROSSMITH.)

Sir Joseph Porter, as First Lord of Her Majesty's Navy, would never wear his hat at an angle, Mr. Grossmith. Straighten it! A little more. Right: keep it like that!

(GILBERT turns to BARRINGTON.)

I know Captain Corcoran is not the most effective commander, Mr. Barrington, but I'm sure he would still know how to stand like a naval officer. Heels together, man! Chest forward! Toes straight ahead! And pull in that stomach!

BARRINGTON: If I really were Captain Corcoran, Mr. Gilbert, I doubt whether a non-naval person would speak to me like that.

GILBERT: If you really were a naval officer, Mr. Barrington, you would *know* how to carry yourself.

(He turns toward Leonara BRAHAM, speaks pleasantly.)

Now, Miss Braham: 'Josephine'. Come over here, will you? Stand between these two gentlemen and take your positions for 'Never mind the why and wherefore'.

(He consults a drawing, ushers the three forward, and again addresses BRAHAM.)

The audience knows you want to marry one of the seamen. Right? *(she nods)* But—as the Captain's daughter—you are not sure such a union would be viewed as appropriate. Am I not correct? *(she nods, then he points to GROSSMITH)* You are also aware that Sir Joseph Porter, who you do not particularly like, has asked your father for your hand in marriage. Right?

(BRAHAM nods; GILBERT turns to GROSSMITH.)

Now, pick up the dialogue from the point where you and the Captain join Josephine. *(he steps back)*

SIR JOSEPH: *(to* JOSEPHINE*)* Madam! It has been represented to me that you are appalled by my exalted rank. I desire to convey to you officially my opinion that love is a platform upon which all ranks meet.

*(*GILBERT *nods approvingly, encourages* BRAHAM *to respond.)*

JOSEPHINE: I thank you, Sir Joseph. I did hesitate, but I will hesitate no longer. *(aside)* He little thinks how eloquently he has pleaded his rival's case!

(The trio sing.)

CAPTAIN: Never mind the why and wherefore,
               Love can level ranks, and therefore,
               Though his lordship's station's mighty,
                  Though stupendous be his brain
               Though your tastes are mean and flighty
               And your fortune poor and plain,

CAPTAIN *and* SIR JOSEPH:
                  Ring the merry bells on board-ship,
                      Rend the air with warbling wild,
                  For the union of [his/my] lordship
                  With a humble captain's child!

CAPTAIN: For a humble captain's daughter—

JOSEPHINE: For a gallant captain's daughter—

SIR JOSEPH: And a lord who rules the water—

JOSEPHINE: *(aside)* And a tar who ploughs the water!

ALL: Let the air with joy be laden,
                Rend with songs the air above,
            For the union of a maiden
                With the man who owns her love!

> **Option**: *The actors turn 50 degrees toward stage left and a spotlight comes up on SULLIVAN, in evening dress, conducting the first performance. Only the upper half of his body is visible.*

(The lights fade and extinguish on Gilbert and all other cast members, until only the three singers are spot-lit.)

SIR JOSEPH: Never mind the why and wherefore,
    Love can level ranks, and therefore,
Though your nautical relation
(alludes to Captain)
    In my set could scarcely pass—
Though you occupy a station
    In the lower middle class—

CAPTAIN *and* SIR JOSEPH:
    Ring the merry bells on board-ship,
        Rend the air with warbling wild,
    For the union of [my/his] lordship
        With a humble captain's child!

CAPTAIN: For a humble captain's daughter—

JOSEPHINE: For a gallant captain's daughter—

SIR JOSEPH: And a lord who rules the water—

JOSEPHINE: *(aside)* And a tar who ploughs the water!

ALL: Let the air with joy be laden,
    Rend with songs the air above,
For the union of a maiden
    With the man who owns her love!

JOSEPHINE:
    Never mind the why and wherefore,
        Love can level ranks and therefore
    I admit the jurisdiction,
        Ably have you played your part,
    You have carried firm conviction
        To my hesitating heart.

CAPTAIN *and* SIR JOSEPH:
    Ring the merry bells on board-ship,
        Rend the air with warbling wild
    For the union of [my/his] lordship
        With a humble captain's child!

CAPTAIN: For a humble captain's daughter—

Chords, Accords and Discords

JOSEPHINE: For a gallant captain's daughter—
SIR JOSEPH: And a lord who rules the water—
JOSEPHINE: *(aside)* And a tar who ploughs the water!
           (to the others) Let the air with joy be laden.
CAPTAIN *and* SIR JOSEPH:
           For the union with his lordship
           Rend with songs the air above
           For the man who owns her love!

(Recorded applause from stage left. The lights fade center stage and come up on Gilbert's study. GILBERT and CARTE are seated.)

CARTE: The Americans were extraordinarily helpful. Their enthusiasm is incredible.

GILBERT: Their enthusiasm for using our scripts and music without license also is incredible! I assume you checked their copyright laws?

CARTE: I did. But they are only loosely interpreted, and to their advantage.

GILBERT: So, we are not protected?

CARTE: Unless the first production of a work occurs in America, there is no protection. They choose not to recognize British copyright.

GILBERT: It's not the money I mind, it's the principle. It upsets my digestion.

(CARTE laughs lightly. SULLIVAN enters with LUCY.)

SULLIVAN: Ah! Carte! Welcome back.

(They shake hands.)

I trust New York was good to you?

CARTE: Yes, indeed.

(GILBERT indicates for SULLIVAN to sit, and for LUCY to sit beside GILBERT.)

SULLIVAN: Did you see any of the pirate productions?

CARTE: Three, actually. There are eight productions of Pinafore running in New York alone. Lord knows how many in other cities.

SULLIVAN: Do they do justice to Gilbert's words? To my score?

CARTE: The casts have excellent voices. Surprisingly good. But they have no idea how to put the piece together: the acting...the costumes...the timing...your music...

SULLIVAN: And still they stay in business?

CARTE: Playing to packed houses, some of them.

SULLIVAN: This *is* upsetting. Of course I like to be paid for my work—we all do—but I am more disturbed that my music is not being performed correctly.

CARTE: Well, gentlemen. Eleven days on the ocean have given me time to think of a solution.

LUCY: *(starts to rise)* Perhaps I should...

(GILBERT places his hand over hers, draws her back into her chair, keeps his hand there.)

GILBERT: No. Stay, Kitten.

CARTE: The three of us will sail to America next autumn. We'll let it be known we're going to mount the original—the *authentic*—version of Pinafore, in New York. We'll hold a grand opening night, just as we do in London. You'll conduct, Sullivan, which in New York will be a special attraction. Your name's well-known there.

(Pause; CARTE lowers his voice.)

What we will not announce—even to the cast—is that we will take the manuscript for the next comic opera with us. And produce it right there, first. In New York!

GILBERT: Damnably clever! We'll secure copyright because it will be the first production, and on American soil.

CARTE: *(mimics GILBERT)* Exactly!

(LUCY notices, giggles. GILBERT doesn't notice.)

Mind, **nothing** is to be said outside this room!

(Immediately Jessie BOND can be heard, as MABEL in The Pirates of Penzance.)

MABEL: *(sings)* For shame, for shame, for shame!

> **Video Option:** *A passenger liner sailing westward over the Atlantic Ocean.*

(A spotlight comes up on BOND and the lights extinguish on Gilbert's study. BOND holds a handwritten script and refers to it as she sings. She wears her own clothes.

(Although they cannot be seen yet, BOND *is surrounded by members of the* CAST, *who are sitting around the bare stage of the Fifth Avenue Theatre in New York. [*GROSSMITH *is wearing the uniform of Major General Stanley; a tailor is adjusting it, placing pins in appropriate places.]* BOND/MABLE *sings to a young actor standing beside her, who plays* FREDERIC. *As she sings the lights come up to show a rehearsal in progress.)*

MABEL: *(continues singing)*

> Poor wandering one!
> Though thou has surely strayed,
> > Take heart of grace,
> > Thy steps retrace,
>
> Poor wandering one!

*(*SULLIVAN *and* GILBERT *enter, watch.)*

> Poor wandering one!
> If such poor love as mine
> > Can help thee find
> > True peace of mind—
>
> Why, take it, it is thine!
> Take heart, fair days will shine;
> > Take heart—take mine!

FEMALE CHORUS:

> Take any heart; no danger lowers;
> Take any heart – but ours!

*(*MABLE *and* FREDERIC *move from center stage and seat themselves.* EDITH *and* KATE *read their lines from a single script they hold as they sing.)*

EDITH: What ought we do,
>   Gentle sisters, say?

(She appeals with a gesture to the other women.)

> Propriety, we know,
> > Says we ought to stay;
>
> While sympathy exclaims,
> > 'Free them from your tether—
> > Play at other games—
> > > Leave them here together'.

*(*CARTE *enters hurriedly, whispers to* GILBERT.*)*

KATE: Her case may, any day,
Be yours, my dear, or mine.
Let her make hay...

(GILBERT steps forward, interrupts.)

GILBERT: Ladies and gentlemen! I apologize for interrupting, but Mr. Carte has just informed me that two gentlemen from the press are here!

SULLIVAN: Give me the scripts. Quickly!

(SULLIVAN and CARTE go among the cast gathering up sheet music and words. There is a general bustle.)

GILBERT: Mr. Grossmith! Will you sing something? From Pinafore. Anything!

(GROSSMITH nods, moves to center stage, calls to the pianist.)

GROSSMITH: 'I am the Monarch.'

(The pianist turns over sheet music, starts to play. GROSSMITH [as SIR JOSEPH] starts to sing.)

I am the monarch of the sea,
The ruler of the Queen's Navee...

GILBERT: *(shouts)* No! No, you're not!

(GROSSMITH stops.)

You're wearing the uniform of an army major general! From the new play!

GROSSMITH: Oh! Good lord!

(He rapidly unbuttons his jacket, passes it to an actor who folds it inside out and sits on it. A second actor runs up with the First Lord's naval jacket from H.M.S. Pinafore. GROSSMITH struggles into it and the actor helps him button it. GROSSMITH nods to the pianist and starts singing before the buttoning is complete.)

SIR JOSEPH: *(sings)*

I am the monarch of the sea,
The ruler of the Queen's Navee,
Whose praise Great Britain loudly chants,

COUSIN HEBE (Brandram):

And we are his sisters, and his cousins, and his aunts!

FEMALE CHORUS:
>And we are his sisters, and his cousins, and his aunts!

(SCHACTER and O'LEARY enter, pause to watch.)

SIR JOSEPH:
>When at anchor here I ride,
>My bosom swells with pride,
>And I snap my fingers at a foeman's taunts;

COUSIN HEBE:
>And so do his sisters, and his cousins, and his aunts!

CHORUS: And so do his sisters, and his cousins, and his aunts!

(CARTE notices reporters and crosses to them.)

SIR JOSEPH:
>But when the breezes blow,
>I generally go below,
>And seek the seclusion that a cabin grants;

COUSIN HEBE:
>And so do his sisters, and his cousins, and his aunts!

CHORUS: And so do his sisters, and his cousins and his aunts!
>His sisters and his cousins,
>Whom he reckons up by dozens,
>And his aunts!

(CARTE shakes hands with the reporters.)

SCHACTER: We didn't mean to interrupt your rehearsal.

CARTE: No. That's all right. You are...?

SCHACTER: Harry Schacter, New York Herald.

O'LEARY: Fred O'Leary, New York Sun.

CARTE: Welcome, gentlemen. I am Richard D'Oyly Carte. I manage the production. *(leads them to GILBERT)* May I introduce you to Mr. William Gilbert. He wrote the words for H.M.S. Pinafore.

(GILBERT and REPORTERS shake hands, "How do you do," "Glad to meet ya," etc.)

And this is Mr. Sullivan. He composed the music.

(Handshakes, etc.)

O'LEARY: Your name has preceded you, Mr. Sullivan.

(SULLIVAN inclines his head in acknowledgment.)

SCHACTER: This is the new opera, you're rehearsing?

SULLIVAN: It will be a long time...) *(shocked, in unison,*
GILBERT: What new opera?) *with awkward looks*
CARTE: Oh, no! Hardly.) *at one another)*

CARTE: This is H.M.S. Pinafore.

O'LEARY: Why would you be rehearsing H.M.S. Pinafore, when it has already been running for a week?

GILBERT: We...er...we like to try new stage movements.

CARTE: And let the understudies practice singing the principal roles.

SCHACTER: *(points to* GROSSMITH*)* This is an understudy?

SULLIVAN: Oh, no. That's Mr. Grossmith. Sir Joseph Porter, in naval uniform.

CARTE: He was demonstrating how the First Lord presents his introductory song.

SCHACTER: Uh-huh...

O'LEARY: Mr. Gilbert: Is the version of H.M.S. Pinafore you're showing in New York the same as in London?

GILBERT: Exactly.

SHACTER: You don't have to change the words to suit an American audience?

GILBERT: Absolutely not! New York audiences are just as knowledge-able as London audiences. They just take a little longer to—using one of your own expressions—to catch on.

CARTE: To understand the accent, Mr. Gilbert means. The British accent.

SCHACTER: Uh-huh.

O'LEARY: *(to* GILBERT *and* SULLIVAN*)* What is it about your particular production of H.M.S. Pinafore that makes it such a success? I mean, there are many other local productions.

GILBERT: Discipline! Absolute discipline.

SULLIVAN: It has a lot to do with the performers. They are professionals. Every one of them.

(The CAST *glance appreciatively at one another.)*
Under Mr. Gilbert's expert direction they have studied the...er...the articulation necessary to create unprecedented clarity of expression.

SULLIVAN: *(continuing)* And musically they are extremely sound.

SCHACTER: Well, which do you write first: the music or the words?

SULLIVAN: Oh, Mr. Gilbert writes the libretto first. Always.

SCHACTER: There's no music yet?

SULLIVAN: No. Not until Mr. Gilbert hands me the complete script. Then I write the music: solos, duets, the score.

(Pause. SCHACTER makes notes.)

O'LEARY: How do you go about writing your lyrics, Mr. Gilbert?

GILBERT: By applying the tip of a hard pencil to a firm pad. And concurrently applying a firm pad *(he slaps his buttock)* to a hard chair!

(The CAST laugh quietly; O'LEARY has not realized it's humor.)

O'LEARY: Word has gotten around that you're preparing a new opera, which you'll present in New York. Can you comment on that, Mr. Gilbert?

GILBERT: I would love to comment on that, Mr. O'Leary, if there was something to comment on.

SCHACTER: Well, it's common knowledge along Broadway you're writing about burglars.

SULLIVAN: Burglars!

GILBERT: At one time Mr. Sullivan and I did consider such a plot. But the next piece... *(shrugs)* has yet to be devised. Yet you can be sure our approach will remain the same: it will be similar to 'Pinafore.'

SULLIVAN: It will treat a farcical subject in a very serious manner. Won't it, Mr. Gilbert?

GILBERT: Exactly!

O'LEARY: *(to GILBERT)* Will you be casting an unattractive, middle-aged contralto in an unsympathetic role?

GILBERT: Only if an unattractive, middle-aged, unsympathetic contralto comes to audition for us.

O'LEARY: You have written one into your previous productions.

GILBERT: Well, if you know of one, do encourage her to apply.

SCHACTER: Mr. Sullivan: do you prefer to compose music for comic opera, or write more serious works?

SULLIVAN: There is great pleasure in collaborating with Mr. Gilbert. At other times I prefer to compose more serious works.

O'LEARY: What were you doing, Mr. Gilbert, before you met Mr. Sullivan? Your name's new to me.

GILBERT: *(slightly miffed)* Oh, I've done a number of things. For a while I was a barrister: a lawyer, in your country. And I was in the reserve army. More recently I've been doing some dramatic writing. Plays. Nothing you would have heard of.

(CARTE senses Gilbert's irritation.)

CARTE: Perhaps this would be an appropriate moment to resume the rehearsal.

SCHACTER: Yeah! I'd like to see some of that discipline Mr. Gilbert talked about.

SULLIVAN: *(to GILBERT)* Then perhaps they should sing 'The Cat'.

GILBERT: *(still miffed)* As you wish.

SULLIVAN: *(to CAST)* Start with 'Carefully on tiptoe.'

(He looks at the pianist, who nods; the CAST move into position. DICK DEADEYE is sung by Courtice Pounds; the CAPTAIN by Richard Temple.)

Are you ready?

(The cast nod, say "Aye", "Yes". The REPORTERS sit to one side. SULLIVAN moves to side stage, beside GILBERT and CARTE. As the cast sing the lights fade on SULLIVAN, GILBERT and CARTE, who exit. The crew cross the stage stealthily on tiptoe, from one side; JOSEPHINE and BUTTERCUP approach stealthily from the other. The CAPTAIN is partly concealed by a cloak.)

ALL: Carefully on tiptoe stealing,
    Breathing gently as we may,
Every step with caution feeling,
    We will softly steal away.

(The CAPTAIN stamps, accompanied by a chord.)

ALL: Goodness me,
    Why, what was that?

DICK DEADEYE:
    Silent be, ... it was the cat!

ALL: It was – it was the cat!

(The CAPTAIN produces the cat-o-nine-tails.)

CAPTAIN: They're right! It was the cat!

ALL: Pull ashore, in fashion steady,
    Hymen will defray the fare,
For a clergyman is ready,
    To unite the happy pair!

(The CAPTAIN stamps; chord.)

    Goodness me,
        Why, what was that?

DICK DEADEYE:
    Silent be … Again, the cat!

ALL: It was again that cat!

(The CAPTAIN throws off his cloak, reveals himself.)

CAPTAIN: They're right! It was the cat!

JOSEPHINE, BUTTERCUP *and* RALPH:
    Every step with caution feeling,
    We will softly steal away.

ALL: Every step with caution feeling,
    We will softly steal away.

(The lights fade and extinguish. Orchestration of the song continues as a spotlight picks out a large poster set downstage right.)

Fifth Avenue Theatre
Final Performance Tonight

H.M.S. PINAFORE

Sold Out!
Again!

(The spotlight sweeps across to pick out a PIRATE as he enters downstage left. He carries a second poster and takes it across to stage right.)

> **Fifth Avenue Theatre**
>
> Opens New Year's Eve, 1879
>
> ## *The Pirates of Penzance*
>
> **A GRAND NEW OPERA**
> **by Messrs**
> **Gilbert and Sullivan!**

(As the PIRATE crosses, the orchestration subtly changes to 'For I am a Pirate King' from the overture to The Pirates of Penzance. *The PIRATE sets the new poster down in front of the old poster. He points to the new poster, bows to the audience, and then exits stage right.)*

> *Video Option: The 'Pirate/Poster' sequence can be pre-recorded and shown on screen, followed by the camera homing toward an imposing hotel in New York.*

(The music continues into the next scene, which opens on a formal reception in a hotel room. Invited New York playgoers are in evening dress, and the principal actors are still in their stage dress from The Pirates of Penzance. *CARTE is talking to guests, as are BARRINGTON in a policeman's uniform and GROSSMITH as Major General Stanley. LADY 1 is talking to GROSSMITH and BARRINGTON. The music fades.)*

LADY 1: Does a British general really dress like that?

GROSSMITH: Not every day, madam. This is a ceremonial uniform, worn on special occasions.

BARRINGTON: Exact in every detail. Mr. Gilbert sees to that.

LADY 1: It must be very hot in there.

Chords, Accords and Discords

GROSSMITH: Worse on stage, madam. With all those gas lamps.

(SULLIVAN enters, goes up to CARTE, hands him a locked music case.)

CARTE: *(to the HOST)* Tonight was the very first production of The Pirates of Penzance. It's not running in London yet.

HOST: A-a-h! So that gives you the copyright here. But not in England?

CARTE: Oh, we have taken care of that. Haven't we Mr. Sullivan? Earlier today, one of our touring companies gave a first performance in a small theatre in Devon.

HOST: Very clever! *(taps on a glass, waits for silence)* Ladies and gentlemen! I wish to propose a toast. To Mr. Sullivan and Mr. Gilbert, who have given us so much pleasure by choosing to come to our shores.

GUESTS: Hear, hear! *(etc)*

HOST: I know I reflect the thoughts of everyone here, when I say that you have done us a great honor, permitting The Pirates of Penzance to have its premiere in New York. *(raises glass)* For giving us such a grand spectacle, Mr. Sullivan and Mr. Gilbert!

GUESTS: *(raise glasses)* Mr. Sullivan! Mr. Gilbert!

GILBERT: *(to SULLIVAN)* Will you respond?

SULLIVAN: No, no! You do it.

GILBERT: You are better than I, at such civilities.

SULLIVAN: But you are the one who writes the words!

GILBERT: Not these types of words!

SULLIVAN: *(after an awkward pause; to the guests)* Your honor. Ladies and gentlemen. You have just witnessed Mr. Gilbert and I having our first difference of opinion!

(Polite laughter.)

We had heard in England that American audiences are outspoken and generous, but we certainly were not prepared for the overwhelming welcome we have received. Your kindness cheers us immensely, and has made worthwhile the discomfort of a winter journey across the Atlantic Ocean. We, and the casts of both H.M.S. Pinafore and The Pirates of Penzance, thank you for your exceedingly warm reception.

GILBERT: Hear, hear!

(Guests applaud.)

GUEST VOICES: Sing for us!
                  Yeah!
                  Something from the new play!
                  The Pirates!
SULLIVAN: A musician I may be. A singer I am not.
GILBERT: Perhaps we could persuade Mr. Grossmith. Or Mr. Barrington…?
GUEST VOICES: *(overlapping)*
   The policeman's song!
   Oh, yes. Please!
   A policeman's lot is not a nappy one!
   Best song in the show!
SULLIVAN: Would you mind, Mr. Barrington?
   (BARRINGTON smiles broadly, steps to center stage; someone sits at a piano.)
BARRINGTON: Are we ready, then!
GUESTS: *(overlapping)*
   Sure!
   We're ready!
   Got your truncheon?
   (CARTE has stepped to the side and during the early part of the song he exits.)

BARRINGTON: *(sings)*
   When a felon's not engaged in his employment—
GUESTS: (singing raggedly)
   His employment,
   (SULLIVAN steps forward, encourages guests to sing. After a while GILBERT follows suit.)
BARRINGTON:
   Or maturing his felonious little plans—
GUESTS: Little plans,

BARRINGTON:
   His capacity for innocent enjoyment—
GUESTS: 'Cent enjoyment,
   (Gradually the guests join in boisterously.)
BARRINGTON:
   Is just as great as any honest man's—
GUESTS: Honest man's,

BARRINGTON:
>Our feelings we with difficulty smother—

GUESTS: 'Culty smother,

BARRINGTON:
>When Constabulary duty's to be done—

GUESTS: To be done,

BARRINGTON:
>Ah, take one consideration with another—

GUESTS: With another,

BARRINGTON:
>A policeman's lot is not a happy one.

GUESTS: When constabulary duty's to be done—
>To be done,
>The policeman's lot is not a happy one.

BARRINGTON:
>When the enterprising burglar's not a-burgling—

GUESTS: Not a burgling,

BARRINGTON:
>When the cut-throat isn't occupied in crime—

GUESTS: 'Pied in crime,

BARRINGTON:
>He loves to hear the little brook a-gurgling—

GUESTS: Brook a-gurgling,

BARRINGTON:
>And listen to the merry village chime—

GUESTS: Village chime,

BARRINGTON:
>When the coster's finished jumping on his mother—

GUESTS: On his mother,

BARRINGTON:
>He loves to lie a-basking in the sun—

GUESTS: In the sun,

BARRINGTON:
>Ah, take one consideration with another—

GUESTS: With another,

BARRINGTON:
>The policeman's lot is not a nappy one.

GUESTS: When constabulary duty's to be done—
             To be done,
             The policeman's lot is not a nappy one—
             Happy one.

(BARRINGTON *bows to wild applause. He wipes his brow, is patted on the back. The lights dim, then extinguish.*)

(*The lights come up on Gilbert's study.* LUCY *and* CARTE *are seated.* CARTE *carries several New York newspapers.*)

CARTE: I thought you might like to hear what the Americans are saying about Mr. Gilbert.

LUCY: Do they understand him?

CARTE: Oh, yes! This is the New York Herald. (*reads*) "The appearance and manner of the famous Englishman greatly belie the published accounts which have found their way across the ocean, and which represented Mr. Gilbert as a man of austere and haughty temperament..."

LUCY: Oh, dear. Is that how people see him?

CARTE: "Two more amiable, modest, simple, good-humored and vivacious men could not easily be imagined."

(CARTE *peers at* LUCY *over his pince-nez.*)

LUCY: That hardly sounds like William!

CARTE: (*laughs; reads*) "Mr. Gilbert's voice has a hearty, deep ring, and his utterance is quick and jerky—as though he were almost tired of keeping up this business of saying funny things, which everybody more or less expects of him..."

LUCY: (*nods, laughs*) Yes-s-s.

CARTE: (*reads*) "Mr. Sullivan is quite different. In his appearance, gentle feeling and tender emotion are as strongly expressed as cold, glittering keen-edged intellect is in Mr. Gilbert."

(CARTE *lowers the newspaper, hands it to* LUCY.)

LUCY: How very observant the American reporters are. Thank you, Mr. Carte. (*slight pause*) Mr. Gilbert keeps well?

CARTE: Oh, yes. His usual self.

LUCY: And Mr. Sullivan?

(CARTE *hesitates.*)

He is unwell?

CARTE: Not as well as I would like him to be.

LUCY: Oh...I am sorry.

CARTE: *(slight pause)* You know Mr. Gilbert is working on another opera?

LUCY: So soon?

CARTE: He wants to poke fun at the aesthetic movement.

(LUCY looks questioningly at him. He poses.)

Oscar Wilde. The painter Whistler. And the poet Swinburne.

(The lights dim rapidly on Gilbert's study and a spotlight comes up on GROSSMITH, *stage left, as Reginald Bunthorne. He is dressed foppishly and carrying a lily. There is a second poster downstage right, with* PATIENCE *standing beside it.)*

> **Video Option:** *This and the following sequence of two more posters are shown on-screen. Patience is onstage to draw Bunthorne's attention to the screen.*

At Madam Dolaro's
Opéra Comique

A New Musical
Extravaganza!

Patience

Opens 23rd of April 1881

BUNTHTHORNE: *(sings)*

    If you're anxious for to shine in the high
        aesthetic line as a man of culture rare,
    You must get up all the germs of the
        transcendental terms,
    And plant them everywhere.

*(*PATIENCE *taps her foot on the floor and raises her hand vertically to indicate* BUNTHORNE *is to stop.)*

(BUNTHORNE pauses questioningly [the music continues in the background]. She nods, lifts the first poster to reveal a second poster behind it.)

> **We are moving!**
> From 10th October 1881
>
> *Patience*
>
> Will be at the new
>
> **Savoy Theatre**
>
> **ELECTRIC LAMPS !**

(BUNTHORNE acknowledges PATIENCE's foot-tapping with an 'Ah! Of course!' gesture. PATIENCE curtsies and indicates he should continue his song.)

BUNTHORNE: *(sings)*
      You must lie upon the daisies and discourse in
         novel phrases of your complicated state of mind,
      The meaning doesn't matter if it's only idle chatter
         of a transcendental kind.

         And everyone will say,
           As you walk your mystic way,
    'If this young man expresses himself in terms
        too deep for me,

    Why, what a singularly deep young man this
        deep young man must be!'

(There is applause, BUNTHORNE bows, then indicates for PATIENCE to do the same. Rosina BRANDRAM, dressed as the FAIRY QUEEN in Iolanthe, enters upstage center. She imperiously indicates that BUNTHORNE and PATIENCE withdraw. They exit, PATIENCE taking the poster with her. The FAIRY

QUEEN *gestures for a Fairy to come to her from offstage.* CELIA *enters, carrying a new poster, and sets it up. The action is accompanied with music from the Overture to* Iolanthe, *leading in to Iolanthe's call.)*

Savoy Theatre

Iolanthe

or

The Peer and the Peri

**Will open on
25th November 1882**

FAIRY QUEEN: *(sings)*
    Iolanthe!
        From thy dark exile thou art summoned!
        Come to our call—
        Come, Iolanthe!

(CELIA looks into the wings, as though searching.)

CELIA: Iolanthe!

(Fairy LEILA enters, as though searching.)

LEILA: Iolanthe!

FAIRY CHORUS: *(offstage):*
    Come to our call,
    Come, Iolanthe!

(Lights fade on the singers, who exit. Iolanthe *music carries over the transition and into the next scene.)*

Video Option: *Horse-drawn coaches draw up at a London house, passengers alight, enter.*

(Lights come up on Sullivan's sitting room, which is more sumptuous than his study. Guests in evening dress are entering from the dining room. They include the Prince of Wales, Lord Cranmore, Lady Frederic, plus two others.)

LORD CRANMORE: *(entering with* SULLIVAN*)* I find the music for Iolanthe more serious than I have become accustomed to.

SULLIVAN: Ah… Well the subject is hardly serious, Lord Cranmore. So I had to treat it with some solemnity, to offset the…absurdity…of the situation. With Mr. Gilbert's full agreement, I might add.

LADY FREDERIC: Where does Mr. Gilbert get his ideas? I mean, to make the main male character half a human and half a fairy!

SULLIVAN: Theatre audiences seem to like the topsy-turvy world he creates.

CRANMORE: You must work very closely together.

SULLIVAN: Yes, I suppose we do. Not physically, mind. Most of the time we exchange our ideas by correspondence.

LADY FREDERIC: You mean, you just write to each other?

SULLIVAN: Yes, Lady Frederic, we send the script back and forth. Or parts of it.

LADY FREDERIC: But how do you resolve differences? I mean, you must have had some disagreements along the way. Surely? Even by post!

(The PRINCE *strolls over and listens to the conversation.)*

SULLIVAN: A few. *(laughs)* No, very few really. Oh, with the next play – we're thinking of calling it Princess Ida – I couldn't accept Mr. Gilbert's original idea: to base the plot on a magic lozenge which would cause its eater to change into another character.

PRINCE: The lozenge stuck in your throat?

(Laughter.)

SULLIVAN: Yes, Your Royal Highness. I couldn't swallow the idea. But now we have agreed on a different theme.

LADY FREDERIC: And who among us is to be the target of Mr. Gilbert's satire this time?

SULLIVAN: Oh, it's too early to say what direction the plot will take. For now, can you accept it will be about you ladies?

SULLIVAN: *(continuing)* It will be something about the feminist movement. You ladies will be center stage!

LADY FREDERIC: Oh! But is that all you can tell us?

SULLIVAN: *(smiles)* Yes, I'm afraid so.

(The PRINCE draws SULLIVAN aside, to speak on a private matter. Lights fade on all but these two.)

PRINCE: Sullivan! Correct us if we are wrong, but we have the impression that your orchestra plays too quietly in the theater. More than one would expect.

SULLIVAN: That may well be so, Your Highness. Unlike grand opera, which often is sung in another language, in comic opera the singers' words must be clearly heard.

PRINCE: Do you not find that difficult? Having to subjugate your work to Gilbert's?

SULLIVAN: *(carefully; this is a sore point)* Yes, I cannot deny that. But Gilbert is right. The audience must understand what is happening.

PRINCE: Then will you accept our advice, Sullivan?

(SULLIVAN inclines his head in acquiescence.)

You should be composing more important works; works in which your music will take a predominant position. *(slight pause)* Her Majesty wishes you to write a symphony for her. Or, better still, a full opera.

SULLIVAN: Her Majesty's wish is my command.

PRINCE: Then Her Majesty can look forward to hearing music from you on a grander scale?

(SULLIVAN bows. A servant enters with the PRINCE's cloak, which he helps the PRINCE don. The PRINCE adopts a confidential tone.)

We have to congratulate you on the great honor Her Majesty has in store for you.

(The lights fade rapidly, accompanied by the first bars of 'Loudly let the trumpets bray.')

(The lights come up on Gilbert's study. GILBERT is writing. LUCY is reading a newspaper. She lowers it and looks at him with some surprise.)

LUCY: Mr. Sullivan is to be knighted!

(GILBERT taps a folded newspaper on his desk.)

GILBERT: So I see.
LUCY: But…only Mr. Sullivan?
GILBERT: Exactly.
LUCY: But shouldn't… *(she pauses)*
GILBERT: Now, Kitty. You know how I feel. About patronage appointments.
> *(GILBERT turns back to his writing. LUCY shakes her head: she is genuinely sorry for him, feels his pain.)*

LUCY: Oh, William…
> *(Immediately, the opening to the peers' chorus from* Iolanthe *can be heard. The lights dim slightly on Gilbert's study and come up on the male chorus of peers standing in a semicircle at upstage center; they sing.)*

CHORUS: Loudly let the trumpet bray!
> Tantantara!
> Proudly bang the sounding brasses!
> Tzing! Boom!

(SULLIVAN enters stage right, wearing a top hat and cloak. A liveried manservant helps him remove them, holds them.)

CHORUS: As upon its lordly way
> The unique procession passes,
> Tantantara! Tzing! Boom!

(The lights come up on QUEEN VICTORIA, in profile, seated on a dais at stage left, facing stage right. An equerry stands upstage of her, holding a sword.)

(GILBERT turns from his desk and watches, his expression impassive, unmoving, expressionless. Slowly the lights fade on him.)

> Bow, bow, ye lower middle classes!
> Bow, bow, ye tradesmen; bow, ye masses!
> Blow the trumpets, bang the brasses!
> Tantantara! Tzing! Boom!

(SULLIVAN approaches the QUEEN and goes down on one knee before her.)

CHORUS: Composer of highest station,
> Here with greatest commendation,

CHORUS: *(continues singing)*
> Pillar of the British nation,
> > Tantantara! Tzing! Boom!

(The music and singing pause briefly. The QUEEN *stands, takes the sword, lifts it, touches its tip to each of* SULLIVAN*'s shoulders.)*

QUEEN: Sir Arthur!

*(*SULLIVAN *rises, steps back, bows.)*

SULLIVAN: Your Majesty.

(The final chorus of the song booms out as SULLIVAN backs away.)

CHORUS: Blow the trumpets, bang the brasses!
> Tantantara! Tzing! Boom!

CURTAIN

Seven Plays with a Light Touch

Act 2 – Discords

*(**Introductory music:** excerpts from one or more of the songs from the operettas mentioned in Act Two:* The Mikado, Yeoman of the Guard, *and* The Gondoliers.*)*

> ***Video Option**: Alternatively, The front of a theatre with audience arriving, and the words below streamed across the lower part of the screen, much as is done in television newscasts. Alternatively, a newspaper article is shown on screen, with these words in bold print:*
>
> 'It will look rather odd to see announced in the papers that a new comic opera is in preparation, the book by *Mr* W. S. Gilbert and the music by *Sir* Arthur Sullivan'.

(The lights come up on Gilbert's study, where GILBERT *is penning a letter. His recorded voice can be heard. Part way through the following dialogue, the lights come up on Sullivan's study, where* SULLIVAN *is reading the letter.)*

GILBERT: *(v.o.)* My dear Sullivan. I have learnt from Carte, to my unbounded surprise, that you do not intend to write any more operas with me. You are, of course, aware that by our agreement we are *bound* to supply Carte with a new opera? And, if we fail to do so, we are liable to him for any losses that may result from our default? Of course you are! So I have busied myself with a new libretto and now I need your advice. As you know, in all the pieces we have written together I have invariably subordinated my views to your own...

SULLIVAN: Oh, no! No, no.

GILBERT: *(v.o.)* I am therefore absolutely at a loss to account for your decision.

*(*SULLIVAN *shakes his head in disbelief, pulls a pad of paper onto his lap, starts writing.)*

(LUCY *enters Gilbert's study, hands* GILBERT *the letter, which he opens as* SULLIVAN *speaks.)*

SULLIVAN: *(v.o.)* Dear Gilbert. I will be quite frank. I have come to the end of my tether. My tunes are in danger of becoming mere repetitions of former pieces. I have always looked upon your words as being of such importance that I have been continually keeping the music down so that not one word should be lost.

GILBERT: He keeps the music *down*?

SULLIVAN: *(v.o.)* I should like to set a story of human interest and probability, where the words derive naturally from the situation. Then there would be a feeling of reality which would give fresh interest to my writing, and fresh vitality to our joint work.

(GILBERT closes the letter.)

GILBERT: Hmmph!

(He reaches for a pen, starts writing furiously; v.o.)

My dear Sullivan. Your reflections on the character of my libretti have caused me considerable pain. However I cannot suppose you intended to gall and wound me. I must assume your letter was written hurriedly. *(slight pause)* I have sketched out the idea for the new plot and am enclosing it with this letter…

(SULLIVAN opens several manuscript pages and starts to read them. Almost immediately he shakes his head. SULLIVAN remains seated but turns and faces GILBERT across the stage; he holds a page in his hand and speaks as though he is reading from it.)

SULLIVAN: The plot you have sent me seems little different to plots you have shown me previously concerning a magic lozenge. It is going back to the topsy-turvydom which I had hoped we had now done with.

(GILBERT throws up his hands in despair and desperation. Still holding the letter, he stands and faces SULLIVAN across the stage. They are now speaking directly to each other, yet reading from their letters.)

GILBERT: My dear Sullivan. Your letter has caused me the gravest disappointment. Indeed, your objections to my libretto seem arbitrary and capricious! I regret I cannot consent to construct another plot.

SULLLIVAN: *(resigned)* The tone of your letter, Gilbert, convinces me that your decision is final and therefore further discussion is useless. I regret it very much.

(The lights extinguish quickly on Sullivan's study. GILBERT, vexed and frustrated, strides over to his desk,

throws down the letter, picks up the script, riffles through the pages, throws it down, strides to the window, looks out, strides to the door, pulls it open, calls.)

GILBERT: Kitten? Are you there? *(slight pause; irritated)* Lucy!

(GILBERT waits momentarily and then turns angrily back into the room, slamming the door shut behind him. The vibration causes a long Japanese sword to fall from the wall above the door. Startled, he picks it up, strokes it, looks at it in a bemused way.)

(Quietly at first, the opening bars of The Mikado *are heard. As they rise in volume,* GILBERT *grins, smacks his leg, strides to his desk, picks up pen and paper, carries them to his armchair, sits, leans the sword against the stool at his feet, and starts to write. The lights dim slowly in the room.)*

(Simultaneously, the MALE CHORUS *is spotlighted in the stage area, dressed in Japanese costume. As they sing,* LUCY *enters and lights the gas lamp in Gilbert's study.* GILBERT *folds the papers he has written, places them in a large envelope, gives the envelope to her with mimed instructions to post it.* LUCY *exits.)*

CHORUS: *(sings)*
    If you want to know who we are,
        We are gentlemen of Japan;
    On many a vase and jar—
        On many a screen and fan,
    We figure in lively paint,
        Our attitude's queer and quaint—
    You're wrong if you think it ain't, oh!

(The lights come up on Sullivan's room. His VALET *enters with the large envelope, hands it to* SULLIVAN, *then exits.* SULLIVAN *opens the envelope, reluctantly reads. [These actions occur as the song continues].)*

CHORUS: If you think we are worked by strings,
        Like a Japanese marionette,
    You don't understand these things;
        It is simply court etiquette.
    Perhaps you suppose this throng
        Can't keep it up all day long?

CHORUS: *(continues singing)*
>If that's your idea, you're wrong, oh!

SULLIVAN: This is more like it!
>*(SULLIVAN reaches for some blank sheet music, starts to write. Both men are now writing, and pleased with what they produce. The chorus continues to sing. Gradually, the lights fade and extinguish on both GILBERT and SULLIVAN. GILBERT rises, walks into center stage and joins a dress rehearsal.)*

CHORUS: Behold the Lord High Executioner
>A personage of noble rank and title—

(GROSSMITH enters, dressed as KOKO.)

>A dignified and potent officer,
>>Whose functions are particularly vital!
>
>Defer, defer
>To the Lord High Executioner!

KOKO: *(sings)*
>Taken from the county jail
>>By a set of curious chances;
>
>Liberated then on bail,
>>On my own recognizances;
>
>Wafted by a favouring gale
>>As one sometimes is in trances,
>
>To a height that few can scale,
>>Save by long and weary dances;
>
>Surely never had a male
>>Under such like circumstances
>
>So adventurous a tale
>>Which may rank with most romances.

CHORUS:
>Defer, defer,
>To the Lord High Executioner—
>A dignified and potent officer,
>>Whose functions are particularly vital!
>
>Defer, defer,
>To the Lord High Executioner!

(GROSSMITH/KOKO is now downstage center. The lights are fully up on the stage area. He turns to face the chorus, so his back is to the audience.)

KOKO: Gentlemen, I'm much touched by this reception. I can only trust that by strict attention to duty I shall ensure a continuance of those favors which it will—

GILBERT: *(sharply)* The only favor you're conferring is on the audience.

(GROSSMITH turns, faces GILBERT.)

GROSSMITH: I beg your pardon?

GILBERT: Your back is to the audience!

GROSSMITH: Well, how do I...?

(GILBERT points to a position upstage and to one side.)

GILBERT: According to the stage plan you should be there at the end of your solo. You do have a copy of the stage plan?

GROSSMITH: Yes, but I was concentrating first on becoming familiar with the words.

GILBERT: *(with heavy emphasis, smacking the back of one hand into the palm of the other)* The words *(smack)* and the music *(smack)* and the movements *(smack)* work together to integrate *(smack)* the effect *(smack)*. I suggest you step off the stage until you know for certain exactly where you should be at any given moment.

(GILBERT turns away from GROSSMITH who, annoyed, backs to the periphery of the group and sits.)

(GILBERT peers around, speaks reasonably, pleasantly.)

Now! Where are the three little maids? Miss Braham! Miss Bond! Miss Grey! Up front, if you please!

(The MAIDS come forward. GILBERT crosses to a real Japanese woman, in full Japanese dress, sitting on the edge of the group. She holds five fans. GILBERT leads her toward the MAIDS.)

Ah, ladies! This is Miss Sixpence. I cannot pronounce her real name. Found her in the Japanese Exhibition in Knightsbridge. She speaks very little English. *(to SIXPENCE)* Do you, my dear?

(SIXPENCE does not understand, smiles demurely, flutters a fan. GILBERT turns to the MAIDS.)

Now watch Miss Sixpence and see how she uses her fan. Japanese women use their fans to show their emotions: their delight, wrath, homage to a man.

(GILBERT turns to SIXPENCE, speaks slowly and carefully.)

GILBERT: *(continuing)* Show the ladies you are pleased.

(SIXPENCE looks vacantly at him.)

You are happy!

(Another vacant look.)

Happy! Happy!

(He tries to demonstrate happiness. SIXPENCE giggles and displays a fan movement.)

Good! Good! Now you are angry.

(No response)

Angry. Angry!

(He acts out 'wrath.' SIXPENCE nods, displays fan and body movements. GILBERT takes four fans from her, hands one to each MAID, keeps one himself, turns back to SIXPENCE.)

Now! You show them how to do it.

(He instructs the MAIDS.)

And you follow her every move.

(He urges SIXPENCE to start.)

(In the short sequence that follows, SIXPENCE demonstrates various movements with the fan, hissing and giggling at appropriate moments. The MAIDS try to copy her movements but are only partly correct. They make brief remarks such as "I see!", "Like this?" and "Is this right?" GILBERT copies the fan movements from the side, handling his fan and bodily movements correctly.)

(During the above sequence, SULLIVAN enters and sits to one side.)

GILBERT: *(to the MAIDS)* Now, try incorporating the fans into your first song together. Take your positions.

(GILBERT leads SIXPENCE to one side, shows her a seat.)

Thank you, Miss Sixpence. Do not go. We may need you yet.

(GILBERT signals to the pianist to start.)

THREE MAIDS: *(sing)*
    Three little maids from school are we,

THREE MAIDS: *(continue singing)*
> Pert as a school-girl well can be
> Filled to the brim with girlish glee,
> Three little maids from school.

GILBERT: *(as they sing)* Bend over slightly!...Look coy!...Start again.

MAIDS: Three little maids from school are we,
> Pert as a school-girl well can be
> Filled to the brim with girlish glee,
> Three little maids from school.

(The MAIDS' handling of the fans is inexpert.)

GILBERT: You have to chuckle! Giggle! Bring the fans into play. *(demonstrates)* Three little maids from school...Try it! Three little maids from school...

MAIDS: Three little maids from school...

GILBERT: Again.

MAIDS: Three little maids from school...

GILBERT: No. No. No!

(Although exasperated, GILBERT displays the immense patience he always seems to be able to muster when working with attractive young women. He steps into the group, speaks to BRAHAM, who is YUM-YUM.)

Step over there, Yum-Yum. I will demonstrate.

(He takes the middle position, between PEEP-BO and PITTI-SING, turns to BRAHAM.)

You sing your part, just as though you are standing here. I'll go through the movements.

(GILBERT turns to the two MAIDS beside him.)

Ready?

(They nod. During the song and dialogue that follow, GILBERT plays his role absolutely sincerely—there should be no attempt to clown the part, since the humor comes naturally from the situation. The onlookers on stage smile, affected by the humor that GILBERT is inadvertently creating.)

MAIDS:	Three little maids from school are we,
	Pert as a school-girl well can be,
	Filled to the brim with girlish glee,
	Three little maids from school!
YUM-YUM:	Everything is a source of fun. *(chuckle)*
PEEP-BO:	Nobody's safe, for we care for none! *(chuckle)*
PITTI-SING:	Life is a joke that's just begun! *(chuckle)*
MAIDS:	Three little maids from school.

(The two MAIDS and GILBERT dance.)

    Three little maids who, all unwary,
    Come from a ladies' seminary,
    Freed from its genius tutelary,
    (demure) Three little maids from school!

YUM-YUM:	One little maid is a bride, Yum-Yum—
PEEP-BO:	Two little maids in attendance come—
PITTI-SING:	Three little maids is the total sum.
MAIDS:	Three little maids from school!
YUM-YUM:	From three little maids take one away,
PEEP-BO:	Two little maids remain, and they—
PITTI-SING:	Won't have to wait very long, they say—
MAIDS:	Three little maids from school!

(dancing) Three little maids who, all unwary,
    Come from a ladies' seminary,
    Freed from its genius tutelary—
    (demure) Three little maids from school!

(As the song nears its end, GROSSMITH [as KOKO] signals to BARRINGTON [as POOH BAH] to join him in the dialogue that follows. Although the inferences in the exchanges between KOKO and GILBERT (as Yum-Yum) are amusing to the onlookers, GROSSMITH and GILBERT play their roles absolutely sincerely.)

KOKO: At last, my bride to be!

(KO-KO is about to embrace GILBERT who, looking surprised, glances at BRAHAM, expecting her to answer. When she does not, he speaks Yum-Yum's lines.)

GILBERT: You're not going to kiss me before all these people?

KOKO: Well, that was the idea.

GILBERT: *(as* Yum-Yum, *aside to* PEEP-BO*)* It seems odd, doesn't it?

PEEP-BO: It's rather peculiar.

PITTI-SING: Oh, I expect it's all right. Must have a beginning, you know.

GILBERT: *(as* Yum-Yum*)* Well, of course I know nothing about these things; but I've no objection if it's usual.

KOKO: Oh, it's quite usual, I think. *(appeals to* POOH BAH*)* Eh, Lord Chamberlain?

POOH BAH: *(trying not to laugh)* I have known it done.

*(*KOKO *embraces* GILBERT.*)*

GILBERT: *(as* Yum-Yum*)* Thank goodness that's over!

(The whole CAST *burst into laughter.)*

SULLIVAN: My dear Gilbert! Is there no way we could have you perform in the production? There's more humor in the moments you have just created than in the whole opera!

GILBERT: I fear a Savoy audience would hardly find it acceptable.

*(*GILBERT *turns abruptly to* RICHARD TEMPLE, *who is dressed as* THE MIKADO.*)*

Your solo, Mr. Temple. I have had to change the words. I suggest you practice them.

*(*GILBERT *hands* TEMPLE *a sheet.* TEMPLE *studies it and invites the pianist to play.)*

MIKADO: *(sings)*

>My object all sublime
>I shall achieve in time—
>To let the punishment fit the crime—
>>The punishment fit the crime;
>And make each prisoner pent
>>Unwillingly represent
>A source of merriment!
>>Of innocent merriment!

(As The MIKADO *sings he beckons to offstage. A member of the Japanese male chorus enters, carrying a poster, sets it up.)*

> **Savoy Theatre**
>
> # The Mikado
>
> **Second Year!**

> **Video Option:** *A video of the front of the theater shows a regular poster. A Japanese worker enters and glues a strip of paper announcing* SECOND YEAR! *diagonally across the poster.*

(If the video option is not used, during the chorus the MIKADO *and the* WORKER *bow to each other Japanese style, turn about, and walk off in opposite directions.)*

(During the MIKADO'*s song,* GILBERT *exits unobtrusively.)*

CHORUS: His object all sublime
       He shall achieve in time—
    To let the punishment fit the crime—
          The punishment fit the crime;
       And make each prisoner pent
       Unwillingly represent
   A source of merriment!
       Of innocent merriment!

(The lights fade and extinguish on the scene and come up on Gilbert's study. CARTE *is seated.* GILBERT *stands beside his desk, sorting papers. The two men are making small talk, aware that something deeper has to be brought into the open.)*

CARTE: You realize The Mikado is expected to have a remarkably long run? It will be *months* before I have to call on you for a new libretto.

GILBERT: Does Sullivan know that?

CARTE: I'll drop him a line.

(GILBERT crosses to a chair. He limps. CARTE notices.)

GILBERT: Gout! A nuisance I have recently acquired. *(he sits)* You have my letter?

CARTE: You feel I have too much control?

GILBERT: Exactly.

CARTE: Perhaps we should review the agreement and define—

GILBERT: We both know what's in the agreement!

CARTE: But I think we are interpreting it differently.

GILBERT: How do *you* interpret it?

CARTE: You and Sullivan write the operas, select the principal actors, and have complete control over rehearsals right up to the first performance. I keep an eye on production after that. I also look after all business matters: purchasing, making payments, all the little details.

GILBERT: In other words, you have complete control.

CARTE: Only when a production is running. Then I manage the business for you and Sullivan.

GILBERT: So you have complete control. I thought the agreement implies equal management, by the three of us?

CARTE: That would be impractical.

GILBERT: Which means I have no voice in the control over the theater?

CARTE: Of course you have a voice.

GILBERT: In your view I am merely a casual author you employ to supply you with manuscripts!

CARTE: If I could be an author like you, I would not want to be a manager. Have you ever thought that I'm no more than a tradesman, a tradesman who sells the operettas you write?

GILBERT: If you alone are in control, how do Sullivan and I know you won't make poor decisions? Decisions that could jeopardize the whole business?

CARTE: In nine years, have I ever given you evidence of mismanagement?

GILBERT: An agreement in which only one person has any real control...no, it simply will not do. I have informed Sullivan that he and I must share in the management of the theater.

CARTE: Sullivan does not wish to be drawn into the matter.

(GILBERT reacts with surprise.)

He wrote to me.

GILBERT: So Sullivan is taking your side?

CARTE: No, no! He just doesn't want to be bothered with the day-to-day management of—

GILBERT: *(explosively)* It's a conspiracy!

CARTE: If you want to talk to Sullivan you—

GILBERT: We have a 'loaded' agreement! The sides of the triangle are not equal!

CARTE: *(sharply)* The *risk* certainly is not equal. Has it occurred to you, Gilbert, that the difference is in *your* favor?

(GILBERT does not respond.)

We share the profits equally, do we not? But do we share the risks equally?

GILBERT: You deduct the expenses from the profits—

CARTE: Suppose you and Sullivan do the most unlikely thing and write an operetta that drives audiences away? Who, then, will be most affected financially? True, you and Sullivan won't have any profits. But I alone would bear *all* the expenses: over three thousand pounds to produce The Mikado! *(slight pause as he becomes calmer)* It's a matter of trust. I trust you and Sullivan to produce pieces that will be popular. You trust me to manage the business well. We are all experts in our own fields, and we have to trust each other. It certainly is not just one against two!

(Pause as they weigh each other up.)

GILBERT: *(gruffly conciliatory)* Then I suggest we let the matter drop.

CARTE: Gladly. *(extends his hand)* It's already forgotten.

(They shake hands. The lights extinguish on Gilbert's study and come up on a poster. Music from The Mikado *can be*

heard. *The* MIKADO *enters, walks to the poster, studies it, then beckons off-stage.)*

> **Savoy Theatre**
>
> ## The Mikado
>
> **650 Performances!**
>
> **Closing 2nd January**

(The JAPANESE MAN *enters and, in response to the* MIKADO's *mimed directions, turns the poster around. A new poster, advertising* Ruddigore, *is on the reverse side.)*

> **Savoy Theatre**
>
> # Ruddigore
>
> or
>
> ## The Witch's Curse!
>
> **Opens**
> **22nd January 1887**

(The MIKADO *and the* JAPANESE MAN *bow to one another and exit in opposite directions. A short piece from* Ruddigore *is heard as the lights fade slowly on the poster.)*

> ***Video Option:*** *The posters can be projected, showing the front of a theater with the Mikado and Japanese Man videotaped, performing the action. Or the announcements can be streamed. as in a newscast.*

(The lights come up on Sullivan's office, with GILBERT, CARTE *and* SULLIVAN *present.)*

Chords, Accords and Discords

CARTE: Gentlemen! I asked you to meet here this morning because we have to find a successor to Ruddigore. Houses are thinning.

SULLIVAN: One cannot just churn them out, Carte, like a string of sausages!

CARTE: No. I'm not unaware you have…other commitments. *(to GILBERT)* How soon can you promise me a new libretto?

GILBERT: I have one now. Ready.

SULLIVAN: *(with heavy emphasis)* A *new* one?

GILBERT: I sent it to you. A fortnight ago.

SULLIVAN: And I returned it. *(to CARTE)* I have to work on a plot that has more depth. It's too contrived: the same kind of story. No substance to it. *(to GILBERT)* If I were to use the same basic melodies again, for the next piece, would you not object?

GILBERT: I told you. I have a tin ear.

(Exasperated and frustrated, SULLIVAN gestures an appeal to CARTE.)

CARTE: Gentlemen. I know we have an agreement, but I would rather not be strident about it. I'll put on a revival. Probably H.M.S. Pinafore. That should give you three to four months.

SULLIVAN: *(reluctantly conciliatory; not with very good grace)* I suppose that's reasonable. *(to GILBERT)* If you can present me with a libretto that has both realism and humor in it, then… alright, I'll work on it with you.

GILBERT: I cannot see why I should start scrambling for another plot, when I've already provided you with a perfectly sound one! *(he rises, prepares to leave)* I'll leave it to you, Carte. You convince him! Good-day to both of you. *(he pushes through the door and exits.)*

CARTE: That's the gout talking.

SULLIVAN: Is it? *(sighs)* I wonder, sometimes, whether the time has come for Gilbert and me to go our separate ways.

CARTE: You can't be serious? You and Gilbert *created* the current comic opera genre.

SULLIVAN: I would rather retire gracefully now than be laughed at because Gilbert is incapable of coming up with something original. The new piece *has* to be on a much grander scale. On that I insist.

(CARTE throws his hands up in desperation as the lights extinguish and come up on a backdrop of part of a railway station with a ticket office and two signs: UXBRIDGE and GREAT WESTERN RAILWAY. On the wall, beside the ticket office, there is a large advertisement for Beefeater Gin showing a Beefeater standing in front of the Tower of London. There are steam-train engine sounds.)

(GILBERT enters, looks along the line, studies his pocket watch, looks up, sees the poster, studies it. He nods, taps the side of his head: he has an idea.)

(Quietly, the opening bars of the overture to The Yeoman of the Guard *can be heard.)*

> **Video Option:** *Instead of the physical presence of the railway station, it is shown on screen with a steam train pulling in, Gilbert boarding it, and the train departing.*

(The lights extinguish on the rail station and come up on Sullivan's study, with SULLIVAN seated. GILBERT marches from the station into the study, stands across from SULLIVAN, leans toward him.)

I want to use the Tower of London—Beefeaters and all—as the scene for the new opera.
(SULLIVAN nods cautiously, enquiringly. GILBERT paces.)
A romantic and dramatic piece, set in Elizabethan times.

SULLIVAN: *(gestures)* Oh, do sit down!

GILBERT: *(sits; enthusiastic)* I've got the plot pretty well combed out…almost a historical tale. D'you think a Savoy audience could stand a sad ending?

SULLIVAN: Without knowing the full story, I—

GILBERT: Not entirely sad! Three couples: one more or less happily wed. Two marriages, of shall we say…convenience? And one person—a jester—broken-hearted. *(defensive)* It's complicated to describe, but visually it will be clear.

(Slight pause; Sullivan nods: shows he is interested.)

There's a prisoner in the Tower—I'll call him Colonel Fairfax—and he's to be executed. Tomorrow.

GILBERT: *(continuing)* Because he doesn't want his conniving brother to inherit his estate, he asks the Tower Warden to find him a woman to marry. And that very day!

SULLIVAN: *(clearly interested)* Go on...

GILBERT: Now! At that moment two strolling singers arrive—a man and a woman. The woman agrees to go through with the marriage, for a sum of money. The man—the court jester—he loves the woman, which means he's not happy with the arrangement. But eventually he agrees. Because of the money. And because he knows the woman will be a widow almost immediately.

SULLIVAN: It sounds complex, but I follow you.

GILBERT: But a last-minute escape is arranged and Colonel Fairfax is *not* executed. By then, he's married to the woman—not too unhappily, I might add. And of course now the court jester has lost his love. *(Slight pause)* I realize it's not our normal kind of light opera...

SULLIVAN: It sounds splendid, Gilbert!

GILBERT: *(surprised; gruffly)* Thought it might appeal to you.

SULLIVAN: *(nods his agreement; now enthused)* Tell me more...

GILBERT: The piece will even open dramatically. Phoebe—she's the warden's daughter—alone on the stage, spinning at a wheel, lamenting an unrequited love...

(A spotlight identifies JESSIE BOND, *as* PHOEBE. *The lights dim on* GILBERT *and* SULLIVAN.*)*

PHOEBE: *(sings)*

> When maiden loves, she sits and sighs,
> > She wanders to and fro;
> Unbidden tear-drops fill her eyes,
> And to all questions she replies
> > With a sad 'heigho!'
>
> 'Tis but a little word—'heigho!'
> So soft, 'tis scarcely heard—'heigho!'
> > An idle breath—
> > Yet life and death
> May hang upon a maid's 'heigho!'
>
> When maiden loves, she mopes apart,
> > As owl mopes on a tree;
> Although she keenly feels the smart,

PHOEBE: *(continues singing)*

> She cannot tell what ails her heart,
> With its sad "Ah me!"
>
> 'Tis but a foolish sigh—"Ah me!"
> Born but to drop and die—"Ah me!"
> Yet all the sense
> Of eloquence
> Lies hidden in the maid's "Ah me!"

(She pretends to weep.)

(The lights come up and we see BOND *is in rehearsal. The* CAST *are sitting around the stage.* GILBERT *and* SULLIVAN *are present, but sitting apart.)*

SULLIVAN: Splendid, Miss Bond! Don't be afraid to let a catch in your throat be heard, the second and third time you sing 'Ah me!' A quick indrawn breath: "Ah me!" Prepare the audience for your weeping. Do you agree, Mr. Gilbert?

GILBERT: In essence, yes. But not *too* tearful, Miss Bond. Discreet weeping, if you please. It's still a *comic* opera.

(GILBERT consults a list, turns to GROSSMITH.)

Now! Mr. Grossmith.

GROSSMITH: Yes, Mr. Gilbert.

GILBERT: And Miss Ulmar.

(They approach. GROSSMITH *wears a jester's outfit;* ULMAR *a peasant dress.)*

Yesterday's rehearsal: 'I have a song to sing, O!' There's too much similarity between the two occasions you sing it. *(to* SULLIVAN*)* Do you mind if we rehearse it again?

SULLIVAN: No, that would be useful. *(To* GROSSMITH*)* The first time, the song must be joyful, cheerful: you're dancing and singing with the woman you love *(indicates* ULMAR*)*. You *know* you have a future together.

GILBERT: Exactly. The audience needs to empathize with you; feel your joy.

SULLIVAN: *(to* GILBERT*)* You go ahead. I'll watch from the auditorium. *(he exits into the audience)*

GILBERT: *(to* GROSSMITH *and* ULMAR*)* You're strolling singers and you burst into the scene. The crowd *(indicates the* CAST*)* expects some fun from you. So does the audience.

GILBERT: *(continuing)* Especially from you, Jack Point. So make the song merry, even though the subject is doleful.
(JACK POINT [Grossmith] and ELSIE [Ulmar] sing exuberantly, interacting with and dancing in and out of the CAST assembled around them.)

POINT: I have a song to sing, O!

ELSIE: Sing me your song, O!

POINT:
    It is sung to the moon
    By a love-lorn loon,
Who fled from the mocking throng, O!

It's a song of a merryman, moping mum,
Whose soul was sad, and whose glance was glum,
Who sipped no sup, and who craved no crumb,
    As he sighed for the love of a ladye.
        Heighdy! Heighdy!
        Misery me, lackaday dee!
He sipped no sup, and he craved no crumb,
    As he sighed for the love of a ladye.

ELSIE: I have a song to sing, O!

POINT: What is your song, O!

ELSIE:
    It is sung with the ring
    Of the song maids sing
Who love with a love life-long, O!

It's the song of a merrymaid, pearly proud,
Who loved a lord and who laughed aloud
At the moan of the merryman, moping mum,
Whose soul was sad, and whose glance was glum,
    As he sighed for the love of a ladye.
        Heighdy! Heighdy!
        Misery me, lackadaydee!
He sipped no sup, and he craved no crumb,
    As he sighed for the love of a ladye.

(GILBERT interrupts.)

GILBERT: That's fine. That's fine. *(to SULLIVAN, in audience)* What do you think, Sir Arthur?

SULLIVAN: *(from the audience)* You have caught the spirit well. I suggest we go straight to the final scene.

ULMAR: Then let me put on the wedding gown.

(A cast member hands a formal, flowing gown to ELSIE/ULMAR, *which she pulls over her peasant dress.)*

It's not really a bridal gown, but the audience will think it is.

*(*COURTICE POUNDS, *dressed as Colonel Fairfax, approaches; two* CAST *members push a platform to center stage. There are three steps leading to its top level.)*

GILBERT: *(to* POUNDS, *indicating the top of the platform)* We need you here, Colonel Fairfax. You stand beside Elsie. Closer! You've just discovered you are married to her, and you are not entirely displeased. Elsie: you find him attractive, too, yet your heart still seems to be with the jester. Now, we'll pick up from the moment when Jack Point enters. Is everyone ready?

GROSSMITH: No, not yet. How do you want me to play this scene?

SULLIVAN: *(from audience, walking toward stage)* You must be mournful, woeful.

GILBERT: You have just lost your sweetheart *(indicates* ELSIE*)*. You're heartbroken. Yet you're still the jester, and have to continue in your role.

GROSSMITH: So, do you want it to be tragic or comic?

GILBERT: How do you feel when you sing it?

GROSSMITH: You wrote the words!

GILBERT: You're the actor. You're the person out there, interpreting them. Not me.

GROSSMITH: *(exasperated)* Well, what do you mean by "insensible"?

GILBERT: Insensible?

GROSSMITH: In your libretto. The very last words before the curtain falls: "Jack Point falls insensible at her feet."

GILBERT: Exactly what it says.

GROSSMITH: *(frustrated)* Have I died of a broken heart? Or have I just fainted? Or am I only acting, as a jester might?

GILBERT: *(with finality)* Play it the way you *feel* it, when you get there.

*(*GROSSMITH *shakes his head in frustration and exits.* GILBERT *moves to stage right of the acting area.)*

All right, Jack Point. Make your entrance.

(POINT *enters, sees* FAIRFAX *and* ELSIE *on the platform, clearly attracted to each other. He breaks into song, but this time the tempo is slower and the song is affecting, moving.*)

POINT: Oh, thoughtless crew!
    Ye know not what ye do!
    Attend to me, and shed a tear or two—
For I have a song to sing, O!

CHORUS: Sing me your song, O!

POINT: It is sung to the moon
    By a love-lorn loon,
Who fled from the mocking throng, O!
It's the song of a merryman, moping mum,
Whose soul was sad, and whose glance was glum,
Who sipped no sup, and who craved no crumb.
    As he sighed for the love of a ladye!

CHORUS: Heighdy! heighdy!
    Misery me, lackadaydee!
He sipped no sup, he craved no crumb,
    As he sighed for the love of a ladye!

ELSIE: I have a song to sing, O!

CHORUS: What is your song, O!

ELSIE: It is sung with the ring
    Of the song maids sing
Who love with a love life-long, O!
It's the song of a merrymaid, nestling near,
Who loved her lord—but who dropped a tear
At the moan of the merryman, moping mum,
Whose soul was sad, and whose glance was glum,
Who sipped no sup, and who craved no crumb,
    As he sighed for the love of ladye!

CHORUS: Heighdy! heighdy!
    Misery me, lackadaydee!
He sipped no sup, he craved no crumb,
    As he sighed for the love of a ladye!

(*During the last chorus,* FAIRFAX *embraces* ELSIE. POINT *sees, kisses the hem of her dress, and falls inert at her feet.* FAIRFAX *and* ELSIE *turn and walk down the steps, leaving* POINT *spot-lit, alone. They pause at the side of the stage, where other members of the cast are gathered, silent, emotionally affected by* GROSSMITH*'s performance.* ULMAR *is weeping.)*

GILBERT: *(approaching* ULMAR*)* Come, come, my dear. It's only make-believe.

*(*ULMAR *shakes her head.* GROSSMITH *rises, approaches.)*

ULMAR: Oh, Mr. Grossmith...you made it seem so real! To see you lying there, dying, as I walked away... *(sniffles)*

GILBERT: You see, Grossmith. I said for you to play it the way I wrote it.

(The lights extinguish quickly to a blackout, then come up immediately on Sullivan's room. SULLIVAN *is seated, a rug over his knees, reading a letter.)*

GILBERT: *(v.o.)* Dear Sullivan. I write in the earnest hope that the soft breezes are restoring you to good health. D'Oyly Carte has given me notice that a new comic opera will be necessary in due course. The only moderate success of The Yeomen of the Guard has not convinced me that the public will want something more earnest still. So I have started working up a plot for a light-hearted peek at the people of Venice, and particularly two young gondoliers.

*(*SULLIVAN *starts to write in reply. The lights come up on* GILBERT *in his study. He reads the letter.)*

SULLIVAN: *(v.o.)* My dear Gilbert. I confess that the public's indifference to The Yeomen of the Guard has disappointed me greatly. I had hoped its success would open out a large field for works of a more serious and romantic character. If this means returning to our former style of piece, I must say at once, and with deep regret, that I cannot do it.

(For the remainder of the correspondence, GILBERT *and* SULLIVAN *face each other across the stage, speaking the words when the recipient is 'reading' the letter.)*

GILBERT: It would be an understatement to say that I was disturbed by your letter. To hear that you will work only on grand opera confounds me beyond imagination. In grand opera the work of the librettist is always swamped in that of the composer, and I have little taste for it.

SULLIVAN: You say that in serious opera you must sacrifice yourself. I say that this is just what I have been doing, and must go on doing if I continue to work with you on comic opera.

GILBERT: If you are really under the astounding impression that you have been effacing yourself during the last twelve years, then there most certainly is no 'modus vivendi' satisfactory to both of us. If we are to meet, it must be as master and master—not master and servant.

SULLIVAN: There is one point in your letter with which I completely agree: if we meet it must be as master and master. For it has been my sad experience that I have become a mere cipher in the theatre: they are your pieces with music added by me.

(CARTE enters and sits across from SULLIVAN.)

GILBERT: *(very angry)* Your letter has hurt me beyond measure. If you seriously believe that by working with me for twelve years you have been rebuffed, ignored, set aside, extinguished, and generally effaced by your librettist, then I see no point in our continuing this correspondence!

(Blackout on GILBERT.)

SULLIVAN: Why does he have to be so intransigent?

CARTE: *(laughs lightly)* He feels *you* are being intransigent. But, then, he feels that way about anyone who disagrees with him.

SULLIVAN: *(after a slight pause)* Are you here to hand me an ultimatum?

CARTE: No. I come as an emissary.

SULLIVAN: From Gilbert?

CARTE: For myself. And, indirectly, the cast. Gilbert is unaware I am here. I have to be cautious. As you know, he has a tendency to draw inferences.

(SULLIVAN nods glumly.)

I need to go back to him knowing you will compose the music for the new piece. But this time with you and Gilbert as master and master.

SULLIVAN: You are asking me to back down?

CARTE: No. Neither of you has to back down. You have both made the same stipulation. But Gilbert won't agree if he thinks *you* think he's backing down.

SULLIVAN: *(sighs)* Have you seen his manuscript?

CARTE: Yes.

SULLIVAN: Do you think it's...acceptable?

CARTE: Yes. Very much so.

SULLIVAN: *(slight smile)* You...er...you wouldn't just happen to have it with you?

CARTE: *(laughs)* I have.

> *(CARTE reaches into his briefcase, pulls out a sheaf of pages, hands them to SULLIVAN. The lights fade on Sullivan's room, come up on the stage as GILBERT marches in. The CAST are assembled in their street clothes. GILBERT is very business-like.)*

GILBERT: I trust you have all read the script?

> *(Nods from the CAST.)*

And marked your own lines?

> *(More nods.)*

And have noticed the major difference between The Gondoliers and The Yeomen of the Guard?

> *(GILBERT looks around, questioningly. There is no response.)*

Well?

BOND: *(hesitantly)* The Gondoliers seems to be a much happier story?

GILBERT: Exactly, Miss Bond. Cheerful, not tearful.

> *(SULLIVAN enters, carrying his music case.)*

BARRINGTON: There seems to be a lot more music.

GILBERT: Exactly! And it's right at the start. A full seventeen minutes, before there's a line of dialogue. Sir Arthur will be rehearsing that part with you. *(to SULLIVAN)* Right, Sir Arthur?

SULLIVAN: Well, yes.

GILBERT: Perhaps you would like to rehearse it, right now?

SULLIVAN: Perhaps just one song. To set the mood.

GILBERT: Right, then.

> *(GILBERT sits to one side, making it clear that SULLIVAN is in control.)*

SULLIVAN: Miss Bond. Miss Ulmar. How about singing 'Thank you' to the two gondoliers who have chosen you to marry them? It's on page fourteen.

BOND: Oh, yes, Sir Arthur.

ULMAR: I would love to!

SULLIVAN: Then you shall. Mr. Barrington? Mr. Pounds? Will you come up here, too, please? *(to* CAST*)* And you ladies: will you pick up the first chorus? *(to* GILBERT*)* I gather you intend the two ladies should tease their men?

GILBERT: Quite right! Teasing comes naturally to women. They can't help it.

SULLIVAN: Shall we start, then?

*(*BOND *and* ULMAR *nod. During the song,* SULLIVAN *'conducts' the cast.* ULMAR *is* GIANETTA *and sings to* POUNDS; BOND *is* TESSA *and sings to* BARRINGTON. *They all sing from scripts; Gilbert exits unnoticed.)*

GIANETTA: Thank you gallant gondolieri!
    In a set and formal measure
  It is scarcely necessary
    To express our pleasure.
    Each of us to prove a treasure,
  Conjugal and monetary,
    Gladly will devote our leisure,
  Gay and gallant gondolieri!
    Tra, la, la, la, la, la, *etc*

TESSA: Gay and gallant gondolieri,
    Take us both and hold us tightly,
  You have luck extraordinary;
    We might have been unsightly!
    If we judge your conduct rightly,
  'Twas a choice involuntary;
    Still we thank you most politely,
  Gay and gallant gondolieri!
    Tra, la, la, la, la, la, *etc*

WOMEN'S CHORUS:
    Thank you, gallant gondolieri,
    In a set and formal measure,

WOMEN'S CHORUS: *(continue singing)*
> It is scarcely necessary
> To express our pleasure.
> Each of us to prove a treasure
> Gladly will devote our leisure
> Gay and gallant gondolieri!
> Tra, la, la, la, la, la, *etc*

FULL CHORUS:
> Fate in this has put his finger—
> Let us bow to Fate's decree,
> Then no longer let us linger,
> To the altar hurry we!

SULLIVAN: Splendid! Splendid! Now you two couples can run off hand-in-hand. *(clearly pleased)* This is such a happy occasion!

(The lights fade on the rehearsal area and come up on Carte's office. CARTE *and* HELEN CARTE *are seated.* GILBERT *is standing, leaning on his stick and waving a sheaf of papers at* CARTE.*)*

GILBERT: If I hadn't *asked* to see the accounts, I would never have known!

CARTE: The pre-production costs were a bit above average, but in the light of The Gondoliers' extraordinary success—

GILBERT: A *bit* above average! You are calling forty-five hundred pounds only 'a bit' above average?

CARTE: I cannot stage the kind of production you and Sir Arthur expect without incurring—

GILBERT: *(studying papers)* Look at this! Seventy-five pounds for Miss Moore's dress! One hundred for Miss Brandram's! Incredible! Four hundred and seventy pounds for carpenters' wages! I could build a decent bungalow for that. Four hundred and sixty pounds for the gondola. It's used only once each night!

CARTE: You insisted it should be exact in every detail—

GILBERT: *(waving the accounts at* HELEN*)* You informed me, Mrs. Carte, that all these expenses are pre-production costs.

HELEN: So they are.

GILBERT: Then can you explain why they include carpet for the *front* of the theater?

HELEN: After seven years the carpet has become quite worn—
GILBERT: What has the *front* of the house got to do with *production* costs?
CARTE: It's part of the general upkeep.
GILBERT: Four hundred and fifty pounds to carpet just the *front* of the theatre? I should like to see how you have carpeted your new home!
CARTE: That is entirely unwarranted. I demand you withdraw your accusation!
GILBERT: Unwarranted? Perhaps. But four hundred and fifty pounds is totally beyond reason for—
CARTE: I asked you to withdraw—
GILBERT: You have not explained to my satisfaction why the carpet should be charged against *production* costs?
HELEN: *(who has been leafing through some papers)* Mr. Gilbert! Do take a look at the entry for carpets. My sheet shows the cost to be *one* hundred and fifty pounds. Not *four* hundred and fifty. Is there, perhaps, an error, on your sheet?
GILBERT: *(peers at his sheet)* Atrocious lettering. Hardly readable! Possibly it's one hundred and fifty. Regardless, it's the principle I'm concerned about.

(SULLIVAN enters, looks around, is concerned He looks wan and drawn.)

Ah! Sullivan. You received my letter?
SULLIVAN: I came immediately.
GILBERT: I am trying to elicit from this rogue *(indicates* CARTE*)* why the expenses for the Gondoliers were so impossibly high. It's all in here.

(GILBERT shoves the sheaf of papers in front of SULLIVAN and pokes his finger at them.)

Look at this: four hundred and fifty pounds for carpet for—
HELEN: *(firmly)* One hundred and fifty pounds, Mr. Gilbert.
GILBERT: The amount is of little significance, madam. *(to* SULLIVAN*)* You and I are being robbed to pay for carpet for the *front* of the theatre!
SULLIVAN: Oh, I'm sure D'Oyly Carte has good reason—
GILBERT: I have been unable to obtain a single satisfactory answer. Not one!

SULLIVAN: Well, perhaps we should pause a minute to give Mr. Carte the floor. *(To* HELEN*)* Do you mind, madam, if I sit?

HELEN: Please do.

*(*SULLIVAN *sits wearily.)*

GILBERT: Well, Carte, we're waiting.

CARTE: *(angry, but controlling it)* There seem to be two points of contention: the production costs, and the carpet costs. May I take the production costs first?

GILBERT: *(curtly)* If you wish.

CARTE: I agree, the production expenses for The Gondoliers were enormously and unnecessarily high—

GILBERT: Ah, ha!

CARTE: But I have to lay the blame at your door.

GILBERT: At *my* door? You conceal the accounts and then—

SULLIVAN: *(interposing quietly but firmly)* Let him speak, Gilbert.

CARTE: It has always been my policy to get estimates before placing an order. Many times you ordered materials and costumes, or work to be done, without informing me or consulting me.

GILBERT: I have to *consult* you every time I want to order—?

CARTE: I tried to get estimates, but always it seemed you had not settled this, or couldn't decide that... *(he shrugs; to* SULLIVAN*)* You know how it can be! *(to* GILBERT*)* So, rather than get involved in an argu...in a lengthy discussion, I stood back and let you go ahead.

GILBERT: Humph! And the carpet?

CARTE: The carpet was rightly charged as an expense to the production.

*(*GILBERT *looks incredulous.)*

When a production company rents a theatre, they are expected to return it at the completion of the engagement in the same state as when they first rented it. We three *(indicates* GILBERT, SULLIVAN *and himself)* rent the Savoy from me. I built and own the theatre. After seven years the carpet has been worn down by *our* audiences.

SULLIVAN: Standard practice.

GILBERT: That's the core to the whole problem: our friend Carte, here, is biased!

Chords, Accords and Discords

SULLIVAN: Oh, come now, Gilbert—

GILBERT: Here me through. We've got to have a new agreement. It's essential!

HELEN: I think you are overlooking one rather important fact, Mr. Gilbert. Under the terms of your present agreement, you and Sir Arthur and Mr. Carte share the profits *equally*.

GILBERT: If any happen to be left, madam, yes. After the expenses have been deducted, over which Sir Arthur and I seem to have no control!

CARTE: *(indignant and passionate)* While you have been on holiday, Mrs. Carte and I have been working like slaves keeping your productions running. Then, on your return, you come straight here and present us with this ridiculous disturbance. I should be sorry to lose the financial advantage of producing further operettas for you, but this earth does not contain enough money for me to put up with you any longer!

GILBERT: *(irrationally angry)* You, sir, have been making too much money out of my brains! And for more years than I care to count. I have written my last opera for the Savoy. After December you are to withdraw The Gondoliers. Sir Arthur's and my work—our *united* work—will no longer be heard in public!

SULLIVAN: Gilbert, I—

GILBERT: There is little point in your addressing me, Sir Arthur. It has been apparent for some time that you and Mr. Carte have your own agreement, which clearly excludes me. *(he pushes past* SULLIVAN*)* Kindly let me pass! *(at door)* The two of you are a pair of out-and-out blackguards! I have no recourse but to place the matter in the hands of my solicitors!

(Fast blackout on office scene.)

(Lights up on a London street scene. A newspaper seller's poster leans against an upended crate piled with newspapers.)

> **Video Option:** *The sequence from the moment the poster is seen is pre-recorded and projected onscreen, opening with the poster being in close-up and then the camera pulls back to reveal the street scene.*

THE STAR

***

GILBERT AND SULLIVAN IN COURT

(Two women in their mid-to-late-thirties converse stage left, shopping baskets over their arms.)

NEWS VENDOR: Star! Gilbert sues Sullivan. All the latest. Star!

(A man [ERNIE] approaches, buys a paper.)

WOMAN 1: *(inclines head toward poster)* Better than going to the theater, love.

WOMAN 2: Well, 'e can't need the money, now can 'e? My Jack, 'e says they makes a thousand quid a month. Each!

WOMAN 1: They're all the same. Them that 'as it, it's them that wants more.

(ERNIE walks toward the women as he reads.)

WOMAN 2: 'Ere, Ernie! Don't keep it to yerself.

ERNIE: The Star says it's like Trial by Jury. Their first play.

WOMAN 1: Bit before my time, Dearie.

(WOMAN 1 eyes WOMAN 2 doubtfully.)

ERNIE: *(reads)* "It would be a pretty piece of courtesy if the judge were to open the proceedings in the proper comic style laid down by the librettist."

(During ERNIE's speech the lights have come up on stage right, where a bewigged JUDGE [FRED] sits at the bench and a bewigged COUNSEL [POUNDS] stands beneath the bench.)

COUNSEL: *(sings)*
>May it please you, my lud!
>>Gentlemen of the jury!
>
>With a sense of deep emotion,
>>I approach this painful case,
>
>For I never had a notion
>>That a man could be so base
>
>As to doubt a gentleman's word,
>>And bring this case to be heard.

CHORUS: He doubted a gentleman's word
>>And brought this case to be heard.

JUDGE: A nice dilemma we have here
>>That calls for all our wit!
>
>And at this stage, it don't appear
>>That we can settle it!

(The lights extinguish on the JUDGE, COUNSEL, ERNIE and the two WOMEN, and come up on Sullivan's study, with CARTE and SULLIVAN sitting. SULLIVAN is clearly ill.)

CARTE: I have instructed my counsel to make still another offer to Gilbert. This time he has accepted.

SULLIVAN: Thank God! I am physically and mentally ill over this wretched business.

CARTE: Already he seems to regret having let it go so far. He has written to Mrs. Carte to apologize.

(SULLIVAN picks up and waves a letter.)

SULLIVAN: I have one too. *(reads)* "In a moment of anger I applied an epithet to you and Carte which, on reflection, I consider to be unjustifiable. I am sorry that I used it and I unreservedly withdraw it."

CARTE: Gilbert lives only in black and white. He has no room for a gray area in between.

SULLIVAN: I am neither expecting nor encouraging a personal reconciliation. I cannot overcome the shock of seeing my name coupled with Gilbert's, not in the happy collaboration we have known but in hostile antagonism over a few miserable pounds.

(The lights extinguish on Sullivan's study and come up on Gilbert's study. GILBERT *is limping toward his large chair and is leaning on a stick. In his other hand he holds a writing pad and pen. He seats himself and writes.)*

GILBERT: *(v.o.)* My dear Sullivan. It is, as you know, a long time since we corresponded, but it would indeed be remiss of me to let the moment pass without passing comment on your grand opera Ivanhoe. Even I was caught up in the splendor of the piece. I had expected to be bored, but was surprised to find myself awake and following every song with interest.

(The lights come up on Sullivan's study, where SULLIVAN *is sitting in a wheelchair with a rug over his knees; he is reading Gilbert's letter.)*

I have a second reason for writing. Helen Carte has called on me. D'Oyly is ill and she is preparing a revival of The Pirates of Penzance on his behalf, to open in November. She feels it would do him much good if some sort of reconciliation could be arranged on stage between yourself, D'Oyly and myself. I have told her that I am in agreement. Would you be willing—and well enough—to come?

*(*SULLIVAN *lowers the letter, thinks briefly. Very quietly, the Policeman's chorus from The Pirates of Penzance can be heard. It rises in volume as* SULLIVAN *wearily reaches for a pad and paper and writes. The* POLICEMEN *can be scene dimly lit at the back of the stage.* GILBERT *turns and looks across the stage toward* SULLIVAN.*)*

SULLIVAN: *(v.o., shaky)* My Dear Gilbert. For three such frightful wrecks to appear on stage at the same time would create something of a sensation! Perhaps we could ask Mrs. Carte to arrange for the three of us to be wheeled on in wheelchairs.

(He and GILBERT *smile at the thought.)*

Do tell her that if it will please D'Oyly—and you—to have me there, then I will do my best. But, frankly, of the three of us, I fear I am the least likely to keep my appointment.

(The lights extinguish on Gilbert's study and come up on the chorus. SULLIVAN *folds the letter and leans back in the wheelchair. During the following song, the lights fade slowly over his study and extinguish completely about four lines from the end.)*

SERGEANT: (sings)
        When the foeman bares his steel,
CHORUS: Tarantara! Tarantara!!!
        We uncomfortable feel,
            Tarantara!
        And we find the wisest thing,
            Tarantara! Tarantara!
        Is to slap our chests and sing
            Tarantara!
        For when threatened with emeutes,
            Tarantara! Tarantara!
        And your heart is in your boots,
            Tarantara!
        There is nothing brings it round,
            Tarantara! Tarantara!
        Like the trumpet's martial sound,
            Tarantara! Tarantara!

(All lights fade to blackout.)

CHORUS: Tarantara-ra-ra-ra-ra!
        Tarantara-ra-ra-ra-ra!

(The lights come up on Gilbert's study. LUCY and HELEN are seated. HELEN is dressed entirely in black.)

HELEN: *(responding to a question)* Yes, it has indeed been a sad six months. Sir Arthur, last November. Then the Queen—God bless her. And now my dear D'Oyly.

LUCY: What will you do now?

HELEN: I will run the company. Put on revivals of the Savoy operas, for as long as the public wants to see them. D'Oyly wanted it that way. I plan to set up a trust, to protect Mr. Gilbert's and Sir Arthur's works. And form a permanent company to present them. I want to maintain the high standards Mr. Gilbert has set.

(GILBERT enters, limping. he wears a black armband.)

LUCY: And no more pirated productions?

HELEN: No. In America, the Savoy operas will—

GILBERT: *(crossing to her)* The Savoy operas will be protected, thanks to D'Oyly's many representations in Washington. *(takes her hand)* And you, good lady: Are you bearing up?

HELEN: Yes. I am, thank you.

GILBERT: Capital! Your daughter too?

HELEN: She misses her father, but she is learning to accept it. (slight pause) I came, because Sir Boscombe John has asked me to see you. He's designing a memorial to Sir Arthur, to be erected in the Embankment Gardens. Can you write a suitable inscription, for him to carve on it?

GILBERT: An epitaph?

HELEN: Oh, no. Too forbidding.

GILBERT: Something from one of the operettas, then?

HELEN: If you can find something suitable.

GILBERT: Hmmm. *(ponders; then suddenly definite)* The Yeomen of the Guard. Always his favorite.

(GILBERT goes to his desk, picks up a book, leafs through it. He holds the open page in front of HELEN.)

Act one. Colonel Fairfax. Here!

(A spotlight picks out POUNDS, dressed as Colonel Fairfax. The lights extinguish slowly on the study.)

FAIRFAX: (sings)
>Is life a boon?
>>If so, it must befall,
>>That death, whene'er he call,
>Must call too soon.
>
>>Though fourscore years he give,
>>Yet one would pray to live
>Another moon!
>
>What kind of plaint have I,
>>Who perish in July?
>>I might have had to die,
>Perchance in June?

> ***Video Option:*** *As Fairfax sings, a DVD is shown of Sir Arthur Sullivan's monument in the Embankment Gardens in London, with the camera homing in on the inscription.*

(The spotlight extinguishes on POUNDS. *the lights come up again on Gilbert's study. It is now seven years later.* GILBERT *is reading mail.* LUCY *is embroidering.)*

GILBERT: *(tone is matter of fact)* My dear. I have received an invitation…from His Majesty. *(paraphrasing as he reads)* "I am commanded to present myself at Buckingham Palace at eleven o'clock on the fifteenth day of July, 1907."

LUCY: You are to be knighted!

GILBERT: A tap on the shoulder. I wonder for what?

LUCY: Oh, for your writing! For your plays. For your operettas.

GILBERT: *(wryly)* Twenty-four years after Sullivan.

LUCY: You were upset about that!

GILBERT: Because I was overlooked? Of course not!

LUCY: *(suddenly doubtful)* You will go?

GILBERT: *(shrugs)* It means very little…

LUCY: Oh, William!

GILBERT: *(gently)* Well, if it will please you. Oh, it's not so much for me, Kitten. If I am to accept, it will be for all of this country's writers. By setting a precedent—by tapping me on the shoulder—the King will be opening the doors for tomorrow's writers.

(As he speaks, GILBERT *stands and steps out of the study into the open area (he still has a limp).* LUCY *brings him a formal jacket, which matches his trousers. In the background, a few bars from* H.M.S. Pinafore*'s 'For he is an Englishman' can be heard. He kisses her on the cheek and turns toward center stage.* LUCY *exits.)*

(The lights come up on the KING *[previously Prince of Wales] seated on the throne and dais where Queen Victoria sat in Act 1. The male chorus sings the last lines of* H.M.S Pinafore *as* GILBERT *approaches, bows, and kneels before the* KING.

CHORUS: For he is an Englishman,
              And he himself hath said it,
              And it's greatly to his credit
              That he is an Englishman!

(The KING takes the sword from an equerry and taps GILBERT on each shoulder.)

KING: Sir William!

CHORUS: Hoorah! Hoorah! Hoorah!

(GILBERT stands, bows, backs away. The lights extinguish over the KING. GILBERT, alone, turns toward the audience.)

GILBERT: *Sir* William. Ha!

*(This is **not** a derogatory or derisive 'Ha!')*

(GILBERT turns and slowly walks stage left into a London street scene. A MAN crosses the stage whistling 'A Pair of Sparkling Eyes'. He nods as he passes GILBERT, who amusedly returns the nod. Other Londoners enter, some following a man pushing a hurdy-gurdy [barrel organ]. The organ-grinder stops, turns the handle, churns out 'A Wandering Minstrel' from The Mikado. *The Londoners gather as one man starts to sing.)*

> **Video Option:** *The organ grinder and the hurdy-gurdy are shown on a DVD screened above the action.*

MAN:
>> A wandering minstrel, I—
>>> A thing of shreds and patches,
>>> Of ballads, songs and snatches,
>>> And dreamy lullaby!

(GILBERT walks over and watches the group; several nod to him.)

>> My catalogue is long,
>>> Through every passion ranging,
>>> And to your humours changing
>>> I tune my supple song!

(The singing MAN encourages the onlookers to sing with him, who boisterously take part.)

CHORUS:
>> A wandering minstrel, I—
>>> A thing of shreds and patches,
>>> Of ballads, songs and snatches,
>>> And dreamy lullaby!

(GILBERT looks from one to the other, smiles, slaps his hand against his thigh, pushes out his chest, and marches briskly off.)

CHORUS: My catalogue is long,
        Through every passion ranging,
        And to your humours changing
    I tune my supple song!

CURTAIN

Character Descriptions
(Principal Characters)

W. S. Gilbert

William Schwenck Gilbert is tall with a military bearing, a full head of hair, and a walrus-like moustache. He is brusque, impatient and outspoken, and has an acid tongue famed for uttering cutting remarks. He constantly makes fun of other people, but cannot forgive any person who makes fun of him.

His legal training has made him very exacting and has exacerbated his natural tendency to be suspicious of anyone he thinks is trying to take advantage or get the better of him. Consequently he has few really close friends and many enemies. He has little use for or patience with older women, and particularly those who are less than attractive, have pretensions to higher rank, or who aspire to love a younger man (as can be seen from his libretti).

Yet he can be immensely patient with and go far out of his way to help pretty *young* women. This does not imply that he has affairs with them: indeed, the reverse is more true, for he is a man of impeccable moral character. He married Lucy Agnes Turner when she was 17 and he was 30, and they enjoy a devoted but childless marriage.

Gilbert is 38 when we first meet him in 1875, already a successful writer of humorous plays and poems. He is 71 at the end of the play.

It should not be the intent of the actor playing Gilbert to make him an unsympathetic character. He has some excellent traits but they tend to be hidden by his irascibility.

Arthur Sullivan

Arthur Seymour Sullivan is short, inclined to be overweight, 32 when we first meet him, a bachelor (and remains so throughout his life), a quiet womanizer, loves a fling at the gaming tables, and wears a monocle in front of his right eye. He is dedicated to music and has been since a young child, winning scholarships to music academies because his parents were too poor to give him more than moral support. He has a gentle manner and a kind word for everyone, with the result that he is almost universally liked and respected. Behind his serious manner lurks a quiet sense of humor.

He also is a sick man, for he is contending with the pain of kidney stones. These, and a natural indolence and tendency to procrastinate, constantly make him start composing very late—often only days before a work is to be produced—resulting in very late nights during which he often works until 4 a.m. and starts again at 8 a.m., and so further impairs his health.

At the start of the play he is already a well-respected composer of oratorios, church music, and a symphony. Throughout the action of the play he ages 25 years and becomes progressively more ill. Toward the end of the play he looks grey and 10 years older than his actual age of 58.

Richard D'Oyly Carte

Richard D'Oyly Carte is an astute businessman in theater management (today we would refer to him as an entrepreneur). He is not quite a manipulator, but he uses excellent intuition and judgment to ferret out and mold good business deals that result in a high return on the money he has invested in them.

He is slim, of medium height, wears pince-nez glasses, and has a sharp mind and an equally sharp tongue when aroused. He is 31 at the start of the play and 49 when we last see him. He dies in 1900 at age 56, within six months of Queen Victoria's and Sullivan's deaths.

Lucy Gilbert

Lucy Gilbert is petite, very attractive, and fully understands her role as a supportive wife for her vituperative husband. She quietly encourages him in his endeavors and bears his unequable temperament with ease.

Seemingly a colorless character, she has an inner strength seldom apparent to those who do not know her well. Gilbert always refers to her as Kitten. Married at 17, she is 25 at the start of the play and 57 when it ends.

Helen Carte

Helen Carte provides the perfect balance for her entrepreneur husband. She is an excellent business administrator with a strong hand for organizing detailed activities. Originally D'Oyly Carte's secretary, when she married him she continued to help him run the business and took over fully when he became ill and subsequently died. She reasons rationally and with considerable firmness. She also commands Gilbert's absolute respect.

Helen is 35 when we first meet her half way through the play, and about 50 when we last see her in 1901.

Obtaining Performance Rights

All seven plays in this book are fully protected under the copyright laws of Canada, the United States of America, the British Commonwealth, and all other countries forming part of the Copyright Union. No part of this book may be reproduced in any form, either print or electronic, or transmitted to others.

Amateur and professional rights for live stage performance can be obtained by accessing our web site:

www.r-group.ca

Performance rights must be acquired at least six weeks before the first performance.

Where royalty rights apply, they are reasonable. They are based on the particular play, whether the play is being performed by a professional or amateur group, the production opening date, and the number of performances.

Some further guidelines apply:

1. No changes may be made to the plot, the dialogue, and the stage directions without the prior approval of the author or his representative. If a change is necessary, write to the address at the foot of this page.

2. The author's name must appear on all documents associated with the production, such as the program and marketing literature, and be placed on a separate line immediately below the play's title.

3. Sometimes the author can be available to attend a performance, particularly as part of a media-related event. Alternatively, the author can be available by remote means such as Skype.

If difficulties are encountered in reaching the web site, write:

rgrouppubs@gmail.com

About the Author

Ron Blicq was a flyer in the Royal Air Force who later became a technical editor for CAE Industries, and then a teacher of technical communication at Red River College in Winnipeg, Canada.

On his 'retirement,' he tried his hand at writing stories and novels. But when he discovered he preferred writing dialogue far more than descriptive scenes, he turned to playwriting. Since then he has written 14 plays, 11 of which have been produced. His play *Closure,* in which a key role is played by a nine-year-old boy (see below), won the Samuel French award for Best Canadian Play in 2008, and is now being performed in several countries.

Blicq particularly enjoys writing for young audiences. Although he lives in Winnipeg he frequently travels to the UK, and especially to the Island of Guernsey, where many of his plays have had their first performance.

In 2005, young Alex Crossan played the role of Gordie in **Closure**. *(In the upper photograph on the front cover he is seen building a model airplane with John Gaisford, in a memorable scene from the play.) Then in 2009 he was again on stage in another Blicq play, this time in the role of Cyril in* **Adventures With a Psammead.**

(Photo by the author)

Closure is published by Samuel French Inc. and is available from the publisher (Samuel.french.com), Amazon, or most bookstores. The ISBN is 978-0-573-66400-7.

Printed in Canada